Lynne Graham was born in Northern Ireland and has been a keen romance reader since her teens. She is very happily married, to an understanding husband who has learned to cook since she started to write! Her five children keep her on her toes. She has a very large dog, who knocks everything over, a very small terrier, who barks a lot, and two cats. When time allows, Lynne is a keen gardener.

After spending three years as a die-hard New Yorker, **Kate Hewitt** now lives in a small village in the English Lake District, with her husband, their five children and a golden retriever. In addition to writing intensely emotional stories, she loves reading, baking and playing chess with her son—she has yet to win against him, but she continues to try. Learn more about Kate at kate-hewitt.com.

D0256457

THE ITALIAN IN NEED OF AN HEIR

LYNNE GRAHAM

VOWS TO SAVE HIS CROWN

KATE HEWITT

MILLS & BOON

First Published in Great Britain 2020
by Mills & Boon, an imprint of HarperCollins*Publishers*
1 London Bridge Street, London, SE1 9GF

The Italian in Need of an Heir © 2020 Lynne Graham

Vows to Save His Crown © 2020 Kate Hewitt

ISBN: 978-0-263-27821-7

MIX
Paper from
responsible sources
FSC® C007454

This book is produced from independently certified FSC™ paper
to ensure responsible forest management.
For more information visit www.harpercollins.co.uk/green.

Printed and bound in Spain
by CPI, Barcelona

THE ITALIAN IN
NEED OF AN HEIR

LYNNE GRAHAM

CHAPTER ONE

SILHOUETTED AGAINST THE moonlit sky, the huge house outside Naples looked as if it belonged in a gothic horror movie. All it lacked was the ubiquitous thunderstorm to set the scene as it already had bats flying around the turrets, Raffaele Manzini conceded with wry amusement as he climbed out of his car and his bodyguards clambered out of the car behind him.

'Some place,' Sal, the middle-aged head of Raffaele's protection team, remarked, with the privilege of a man who had been responsible for Raffaele's physical safety since he was a child. 'I'm going to stick to you like glue tonight whether you like it or not. I don't trust your great-grandfather. Back in the day, the word is he was a ruthless killer.'

'Probably all smoke and mirrors.' Raffaele laughed.

'He treated your father badly. A man who casts his own grandson out of the family isn't doing right by his own blood and I'd believe him capable of anything.'

Raffaele said nothing, knowing the older man well enough to know that he had always been a fervent believer in the strength and importance of family ties. But the concept of family was meaningless to Raffaele. His mother had suffered brain damage in an adolescent accident and in spite of her unpredictable rages, obsessional behaviour and wild impulses she had still been allowed to raise him, her only child. Not that she, a Spanish billionairess, had done any of the actual raising. Naturally not. Raffaele had been brought up by nannies, few of whom had endured his volatile mother's employment for long. He had never known a hug, physical affection being something his mother had put on the 'grounds for dismissal' list. He had never known his father until he grew into a man. And he had nothing in common with him either.

To be fair, Raffaele had long known that he wasn't quite normal. There was a giant black hole in him where other people had emotion. Very little touched him. Only business, profit and power revved his engines. And just as he knew that, he knew that all that had brought him to his great-grandfather's doorstep was curiosity.

Aldo Manzini might be ninety-one, but he had retained his sinister reputation. Rumours of Mafia connections, corruption and killings, not to mention brutal business tactics, still clung to his name. Even though his son had died, Aldo had still cut his grandson, Tommaso, out of his life for defying him and he had never forgiven him, which made it all the stranger that he should have extended an invitation for Tommaso's son, Raffaele, to visit him at his fortified estate.

And if Raffaele hadn't been bored, he wouldn't have come. It was that simple. Family ties had nothing whatsoever to do with Raffaele's arrival. His heiress mother's death from an epileptic seizure had left him wealthy beyond avarice at eighteen and his own business achievements since then had made him untouchable. On the international stage, he was an infinitely more powerful man than Aldo Manzini had ever been in his Italian home. He was feared, flattered and feted wherever he went. Needless to say, that got tedious.

Boredom set Raffaele's teeth on edge. He had tried to combat it every way he knew how. The turnover of women in his bed had moved even faster. He had skydived, scaled mountains, deep sea–dived, always searching to find what he needed to stop being bored. Because he *knew* how lucky he was to be born healthy and rich and to have the power to get just about anything he wanted. And at the age of twenty-eight, he had had it *all*: the beautiful women, the decadent parties, the travel, the ultimate of life's experiences. And yet, he was *still* bored…

An ancient manservant ushered them into the creepy mansion. The giant hall rejoiced in the antiquated splendour of a bygone age, the very antithesis of what Raffaele liked but, for the first time in a very long time, Raffaele was not bored. A long wood-panelled corridor ornamented with a line of grim family portraits led into what the old man called the 'master's office'. Raffaele was surprised to register that he would have liked a moment or two to study his paternal ancestors but he suppressed that startling impulse, every skin cell in his very tall and powerful body firing as he saw the even older man seated behind the desk with an assistant hovering by his side. He had drawn hawkish features, but his dark eyes were still as keen as a raptor's.

'You're very tall for a Manzini,' Aldo remarked in Italian.

'Must have caught the tall gene,' Raffaele responded

in the same language, which he spoke as fluently as he spoke half a dozen other languages.

'Your mother was taller than your father. Couldn't have abided that in a woman,' Aldo admitted.

Raffaele shifted a broad shoulder clad in a casual cotton shirt. 'Presumably you didn't invite me here to get sentimental about my antecedents.'

'Your hair's too long as well,' Aldo commented, unconcerned. 'And you *should* have dressed for the occasion. Dismiss your bodyguard and I will dismiss mine. What I have to tell you is confidential.'

Raffaele angled his head at Sal, who frowned but backed out of the door again obediently, closely followed by Aldo's companion.

'Better,' Aldo pronounced. 'You can pour us a drink if you like.' A gnarled hand indicated the drinks cabinet by the wall. 'A brandy for me.'

Mouth quirking at the old man's strength of character and imperious attitude, which defied the frail shell of a body trapped in a wheelchair, Raffaele crossed the room and it was one of those very rare occasions when he did as someone else told.

'Do you see much of your father?' Aldo enquired as his great-grandson set a brandy goblet down within his reach.

'No. By the time I had access to him, I was an adult. I see him a couple of times a year,' Raffaele responded carelessly.

'Tommaso's a disgrace to the Manzini family, as spineless as a jellyfish!' Aldo proclaimed bitterly.

'He's happy,' Raffaele replied with complete assurance. 'And that, his small business and his family are all he wants out of life. We all have different dreams.'

'I would hazard a guess that a white picket fence and a bunch of kids isn't *your* dream,' the old man murmured very drily.

'It's not, but I don't begrudge my father his,' Raffaele countered, his dark eyes a brilliant gold that flared in warning as he studied his great-grandfather, wanting the miserable old codger to get the message that while he might not be exactly close to his father, Tommaso, his father's second wife or his three little half-sisters, he would protect both him and them from anyone who sought to harm them.

'Let me bring you up to date on old history.' Aldo leant back in his wheelchair.

A whiskey cradled in an elegant brown hand, Raffaele sprawled down in an armchair, hoping it wasn't going to be a long story because he was already beginning to regret the impulse that had brought him.

'When I was twenty-one I was engaged to Giulia Parisi. Our family businesses were competitors. Both our fathers wanted the marriage to take place but, make no mistake—' Aldo lifted his bony chin to punctuate the point '—I was very much in love with her. The week before the wedding I discovered that she was sleeping with one of her cousins and was not the decent young woman I believed. I was young, *hurt*... I jilted her at the altar because I wanted to shame her the way she had shamed me.'

'*And?*' Raffaele pressed when the old man seemed to be drifting back into the past.

'Her father was enraged by my disrespect and he changed his will. The Parisi business could never be bought or otherwise acquired by a Manzini. It could only pass through a marriage between the two families and the birth of a child.'

Raffaele rolled his eyes. 'A bit short-sighted to say the least—'

'That business is now one of the biggest technology companies in the world,' Aldo informed him, having reached his punchline. 'And if you do what I want you to do it will be *yours*—'

'Which company?' Raffaele prompted, his interest finally engaged as he ran through various names before Aldo nodded confirmation. '*Seriously? And it could be mine? For the price of a wife and a kid?'* His lean bronzed features snapped taut with distaste. 'As you guessed, not my style.'

'Ever since Giulia, it has been my ambition to acquire that company. The question didn't arise with my son's generation because the Parisi clan had no daughters to target but by the time my grandson, Tommaso, was of age, there was a daughter called Lucia available.'

'And my father blew his opportunity,' Raffaele filled in. 'He's already told me that part of the story. You wanted him to marry Lucia but he was already in love with my mother and picked her instead.'

'Great foresight there,' Aldo quipped with a curled lip. 'She only stayed married to him long enough to have you and then dumped him. How many stepfathers did you have?'

Raffaele shrugged. 'Half a dozen. My father may not have been the sharpest tool in the box, but he was the best of a bad bunch.'

'You don't know the whole story,' Aldo condemned. 'Not only did Tommaso not marry Lucia, but he also *paid* for Lucia and her lover to run off to the UK and escape the wrath of her family using *my* money!'

Raffaele compressed his wide sensual mouth, almost betrayed into laughter by that dire announcement, which still, even after all the years that had passed, seemed to rankle the most with the old man. 'That was enterprising of him,' he pronounced stiffly. 'However, I believe she was already pregnant by her lover and you can hardly have expected my father to still marry her in—'

'Why not?' the old man shrilled at him with lancing bitterness. '*Any* child would have met the terms of the will if he'd married Lucia Parisi!'

Raffaele registered that he was not dealing with a reasonable man and was not at all surprised that his father had fled to the UK and a humble lifestyle far removed from his wealthy beginnings. A quiet, gentle man, Tommaso could never have stood up to the force of his domineering grandfather's personality or his demands. In much the same way, Raffaele's mother, Julieta, had run over Tommaso like a steamroller. 'That was unfortunate,' he said, setting his glass down, resolving to get himself back out of the mansion again without further time wastage.

'But not half as unfortunate as it would be if you were equally blind to the possibilities of marrying a Parisi.'

'I'm not prepared to marry anyone,' Raffaele spelt out with cool finality.

'This one's a beauty though, and you wouldn't have to *stay* married to her,' Aldo Manzini pointed out, tossing a file across the desk. 'Have a look…'

Raffaele had no intention of having a look at some

scion of the Parisi clan. The old man was unbalanced and obsessional and Raffaele had had quite sufficient experience of such personalities growing up with his tragically damaged mother. 'I'm not interested. I need neither the money nor the company,' he responded smoothly, rising from his chair.

'Agree to consider it and I will sign over *my* business empire to you here and now. My lawyer is waiting in the next room,' Aldo told him. 'As for the former Lucia Parisi and her family, I already own them lock, stock and barrel.'

'What are you talking about?'

'Lucia married a fool. They're in debt to their eyeballs and I *own* their debts. What do you think I intend to do with them?'

'I couldn't care less,' Raffaele countered truthfully while thinking about that offer of Aldo's business empire. A fading technology company in need of a fresh innovative makeover, the sort of business challenge he most enjoyed. That attracted him, not the money, no, it was the sheer challenge of rebuilding, redesigning, reenergising that kicked his shrewd brain into activity for the first time since he had entered the room. He *enjoyed* order, structure, after the chaotic nature of his childhood.

'And if you want to acquire the other company, which will dovetail perfectly with mine, you marry the beauty. I know that nothing less than a beauty would tempt a man of your…shall we say…appetites?' Aldo savoured, delighted by the reality that he had contrived to freeze Raffaele in his tracks and that the homework he had done on the nature of his great-grandson had paid off.

Like Aldo, Raffaele was a ruthless bastard in business, a tough and demanding employer and bone-deep ambitious. As Aldo had once been, he was a connoisseur of beautiful women. Like Aldo, what excited Raffaele the most was a challenge in the business field. But Raffaele had had too much too soon and too young, too much money, too much success, too many women. He needed something or someone to ground him back in the real world. Inwardly chuckling, Aldo watched Raffaele lifting the file he had, moments earlier, refused to even look at: *the honey trap.*

Raffaele stared down at the colour photograph. She was tall and she was naturally fair with long silky hair to her waist, flawless porcelain skin and eyes the fresh colour of spring ferns. Her features were…perfect, classical. But beautiful women were two a penny in his world and he would sooner have cut off his right arm than marry anyone and have a child. He flipped past the photo and discovered that she had an IQ higher than his own and Raffaele was twice as clever as most people. Now the thought of an intelligent beauty had considerable appeal to a man long convinced that all truly beautiful women were either mad as hatters like his late mother or insipid and shallow and so in love with their own looks that they had never bothered to work on having anything else to offer the world. Maya Campbell, Lucia Parisi's daughter, however, would be another experience entirely…

'I'm handing her to you on a plate. My representatives are already calling in the debts her family owes. You can ride in like a white knight and offer her a rescue package.'

'To be blunt, I'm not the "white knight" type,' Raffaele interposed drily. 'If I go for this, I'll be straight all the way. I don't put on an act. I refuse to be anyone other than who I am.'

'So speaks an immensely privileged young man,' Aldo commented.

A carelessly graceful shrug was Raffaele's response. He had few illusions about his own character but there were few people alive who knew what he had suffered as a child and adolescent, a live toy for a woman with mental health issues to play with, abused one day, over-indulged the next. He didn't do self-pity any more than he did compassion. He didn't trust people and it hadn't harmed him. He didn't *care* about people and it had kept him safe as an adult from the nightmares that had haunted his childhood. If you had no expectations, you didn't get disappointed. That approach worked efficiently for him.

He hoped it would work for Maya Campbell as well because he wanted those companies. He would take them and, whatever it took, he would whip them into shape again, restoring both business enterprises to fresh growth and profitability.

'I'm getting tired,' Aldo was forced to admit, his head starting to droop. 'Will I call in my lawyer?'

Raffaele smiled his very rare smile. 'Thank you for an entertaining experience, Aldo. And the prospect of even more entertainment on the horizon.'

'She *is* a beauty.'

'Not the woman, the businesses!' his great-grandson contradicted in impatient rebuttal.

The papers for the handover of Aldo's estate were already prepared for signature. The lawyer appeared, accompanied by two witnesses, both of whom were doctors.

Only on exiting the mansion did Raffaele learn what had driven Aldo Manzini to his decision to sign over his empire *before* he passed away.

'Dementia,' one of the doctors told him with a shake of his head. 'In a few months, who knows what he will still be capable of doing? At his age, the degeneration can be rapid, and he knows that.'

And an utterly unexpected pang of regret stung Raffaele and he knew he would visit again, whether he married to acquire the second company or not.

'Oh, my word, I've never seen a more beautiful man!' Nicola, the bride-to-be, carolled at Maya's side.

'Where?' One of Maya's other companions demanded to know.

'Over by the bar...isn't he just dreamy?' Nicola sighed in a languishing tone.

Maya flicked an instinctive glance over to the bar and saw *him*. Man whore, her brain labelled instantly. There he was, at least six feet four inches tall, powerfully built but somehow lean and lithe at the same time, lounging back against the bar of the VIP section of the club with a glittering confidence that blazed like an angel's halo. A man supremely comfortable with being the cynosure of every female eye in the room, coolly accustomed to attention and appreciation in spite of the fact that he was dressed down in ripped jeans, a black tee shirt and what looked like motorcycle boots. It was a certainty that he got admired every place he went.

And it showed. He *knew* exactly how gorgeous he was. Luxuriant black hair brushed his shoulders, a dark shadow of stubble accentuating his strong jaw line and perfect mouth, throwing his swoon-worthy high cheekbones into prominence. Without the stubble, the muscular development and the tousled hair, he might have looked too pretty or clean-cut as some male supermodels did. Nice wallpaper, she categorised him, but very probably highly promiscuous and definitely not her type. That fast, she dismissed him from her interest and glanced away.

But then she didn't 'do' men in the same way as her university friends did. Maya didn't have time to date, and sleeping around for the sake of a quick physical thrill had never appealed to her either. Life was too short to waste on a man. Her soft mouth curled at the thought and she wondered if her utterly hopeless nice guy of a father had ruined her for all other men and embittered her to a certain extent.

After all, her father was a lovely man, loving, good-natured and caring, but when he went into business, he was a disaster and that truth, matched with the debts he had accrued, had dominated Maya's life for far longer than she cared to recall. Her teenaged years had been a blur of bailiffs, debt collectors and threatening letters and the constant worry of how to keep her family fed and safe. She had her parents, her twin sister, Izzy, and Matt, her eleven-year-old brother in a wheelchair, to look after. Izzy never seemed to resent the harsher realities of their lives and the part their feckless parents had played in depriving their daughters of a normal youth. But Maya had often wondered what it would be like to have ordinary self-sufficient parents, who did the caring, rather than relying on their kids to look after them.

And then, just as quickly, she felt like a bad person for even thinking that way, for being mean and selfish and resentful.

It wasn't her parents' fault that they had always been poor. Neither of them had the desirable talents or educational achievements required by employers and, in any case, her mother had only ever been able to work part-time hours with a disabled son to look after. Indeed, Maya had never contrived to work out how any of her father's car-crash businesses could ever have done well enough to enable her parents to buy a house in London, but they had had the house before she and Izzy were born and that small property was the only stable element in their catastrophic financial world. It was the one plus they had as a family.

Maya had completed two doctorates in mathematics at university after first graduating at eighteen. Being a prodigy from an early age had only two benefits that she recognised. Firstly, academic brilliance had enabled her to finance her studies by allowing her to win scholarships and prizes and, secondly, it had given her higher earning powers in part-time jobs and projects that required a maths whizz. Extra work had always been available to Maya but had she had a choice she would have gone into academic research because, aside of her family's needs, money didn't mean that much to her. There were so many more important, lasting things than cash, she thought ruefully on the dance floor, wondering why Nicole was giving her meaningful glances until a hand lightly touched her shoulder to attract her attention.

Maya spun round and, even in her very high heels which took her to five feet eleven, she had the unfamiliar experience of having to tip her head back to see the man who had approached her. And it was *him*, the guy from the bar, and she was stunned because she was not a good bet and she would have assumed such a man would have already worked that out for himself. Her outfit was conservative, her demeanour quiet and she didn't drink, all of which should have loudly signalled her unavailability in the 'fun for a night' stakes.

'Join me for a drink,' he told her. He definitely didn't *ask*; it was a command.

Maya simply laughed, plucking an explanatory hand at the silly pink sash she had been forced to wear. 'Sorry, I'm on a girls' night. No men allowed.'

He had dark deep-set eyes as hard as black granite with little gold highlights and he couldn't hide the fact that the rejection had disconcerted him because for a split second those eyes flared like fireworks against a night sky. And she forgave him because close up he was even more devastatingly gorgeous than he had looked at a distance and she assumed that he had little experience of meeting with female dismissal. He emanated an aura of golden vibrancy comprised of bronzed skin, vital good health and leashed masculine energy. And like all men, he had an ego and she had briefly dented it.

'Are you crazy?' Nicole hissed in her ear, grabbing her arm to march her back to their table and tell the rest of the hens what Maya had done.

And there was a whole chorus of voluble protests. The mood did not go in the direction Maya expected. Indeed, her companions were ready to gift-wrap her for him and hand her over. A bunch of arguments in that line came her way unasked for: she was single, allowed to stray from the hen party, should grab male opportunity when it beckoned and was far too much of a nerd to appreciate that a man like that only came along once in a lifetime.

'He said, "Join me for a drink." It wasn't a request, it was an *order*,' Maya told them defensively when she could finally get a word in. 'He's an arrogant bastard.'

'Got to expect some flaws in all that perfection,' someone gibed, unimpressed.

'Are you seriously telling me that a guy like that isn't worth more than sitting in swotting prissily every night over your computer like you do?' someone else piped up.

And Maya's polite smile froze a little because there was envy in those comments and she was, sadly, used to dealing with that, after being horribly bullied at school for her scholastic attainments. Her peers preferred to believe that she had to swot from dawn to dusk to gain the results she did, and she let them believe that even if it was a lie. Evidently a nerdy swot was more acceptable than someone gifted at birth with a photographic memory and an IQ that ran into the highest possible triple figures. Maya had been doing algebra at the age of three; she didn't need to swot.

Raffaele returned to the bar, seriously unsettled. He had wanted to meet her on level ground on his own terms but from the first glimpse she had not met his expectations. She dressed badly: there was no avoiding that obvious flaw. The high-necked black dress she wore had as much shape as a sack but still couldn't hide the length of her show-stopping long legs or the delicacy of her curves at breast and hip. As for her face, she was, unbelievably to Raffaele, a cosmetics-free zone. Her face was *bare*, not even liner or mascara applied. Lucky for her that her porcelain-pale skin was smooth and faultless, he mused irritably, and her green eyes so arresting that she could get away without artificial definition. But she had turned *him* away. Ordering up a rare second drink, Raffaele gritted his perfect white teeth.

Women didn't walk away from Raffaele Manzini. It didn't happen. He was as bemused as if a tame dog had suddenly bitten the hand off him. Other guys got blown off by women, Raffaele *didn't*. She had barely glanced at him, dismissing him instantly, he reasoned, his jaw line clenching even harder. He ordered her a fancy cocktail and sent it over to the table. She waved a bottle of sparkling water in an apologetic gesture in his direction and passed the cocktail over to another woman at the table. By that point Raffaele was ready to strangle her because she wasn't the pushover he had assumed she would be. It annoyed him when those around him refused to fit the frame he had set them in. He departed from the club in a brooding mood, raging frustration bubbling only an inch beneath it as he stole a last lingering glance at her.

Madre di Cristo... For some peculiar reason she looked even more beautiful now, light blonde hair shimmering in a veil down her back as she shimmied her curvy little bottom to the music beat with one of the other women, long perfect legs flashing, that determined little chin at an upward angle, signalling that she didn't give a damn about anything, anyone. Well, she would learn different, Raffaele swore to himself soothingly, denying the all too ready pulse at his groin that had a mind of its own; she would learn *not* to tangle with Raffaele Manzini and expect to walk away free and undamaged.

'I think she's a nice girl…didn't mean any harm.' Sal broke into speech unexpectedly on the pavement as the limo door was flipped open for Raffaele's entry. 'Not your usual hook-up. Nothing flirtatious about her, nothing suggestive in her dress, just not your usual type.'

Raffaele bit out a curse in Italian, enraged by that comforting assurance from a man who was probably closer to a father than any he had ever known.

'I wouldn't know what to do with a nice girl.'

'Most of us marry the nice ones,' Sal riposted cheerfully.

Of course, Sal knew she was a Parisi from the investigation agency he had employed to track her down for Raffaele to meet. And yet they hadn't officially met as yet. Maya Parisi… Raffaele savoured the name. It suited her better than Campbell, which was too ordinary for a blonde that could catch his eye garbed in a dress like a sack and without make-up or silicone or Botox or, indeed, any of the artificial enhancements that Raffaele was more accustomed to finding featured in the women he bedded.

But if he married Maya, it wouldn't be to *keep* her as Sal implied. It would be to bed her and get her pregnant, Raffaele reflected coldly, and strangely enough that idea no longer repulsed him in the way it had only a week earlier. In fact, he discovered it was more of a turn-on for his jaded libido because it was something new, something different. *But* only for a short time until the task was accomplished. And no, he wouldn't

be keeping her, he would be corrupting her with pleasure and then discarding her again, which was pretty
much the norm for him. After all, the window of his
attention span for a woman was notoriously short.

CHAPTER TWO

MAYA WAS TREMBLING and struggling to hide it as she watched her little brother being boarded on the bus that took him to his special school every morning. Matt was grinning as a friend with a similar disability shouted something out to him, an eleven-year-old boy, still wonderfully innocent about the world he and his parents lived in. A world of debt and disaster, she acknowledged wretchedly, as if Matt hadn't already endured enough in life after losing the use of his legs at the age of four following a fall from the ladder of a playground slide.

The bus pulled away and she closed the front door again. In her mind's eye, every word of the letter that had been delivered and the papers that had been served first thing that morning were still etched inside her pounding head. Official documents containing a court summons and a *threatening* letter had disclosed alarming facts she had not known about her family's financial history.

And that her parents should have left her in ignorance was unacceptable. *That* shouldn't have been possible when she had spent years borrowing from one loan company to pay another, performing mathemati-

cal acrobatics to stave off her parents' bankruptcy and
the loss of the home her little brother needed for security! Her twin, Izzy, had made so many sacrifices too,
working in low-paid jobs to earn every extra penny
she could and bring it home. Maya was so angry she
wanted to scream. A legal summons to court had been
served on her parents, threatening them with bankruptcy.

'Don't look at us like that!' Her mother, Lucia
gasped, an attractive brunette in her forties, her brown
eyes crumpling as she broke down into sobs. 'We c-
couldn't *face* telling you the truth!'

'All these years you've allowed me to believe that
you *owned* this house and, because I believed you, now
I could be in trouble for fraudulently helping you to
borrow money against an asset that doesn't belong to
you!' Maya condemned, out of all patience with her
parents, watching stony-faced as her father closed a
supportive arm round his sobbing wife's shoulders.

'Maya…*please,*' her father, Rory, begged with tears
shining in his own eyes.

Scolding her parents was like kicking newborn puppies. And not for the first time, as she turned away in
a mixture of guilt and angry discomfiture she wondered if she was a changeling, because she had nothing
whatsoever in common with either her mother or her
father. She loved them but she couldn't comprehend the
way their minds worked or the dreadful decisions they
made, or the half-lies they would employ to evade any
nasty truth. But she had, naturally, worked out certain
things. Neither of them was particularly bright, neither
of them capable of planning or saving or budgeting,
so where *had* her sharp calculating brain come from?

One of those gene anomalies, she thought with an inner sigh, knowing such rambling reflections were getting her precisely nowhere in the midst of a crisis.

It was also, by far, the worst crisis they had ever faced as a family and she felt sick and shaky and scared, knowing that no matter what she did she could not possibly drag them out of trouble this time around. There was far too much money owed and, even worse, they had not made a single payment on the private loan that had purchased the house they now stood in.

'Not one single repayment in over twenty years,' Maya reminded her parents out loud. 'That means, you don't *own* this house, the person who gave you this loan *owns* this house and now they want the money back or you have to move out.'

'Tommaso wouldn't do that to me,' Lucia protested. 'His family's too rich and he's too kind.'

Maya slapped the letter that had arrived in the post down on the table. 'They're demanding that the loan be repaid immediately and *in full* or they will take the house and sell it. Whoever Tommaso is, he is no longer prepared to wait for his money.'

'Tommaso is a Manzini,' Lucia informed her in an awed tone, as if that surname alone belonged to some godlike clan. 'The man I was supposed to marry, but he didn't want to marry me either. He helped your dad and I to leave Italy and buy a home here.'

'He gave you a loan,' Maya contradicted. 'The money *wasn't* a gift.'

'Well, *we* certainly thought it was a gift,' her father, Rory, confided in a long-suffering tone.

'It doesn't matter what you thought because you were wrong. You signed a loan agreement.'

'But that was only a sham to cover the paperwork for his grandfather's benefit!' her mother piped up. 'Tommaso promised that he would never ask for any of it back.'

'He *lied*.' Maya slapped the letter again and pushed it across for her mother to see the Manzini Finance logo at the top. 'Although I've got to give the guy his due. He did wait for over twenty years to raise the subject and, if we could afford it, I would take this to court to see how it played out because I'm pretty sure it's *not* legal to wait this long to demand a repayment. *But* we don't have a penny to bless ourselves with, so we won't be going to court on that score.'

'Never mind, we've got an appointment with Manzini Finance,' Lucia objected with a sudden insanely inappropriate smile, as if she were pulling a rabbit out of the hat that would magically save them all. 'We'll just explain and it will all be fixed. This is just a misunderstanding, that's all. You're such a worrier. You're getting all worked up over nothing, Maya.'

'You've been summoned to a bankruptcy court as well,' Maya delivered with clarity. 'Nothing is going to protect you from that. Your debts have caught up with you and we don't have the money to repay them. I hate to say it because I'm not a quitter, but this is the end of the road as far as the debts go. Whoever had the bankruptcy summons served probably assumes they can sell the house to cover the debts.'

'If it wasn't for Matt, we could,' her mother burbled as if the earlier conversation had not taken place.

'No, you couldn't, Mum, because you don't own the house,' Maya parried wearily. 'And I'll be keeping the appointment with Manzini Finance, not you and Dad.'

Rory squeezed his wife's shoulder comfortingly. 'Maya understands all this financial stuff better than us,' he said with confident pride in his daughter's abilities. 'She'll sort this out in a trice.'

Maya studied her parents with quivering lips, which she had to compress to stay in control of her tongue. There would be no sorting it out this time. It was a case of pay up and move out, but she supposed only the actual experience of being homeless would persuade her parents that their mindset of running away from their debts was no longer sustainable. And that was all very well, but what about Matt?

It was her kid brother that her heart bled for the most. The house had been specially adapted for his needs and he had a place in a special school nearby. It was unlikely that her family would be able to stay in the same area. He would lose his schooling and his little circle of mates, lose his home and the few freedoms he still had. Even for an able-bodied child that would be a tough proposition but for a disabled child, it was absolutely tragic.

'I wouldn't mind seeing Tommaso again,' her mother sighed. 'He was like my big brother. Honestly, he was the nicest, kindest man.'

'I seriously doubt that someone as important in Manzini Finance as this Tommaso must be will be present at the meeting,' Maya pointed out, striving not to add the reminder that a *nice* guy wouldn't have allowed such a letter to be sent to his pseudo little sister. As usual, her mother's expectations were far removed from the reality of what was likely to happen.

'You're probably right,' Lucia conceded. 'As a family member, Tommaso must be very senior now in his grandfather's business.'

'I need to dress for the appointment,' Maya pointed out, escaping the small lounge to flee down the corridor of their semi-detached bungalow home into the bedroom she had grown up in with her twin. It still had bunk beds, there not being the space for any other option.

It was fortunate that she kept her interview suit at her parents' home, although she doubted if it mattered what she wore in the circumstances. Short of selling her soul to the devil, there was no way anyone was going to extend further understanding to her financially incompetent parents, but it was equally fortunate that she had had the foresight to have her father sign a power of attorney in her name so that she was able to deal with their money problems on their behalf. At least that gave her the scope to *try* to find a resolution.

After all, now that her academic studies were complete, she had already accepted a high-earning position as a trader with a top city firm and would be starting work at the end of the month. She hadn't yet mentioned that news to her family because she wasn't exactly looking forward to the prospect. It was ironic that she didn't revere money and the ability to earn lots of it when, right now, her family was in desperate need of cash. Was there the smallest chance that she could pledge most of that future salary towards her parents' debt and gain her family a little breathing space to stay on in the house? It was a far-fetched idea and she knew it, but it was the only offer of repayment she had within her power to make. Maybe someone at Manzini

Finance would prove to have a heart but she wasn't her mother: she was a pessimist.

It was a simple fact of life that people who handled money took good care of it to make a profit, and people who didn't or couldn't pay up, like her parents, were a losing investment.

Maya donned her black interview suit and braided her long hair into a more restrained, adult style, her anxious strained green eyes meeting her in the mirror. *Oh, please, God*, she thought fearfully, thinking of her brother's needs, let me be meeting with a man or a woman with a heart…

It was a very fancy office in the centre of the City of London at a prestigious address. Maya was trying not to be impressed but she *was* impressed, by the elegant receptionist clad in designer clothes, the contemporary architectural design of the building and the buzz of a busy city office space that screamed cutting edge and modern. She sat in the waiting area rigid as a stick of rock, reckoning that there was little chance of meeting with compassion in such a place as Manzini Finance.

All smiles, the receptionist approached her to usher her in for her meeting, her attitude almost fawning, which disconcerted Maya, who was good at reading body language. As the door opened she mustered her courage, her eloquence, her top-flight brain and then all of it fell away in a split second when she stared across the vast office at the very tall, well-built and denim-clad man standing there. And it was unnervingly impossible to hang onto her self-discipline when she saw the same guy she had first seen the night of the hen do at the club with her friends.

'What…what are you doing here?' she muttered in disbelief.

Raffaele was never petty, but he enjoyed the sight of Maya being knocked off her cool, self-contained perch, the widening of the witchy green eyes, the faint pink feathering across her cheeks and the surprised pout of her luscious pink lips. He shifted position, his big powerful frame tensing as the cut of his jeans tightened across the groin. He didn't know what it was about her, certainly not the atrociously ugly suit she sported, but she aroused him. And that was fortunate in the circumstances, wasn't it? he reasoned, but he knew he didn't like that instinctive physical reaction to her. He didn't like anything outside his control, didn't want to be troubled by the suspicion that anything with her could mean anything beyond a business deal.

'I am Raffaele Manzini. It was my father who gave your parents the original loan.'

'Tommaso? My mother said he was a very nice man.'

'He is. Unfortunately for you, however, he is no longer involved in Manzini business. He cut ties with his family around the same time as your mother ran away from hers.'

Maya was trying hard not to stare at him but, really, it was very difficult. In a dark nightclub he had been strikingly good-looking, in broad daylight, he was almost impossibly beautiful, sunlight glinting off his blue-black hair, lingering on cheekbones sharp as blades, a strong straight nose, a full wide mouth. And then those eyes, deeply densely dark, enhanced by lush black lashes yet disturbingly expressionless.

'Why unfortunately for me?' Maya queried.

'My father was probably the only *nice*—' he stressed the word with a sardonic twist of his mouth '—person in his family. I'm not nice and I have no ambition to be. You do, however, have something that I want, which I consider very providential for you in this scenario.'

'P-Providential?' she stammered, knocked off-balance by that unexpected statement because how could she possibly have anything that *he* could want?

'I have the power to make all the bad stuff in your life vanish,' Raffaele spelt out with blazing assurance. 'I know about *all* the debts your family have, so don't waste your time trying to bluff me. Now take a seat and we'll talk.'

His attitude set her teeth on edge, but she fought the sensation because, whether she liked it or not, he was the guy with the power. She settled down in an armchair in the seating area in the corner while he rang for coffee. It arrived at supersonic speed, on a tray carried by the receptionist, who didn't seem able to take her eyes off Raffaele. Like a mesmerised groupie she giggled when he spoke, and backed out again in a smiling daze as if she had touched liquid sunlight. Maya resisted the urge to roll her eyes, wondering if that was how women usually reacted to him, recalling how her own friends had behaved, and suppressed a sigh, wondering if she should ask what he had been doing in that club that night, wondering if it was wiser simply to leave the topic alone. But she didn't believe in a coincidence that far-fetched.

'So…tell me, why haven't you ditched your family yet?' Raffaele enquired as she took her first sip of coffee.

Maya almost choked and cleared her throat in haste,

scanning him for a clue as to whether or not he was joking. He didn't look as if he was joking. 'Why would you ask me that?'

'It's an obvious question. Your family are like an albatross round your neck dragging you down,' Raffaele informed her. 'With your brain and your prospects, I would have ditched them long ago and moved on to make my own life.'

He was deadly serious. 'Your attitude tells me that you're not particularly close to your own family, because if you were you wouldn't need to be asking me that question,' Maya countered. 'I love them a great deal, even though they're flawed. But then nobody's perfect. I'm not either.'

'Your fatal flaw is that you're sentimental. I don't get attached to people,' Raffaele revealed, disconcerting her again.

'Why are we having this weird conversation?' she asked. 'I mean, we're strangers and this is supposed to be a business meeting.'

'How can we have a business meeting when I already know that you and your family are broke and completely unable to settle their debts? In that field, there is nothing to discuss. I don't waste time playing games for the sake of it.'

Maya sipped at her coffee, striving not to look at him, but somehow he commanded the room, drawing her attention continually back to his corner where he sat in a fluid sprawl of long limbs, a black tee stretched across his broad torso, faded, ripped and frayed designer denim clinging to long muscular thighs. Aware of where her gaze had strayed, she flushed, choosing in preference to focus on his lean bronzed face. 'You were in that club I was in, you approached me…*why*?' she asked starkly, wishing that steady but uninformative dark regard of his weren't quite so unsettling.

'I wanted to see you in the flesh. I was curious. How up to date are you on our respective families' histories?'

'I know nothing about your family and only that my mother's family once wanted her to marry your father,' she admitted.

'Allow me to bring you up to speed,' Raffaele murmured, his concentration shot when she crossed her legs, revealing for a split second a tiny slice of pale inner thigh that was inexplicably outrageously erotic.

Raffaele clenched his strong jaw, questioning his libido's overreaction to such a tame glimpse of the female body. He didn't like how she turned him on hard and fast. He didn't like that he wanted to unbraid her hair to see it loose again and rip off that ugly suit and put her in clothing that would flatter her tall, slender figure. Such reactions didn't come naturally to him— at least they never had before with any other woman.

'You were saying,' she prompted, irritating him more.

He gave her a potted history of their families' marital misses and the news about her ancestor's will and the company. Her eyes widened. 'But that was really stupid of him… I mean, what if—?'

'Exactly,' Raffaele interposed. 'And all sorts of complications have arisen since with the company, particularly now that they have a dearth of Parisi talent to run it. It's going downhill and I want to acquire it.'

Maya glanced up, still mulling over the tangled tale

he had spun. 'But you can't acquire it,' she said. 'Not without marrying and producing a child.'

'The mathematician can put two and two together.' Raffaele shifted his cup in a mocking congratulatory gesture. 'That's why you're here. You're my chance to buy.'

Maya was frowning, her incredulity rising in a great tide so that she set down her coffee cup and stood up, all flustered and defensive. 'And that's why you wanted to catch a look at me in the club,' she realised out loud. 'But I'm *not* your chance to buy the company... I couldn't marry you and have a child with you!'

'Never say never, Maya,' Raffaele advised with inhuman calm. 'Once you think it through, you'll realise that I'm offering you an unbeatable deal. Sit down again.'

'There's no reason for me to sit down again when I wouldn't even consider something so barbaric!' she exclaimed. 'And only a man very far removed from reality could label conceiving a child as an unbeatable *deal*!'

Raffaele angled his dark arrogant head back and smiled, startling her. 'There's the sentimental flaw coming out.'

'Don't you have *any* sense of decency?' Maya hissed down at him.

'Probably not but I do know that, while some women and men casually conceive kids on one-night stands, asking you to marry me *first* and have a child, whom I will fully support, is not that barbaric a request in today's world,' Raffaele maintained smoothly. 'If I have a child with you, it will probably be the only child I ever have and my heir, so you would be raising a child with every possible advantage and privilege from birth.'

'Money doesn't come into this equation. Right and wrong *do*!' Maya slammed back at him. 'Where's your conscience?'

'Where this issue is concerned it is as quiet as the grave,' Raffaele countered levelly. 'Your family is one step away from being put out on the street with a disabled child.'

'No, you really don't have a conscience,' Maya decided, shocked by that reminder and trembling with the force of her emotions.

'Where has conscience got you dealing with your irresponsible father?' Raffaele enquired silkily. 'As a bonus, I would sort him out for you as well. He needs a job, not another business he can't cope with. You need to be realistic about the future. You can't save them from the consequences of their own stupidity all on your own. You *need* my money. *I* need a Parisi descendant as a wife and to have a child with.'

'You really are the most hateful man!' Maya slung at him wrathfully.

'And there's flaw number two,' Raffaele enumerated coolly. 'You're an emotional drama queen. I'm not an emotional person.'

'That's good,' Maya told him with a razor-edged smile as she snatched up the cream jug on the tray and doused him with what remained of the contents.

Raffaele vaulted upright, towering over her, his lean, devastatingly handsome features still calm and controlled as he shook himself as casually as a dog that had run through a puddle. 'Did that make you feel better, Maya?'

'Yes!' she yelled back at him as she stalked towards the door.

'But it hasn't changed the situation you're in, has it? So, you have some thinking to do,' Raffaele told her with infuriating cool. 'Walk round the block to dissipate the rage. Think *sensibly* about what I'm offering. I'm offering you your life back because I will free you from all responsibility for your family. All their debts will finally be settled. Their lives will only change for the better and so will yours because you won't have to worry about them any more.'

'Dear heaven, who did you take your lessons off? Svengali?' Maya gasped, her heart hammering, her head awash with murderous impulses she had never experienced in her life before. She was so enraged that she was shaking all over.

'I'm more Machiavellian in outlook,' Raffaele paused to tell her gravely. 'You need to take a deep breath and count to ten before you try to deal with me because losing your temper will back you into a corner and ensure that you lose every time.'

'I would sooner *die* than be married to a monster like you!' Maya shouted at him.

'I don't think so, Maya. I think you'll be back here within the hour with a different attitude because I'm the only option you have right now,' Raffaele forecast with a satisfaction that blazed like a neon sign in his scorching dark golden eyes.

Just when she had decided he was a sociopath he'd revealed an emotion, only not the right kind of emotion, while he had reduced her to a mindless state of rage. Had she ever pictured herself burying a knife in a man's chest before? She didn't think so. In a daze she stalked back out and into the lift. She couldn't think straight.

Raffaele immediately got on the phone to Sal to instruct that one of his bodyguards should tail her.

'Why?' Sal asked baldly.

'She's in shock. I don't want her stepping out in front of a bus…or something,' Raffaele murmured. 'Not when she's going to be my wife.'

'She *agreed*?' Sal demanded.

'She will,' Raffaele confirmed with unblemished confidence.

Without any idea where she was going, Maya marched down the street as though she was on a mission. Her brain was awash with conflicting thoughts laced with a depth of anger she hadn't known she had the ability to feel. He had asked her to conceive a baby as part of a business *deal*, apparently quite content to create his own flesh and blood purely in the name of profit, recognising nothing wrong in such behaviour. What a poor little mite that child would be! He was immoral, unscrupulous and totally free of normal civilised constraints, as if he had been reared in a jungle well away from the rest of the human race. She had never met anyone that avant-garde before and he had shocked her to her conservative core. When her feet began to ache in her cheap but presentable black medium-heel shoes she walked into a café and bought a cup of tea.

As the sheer shock value of meeting with Raffaele Manzini ebbed, realities began flocking back in to weigh her down. Just as *he* had forecast, which sent another spear of fury rattling through her slim body. It was pointless to have become so angry when she was powerless, she recognised, ready to kick herself for being so impressionable. She had been traumatised by his shamelessly insouciant suggestion that she go to bed with him to have a baby to allow *him* to acquire a company he wanted. Did he honestly believe that a wedding ring would take away the shock of that proposition? Could any guy be more cold-blooded?

Yet suddenly she was trapped in a corner with an offer of a rescue that had come out of left field at her when she had least expected it. He had spelt out what he would do for her family. He had been blunt. He would settle *all* the debts, an almost unimaginable concept to Maya, who had been struggling for so long and for so many years to keep those debts at bay and protect her family. And then Raffaele Manzini came along, evidently wealthy enough to the point where money could be flung around wastefully because her family was *deep* in debt and it would take an enormous amount to settle what they owed.

Seemingly he could afford it. Who *was* Raffaele Manzini? She looked him up on her phone and broke out in goosebumps when she found out. He was *so* rich he belonged to the tribe of the super-rich. What her family owed would barely be pocket change for him. In fact, in asking her to marry him he was scraping the bottom of the barrel because he was a man who appeared to inhabit an exclusive world featuring crowned heads and oil-rich billionaires. But then he was only asking her because her mother had been born a Parisi. Who she was, what she was, were immaterial facts to him because it *wasn't* personal to him, it was simply business.

And he had put her in a quandary because she was

clever enough to accept that he had given her the only choice she was likely to be given. It was a choice between marrying Raffaele Manzini and her family being made bankrupt and homeless. There was no compassion in him. He wanted what he wanted and to hell with who else got hurt in the process, she reasoned angrily, momentarily overpowered by the idea of having to deal with someone that far removed from her in moral outlook.

Women had had to do worse things in tight corners than marry and reproduce, she told herself fiercely. Oh, how she hated the reality that *he* had foreseen that she would change her mind! How could she marry someone she didn't even like or admire? How could she go to bed with him? Give him a child? In a rush she suppressed those reactions, which now felt embarrassingly weak and *sentimental*. Best not to think about those things, she told herself firmly, determined to reclaim her peace of mind and take a rational view of the situation. It would be much wiser to take it all one step at a time and handle events as they happened.

Raffaele Manzini was offering her family an escape route into a new way of life, a safer, more stable life such as they had *never* enjoyed before. After all, the crash of the very first business her father had started up was still following him with debts twenty years later. It would take so much stress off her parents; best of all it would protect her little brother, Matt, from the consequences of bankruptcy and homelessness. And Raffaele might think it was stupid for her to love her family as much as she did but what did that matter to her? There were no loving grandparents or any other relatives for her family to turn to in a crisis. Izzy, her twin, always tried to help but there wasn't much more she could do. There *was* only Maya and, like it or not, her family *needed* her. And if she could give them that one perfect chance to start afresh with a clean sheet, wouldn't that be the most wonderful gift for the *whole* family?

It wasn't as though she didn't like babies either. She adored babies but she couldn't even imagine having a child with Raffaele Manzini. *You're not allowed to think about the mechanics of the production project*, she reminded herself fiercely. Panic would plunge her back into emotional mode and that got her nowhere. Although he *was* a cold-blooded, callous, four-letter word of a guy to have confronted her as he had, both in the club and in that office.

Don't think about that either, she told herself firmly. If she had to say yes, it was more sensible not to dwell on any of it except in so far as she would have to protect herself in every way possible, she reasoned, tugging out a notebook and beginning to make rapid notes of certain non-negotiable demands she would have to make on her own behalf.

An hour after that Maya was walking back into Manzini Finance. Although she felt cool and in control, she knew it wouldn't last once she was exposed to *him* again. He put her on edge, he outraged her, he continually hogged the drivers' seat. Well, not *this* time around, she decided, wearing a steely expression that none of her family would have recognised.

CHAPTER THREE

'IT TOOK YOU a little longer to get up to speed than I expected,' Raffaele drawled cuttingly, surveying Maya with the complacent look of a cat with a cornered mouse. 'But here we are again.'

'Yes, here we are,' Maya agreed flat in tone, head held high, fingernails biting into her palms viciously because he hadn't been able to resist needling her even though he had won and that told her a lot about Raffaele Manzini. Resistance inflamed him because he wasn't accustomed to having to handle it, but he was going to *have* to learn because intelligence warned her that she and Raffaele were oil and water and would fight every step of the way.

'Take a seat,' he intoned smoothly.

'Don't mind if I do.' Maya settled back into the seat she had vacated in her rage earlier. 'I'll get straight to the point. I don't like you. I don't like anything I've so far seen in you but, as you said, you're the only game in town. If I want to help my family out of a crisis, I don't have a choice.'

'Oh, don't come over all martyr on me, Maya, because it's untrue,' Raffaele sliced in icily, wondering if anyone had ever dared to tell him that they didn't like him before, knowing they hadn't while wondering why that single tiny opinion should sting. 'If you do this, you do it by your *own* choice, not anyone else's.'

Hatred lashed through Maya like a storm unfurling inside her chest and that quickly she wanted to assault him again, because it was as if she were Eve in the Garden of Eden and he wouldn't even allow her a fig leaf to hide behind, no, not even the smallest excuse. 'Right, I do it by my own choice,' she gritted. 'But there are conditions.'

'I set the conditions.'

'No, you can't set *all* of them,' Maya countered steadily. 'I'm entitled to certain safeguards. The first is exclusivity. You stay out of other women's beds while you're with me.'

Raffaele's head flung up and back in surprise, luxuriant tousled black hair tumbling back from his cliff-edge cheekbones, dark eyes awash with gold rebellion. 'No.'

'I am not sleeping with you while you also sleep with other women,' Maya told him curtly. 'That is non-negotiable. If you can't commit to that, then we'll have to use artificial insemination as our method of conception.'

For a split second, Raffaele could not credit that she had said that to him because, in response, *hell no* flared straight through his every skin cell like an alarm bell, firing up his tension because he already knew that he wanted her. No, artificial insemination wasn't an acceptable alternative for him…even though he felt as though it *should've* been? That he shouldn't be so sexually invested in her in what was basically a business deal? So, he was human, after all, he reminded himself wryly.

'That's a yes to exclusivity but, once you're pregnant, all bets are off,' Raffaele conceded, choosing to be reasonable when he himself least felt like being reasonable because there was something about her that continually scratched him the wrong way and made him feel ridiculously like a rebellious teenager.

'That will do…' Almost imperceptibly, Maya's slender body lost some of its tension.

'Fidelity means *that* much to you?' Raffaele shot at her in surprise. 'I've never been faithful to anyone, but then I've never had anyone close enough to be faithful to.'

'As far as I'm concerned fidelity is the bedrock of any relationship.'

'I haven't *had* a relationship with a woman before,' Raffaele clarified without the smallest hint of discomfiture in making that admission. 'I have sexual affairs that rarely last longer than a couple of weeks.'

'That kind of shallow is just a touch adolescent at your age,' Maya remarked.

Raffaele was incredulous when he felt the hit of heat striking his cheekbones. He could not recall when anyone had last embarrassed him. His dark eyes flared bright as gold ingots with anger. 'I've always preferred to steer clear of serious relationships,' he told her.

'I read your profile online. That was kind of obvious. Right, moving on,' Maya continued with an air of efficiency that exasperated him. 'Health screening. That has to be done.'

'I don't have unprotected sex.'

'But you will be having it with me and if I agree to getting tested, you can too,' Maya cut in.

Raffaele spoke through gritted teeth. 'Anything else you feel as though you must air?'

'Yes, what do we do if a pregnancy doesn't happen? It can take up to a year even for a healthy couple to conceive. Were you aware of that?'

No, actually he hadn't been, but he would have preferred flogging to admitting that salient fact to her! Raffaele knew absolutely nothing about conception or pregnancy, only how best to *avoid* that development, which was why he had never taken the tiniest risk in that field.

'We can only deal with that situation if it occurs,' Raffaele fielded impatiently.

'I want full custody of any child we may have,' Maya informed him next.

'I won't agree to anything other than joint custody. For all I know you'll be a terrible mother,' Raffaele responded. 'I will maintain access rights to any child we have for that reason. It's my duty to protect my child too.'

Maya blinked in surprise, disconcerted by his attitude because she had fully expected him to be willing to sign over any rights to that prospective child whom he only wanted in the first place to fulfil a business purpose. That he should actually care about the child's welfare was a plus in his favour, the only plus he had shown her so far, she acknowledged grudgingly.

'Where is all this conception stuff to take place?' she enquired, pleased by her calmness.

'Italy, where we'll get married. I'm already putting the arrangements in order,' Raffaele volunteered.

Maya stiffened. 'You *do* like to put the cart before the horse, don't you?'

'But then I knew you'd come down off *your* high horse and agree,' Raffaele replied, setting her teeth on edge again.

'We'll be living in Italy?' she questioned. 'What am I supposed to tell my family?'

Raffaele shrugged a broad shoulder with magnificent disdain. 'Tell them we're getting married? You don't need to tell the whole truth. You could spin a love-at-first-sight story.'

'I don't like telling lies,' Maya said icily. 'I'll tell them you've offered me a job in Italy and that because of that famously compassionate streak of yours—' her lip curled at that provocative phrase and his teeth clenched again '—you've decided to erase their debts because of the connection that once existed between our families.'

'The *hate* connection, you mean?' A rough-edged laugh parted Raffaele's perfect masculine lips. 'Tell them whatever you like. It's not my business.'

'But you *made* it your business. You own *all* their debts, don't you? It's too big a coincidence that all their debts came home to roost on the same day,' Maya opined in disgust.

Raffaele jerked his chin in unashamed acknowledgement.

'So, you set up me up for this…*literally*,' Maya accused.

'No, you can thank my great-grandfather, Aldo, rather than me for that move. I didn't know you existed until he made me aware of it before informing me that he owned your family lock, stock and barrel,'

Raffaele recounted drily. 'If I hadn't been willing to play ball and go for the deal he offered me, he would have happily bankrupted your parents and made them homeless because he has no reason to like your family.'

An angry smile tilted Maya's lush pink mouth. 'Are you implying that I should be grateful for you and the marriage proposal?'

'Sì...' Raffaele confirmed, golden flames dancing in his arrogant challenging gaze. 'Without me, where would you and your family be?'

Incensed afresh, Maya jumped up. 'You just couldn't be kind for even ten minutes, could you be?' she snapped back at him, her furious voice shaking. 'You want me on my knees in gratitude...don't you?'

A sudden disturbing grin flashed across his lean, devastatingly handsome features as he vaulted upright, towering over her with his superior height. 'Now you're talking my language...what I wouldn't give at this moment to have you there!'

The explicit image she assumed he intended struck her like a mortifying, humiliating blow as she belatedly realised what she had said, and it was too much on top of everything else she had already endured from him. Her hand flashed up and he caught her wrist between long brown fingers before the slap could connect, his reflexes far faster than her own. 'No, don't you *dare*!' he breathed in a raw, wrathful undertone. 'Nobody hits me now.'

Nobody hits me now? What on earth did he mean? For an instant, Maya froze in shock and bewilderment at what he had said and what she had almost done. She was on the very brink of apologising as she moved away in a blindly direct line with the corner of the coffee table when he simply stretched down his long arms and scooped her up from the other side of the table separating them and lifted her bodily into the air. 'I'm sorry...put me down!' she gasped.

'I'm not going to hurt you. I don't *hurt* women. You were about to trip over the table,' Raffaele bit out, almost breathless as he stared down into her bright green eyes and his scorching gaze trailed down her heart-shaped face to the pillowy invitation of her pink lips. A raging beast of sexual hunger was clawing at him, disorientating him. *Nobody* hits *me now?* Why the hell had he let that slip out? He never, ever referred to the abuse he had suffered as a child.

'That's good, and thanks...now put me down,' Maya repeated urgently, her heart hammering so hard inside her chest she thought it might jump right out.

After an instant of hesitation during which she believed he was not about to listen to her at all, Raffaele slowly lowered her back to the floor a safe distance from the table and she snatched in a gasping breath. 'I didn't intend to frighten you,' he said flatly.

'I wasn't frightened, not exactly,' Maya framed, all out of breath and inspiration because, for the count of the ten seconds he had held her, she had experienced panic and then the strangest inner pulse of excitement that had left her quivering and embarrassed and all over the place. 'I'm sorry I went for you like that. You made me very angry. That's not an excuse...well, it is, isn't it? But I have never tried to hit another person before in my life and it won't happen again, I assure you.'

'Forget it,' Raffaele advised carelessly, fighting to suppress the sexual arousal she induced, willing away the desire pushing against his zipper, yes, the thought of her on her knees half-naked, yes, that really pressed every one of his sexual triggers and filled him with lust. 'But, as it looks like we're going to have a confrontational relationship, it makes sense to start working on that problem now.'

'Now?' Still a little dazed from dealing with him, simply being trapped in his energising, maddening radius, Maya looked up at him, her face feeling as flushed as though she had a fever.

'Yes, now. Time you started adapting to me and I start adapting to you because we're going to have to live together, potentially for months,' Raffaele pointed out levelly. 'We'll go and get you some clothes and we'll go out tonight.'

'Get me clothes?' she echoed in bewilderment.

'I hate that rag of a suit. I'll pick clothing for you and we'll go out,' Raffaele repeated, shooting her an assessing appraisal. 'This is your new life, Maya. *Show* me that you can handle it.'

Maya swallowed hard and just nodded, wondering what was wrong with her brain because it seemed to have gone to sleep. He wanted proof that she could act normally and fit into his world and she couldn't blame him for that. Was buying women clothes something he was used to doing?

Half an hour later, she was in a beauty salon, having her hair done and her nails painted, and her face made up. It was like a television makeover except with Raffaele in charge, his opinions sought, rather than hers. And she let him do it, reminding herself of what he would do for her family. He would take the nightmare of debt away. Surely it was a small enough sacrifice in return for her to surrender her independence and her strong will? But she'd never done the feminine stuff before, had never really cared what she wore or how she looked as long as she was decently covered.

Two hours later still, she was standing on a dais in a designer salon, clad in garments she wouldn't have been caught dead in and congratulating herself on her self-discipline in not fighting him. It disconcerted her, though, that Raffaele could be so determined to transform her at what she imagined to be enormous expense into the kind of woman he obviously preferred.

'That'll do,' he eventually conceded, beautiful wilful mouth still down-turning even after about the twentieth outfit that had been tried on for his perusal.

Raffaele didn't know why he was still so dissatisfied with Maya's appearance. Logically, she looked beautiful, hair like a pale shimmering veil loose to her waist, face enhanced with subtle cosmetics, glorious legs exposed in a brocade skirt that was the sort of thing he had seen other women wear. The leather and lace corset top exposed her delicate shoulders and slender arms, her pale, smooth, flawless skin exercising the most weird allure for him—he wanted to see his own hands on that skin with a hunger that was beginning to seriously annoy him because it wasn't cool. But she still didn't look *right* and why would she, he asked himself sarcastically, when he had never in his life before taken it upon himself to choose clothing for a woman?

And why had he done it? The power trip? He couldn't deny the appeal of that aspect. She brought out a bone-deep dominant urge he hadn't known he even possessed. But one look at her had also warned him that *she* didn't have a clue how to dress and surely he could not do worse with that challenge than she already had? In fact, he didn't think she had the slightest interest in what she put on her body because not once...and he had been watching carefully...had she demonstrated even a spark of pleasure at the vast choice of clothing now open to her. And he had watched her grimace at her make-up–enhanced features in the mirror, seemingly indifferent to how beautiful she looked. Didn't she have any normal female traits? Where was her vanity? Her drive to look her best? To impress? Even if it was only to impress other women?

Well, she *still* wasn't looking to impress him, he acknowledged grimly. Shopping, while being a pastime guaranteed to thrill most women, with Maya was like taking a robot out. She behaved as if she had resolved to do whatever it took to satisfy him while remaining determined not to take the smallest ounce of personal enjoyment out of the experience. Her vital spark was missing and it annoyed him. It *hugely* annoyed him. He might have told her that they needed to work on their confrontational vibe but, in truth, he enjoyed that vibe. No woman had ever come back at him as Maya did, refusing to please, refusing to accept her place, refusing to flatter his ego.

'You look good,' he told her almost fiercely.

Maya stepped daintily off the dais in the flamboyantly high heels he had insisted on. 'Well, you can tell what sort of women you're used to,' she commented half under her breath.

'Educate me,' Raffaele urged.

'Isn't it obvious? A skirt too short and tight to sit down in comfortably? Shoes I have to totter in? A top that bares far too much flesh?'

'You're not endowed enough in that sector to be showing too much flesh,' Raffaele riposted.

Maya hitched a naked little shoulder. 'So sorry if I am a disappointment in any department,' she murmured with a tiny poisonous smile.

'Sadly for you,' Raffaele retorted deadpan, resting a big bronzed hand possessively on a slim shoulder, 'you are *exactly* what I like most.'

'Cheap looking,' Maya said, tossing him a mutinous glance.

And disturbingly, Raffaele laughed with rich appreciation and resisted the urge to ask the designer hovering for an opinion because she wasn't likely to diss her own designs. He did not go for cheap-looking women… *did he*? Certainly, nobody could have accused him of going for unadventurous types, he conceded. Possibly he had always instinctively sought out the wilder, freer women, least likely to seek anything other than a bout of exciting sex from him.

No, Maya didn't fit the mould, but if he toned himself down a little and she relaxed a little, they could meet somewhere in the middle, couldn't they? *Madonna mia*… Thunderstruck at the sudden realisation that he was toying with the idea of changing his behaviour to *please* a woman, Raffaele froze in fleeting consternation. No, that was the wrong reading of the situation, he reasoned speedily. He might never have been in a relationship before, but he was required to make that effort with Maya to attain his ultimate goal. He was engaged in an act of persuasion aimed at coaxing Maya into accepting the necessary status quo. *Sì*, that sounded much more like him…calculating and logical.

He took her to a private members' club for dinner.
She walked like a queen through the public dining
room into the private room he had engaged. A momentary hush fell on their entry. Every eye was on her as
diners greeted him with nods and waves, but she looked
at no one, little chin held high, clear green eyes blank.
He had seen models on catwalks with more expression.
It foiled him: he couldn't tell what she was thinking,
and why was that annoying too?

Her slender neck looked bare: she needed jewellery.
He recalled his mother's vast cache of jewels stowed in
a bank vault since her death and he thought, why not
let Maya wear them? They were unlikely to be worn
again in his lifetime because he didn't ever see himself taking a wife for real. Maya wouldn't be able to
keep the jewellery, of course. He would get that written
into the pre-nup already being drawn up for them. He
stabbed a button on his phone, speaking to his Italian
lawyer as they were ushered to their table.

Maya collapsed down with relief into a chair, flexing her crushed toes in the new shoes, wondering if
she dared to slip them off, would she ever get them on
again to walk out? Going out with Raffaele was an educational experience, she mused dizzily. People dropped
everything to attend to his needs. He had walked into
a beauty salon with a busy waiting area and she had
been led straight to a stylist. In the same manner, the
designer had abandoned someone else to deal with her
needs exclusively.

Raffaele was richer than rich, and businesspeople
knew it and fawned on him, granting his every demand without protest or delay. No doubt he paid in
spades for that kind of service but being in the pres-

ence of the power that extreme wealth gave him over others was shocking in its own way, and had taught Maya why he hadn't expected her to argue with anything. He was much more accustomed to those slavishly eager to please, ready to roll over and perform obediently at his first request.

'How do you know so much about me and my family?' Maya enquired over the first course.

'Aldo gave me a file,' Raffaele admitted. 'That's how he does business. He still has a bee in his bonnet about the fact that his grandson, my father, gave your parents the money to set up home in the UK.'

'And it *was* given, not loaned, according to my parents,' Maya cut in curtly.

'But it was Aldo's cash,' Raffaele retorted with finality. 'My father cut ties with his family soon afterwards when he married my mother instead of yours as Aldo had decreed.'

'So, Aldo is bossy like you,' Maya observed.

'I'm not bossy.'

'You *so* are,' Maya told him, lifting a fine blonde brow in emphasis.

Raffaele could feel his patience sliding again. 'Let's leave how we arrived at this point behind us. They're not *your* debts.'

'But I'm the one paying for them,' she pointed out helplessly.

'This topic is closed,' Raffaele dictated.

Silence fell. Maya dealt him an amused glance and concentrated on her food.

'Possibly…' Raffaele breathed tautly. 'I can be a little too dominant.'

'Or…' Maya pondered. 'You just want to leave the

truth behind and make me behave like I'm one of your women.'

'I do not have women in the plural,' Raffaele informed her levelly. 'Why are you so determined to argue with me?'

A faint pink lit Maya's face and she jerked a slight shoulder and fell silent. She felt an intense need to keep him at a distance. Because she disliked him? Or because dredging her attention from that lean, beautiful face of his across the table was becomingly increasingly difficult? This close he had stunning eyes, dark pools laced with fascinating gold highlights, inky black lashes even better than eyeliner at framing that lustrous gaze. Her breath feathered in her throat, her chest tightening as she felt her nipples stiffen, and a hollow ache stirred between her thighs. She was not so dumb that she didn't know what was happening to her even if it hadn't happened to her in a man's company before…

It struck her as cruelly ironic that that surge of physical attraction should strike with Raffaele Manzini. She had been waiting, *wanting* to feel that exciting hormonal buzz with a man and take advantage of it to gain some sexual experience. Her face bloomed with colour because that seemed such an obnoxious thought to have, but as it dawned on her that Raffaele Manzini would be her first lover she found herself wishing that she weren't still a virgin. No man had ever drawn her enough to want to take that final step. Was that why she had been waiting like the Sleeping Beauty, or some such silly creature, for that first love to come along and give her that happy fairy-tale ending?

She almost laughed at how ridiculously naïve she

had been for so many years, honestly believing that that one very special guy was going to just magically appear for her. That wasn't how life worked. Life wasn't that neat and tidy; it wasn't like an exam to prepare for and pass. But Maya had never done anything she hadn't pre-planned because she rarely took risks, had learned at far too early an age that she was the one who had to be mature, sensible and careful to look after her family. There had been no teenaged crushes, no infatuations, no first boyfriend who counted in any meaningful way. The whole sex and romance story had passed her by while she'd worked and studied and passed exam after exam because the academic world was stable and sensible and gave her no nasty surprises.

And it was a very nasty surprise to accept that she could feel her body burn as though someone had turned a blowtorch on her just because a man smiled. Raffaele Manzini, womaniser that he was, had dynamite sex appeal. It had nothing to do with her brain, it was all physical, meaningless, forgettable, she told herself urgently. He was making conversation, smoothly, entertainingly, sticking slickly to the impersonal because she knew that he had decided that *she* was prickly and difficult. But she wasn't, she *wasn't*. He…he just made her angry. And why was he surprised by that when he had virtually blackmailed her into agreeing to marry him and have a child for him? Was he so spoiled by her sex that, no matter what he did, he expected admiration and appreciation?

'I was planning to take you to a club *but* I think you'd prefer to go home.'

'I would but not dressed like this,' Maya confessed.

'I'll tell my family lies tomorrow, not tonight. I'm too tired this evening to tell smiling, soothing lies.'

'I'll take you back to my apartment to change. Your clothes are there,' Raffaele admitted.

'Why are they at your apartment?' Maya asked as she stood up, wincing as she forced her feet back into the new shoes again.

'Obviously because I thought you'd spend the night with me,' Raffaele confessed without hesitation. 'Why would we wait for a ring to get this show on the road?'

Even in her heels she had to tilt her head to look up at him. He had to be six feet four or five. His confession had blown her resolve to be polite and pleasant right out of the water again because it told her so much that she didn't want to see in him. 'You are unbelievable,' she snapped at him, bristling with distaste. 'I only met you properly for the first time this morning!'

'Believe me, it feels like I've known you a lot longer,' Raffaele murmured, sincere for once because he couldn't quite credit that it had only been a few hours since their first meeting. In the strangest way, in a way he couldn't possibly explain, he felt ridiculously comfortable with Maya even though she had sat there damning him with her eyes and acting moody as hell.

But Maya was only winding up, her temper like petrol on a bonfire as she studied his ridiculously beautiful and insouciant face. 'And you thought I would be willing to fall into bed with you *immediately*?' She gasped incredulously.

'A guy can hope—that's not a crime,' Raffaele fielded, shifting to ease the pressure on his jeans because there it was again, that spear of unholy lust that she roused without even *trying*, without even touching him. The sexual charge of her blew him away.

'You don't hope, you *expect*!' Maya corrected angrily, gathering her bag in a quick angry movement and clutching it to her chest. 'Sex and baby-making is off the table *until* we're married.'

'That doesn't surprise me.'

Maya stalked forward, green eyes bright as emeralds. 'Why doesn't it surprise you?'

'Because you don't trust me, you don't trust anyone,' Raffaele told her softly. 'I'm like that too. And on top of not trusting, you're…inhibited.'

'I'm not inhibited!' Maya snapped at him.

Raffaele took her hand and pressed her back against the wall. 'If you're not, kiss me.'

'I'm not kissing you!' Maya spat.

'But secretly you know you want to,' Raffaele purred, leaning down to steal a tiny kiss from her pink pouting mouth, lingering to nibble on her full soft lower lip, sending a shattering flood of sensation snaking right down into her pelvis. 'One kiss…that's all… I promise not to try to take it any further.'

'OK…one kiss,' Maya conceded in a deliberately bored tone. 'Then you let go of me and you *don't* forget about those *health* checks.'

He kissed her and the world fell away. She hadn't believed that could happen, but it did. Her fear surged beneath the drowning electrifying pleasure that consumed her when his tongue licked against hers, unexpectedly subtle, incredibly sexy in technique, like nothing she had ever experienced before in her life, and for the first time ever she wanted more, arms travelling round him, hands smoothing over a broad, warm, strong back before sliding down to curve to lean hips.

'I won't forget about the health checks,' Raffaele breathed, lifting his head, dark eyes flaming bright as the sun with hunger. 'Stay the night with me,' he urged. 'I'll use protection.'

Maya returned to planet earth again, unnerved by his physical effect on her, trembling, all hot and flustered in a way she wasn't used to being. 'No, thanks. I want to go home, please,' she said as tightly as a little girl trying to show that she could be polite even in trying circumstances.

'Stay the night with me. I'll use protection.'

Raffaele had knocked her straight back down to reality again. Nothing romantic or special there, she mocked herself for the quivering hunger still tugging at her unrepentant body. Raffaele was just like all the other men she had met, wanting more what he couldn't have. Reluctance only heightened her appeal with such men.

'As you wish...' Raffaele gritted his teeth. 'But I don't understand you.'

'Of course, you don't. I'm not the type of woman you're used to,' Maya pointed out drily as she opened the door to leave. 'I'm not anyone's one-night stand.'

Raffaele breathed in so deep that he thought the top of his head ought to go flying off. 'We're getting married within the next week.'

Beneath his disbelieving gaze, Maya grimaced. 'I wasn't expecting it to be quite *that* soon—'

'Let's move,' Raffaele urged, planting a hand to her rigid spine, watching male heads turn to watch her progress, those endless perfect legs, that shimmering cloud of naturally fair hair. The whole time he was thinking, She may not know it yet but *she's mine*, will be absolutely totally mine. He marvelled at that thought, smiled with amusement at it, could not get over quite how invested he was becoming in the project to acquire her grandparents' company.

CHAPTER FOUR

RAFFAELE LIVED IN a breathtaking penthouse apartment with a fabulous view of London at night.

Maya, concentrating on the need to escape his company, spared it barely a glance, wincing in her tight shoes as she walked down a tiled corridor to the bedroom he had indicated and shutting the door firmly in his lean bronzed face.

Kicking off the shoes with relief, she scrambled to get into her own clothes again and walked into the adjoining bathroom to do what she could to scrub off the cosmetics she rarely wore. She did not want her family to suspect anything was amiss. Luckily, she had not yet got around to mentioning the job she had already found in London and she would tell them instead that she had got a fabulous job in Italy with Raffaele Manzini. Her story would all tie in nicely together then, with Raffaele starring as the kind and generous guy he, most certainly, wasn't. By the time she finished telling them that he was also writing off their debts, her parents would be extravagantly happy, and it was many months since she had seen them in that state and she couldn't wait to see their faces. That was the pay-off, she reminded herself firmly, her family's security and contentment would be her reward for what she was doing but, no, she wasn't planning to act the martyr even inside her own head.

But she didn't feel the same about lying to her sister because she had never lied to her sister before; she'd possibly told the odd fib to save Izzy from hurt feelings but never anything more than that because, as twins, they were so close. She winced, reckoning that this time around she didn't have much choice.

Raffaele felt a little like he had as a child when he had tried to capture a summer dandelion clock floating through the air and signally failed. He didn't understand Maya. She didn't *like* him. She might be as hungry for him as he was for her, but she wouldn't break even *one* of her doubtless lengthy list of rules to have him. For that reason and for the unavoidable truth that Maya's liking and acceptance were important to him for the foreseeable future, he would make an effort with a woman for the first time in his life, only there was just one small problem: he hadn't a clue *how* to do that. He frowned, exasperated by the uncharacteristic uncertainty engulfing him.

'What sort of clothes do I like?' Maya echoed dimly, several days later, stretching back on her bunk bed with her phone cradled close. 'I've never really thought much about it. Students only dress for important interviews. I like elegant and feminine, not fussy and frilly, though, and never ever short, tight or revealing. Why on earth are you asking?'

'I have a wedding dress to choose since you said you don't care what you wear.'

'I wasn't being awkward,' Maya said apologetically,

wondering why she got on with Raffaele so much better on the phone than she did in person. 'I mean…it's not a *real* wedding, that's what I meant.'

'But we want it to *look* real,' Raffaele countered. 'Aldo's coming, so are some of my friends.'

That was all news to Maya, and it disconcerted her. 'Oh…er…well—'

'Want to join me today?' Raffaele pressed. 'You could pick your own dress.'

His dark deep voice purred down her spine like a caress and she rolled her eyes at the thought. He had rung her every day, asked her out every day while chattering about completely inconsequential things. What on earth was he playing at? Why was he bothering? What nefarious purpose was his uncharacteristic niceness supposed to achieve for him?

'I'm taking my brother out to the British Museum… sorry—' She would have loved to see her sister, Izzy, but knew that would be unwise with all that was going on and the fictions she had had to tell her family. Besides, Izzy had gone strangely quiet herself recently.

'You spent yesterday with him as well,' Raffaele reminded her with an edge.

'I'm going to be parted from my family for months.'

'I've already assured you that you can fly home and visit them any time you want. It's all in the pre-nuptial agreement. Didn't you read it?'

'I read it cover to cover.' Maya set her teeth together before she found herself arguing with him again about the allowance he was insisting she would receive after their marriage terminated, and the even bigger fortune she would walk away with should they have a child. It all seemed so cold and dry and shoddy to her, raised as she had been to look on marriage and child-bearing as something you only did with someone you loved. Only she could hardly say that to Raffaele when she had agreed to those terms, could she?

Maya's breath caught in her throat when she saw the sprawling mansion at the foot of the long straight drive. Somehow she had expected Raffaele's home in Tuscany to be as aggressively modern as his London apartment, and the big graceful property with its landscaped gardens and much older design took her by surprise. Whatever, it scarcely mattered to her, she reasoned apprehensively when her wedding was only a few hours away, to be staged that very afternoon.

How could she possibly be getting married without a single member of her family present? And how could she be marrying a man she didn't love? A kind of panic Maya had never felt before sat like a large immovable stone in her hollow tummy. That panic had nothing to do with logic and had not even been soothed by her family's display of happy relief that week as her parents were freed from all their worst fears and were finally able to contemplate a fresh start in life. Her father, Rory, was actually looking for a job, admitting to her that he had only kept on trying to start up his own business because he had believed that a successful business was his only hope of amassing sufficient cash to pay off their debts.

But, worst of all, Maya missed her twin sister, because Izzy had always been her safe place when the cruel realities of life threatened to crush her. She was used to confiding in Izzy, being soothed by her sibling's more light-hearted and optimistic nature. But she could *not* share her current predicament with Izzy, because she knew that Izzy would've told her not to go ahead, and that their parents' financial problems were not solely their responsibility to fix. Unfortunately, the hard truth of that belief, Maya acknowledged ruefully, was that there *was* nobody else to fix those problems, and that watching poor little Matt suffer alongside their parents was more than Maya could bear when she had been put in a position where she could help. For that reason, there was no excuse for distressing her twin with a situation that could not be changed by wishful thinking. She would tell her sister afterwards, when the whole wretched arrangement was almost over... perhaps once she had conceived.

Of course, that wasn't something she could think about when conception was inextricably linked to the necessity of having sex with Raffaele Manzini. He was gorgeous. Doubtless he would be charming and experienced and pretty much physically what the average woman could only dream of for her first experience. But what mattered most to Maya was that she had no sense of connection with him. Her body operated around him on its own agenda while her brain stayed free, recognising the cold calculation in him, the ruthlessness, the lack of caring. He could flirt, he could talk up a storm, in truth he could be incredibly entertaining, but it wasn't enough for her...

Only it *had* to be enough, she reminded herself doggedly as she climbed out of the limo that had brought her from the airport, fresh from the incredible luxury of her flight in the Manzini private jet. And now it was her wedding day and she had to settle down and accept the conditions she had already agreed, she told herself urgently. Deep down inside she was far too sensitive, far too much of a dreamer, *weak*, she thought, full of self-loathing at that moment. With Raffaele, she needed to be tough as steel and hard as stone to hold her own.

Raffaele watched her emerge from the limo, a slender graceful figure in jeans and a light top, blonde hair braided down her back, and that fast his body reacted. He was amused because that reaction was only telling him what he already knew: Maya had a weird effect on him. The sound of her husky laughter on the phone affected him the same strange way. He only hoped that she would be pleased with the surprise he had helped to engineer for her. Surely she would be delighted? Nobody appeared to be more family-orientated than Maya was.

Maya was disconcerted to find Raffaele poised in the grand hallway. Her luggage was being ferried past her while a maid waited to show her upstairs to her room. A smile curved his shapely sculpted lips and, for once, carried up to lighten his dark eyes to shimmering gold, and her heart stuttered as though he had punched her, she reflected with inner recoil at her response to him. Posed there in sunlight, blue-black hair gleaming, his flawless bronzed features smiling, and his tall, powerful physique casually clad in jeans and a tee, he took her breath away…whether she liked it or not.

'I have a surprise for you. I can only hope it's a good one,' Raffaele murmured quietly. 'Your grandparents are here, hoping to meet you.'

'My… P-Parisi grandparents?' Maya stammered in disbelief.

'Aldo told them about the wedding, and they contacted me to ask if they could attend. They're a little disappointed that your mother and your siblings won't be coming but they're very eager to meet you,' he told her.

'But I thought they wanted nothing to do with any of us!' she exclaimed, taken aback by the development but wondering only briefly how to behave because she had been raised to always be polite and kind.

'I think you'll find that the passage of time and loneliness have changed their outlook. Your mother *is* an only child,' Raffaele reminded her. 'But be warned, your grandmother cries a lot. She's very emotional.'

'So is my mother,' Maya confided with a sudden smile as she braced herself because Raffaele already had a hand at her spine to press her into the room.

Maya focused on the two people who had stood up to greet her. They were older than she had expected, must have been quite an age when her mother was born, she worked out, searching their faces for familiarity and finding it there in her grandmother's damp dark eyes and her small, portly grandfather's anxious expression. She could see her mother's lineage in their faces, and it warmed her into moving forward and extending her arms to the weeping older woman.

'Maya, this is Fortunato and Assunta Parisi, your grandparents,' Raffaele told her.

'I am your *nonna*,' the elderly lady framed on the back of a sob.

'I'll leave you to get acquainted,' Raffaele volunteered, closing the door again.

And there was much chatter and many tears from Maya's *nonna* as the older woman looked in delight at the photos on Maya's phone to see the daughter she had not seen for over twenty years and the pictures of her other two grandchildren.

'You see, now we understand that life had moved on, but we had stayed the same,' Assunta explained. 'We brought up Lucia as we were brought up and expected her to be identical, but the world outside our walls was a different and more modern one and we ignored that influence.'

'You threw her out when she was pregnant,' Maya could not help reminding the older couple.

'We wanted her to agree to have the baby privately adopted, and she wouldn't.'

Maya sighed. 'Thank goodness she didn't or Izzy and I might never have known our parents.'

'I didn't think your father was good enough for her,' her grandfather admitted reluctantly. 'He was penniless and my daughter had never worked a day in her life.'

'They've had their problems with money management,' Maya confided wryly. 'But they are still very much in love with each other.'

Her grandparents looked relieved to hear that news, as if even though that marriage might not have been what they had wanted for their daughter, they were still pleased it had worked out for her.

Raffaele reappeared. 'Sorry to break this up but the bride has to start getting dressed,' he announced.

And her grandmother was up in a trice, keen to accompany Maya. Before Maya left the room, he signalled a maid to show the older woman upstairs and said levelly to Maya, 'Did I make the right choice in letting them come?'

Maya smiled brightly and nodded simultaneously. 'Yes, you did. It was a little embarrassing admitting to them that this is a secret wedding, but I encouraged them to consider contacting my mother and I passed over the phone number,' she confided in a rush. 'I think there will eventually be a reconciliation. Everybody seems to be in the right place now for that to happen.'

'And your family being happy makes you happy?' Raffaele queried in apparent surprise.

'Doesn't yours?'

'I don't have a family. My mother's dead, I *first* met my father when I was twenty-one and my acquaintance with Aldo only began last month,' he told her flatly.

'I didn't realise any of that,' Maya admitted, silenced by those admissions, striving to think of what her life might have been like without the background of support and love that she pretty much took for granted. 'You're very alone.'

Raffaele shrugged and frowned. 'I'm a loner by nature. It hasn't harmed me.'

Maya almost dared to differ with that sentiment because it explained a lot to her—his lack of emotional understanding, for a start. 'You did something kind for me. I didn't think you were capable of that,' she admitted frankly.

Raffaele inclined his arrogant dark head and one of the staff approached with a pile of gift-wrapped boxes. 'It's a wedding gift.'

Her brow furrowed. 'Who from?'

Raffaele tensed, outrageously long black lashes curling up with incredulity. 'From me.'

'Oh…'

'I decided that I didn't want you wearing my mother's jewellery.'

Her facial muscles tightened. 'That's perfectly understandable.'

'No, you're misunderstanding me...*again*,' Raffaele
stressed. 'For me, there's nothing but bad memories attached to my mother's jewellery, and I've now arranged
to have it auctioned off. These jewels are new, and for
you to wear and *keep*.'

Bad memories? Curiosity assailed her, furthered
by the haunting darkness of his gaze. But she was also
disconcerted and embarrassed because it would never
have occurred to her to buy anything for him even as
a token wedding gift. Maya nodded jerkily. 'Thank
you very much.'

Raffaele gazed down at her in mounting frustration,
craving something he wanted from her, unable to label
it, only able to recognise by his own dissatisfaction that
he wasn't receiving it. 'It's no big deal. I've got money
to burn,' he fielded drily.

'I'd better go and start getting dressed,' Maya muttered, backing slowly away, her eyes locked involuntarily to the liquid burning gold of his.

'All I can think about is *undressing* you,' Raffaele
confided without even thinking about it, and then he
watched her face freeze and shutter and knew it had
been the wrong thing to say. But *why* was it the wrong
thing? Once again, he felt at a tactical disadvantage, as
if everyone else but him had the right script in Maya's
radius. She wanted him. He could see that in her eyes,
when she looked at him with need and desire. What
could be wrong with expressing that? Was she really
that shy? And if she *was* shy, how did he handle that?
Because vast as his experience was, he had never been
with a shy woman.

A maid leading the way, Maya hurried upstairs to arrive breathless in an opulent bedroom suite embellished with superb polished antique furniture. There a hair stylist, a make-up artist and her grandmother eagerly awaited the bride's arrival. Her *nonna* addressed the maid in Italian, ordering some drink that Maya had never heard of.

'We drink it at weddings,' Assunta Parisi assured her, her likeness to Maya's mother, Lucia, in her greying dark hair and warm eyes lifting Maya's spirits. 'It's wonderful that you speak Italian. Raffaele didn't mention that.'

'He doesn't know yet. He speaks to me in English. I picked it up from Mum when I was a child and then added Italian in as an additional course at university,' Maya admitted, and when the maid arrived with an elaborate decanter and fancy glasses, she felt that it would have seemed churlish for her to declare then that she didn't usually drink.

Anyway, she thought rebelliously as the preparation of the bride began, perhaps she needed a little pick-me-up to face what lay ahead: sex with Raffaele. Of course, she could get through that as long as she didn't think about the logistics of having to strip off in front of him, open her body to a virtual stranger and act as if it were no big deal. Easy-peasy, she told herself firmly, no silly timid bride here, as she drank down the sweet liqueur. A little while later, a faint buzz hazed her thoughts and she began to feel a tad more relaxed. So, one or two drinks just to grease the wheels of her family-saving marriage and why not? After all, she probably wouldn't be drinking while she was trying to get pregnant, she reasoned ruefully.

She had set the gift boxes on the dressing table when she entered the room and while the stylist was doing her hair, her *nonna* asked what they were and, learning, urged her to open them immediately. With reluctance, because gifts struck her as inappropriate in her non-relationship with Raffaele, she opened the first and everyone present gasped. The opened boxes revealed a king's ransom in jewels, ranging from a superb tiara to a necklace that was a glittering waterfall of diamonds.

Her *nonna* squeezed her shoulder and leant down to whisper, 'He told your *nonno* and I that it was a marriage of business, but he *lied*. No man gives such magnificence in *those* circumstances,' she assured her grandchild with proud satisfaction. 'You are very beautiful and educated and he has fallen in love. Finally, the old bitterness between our families will be buried and forgotten.'

Maya might have been betrayed into laughing out loud at that fanciful conviction had not the maid brought out the wedding gown to display to them. Her breath caught in her throat because it was gorgeous and absolutely not what she had expected when Raffaele had done the choosing. She had been prepared for something tight, revealing and sexy such as he preferred, not a dream of a long dress with fine lace sleeves, a fitted bodice and layers and layers of silk in the skirt that glistened with handmade embroidery and shimmering crystals. The most daring aspect of the gown was the cutaway above the waist, which would bare a section of her back, so not very daring at all, not chosen for him, but chosen by him for *her*, which was another surprise.

And she didn't *like* Raffaele surprising her, especially not after she had believed she understood him to perfection and had set him in stone to play his role as the spoiled, selfish and dissolute bridegroom. As her grandmother enthused about the wedding gown, wild horses could not have dragged the truth out of Maya, that in fact Raffaele had chosen the dress, because suddenly she was ashamed of that truth, that she had agreed to their marriage but had nonetheless *refused* to play *her* role. Shame made her reach for her glass of liqueur again and sip in haste because the alcohol was blurring her dark thoughts. She, who prided herself on being kind, fair and reasonable, had been mean, angry and resentful of a choice *she* had made because she *could* have walked away from Raffaele's offer.

Her fingers curled on her grandfather's arm as he escorted her proudly down the aisle of the picturesque country church, which was festooned with flowers and crammed with smiling, staring guests. The wedding had never felt more real to Maya than it did at that moment as her gaze travelled anxiously to the male awaiting her at the altar. There he stood, Raffaele Manzini, the last man alive she had expected to try to turn their business marriage into a more normal one when she had made no effort whatsoever. And he *was* beautiful, tall and lithe and dark and sleek, for once formally clad in his wedding finery, a light grey morning suit teamed with a cravat, waistcoat and tailored dress pants.

Her throat tightened, butterflies buzzing like bees in her taut stomach, every inch of her reacting to his raw masculinity, and it was so completely, utterly unnerving to Maya, who felt so threatened by that instinctive response, that she hastily dropped her gaze again.

They knelt on velvet cushions and the priest performed the ceremony in both English and Italian, yet once again mutiny and a sense of wrong stirred within Maya, who had only ever expected to wed in all sincerity and love. Raffaele eased a slender platinum band onto her finger and tugged her round to face him as though he intended to kiss her while their guests swelled the church with song in celebration of their rites.

'You look divine…like a breathtakingly beautiful ice maiden,' he whispered, stunning dark tawny eyes locked to her flawless face with an intensity she could feel, and it only made her tremble.

'It's cool in here,' she deflected with a faint shake in her voice, turning her head away from him in denial that he could make her feel so unlike herself.

Maya had never allowed a man to affect her, had believed that that was her choice alone, and now she was discovering different and it scared her. She met Raffaele's eyes and her body lit up like the sunrise at dawn, sexual awareness flooding her in an unstoppable tide, heat and tension gripping her. It made her feel out of control for the first time ever and she hated that.

On the steps of the church he introduced her to his great-grandfather, Aldo, the man she knew she had to blame for masterminding her predicament, she conceded. Yet how could she bestow blame on anyone when her family was finally free of the debts that had stolen their happiness for so many years? Deciding that she could not, she met Aldo's shrewd dark eyes, set in his worn face, with a smile.

'That was generous of you,' Raffaele remarked in surprise as the nurse accompanying Aldo wheeled the elderly man away again.

'As you reminded me,' Maya murmured stiffly, 'I picked this option.'

'We will both adapt to this, to *us* as a couple,' Raffaele pronounced with assurance. 'That you want me as much as I want you gives us a solid foundation.'

'Your idea of a foundation and mine are as far apart as the polar ice caps,' Maya fielded tightly, wishing that she could deny what he said but remembering that kiss with an inner shudder, that kiss that had taught her that she was utterly naïve when it came to sensual temptation. But what was the point in beating herself up about it when she should be grateful for that attraction with a wedding night lying ahead of them?

Her stomach began churning again and the first thing she did when they arrived back at the house, where a reception was being staged, was reach for a glass of champagne being proffered by a uniformed waiter.

Why was she so nervous about sex? Was it only that she didn't love Raffaele? Was it that she knew the first time might very likely hurt to some degree? Or was it simply that Raffaele was *already* making her feel far more than she was comfortable feeling for him? Her emotions were getting involved: he fascinated her.

The truth of that admission slivered through her like a threat because his attraction for her wasn't solely physical. No, the source of that deeper attraction lay in the seeming conflicts she sensed within him. On the surface, Raffaele was cool, logical and ruthless but deep down, where it didn't show to the outside world, Raffaele was actually intense and volatile and highly intelligent, capable of being unexpectedly sensitive to her wants and needs.

That was the man who had searched out her dream wedding gown and who had invited her long-lost Italian grandparents to attend their wedding to foster a family reunion for her benefit. There had also been the jewellery he had given her to replace items he had admitted would only resurrect bad memories for him. All those actions were very personal and specific and the very opposite of what she had expected from him.

'I thought you didn't touch alcohol,' Raffaele commented.

'A wedding should be an exception to any rule like that,' Maya fibbed, determined not to admit that she was so feeble that the alcohol was easing her nervous tension and relaxing her. Dutch courage, she had heard it called—well, today she needed it, lest somewhere in her mind she found that dangerous sexual attraction combining with deeper feelings of a more personalised nature. No, she wasn't foolish enough to make that mistake with the bridegroom.

She had noticed the effect Raffaele had on women, even in the church. Eyes trailing acquisitively over him and lingering before looking enviously at her, a feminine hunger that she recognised now that she had experienced it for herself. But Raffaele wasn't hers and never would be. He wanted the right to buy a giant technology company and she, as well as the child she might conceive, were the price. And that was *all* he wanted. Maya wasn't going to be the idiot who forgot that salient fact for a second.

In the aftermath of the luxury buffet, Raffaele swept her out onto the dance floor and she thought once again about how shockingly fast her life had changed. She had married a man who owned a home large enough to provide a fancy pillared party room with a dance floor. How weird was that?

His hand splayed across her hip as he steered her round the floor and she could feel him, lean and powerful, fingers lifting to her spine to feather against bare skin that had never felt more naked. It was a revelation that that little keyhole of unadorned skin above her waist could be that sensitive and she shivered, still fighting that response to a man she barely knew.

Raffaele tensed as once again his bride moved out of contact. It was as if she didn't want him when he knew she did. That desire was there in her eyes whenever she looked at him. Why did she then back away? His hand lifted from her shoulder and his fingers splayed to lace into the wondrous fall of her pale fair hair, tipping her head back, lifting her face to his. He collided with distrustful green eyes fresh as ferns and before he had even thought about it he was crushing that ripe pink mouth under his, plundering it with raw fervour.

Maya reacted to the burn of his sensual mouth on hers, setting her on fire in places she didn't want to think about but, even so, she was achingly aware of the tautness of her nipples and the yawning ache between her slender thighs. Closing him out didn't work—he burned through her defences like a blowtorch, she conceded grudgingly. Embrace that, her brain urged her; *fight* it, her instincts protested.

'I want a drink,' she told him, angling her head back, stepping away.

'You're driving me crazy. Is that the point?' Raffaele pressed with a ragged edge to his dark deep accented drawl, dark caramel eyes shimmering like gold lighting the shadows.

Maya was feeling dizzy, hazy.

Raffaele stared down at her dilated pupils and murmured, 'I think a drink is the last thing you need. Time for us to leave.'

'Leave?' she exclaimed in astonishment.

'We're leaving on my yacht, *Manzini One.*'

Manzini One? Self-important, much? Her tummy shimmied at the prospect of the sea and she breathed in deep and slow. 'I feel dizzy.'

'Of course, you do. You're drunk,' Raffaele pronounced, suddenly cool and judgemental in tone.

'I'm *not*!' Maya protested fiercely.

And she was still arguing the toss all the way through the polite goodbyes to their guests and into the helicopter, when silence fell because it demanded too much effort to talk over the noise of the rotor blades and, besides, she was beginning to feel a little bit queasy.

Unasked, Raffaele scooped her out of the helicopter and carried her down a wooden dock in silence.

'What are you doing?' she demanded sharply.

'What I have to do,' Raffaele parried grimly.

Maya groaned. 'I didn't intend to drink so much.'

'It's our wedding night,' Raffaele reminded her unnecessarily. 'This is not a good start. But when you said you didn't drink, was that a warning that you *shouldn't* drink?'

'No, this is my very *first* time ever intoxicated,' Maya told him with precision. 'Take that as you will.'

'Not a compliment.'

'Wasn't intended to be.'

'Was the idea of sex with me *that* offensive?' Raffaele growled in apparent disbelief.

'I know that you want me to say that it wasn't but the way I think, it would be wrong,' she framed apologetically.

'You're my bride! This is our wedding night,' Raffaele countered with startling ferocity.

'But you feel like a stranger,' his bride admitted in colloquial Italian before she passed out.

CHAPTER FIVE

MAYA WAKENED WITH a groan, tormented by the waking nightmare of the night she had passed.

Dawn light illuminated surroundings that were still only vaguely familiar. A big room, a glimpse of the sea through a window, a slight rolling gait in tune with the swell of the sea something else to be regretted alongside the amount of alcohol she had imbibed the day before. She scrambled out of bed, her head aching and still swimming, shame almost choking her. But the mortification of her splintered shards of memory was indescribably worse…

She recalled floundering like a landed fish on top of a pale marble floor and wanting to die, literally *die*. Worst of all, she recalled throwing up in that bathroom with Raffaele tugging her hair out of the way. She recalled Raffaele tucking her into bed, trying to get tea down her, failing because her stomach wasn't up to anything but water and even drinking that had been a challenge, she remembered with a shudder. Raffaele had looked after her; she remembered in shock that he had bothered, that he hadn't just stuck her in a yacht cabin to be sick without him as an audience. What did it say about her that she dearly wished he had simply abandoned her to her sufferings?

Sal was out on deck at dawn having a cigarette when Raffaele emerged from the couple of hours of sleep he had snatched and stepped onto the terrace with a cup of black coffee in his hand.

'So?' Sal challenged, smooth as glass. 'Marriage not quite what you expected?'

Raffaele breathed in deep and slow and strove to resist rising to the bait, but the temptation was too great. 'I thought she had more sense.'

'You blackmailed her... I can't imagine why she would be so sensitive,' Sal murmured softly.

Raffaele clenched his teeth together and said nothing at all, waiting until the older man went back inside before making the same move.

Maya emerged from the bathroom, every inch of her washed and shampooed and freshened, her slender body clad in denim shorts and tee shirt, but nothing could take the awful memories away. Her head was still sore. She winced as the cabin door opened. Cabin, she repeated ruefully to herself, for such an ordinary word in no way described the shining expanse of the wooden floor, the opulent upholstery, the glorious built-in furniture or the patio doors that led out onto a private terrace that was also splendidly equipped. When she glanced up to see who had entered and saw Raffaele carrying a tray, her knees gave way and she dropped down on the side of the bed sooner than look him in the eye.

'Feeling pretty rough?' Raffaele murmured flatly.

'Let's be frank… I deserve it,' Maya muttered. 'I can only say sorry—there's not much else I can say.'

Raffaele extended a glass of water to her. 'Painkillers,' he proffered, dropping a couple on her lap. 'No need to suffer if you don't need to.'

Maya snatched in a steadying breath and took the pills, imbibing the water slowly, still terrified that she would start feeling ill again. Mercifully that phase of her recovery seemed to be over. 'I don't usually do stuff like this,' she sighed.

A table settled in front of her and a tray appeared on it. 'Eat.'

'I'm not hungry.'

'The food will help. *Eat,*' Raffaele repeated insistently. 'You speak Italian,' he added, switching languages. 'You didn't mention it.'

'It didn't seem important. You're happy speaking English.'

'But more at home with Spanish or Italian,' Raffaele told her gently.

Maya buttered a piece of toast and ate the egg on offer. She poured the tea, passing him a cup and saucer as he crouched down in front of her, cruelly enforcing eye contact.

And it *was* cruel, she reflected numbly, because in the daylight flooding through the windows they were wickedly beautiful eyes the colour of caramel or melted honey.

'If that wasn't the norm for you, I need to know why,' Raffaele murmured almost softly, as though he was trying to be persuasive or, at the very least, nonthreatening.

Maya swallowed her tea. 'It's just the whole situation,' she mused ruefully. 'I let it get to me. I won't let that happen again.'

'You didn't want to share a bed with me last night… I assume,' Raffaele continued lazily. 'Yet I believed you were attracted to me.'

Maya could feel her face starting to blossom in a dreadful slow-burning blush. 'I was…er… I am,' she admitted tightly, feeling that he deserved that much truth from her.

'So, what was the problem?' Raffaele enquired levelly as he set the tea down that she had handed him untouched.

Maya sipped her tea and stared down into it as if it might provide her with a miraculous rescue from the dialogue. 'I'm not very experienced.'

'Not a problem for me.'

'Actually, not experienced at all,' Maya confided thinly, resenting the need to invade her own privacy, but still feeling that she owed him an explanation for her less than adult behaviour.

Without warning, Raffaele vaulted upright again and moved out of view, utterly astonished by her admission but trying to hide the fact from her. 'Again,' he breathed a little gruffly, 'not a problem… I assume.'

'You…*assume*?' Maya prompted in surprise, glancing across the cabin at him, studying his long, straight, shirt-clad back as he gazed out through the sliding doors onto the terrace.

Raffaele swung fluidly around, dark deep-set eyes settling on her with sudden intensity. 'I'd be a liar if I told you I'd been a woman's first before. I think that the more honest we are with each other, the easier this marriage will be for both of us.'

'I agree with that,' Maya framed round an enormous yawn, her virtually sleepless night catching up with her even as much of her earlier awkwardness with him drained away and somehow without her noticing. 'But, you know, I'm not a child. I wasn't freaking out about the sex as much as…as…what are you doing?' she gasped.

Seeing that yawn, Raffaele had begun moving towards her even while she was speaking and, removing the cup from her hand, he set it down and bent to lift her off the side of the bed and then immediately lower her back down with her head on the pillows. 'You need more sleep,' he told her. 'I'm shattered too.'

Maya watched him toe off his canvas shoes and throw himself down on the other side of the bed with wide anxious eyes.

'I didn't get much sleep last night either,' Raffaele pointed out. 'I'll keep my clothes on though, since I suppose anything else would freak you out.'

'Oh, don't be silly,' Maya mumbled, her face reddening. 'I don't mind if you get undressed.'

He unbuttoned his shirt and sighed, stretching out his long, lean, powerful frame. 'I don't think I can be bothered.'

Maya lifted her head and looked down at him, the curling black lashes resting on his high cheekbones in a flawless masculine face. The shirt lay open now, revealing a long bronzed slice of muscular torso. 'Take the shirt and the jeans off or you'll be uncomfortable,' she instructed drily.

Raffaele's eyes flew open again and a sudden grin slashed his wide perfect mouth and stole away the darkness that often edged his strong features. 'Only if you have the guts to match me.'

Impatience gripping her, Maya peeled off her tee and wriggled free of her shorts, pushing them off the bed. She had forgotten that she wasn't wearing a bra and, flustered by the knowledge that she had bared her breasts for his benefit, she wrenched the sheet back on the bed and scrambled beneath it to close her eyes, acknowledging that she truly felt as if she could sleep for a week.

For a split second as he took in that view of her pale pert breasts, Raffaele had frozen halfway out of his shirt but, gritting his teeth, he shed the shirt in a heap and embarked on his jeans.

'I'm afraid I'm going commando,' he warned her.

'I'm not looking…couldn't care less.'

'Maybe I want you to *want* to look—maybe my male ego is squashed by this amount of disinterest,' Raffaele murmured with sibilant bite.

'A twenty-ton weight couldn't squash your ego,' Maya mumbled soothingly, sliding a hand below a pillow and tucking her cheek gratefully into its soft support because he was correct: she had never felt so tired in her life. It was as if all the stresses, all the fears and worries that had dogged her over the past weeks had all homed in on her at once and she was exhausted, mentally and physically.

'You're doing a very good job all on your own.' Raffaele listened to the soft sound of her breathing ease into a regular rhythm while tension kept his own tiredness at bay.

When had he last been with a woman who didn't *want* anything from him? He couldn't remember. It had started so far back in his life with his mother's incomprehensible demands. If it wasn't attention a woman wanted from him, it was sex or money or the desire to show him off like a trophy in public. That knowledge had forged an iron barrier inside Raffaele and for the first time Maya was making him realise that it wasn't that he was unfeeling, it wasn't that he didn't have emotions, it was that he had walled them up behind that barrier. Every time he had seen someone reveal humanity's worst traits of cruelty and greed, he had felt justified in his outlook, and it had never occurred to him until that moment that he would one day be cruel and greedy too and visit those ugly qualities on the woman he had trapped into marrying him.

No, he *hadn't* blackmailed her, he *hadn't* forced her in any way, he rationalised with confidence. Facts were facts: Maya had made her own choice when she decided to save her parents from their mistakes and had paid with her freedom. But it was also fact that he didn't *need* the Parisi technology company to survive and that he had pushed her into their current predicament simply because he was bored and in search of a fresh business challenge. He wasn't, he decided, a good enough person to decide that he regretted what he had done: *he didn't*. But he was also burning to possess Maya with a hunger that was deeply unfamiliar to him, in spite of his rich, varied past experience of women.

Because she was a challenge? Because she didn't seem to want him as much as he wanted her to want him? Was he really that shallow, that arrogant?

Or was it because she had some strange unidentifiable quality that revved his libido? Was sex really that important to him? He would've claimed it wasn't.

After all, it had been weeks since he had last had sex, because sex had become as lacklustre as everything else in his life. At least, he could be grateful to Maya for returning him to the sexual land of the living, he conceded grimly, amused by the tent in the sheet over his hips. His handsome mouth quirked as she burrowed her hips into his thigh with a sleepy murmur. With care, he gently pushed her back from him because he didn't need the temptation and he didn't do affection. Loving or even highly valuing anyone or anything in his life was too risky, too dangerous, as he had learned at a very early age.

Maya wakened slowly to a room that had been plunged into the warm peach and golden shadows of the afternoon. Checking her watch, she saw that she had slept several hours away and she was about to sit up when the bathroom door opened and Raffaele stalked out stark naked, a towel still in one hand as he dried his wet black hair, leaving it tousled and damp and spiky.

Clothed, Raffaele was intimidating, naked he was even more magnificently overwhelming. He had the physique of a Greek God, carved in vibrant warm bronzed flesh rather than cold marble. From his broad shoulders to his powerful torso, narrow hips and long, strong legs, he was a vision of sleek masculine virility such as she had never seen in real life. Her bemused attention roamed down over the hard contours of his muscular chest to the corrugated lean flatness of his stomach, lingering on the silky line of dark hair that furrowed down over his belly...and there her gaze froze, wide with dismay.

'Well, don't look at me like that if you don't want *that* to happen.' Raffaele laughed with rich appreciation as she reddened and turned her head away. 'You can't be that innocent.'

'I was more into mathematics than men,' Maya fielded as Raffaele, still gloriously, unashamedly naked, came down on the bed beside her and left her breathless.

He lifted a dark brow and frowned, as if he could not comprehend that amount of indifference. 'Always?'

Maya shrugged a bare shoulder. 'It's just the way I'm wired.'

'It's insidiously attractive…'

Maya looked up into brilliant dark eyes that had the glitter of stars below his curling lashes and her heart jumped beneath her ribs and began a slow heavy pound, her body in a sort of heavy stasis that seemed to have nothing to do with her brain. He lifted a hand slowly, brown fingers curving to her cheekbone, and those stunning eyes of his, as dark and riveting as polished jet, held hers, heat pulsing through her in an involuntary rush, the sheer basic attraction that had freaked her out the day before flowing through her, and suddenly she was questioning why she was fighting what she was feeling because he no longer felt like a stranger.

He had reunited her with her grandparents, given her fabulous jewellery and looked after her when she was drunk in a way she would never have expected him to do. Underneath that façade of his, he was not inherently cruel, not innately cold, he was a much more enthralling mix.

'…ensuring that I have the greatest difficulty keeping my hands off you,' he confided in hoarsened completion.

And it was as if something simply snapped into place inside Maya and she stretched up a couple of inches to lay her lips against his as she urged, 'Don't—'

'Maya?'

'Less talk, more action,' she muttered boldly, letting the desire and the fascination take charge of her for the first time ever.

And finally, he kissed her, and it was as if her body had been waiting all her life for that sweet wildness to engulf her from her head to her toes, leaving her feeling almost detached from the self she had thought she knew. She moved to sit up, but his hand splayed across her spine, pushing her back against the pillows, controlling the pace with a masculine urgency that she found indescribably sexy. His lips parted hers and his tongue delved deep and tangled with her own, sending a tide of electrifying hunger pulsing through her with the efficacy of a drug in her bloodstream.

That fast, she discovered that she wanted more, was indeed impossibly greedy for more of him, and it shocked her to recognise that deep-down craving she had fought to restrain as though it were toxic when, indeed, it seemed to be exactly what she needed most. As Raffaele lowered his mouth to the straining pout of her rosy nipples and lingered there, toying with the stiff crests, her heartbeat hammered like crazy and a wash of heat engulfed her pelvis. It occurred to her that, only hours earlier, she had been ducking behind a sheet, pretty much embarrassed to show off that part of her because she didn't have very much to offer in the boob department, as he himself had once noted.

'I like...' Raffaele told her with a brazen smile that was very Manzini, framing the small mounds in splayed fingers, a thumb caressing each throbbing tip. 'Just enough, not too much and real.'

'Hope you can say the same about your own anatomy,' Maya quipped, shocked at herself for that response and staring at him with shaken eyes, thinking, I did not say that, that is not me.

Raffaele burst out laughing and gazed down at her with startled dark golden eyes. 'You give as good as you get…right? That's good. It's a quality you need with me, *bellezza mia*,' he told her with surprising sincerity. 'I can be—'

'Challenging?' Maya slotted in helplessly. 'I noticed.'

Raffaele grinned and kissed her again, his hands roaming over a body that already felt fiercely sensitised to his touch. The throb pulsing at the apex of her thighs was new to her, making her shift restlessly, her hips rising with a hunger she only recognised subliminally because thought didn't seem possible in the midst of her growing physical excitement. The feather-soft touch of a finger just *there* and she could feel herself lighting up like a forest fire, nerve endings jumping, a mesmerising warmth enthralling her feminine core while the slick dampness gathered.

'It's like an equation. You and me and the parameters,' Maya pronounced with a glorious smile of discovery.

'OK,' Raffaele agreed, because he didn't know what she was talking about but it seemed to be making her happy.

'I bet I could make a model of it!' she exclaimed, her brain already homing in on the possibilities.

And Raffaele could see that she was ready to leap

out of bed and look for a whiteboard or some such thing to engage in the kind of mathematics that inflamed her meteoric brain. 'But not right now,' he told her urgently. 'Right now, we stay on task.'

Maya blinked up at him, green eyes limpid as ferns with sheer disappointment, and he kissed her again because it felt like the only thing he could do to distract her. And it worked, mercifully it *worked*, he conceded, shaken up by that experience when he himself was utterly lost in the magic of her response to him.

'I'm burning up for you, *bellezza mia*,' he growled.

'Oh…' Maya trailed gentle fingers through his wildly tousled black hair. 'I've messed up your hair, clutching it.'

'Go right ahead,' he encouraged, dragging in a sustaining breath, his broad chest expanding that something about him could hold her interest.

'You don't mind?' That glorious smile was angled at him again.

Out of words, Raffaele crushed her mouth under his again, struggling to stay in control, fighting not to fall on her like an animal, a hunger of storm-force potency driving him. It was, without a doubt and yet utterly inexplicably to him, the most exciting sexual experience of his life.

'I want you too,' she whispered unevenly, her body quivering, shifting up to his in invitation as the unbearable longing stabbed at her afresh.

He slid over her, easing into her, giving her time to adjust to that unfamiliar intrusion. Maya tried not to tense and looked up into his taut, intent face, the lustrous dark eyes alight with a hunger as deep as her own. Something she hadn't even known she was worrying about quieted within her because she saw that he was fighting for control as much as she was. There was a momentary sharp piercing pain and then that introduction was over and there was only the rousing stimulation of feeling her own body stretch to accept the fullness of his. From the first subtle shift of his hips, she was needy, wanting, aglow with the discovery of that enthralling newness.

Fierce sensation assailed her, and her eyes widened, the spark of excitement flashing into a flame that burned in the most pleasurable of ways. More, she wanted to shout, *more*, and it took effort to stay silent while the raw excitement roaring through her built and built until finally he was slamming into her, wonderfully wild and passionate, and she was urging him on with her body in the only way she knew how, legs wrapping round him, nails turned into talons raking down his smooth spine in her insistence.

She soared to a peak that sent her flying into a million pieces, her whole body consumed by that intensity that lifted her to an unimaginable high and then left her floating in a sea of drowning pleasure.

'That was amazing,' Maya sighed. 'Thank you.'

And that quickly, Raffaele knew what it was about Maya that intrigued him. He had never met a woman like her, never had sex with a woman like her, never even dreamt that a woman like her even existed because she was *so* different that she smashed every one of his trite expectations.

'That was my line,' Raffaele husked in an informative tone as he lifted his head from the tumbled swathes of her blonde hair, which smelled like strawberries, he noted abstractedly as he levered his weight off her and slid to one side.

'No, that's basic relationship stuff,' Maya informed him with superiority. 'If you do something well, I should praise you for it.'

'Like you're training a pet?' Raffaele derided.

'Well, if you're going to take offence at the most innocent comment,' Maya countered.

'Allow me to warn you…tact is not your biggest strength,' Raffaele pointed out with another grin.

'Oh, I know that,' Maya replied without concern. 'You're not the first person to label me socially awkward. I live inside my head most of the time. I'm not observant either.'

In wonderment, Raffaele watched her slide out of the bed and away from him, no hanging around, no after-sex fondling, cuddling, absolutely nothing sought from him. 'Where are you going?' he asked lazily.

'I need a shower. Sex is messy,' Maya sighed.

Raffaele raised an ebony brow. 'I think you're supposed to lie flat for a while afterwards if you're trying to get pregnant,' he murmured silkily.

Maya blinked and walked back to the bed like a naked forest nymph with her hair flowing round her. Beneath his arrested gaze, she lay down again. Felled by an old wives' tale, he conceded in fascination, but for some strange reason he didn't want her washing him off her again and walking away from him.

'How long do I have to lie here for?'

'Ten minutes should be enough,' Raffaele breathed, trying very hard not to laugh because she looked as trapped as he had often felt when women tried to hold *him* by their side and that was a novel experience, not entirely to his satisfaction. He would, he appreciated, have to learn how to cuddle if he wanted her to stay with him afterwards. And *why* would he want that?

'This is *so*...do you have a pen and paper?' Maya asked suddenly, wondering if she could come up with an equation that matched them as a couple and their relationship and calculating the probabilities.

Raffaele reached over and provided her with both from the nightstand nearest him. He lay back watching as she covered line after line with what to him were incomprehensible mathematical notations. Every so often she paused, smooth brow furrowing while she pondered, and then she would be off onto a fresh page, so wrapped in her calculations that he reckoned that a volcanic eruption would not have penetrated her concentration.

He went for a shower and when he emerged, she was still at it and she hadn't glanced up once. It was as if he had vanished; it was as if he didn't exist. He discovered that he absolutely loathed that sensation. It reminded him of the frequent occasions when his mother had forgotten his needs as a child, overlooking the necessity of his eating or sleeping. Of course, his mother, Julieta, had often lived in her own world, cocooned from reality.

'We're getting off the boat,' he told her loudly.

A thousand miles away, for all he knew mentally on another planet, she looked up at him, beautiful sea-glass eyes distant.

'We've arrived at the island where we're spending our honeymoon,' Raffaele extended.

'Oh...' Maya gasped, blinking to take in the sea of

paper surrounding her and her still naked, unwashed state. 'I zoned out, didn't I?'

'You did,' Raffaele agreed.

'Don't dump anything!' she warned him as she leapt off the bed and vanished into the bathroom.

Raffaele picked an outfit out of the new wardrobe she had yet to discover, gossamer-fine undies in lilac, a strappy sundress. He knocked on the bathroom door and entered when she shouted out, *'Yes?'* sounding very harassed.

'Clothes,' Raffaele announced, resting them down on a chair, thinking for a second and then yanking out towels for her use as well because he wasn't sure she would find them on her own. He had never had to look after anyone or anything in many, many years and it felt weird.

'Marriage not quite what you expected?' Sal had mocked. Raffaele conceded that at least he wasn't bored.

'Oh, that was kind of you,' Maya remarked, swathing herself in a towel. 'That's what Izzy does when she's trying to hurry me up...my goodness, those aren't *my* clothes—'

'They are now. I bought them for you.'

Maya sent him a glance that suggested that he was in some way strange and sort of shrugged, not interested enough in clothes, it seemed, to enquire any further. Raffaele stepped back out again and within minutes she emerged, none of the lengthy feminine preparation for his company that he was used to receiving apparent in her appearance. She had combed her wet hair, hadn't bothered to dry it, only braid it, and yet *still* she drew his gaze like a magnet. Something about that slender, leggy, graceful figure, those delicate features or that unexpectedly luscious pink mouth exuded radical appeal.

Maya focused on Raffaele, a sort of creeping shyness briefly enfolding her as she allowed herself to finally recall that experience in the bed with him. Transcendent, earth-shattering, she mused with a little inner quiver she could not suppress. She had never dreamt that sex might be addictive like that. Was it only because she had been with *him*? Or was something deeper involved? Was she starting to feel more than she should for him? Surely not? She was not stupid. And yet the pull he exerted over her was extreme, her eyes constantly needing to stray back to him.

That seemed to be what that physical chemistry could deliver, and she should accept a blessing where she could find one in their business marriage, she told herself urgently. At least, trying to get pregnant wasn't going to be a disgusting ordeal. She really should only deal with Raffaele with logic. All the emotion she was fighting around him could be a disaster in the making, she reasoned worriedly, terrified of getting attached to him in any way. She wouldn't *allow* herself to feel anything for him and that would keep her safe from hurt or disillusionment.

The launch carved a sure passage through the deep blue Mediterranean Sea to the small island that lay ahead. It was an exhilarating ride and all Maya could see of the island was a pale sand beach fringed by trees with a glimpse of a low roof somewhere behind them. Honeymoon, she mused uneasily—it hadn't occurred to her that he would take such a conventional path to his objective.

Raffaele gazed stonily ahead, refusing to acknowledge the nightmare glimmers of his memories. He wasn't a sensitive guy, he didn't look back to the past and dwell unhealthily on it, no, he put it behind him, which was why he had chosen to bring Maya there to this superficially very beautiful little islet, which was both convenient and suitable for purpose.

Even so, when he swept a laughing Maya up into his arms and brought her down on the soft pale sand he had often played on as a child, his stomach still churned sickly when he too stepped out of the launch.

'The path's up here,' he murmured, moving ahead of her as guide, refusing to surrender to that queasiness in his gut because only the frightened, traumatised child he had once been would react that way.

'You've been here before?'

'It's one of my late mother's many properties, like the villa where we held the wedding. I used the villa because Aldo isn't able to travel far now and I'm using Aoussa—as it's called—because…because it makes sense to use it.'

As they walked beneath the palm trees lining the walkway, something in that uncharacteristic hesitation in his dark deep drawl furrowed her brow and filled her with a sense of unease. 'Did you grow up here?'

'No, Julieta used it for summer breaks or simply when she was in the mood to be alone…aside of the staff,' he told her curtly. 'She brought all her new husbands here, her lovers. Aoussa was one of her favourite places.'

'Did you lose your mother recently?' Maya prompted,

seeking an explanation for the tension he couldn't hide. It was etched in the taut lines and hollows forming across his strong bone structure.

'Julieta has been gone ten years. I was in my final year at boarding school when she died.' Raffaele strode on, determined to overcome the reactions assailing him because he was not weak or vulnerable any longer, he was a man, a *strong* man.

'You didn't call her Mother?'

'No. She didn't like to be called that,' Raffaele admitted gruffly.

An unexpectedly large building lay beyond the trees. It was all on one level, probably ultra-modern in its day with its many windows looking out over the ornamental gardens or towards the sea and shore exposed on the other side of the island. 'It is beautiful and clearly well maintained,' Maya commented. 'How long is it since your last visit?'

Raffaele thrust open the front door. 'Twenty-odd years,' he admitted grudgingly. 'Julieta went off it.'

In silence, Maya raised a brow, walking off on her own through big airy rooms, furnished in timeless style. She couldn't even begin to imagine owning a house that she hadn't visited in two decades or the level of wealth that could allow such lavish behaviour. She peered out into an interior courtyard and opened the door, turning her head to see where Raffaele was and immediately realising that something was wrong.

He was poised by the full-length windows staring out into the courtyard, his lean hands coiled into fists and trembling by his side, a sheen of perspiration gleaming on his bronzed face. Every muscle in his body was rigid.

'Raffaele…?' she began uncertainly.

'I'm not sure I *can* stay here,' he muttered raggedly, lifting a shaking hand to rake it through his luxuriant black hair. 'I had a flashback. I haven't had one in many years. It happened out there before breakfast.'

Compassion stirred in Maya; her gentle heart touched because that Raffaele could be vulnerable in his own hidden way had not once occurred to her. Instantly she was dismayed by the one-dimensional view she had taken of him. 'A flashback of what?' she pressed, moving across to him, one slender hand closing over one of his, her arm curving round the base of his spine in an effort to urge him towards the seating area to the left of them.

'Of Julieta killing my dogs,' he mumbled sickly.

CHAPTER SIX

REELING WITH SHOCK at that revelation as they sank down, Maya looked up into haunted dark golden eyes and her heart clenched as though someone had squeezed it. 'Why on earth would your mother have done something so dreadful?'

And he told her about Julieta then, and the day she had pulled out a gun over breakfast while he was playing with his childhood pets, how she had accused him of loving the dogs more than he loved her. In her adolescence, his mother had suffered a serious head injury and brain damage in a car accident, and it was after the crash that her mental health issues had developed. Although she had received many different diagnoses and had endured an ever-changing regime of medication, no treatment and no therapy had ever given her peace or normality.

'She can't be held responsible for anything wrong that she did. She was rarely in rational control of herself,' Raffaele pointed out with creditable loyalty. 'Unfortunately for me, her wealth and her lawyers protected her from outside interference.'

'You were eight years old, Raffaele. *Who* was looking after you?'

'The domestic staff generally took care of my physical needs, but they couldn't protect me from her because she sacked them immediately if they tried to intervene,' Raffaele admitted curtly.

'And your father?'

'Julieta shut Tommaso out of our lives while I was still a baby,' he explained. 'They were only married for a couple of years. He offended my mother by trying to compensate some waitress she had had fired in a restaurant and she threw him out. He had been cast off by the Manzinis when he married her and, in the divorce, he didn't get anything because their marriage hadn't lasted long enough. He didn't have the money to fight her through the courts for access to his son. He didn't have any choice in what followed.'

'So, tell me about the dogs,' she encouraged softly, reaching out to link her fingers carefully with his taut ones, noticing how he glanced down at their entangled hands with bemused discomfiture as they sat side by side on the sofa. 'And stop beating yourself up for being human, Raffaele. You went through an appalling experience as a child. It's still totally masculine *and* normal to be upset by the memory of it.'

Faint colour flared over his exotic cheekbones at that assurance but he let it go past. 'Bella and Lupo were puppies when they arrived that summer. I adored them,' he declared simply. 'They were the closest thing to a family that I ever had. They loved me back.'

'Didn't your mother love you?'

'If she did, she wasn't capable of showing it. She was very possessive of me, though. Nannies weren't allowed to show me physical affection, even if I was hurt or ill. With Julieta,' Raffaele revealed absently with a lack of emotion that cut Maya deep, 'it was half beating me to death one week and then a trip to Disneyland with every conceivable extra the next, all extremes, while she flailed from one mood into another.'

'There was physical abuse?' Maya queried with a concealed shudder and only belatedly did she recall him saying, when she had tried to slap him in his office, 'Nobody hits me now.'

'She was subject to uncontrollable rages. I was the most convenient target. Staff just quit on the spot if she lost her head with them.' Raffaele's fingers tensed in hers. 'I have scars all down my back from the time she took a belt to me. There was nobody to stop her except the nanny and Sal, who was a new employee. The nanny waited until the last possible moment to shout for Sal and I almost died from blood loss and shock. It was all hushed up, of course, by her lawyers. Julieta tried to sack Sal afterwards, but the lawyers insisted that he remain to look after my welfare. Julieta hated him but she couldn't get rid of him and there were no more beatings. If only Sal had been around when my dogs were alive, he would have got the gun off her. The night I first met Aldo, he admitted that he'd heard a rumour about my mistreatment around that time and that he'd tried to visit me. But Julieta wouldn't consent to him seeing me.'

Maya sat listening in a growing pool of horror. She had assumed that he had had it so easy all his life...*all that money*. But instead, he had lived a nightmare, rich but unloved, neglected while being both over-indulged and abused. All of a sudden she understood so much more about Raffaele Manzini from his apparent lack of emotion to his granite cool. It was *all* a front, there to convince everybody, not least him, that he had survived and flourished despite his appalling childhood.

'What age were you then?' she whispered.

'At the time of the beating? Maybe nine... I only remember fragments of it,' he muttered uncomfortably. 'Let's not dwell on this, Maya. It happened, it's done, it's over.'

'But you're still feeling it, you're still living it,' she told him gently.

'I don't want to,' he breathed in a raw bitter undertone. 'I don't want to *feel* anything!'

'I know...well...er... I can imagine,' she whispered ruefully, overwhelmed by her new awareness of the inner self he had successfully concealed from her. She also knew that she would never again feel shortchanged for her childhood with parents who were hopeless with money but who had absolutely adored their children and treated them accordingly.

Raffaele snatched in a steadying breath and his ebony brows pleated. 'How did you get all that out of me?' he demanded abruptly. 'I've never talked about it before.'

'I got you at a weak moment. Don't feel bad—we all have them and sometimes it's good for you to talk,' she soothed, looking up into eyes that were pure golden enticement in the sunlight, inky dark lashes enhancing them.

And the silence smouldered.

Raffaele's grip on her hand tightened and he reached down with his other hand to curve it to her hip and lift her up easily onto his lap. 'I want you,' he told her boldly.

Maya rolled her eyes at him. 'That's only because

you feel ill at ease after telling me all that private stuff. It's a natural reaction for a macho male personality. You're trying to compensate.'

'No, it's a natural reaction to being with a very beautiful, compassionate woman, who also happens to be my wife,' Raffaele corrected in a driven undertone. '*I...want...you.* Right here, right now.'

Maya released a long-suffering sigh because he was so irredeemably *basic*, in no way adjusted to his own emotional prompts and what drove him at any given moment. 'Raffaele,' she began.

A split second after she parted her lips, he forced them apart with the delving lick of his tongue and she gasped. Logic became too steep a hill to climb as the burn of the hunger he could induce in her without effort began to infiltrate her quivering body. Beneath her she could feel him hard and ready, the jeans he sported doing nothing to conceal his arousal, and she felt a piercing pulse of hunger kick up between her thighs even though she still ached there from their earlier encounter. Once again, it rewrote all her assumptions that once that desire was sated, it would stay quiet for a good while and wouldn't unduly bother her again. All of a sudden she was hot, needy and desperate and twisting on his lap, grinding down on him with ridiculous enthusiasm, making him laugh, rough and low in this throat in that infuriating way of his, as if he knew some things better than she did, which, she finally conceded, he possibly did...

What followed was wild and passionate in a way she had never envisaged herself being. He hauled her up into his arms and carried her into a bedroom with a ridiculously huge bed surrounded by mirrored furniture that threw up far too many disorientating reflections.

'Yuck,' she commented on the décor.

'*Sì*, I should've organised a refurbishment,' Raffaele muttered in exasperation as he, very briefly, took the opportunity to look around himself and then froze.

Just taking in his pallor, Maya registered that memories had stolen him away from her again and she yanked him down shamelessly on the silly giant bed, slender hands smoothing up over long muscular thighs to gently brush the revealing bulge at his pelvis and, that fast, Raffaele was back in tune with her again, rolling her over on the bed and kissing her breathless. He was frantic for her, which she perfectly understood after the secrets he had shared and the effect on him of having to relive them. What she did *not* understand was that she should be equally frantic for him. After all, nothing distressing had happened to her. She had merely been an observer, an available listener, yet everything he had confided had somehow touched her too and his pain had distressed her.

When Raffaele flipped her over onto her knees and drove into her with urgent force, that scorching passion was somehow what she expected from him in that moment. She was not surprised or shocked or even standing outside herself marvelling because he had already taught her to expect that wild incredible flood of excitement. The sheer physical release of sex was a necessity for Raffaele after those confessions about his unhappy past. He couldn't handle the emotions, but he could vent them the only way he knew how. His hunger, his sudden overpowering need for her, was as much an expression of distress as he was capable of making and it both saddened and delighted her that he had turned to her for comfort. Yet that intense sharing of his had released something in her as well, she acknowledged, and made her feel much closer to him.

'So...' Maya refused to let go of him in the aftermath because even if he didn't know it, she *knew* he needed to be held. Her fingers smoothed down his long spine, feeling the slight roughness of scarring there, remembering what he had told her about that beating his mother had inflicted on him. Her eyes prickled and she stroked a soothing hand over his back, wishing fiercely that she could take the pain of that recollection from him, that knowledge that the person who should have most protected him had damaged him instead. He was still struggling to catch his breath and her body was humming with an unbelievable surfeit of pleasure and she pressed her mouth softly across his shoulder in an affectionate caress she could not withhold. 'Obviously you're not still planning to stay here in this house.'

'Why not?'

'Since it's clear that this is not a happy place for you,' Maya retorted bluntly. 'And what would we do here anyway?'

Raffaele studied her with glittering wicked eyes. 'What we're doing now.'

Maya rolled her eyes.

Raffaele laughed, relaxation winging through him. It was true: he hated the house but it had taken Maya to make him admit the fact. 'I'll visit the spot above the beach where the dogs were buried and then we'll get back on the yacht and tour with lots of sex included,' he compromised.

'Either you should sell this little island or demolish the house and rebuild,' Maya told him, ignoring the 'lots of sex' quip even though it irritated her. 'It shouldn't have been sitting here for so many years empty and unused.'

Raffaele released his breath on a slow hiss. 'I married an alpha woman, keen to remake me. Why didn't I spot the warning signs?'

Beneath his intent gaze, Maya scrunched up her small nose. 'Because you were too full of yourself to believe that an alpha woman could talk common sense?'

Raffaele winced and then suddenly grinned. 'It's possible…but here you are.'

'Here I am,' Maya murmured, both arms wrapped round him as she surveyed him and the lustrous dark golden eyes locked to her like magnets.

And, he reflected, this kind of holding is fine and meaningless. He might not have enjoyed a relationship in which such affection existed before, but he trusted himself enough to believe that emotion didn't come into it for him. How could it possibly when he didn't feel what he was supposed to feel? He should never have brought her to the island, never have told her what had happened in the house, should never have dropped his guard to that extent. He had made three mistakes in succession, he conceded grimly. No good ever came from letting people get too close, he reminded himself stubbornly. Maya was hotter than hot in bed and, in addition to her intelligence, it was a winning combination for their marriage. In fact, he could not have done better, he mused, because she picked up on his moods as well as a weathervane forecasting a storm. But then, she was a clever woman, a very clever woman, and no doubt as detached as he was from anything deeper developing between them.

Maya drifted awake thinking about her sister, Izzy, and missing her. She was alone in bed and that was typical, because Raffaele always rose at the crack of dawn to spend a few hours working in his on-board office. Taking over his great-grandfather's business empire had kept him incredibly busy.

Just over a month had passed since the wedding and the secrecy Maya had embraced on that score had driven a wedge between her and the sister she loved, she conceded unhappily. Although they had talked with apparent openness on the phone during those weeks, Maya was stuck with the lie that she had taken a job in Italy. Yet how could she possibly tell Izzy the truth without upsetting her? Izzy, already dealing with an unplanned pregnancy and a new relationship in a foreign country, would be distraught if she knew what Maya had agreed to do to protect their parents and Matt.

Yet right now, there was a chance that Maya could be pregnant too and it was with a fierce desire to know, one way or another, that Maya slid out of bed. Her head swam dizzily as she straightened and moved into the bathroom to dig out one of the tests she had bought the day before and buried deep in the back of a cupboard. Her hands were a little unsteady as she sat down and unwrapped the box to pull out the instructions. The test was very simple, unlike her marriage, she conceded ruefully.

If she was pregnant, the marriage as such would

be virtually over because that was what had been decided at the outset when she had insisted on exclusivity. Raffaele had agreed to stay faithful only until she conceived. He wanted his freedom back, the freedom to go out and sleep with other women. Why did the idea of that bother her? Why, when she had suspected for more than a week that she could have conceived, had she taken so long to buy the tests?

She had told Raffaele off for imagining he should be more than human that day on the island of Aoussa and now here she was being guilty of expecting more than she should from herself. After all, how could she live in such an intimate relationship with a man who attracted her and feel absolutely nothing for him? That wasn't realistic. At least not for her and her generous heart, it wasn't. Raffaele, though? Now that was a very different ball game.

Unlike her, Raffaele had spent a lifetime carefully ensuring that he felt very little for anyone. That was how he had got over his dysfunctional beginning in life; that was how he had learned to cope. Was he even capable of changing? And why would he even *want* to change when he was perfectly content as he was?

Yet that indifference in him to the more tender emotions scared and intimidated Maya, she acknowledged reluctantly. On his terms, she was just a business project and the child he wanted to conceive merely a useful tool that would give him the right to buy her grandfather's technology company. On her terms, however, Raffaele was the guy she had hated when she married him and then somehow, incomprehensibly to her, he had turned into a man she was learning to love…

How could she be falling for Raffaele Manzini?

How could the impossible have happened? A sea change had taken place inside her that day on the island as soon as she understood what he had suffered because he had *shown* her his vulnerability. With that single act he had broken through her barriers and demolished her defences. She had stood above the beach with him where the dogs were buried and tears had misted her eyes when she'd seen the mound of pebbles he had gathered to mark the spot and the rough cross, cobbled together from driftwood by the gardener, Raffaele had explained. And, unfortunately for her, the way he had treated her since then had only encouraged the warmth of her developing feelings.

To date, being married to Raffaele was nothing at all as she had expected. He was wonderfully caring towards her and always coming up with new ways to please or entertain her. They had cruised the Mediterranean in the yacht, stopping off in random places to shop or explore ruins or sheltered coves and dine out, the very casualness of their itinerary relaxing.

And when it came to anything she might want, nothing was too much trouble for Raffaele. A reference to her interest in archaeology had led to a surprise flight to Egypt and the fulfilment of a lifelong dream to see the tombs in the Valley of the Kings. Raffaele wasn't into any of that and yet he had still patiently, considerately ensured that she also toured the treasures in the Cairo Museum, saw the pyramids and caught another flight to visit the temples at Luxor. He had devoted an entire energetic ten days to her enjoyment of antiquities. Her fingers toyed abstractedly with the gold sphinx necklace he had given her as a memento of their stay.

He had given her a feast of memories that she would remember all her life. He had even had a cabin on the yacht set up for her to work in, complete with whiteboards and cutting-edge technology. Even if she worked all day and late into the night, he didn't complain. No, he certainly wasn't clingy, but he was capable of interrupting her to remind her to eat or to initiate sex, she conceded with a rueful grin.

For over a month she had lived in a fantasy world with a gorgeous guy who behaved as if she was so incredibly beautiful and alluring that he couldn't resist her. Sexually, Raffaele was insatiable and yet the same man had admitted to her that prior to their wedding he hadn't sought the release of sex for weeks because he had become bored with it. Only he could scarcely afford to be bored with sex when his main goal was to conceive a child, she reminded herself sourly. And only an idiot like herself could have forgotten that reality for long enough to become infatuated with him. *I don't get attached to people*, he had warned her at the outset. With an angry snort at her own act of self-destruction, Maya finally stood up to check the test wand and see the result.

And there it was, exactly what she had expected: a positive.

Warm acceptance diametrically opposed to the furious self-loathing she had just been dealing with flooded Maya. No matter how she felt about Raffaele or her reactions to him, Maya wanted her baby and was excited at the prospect of becoming a mother. Yes, it was happening to her when she was younger than she had planned but Maya had always wanted children and could not be anything other than happy with such a result. Pausing only to brush her teeth and run a brush through her tumbled blonde hair, Maya walked back into the bedroom.

'Well?' Raffaele shot at her expectantly.

The sight of him when she was unprepared still left her short of breath and on the edge of the most ridiculous sense of excitement. But there Raffaele stood, sheathed in black jeans and a black shirt, tall, powerful and strong, and the very air in the cabin hummed with the vibrant energy that he radiated. He had been waiting for her to emerge.

'Don't keep me in suspense,' he told her.

Maya blinked in astonishment as she realised that he had somehow guessed exactly what she had been engaged in doing. 'How did you guess?'

'You stopped drinking wine two weeks ago. You've been feeling dizzy. You went to a lot of trouble to make elaborate excuses about why you wanted to visit a pharmacist yesterday. *And* I watch you like a hawk,' Raffaele countered with a wry smile. 'It's a *yes*, isn't it?'

'At least you didn't put a spy camera in the bathroom,' Maya breathed, her clear gaze pinned to his lean, darkly handsome face and the smile already pulling at the corners of his beautiful stubborn mouth. 'Yes, I'm pregnant…'

'I didn't expect it to happen so fast,' Raffaele confessed then, crossing the cabin in one long stride to reach for her, linking his arms loosely round her shoulders as he gazed down at her. 'How do you feel?'

'Excited, weird, pleased, all sorts of crazy things.'

'You're happy?'

'Yes. I love babies,' she admitted a little self-consciously.

'And why shouldn't you?' Raffaele replied lightly.

'How do you feel about this?' she pressed with intense curiosity.

'Delighted,' Raffaele said quietly. 'I wrongly assumed that this result would take a lot longer to achieve.'

And at least one of the happy bubbles inside Maya burst because 'achieve' wasn't the kind of word she wanted him to use. It wasn't an emotional word; it was a businesslike word that went best with other words like target and goal. It was a reminder that she wasn't in a typical marriage, a reminder that, indeed, her marriage as such was probably already winding to an end even as they spoke because that had been what they had agreed.

'And now you've got your freedom back just like you wanted,' Maya pointed out, because she could not resist the urge to speak out loud her greatest fear. She would get used to the idea that he was no longer a real part of her life, she told herself fiercely; she would forget that he had ever begun to mean something more to her.

Raffaele tensed, stunning dark golden eyes suddenly narrowing and veiling, curling black lashes concealing his expression. In silence, he nodded, a faint frown line etched between his ebony brows. 'It's a little soon to be thinking like that,' he murmured tautly. 'In fact, it's kind of insulting. I have more respect for you than you seem to think.'

But Maya wanted much more than respect, she thought painfully, hoping that what she felt for him wasn't really love but some lesser affliction like a teenager's overwhelming crush, which could often be short-lived. She could swiftly recover from a crush, after all. For the sake of her own peace of mind, she knew that she had to start moving on from their relationship as fast as she could.

CHAPTER SEVEN

BARELY FORTY-EIGHT HOURS later, Maya suffered a miscarriage.

The day before, Raffaele had insisted that she should see a Greek doctor to have the test result confirmed and have the usual health checks. Maya would've preferred to wait until they returned to London in a week's time but she had given way in the end because she wanted to follow all the rules. She had told the doctor about the incredible tiredness engulfing her and he had smiled and advised her that that was normal in early pregnancy.

That evening when they were sailing towards the island of Sicily, sheer exhaustion persuaded Maya into having an early night. Cramping pains in her abdomen wakened her after midnight and she sat up with a start, switching on the bedside light and pushing back the sheet to check that her misgivings were correct.

'What's wrong?' Raffaele demanded.

'I'm bleeding,' she whispered sickly. 'I'm having a miscarriage.'

In a matter of seconds, Raffaele leapt out of the bed and lifted the phone to wake his pilot and instruct him in urgent Italian. As if she were standing somewhere outside herself, Maya watched him as he pulled on jeans, reluctantly appreciating his extreme cool in a crisis and the way he took charge. 'There's no point in taking me to a hospital,' she told him ruefully. 'There's nothing they can do to stop what's happening at this stage of a pregnancy.'

'You *must* receive medical care,' Raffaele sliced in fiercely. 'And don't take that pessimistic attitude. It may be something else amiss, something that can be treated.'

He wouldn't let her go for a shower, wouldn't even let her stand up or walk. He bundled her up in a towel and a sheet and carried her up to the helipad where the helicopter was already powering up. Maya stopped arguing. She didn't need a doctor to tell her what had happened, and she knew how common early miscarriages were. Her baby, barely more than a tiny bunch of cells, was already gone. Rationally she knew that even then, but her brain was having a much harder time coming to terms with the knowledge.

The cramps became more severe during the flight and she struggled to hide the fact that she was in pain because there was nothing anyone on the flight could do about it.

Watching her, Raffaele felt sick and powerless, not sensations he was used to feeling. Her eyes were dark with strain in the white taut triangle of her face and her breathing was erratic, her hands clenching in on themselves. He knew she was in pain and he reached for her hand. 'Maya—?'

'I'm totally fine. Let's not fuss about this,' she told him briskly, snatching her fingers free of his and turning her head away, tears burning free of her lowered eyelids to trickle down her rigid face in silence.

Naturally, Raffaele didn't want her to lose the baby because that would mean starting all over again, she thought painfully. Just when he had been on the very brink of reclaiming his freedom, his neat little plan had fallen apart and they were being thrown right back to where they had begun. He couldn't possibly be feeling what *she* was feeling. The baby itself wasn't real to him the way it was to her. On *his* terms, their precious little baby had only been a means to an end, and she hated him for that, simply couldn't help hating him for it.

The helicopter ferried her to a private hospital in Sicily and she was whisked away from Raffaele. Once she had been examined and scanned, she was given pain relief and finally tucked into a bed in a quiet room where a doctor came to tell her what she already knew: her pregnancy was gone. She had thought she was prepared for that news, but it seemed that she was not and that somewhere deep down inside she had still cherished a dim and foolish little hope that her worst assumptions could yet be proved wrong. Only, unhappily for her, her pessimistic outlook had been correct.

And she felt gutted, absolutely gutted with hurt and disappointment. In the silence of the night, broken only by occasional quiet footsteps of the staff in the corridor beyond her room, she lay wondering if she had done anything that could have contributed to the miscarriage. Maybe she had eaten something she shouldn't have or caught an infection, maybe she shouldn't have had the occasional glass of wine after the wedding, maybe she had been too active scrambling over rocks and along goat paths in Raffaele's energetic wake while they were exploring, maybe her body just wasn't fit enough to host a healthy pregnancy. *Stop it, stop it*, her brain urged her as all the things she could have done wrong tumbled together in a crazed shout of self-condemnation inside her aching head.

It was so pointless to think that way because none of it could change anything: her baby was gone as though it had never been and that absolutely broke her heart. The tears she had struggled to hold back surged then in a blinding, stinging flood and she buried her convulsed face in a pillow to muffle her sobs.

'I'm so sorry...' Raffaele breathed stiltedly from the doorway because he knew how thrilled she had been about the baby.

In fact, he had been sincerely startled by her sheer enthusiasm at the idea of becoming a mother because the kind of women he usually mixed with invariably felt the need to deny the maternal urge as though it were a weakness or an unattractive trait likely to scare off eligible men. But not Maya, no, not Maya, who was who she was without fear or concern as to how she might appear to others and who wanted what she wanted without apology.

Tragically, he didn't know what to say to her and that felt like an enormous failing to him at that moment. He had spoken at length to the medical personnel, had heard every empty cliché that had ever been voiced on the topic of miscarriage and he didn't want to trot those same words out for Maya's benefit. *I'm sorry*, an expression of regret, seemed the only appropriate response.

In dismay at his appearance, Maya rolled over and sat up to focus on him through swollen eyes, angry resentment shooting through her in a heady rush of sudden energy. 'Of course, you're sorry…this development sets back your plans!'

'As of this moment I have no plans,' Raffaele intoned, moving forward, all lithe grace and self-containment. 'We need time to grieve.'

Maya looked at him and truly hated him. *Grieve? We?* She was an emotional wreck and he was calm and assured, which was only to be expected from a man who had no more feelings than a lump of concrete! As she tried to suppress the tumultuous surge of her resentment she studied him, her heart hammering somewhere in the region of her throat, it seemed, teaching her all over again, and when she least required the reminder, how weak she could be around him.

It was the middle of the night and, for once, Raffaele looked tired and under strain, the sculpted lines and angles of his lean dark features clenched taut and shadowing his dark deep-set eyes. But he also looked drop-dead gorgeous and vibrant as if no adversity could do him down for long. His bronzed skin still had the gleam of burnished gold like his eyes, his untidy blue-black hair remained glossy as silk, his arrogant head was high, the athletic flow of his lean, muscular body fluid. She wanted to reach out a hand to him and hold on tightly and she hated herself for that betrayal, for that need for comfort that made her so achingly vulnerable.

'This baby was never real to you the way it was to me!' she condemned bitterly instead. 'You didn't think of our baby as a little girl or a little boy, a child who would be a mix of us both, you only saw our baby as a device to be used to acquire a multimillion-pound company! You didn't see anything wrong with using your own flesh and blood that way! Even though you suffered because your parents broke up when you were a baby, it didn't bother you that you were cursing our child to grow up in a divided family as well!'

'You're right. I saw what I wanted and went for it. I've never had to think about moral boundaries or consequences such as this before and now that I have, I see that I went wrong. But I didn't realise that until I met you,' Raffaele bit out in a rasping undertone. 'Unhappily, I can't change anything I did now. It's too late.'

Maya wasn't even listening properly to him. 'Yes, too late,' she agreed sadly, lying back down and turning her face away. Aware of him hovering at the foot of the bed, she frowned. 'Go back to the yacht, Raffaele.'

'I'll get right on that,' Raffaele breathed through gritted teeth of restraint.

Was she kidding him? His wife suffered a miscarriage and she still expected him to just walk away? Getting it wrong wasn't an excuse to keep *on* getting it wrong. It meant he had to stop and think about what he was doing, but he didn't actually need to think about what to do next. Every fibre of his being told him that he needed to stay with his wife to support her after such a loss, even if she *didn't* want him with her.

It had been *his* loss too, he reflected, striding from the room and finding a corridor window that overlooked the car park to stare out. And he wasn't quite as callous as Maya appeared to believe because he too had been thinking about the child she carried as an individual. He had pictured a little boy with her fair hair and his eyes and then a little girl with his hair and her eyes, before accepting that genes weren't that easy to forecast and that their child might look more like one of their parents or not very like them at all. But the child would still have been *their* child, their flesh and blood. Not, however, a cross between a possession and a plaything, as his late mother had viewed him, not a sacrifice for financially foolish parents, as Maya had become. No, their child would have been safe from such unreasonable demands and expectations, their child would have been left free to become whoever and whatever he or she wanted within safe boundaries. Divided family or not, he would have made it work for their child, no matter what the cost.

But, regrettably, Maya was correct in that he had not started out thinking along balanced, reasonable lines that took a child's needs into consideration. He had simply seen an opportunity to expand his business empire and had leapt on that fresh challenge to alleviate his boredom. He hadn't cared about the position he was putting Maya in, nor had he thought in any depth about the child he was planning to bring into the world with her help. He had been selfish, callous, possibly even cruel, he conceded grimly, and he had few excuses to make for himself. He didn't need that technology company or Aldo's business holdings and properties because he was already richer than sin. He should have thought more than twice about dragging an innocent woman and a child into his bleak, self-indulgent existence.

All of a sudden he was no longer surprised that the situation he had created had blown up in his face. It was what he deserved, after all, for being irresponsible and lacking in compassion. But it wasn't what *Maya* deserved, he thought heavily, and Maya was devastated by the loss of their child. Maya had been ready to love that baby from the instant it was conceived. Her heart, unlike his own, was open and giving.

The dawn light was brightening the room when Maya wakened from her restless doze. Almost immediately the events of the night flooded back to her and her eyes stung afresh, the heaviness in her heart weighing down on her again. A slight sound behind her made her flip over and stare in consternation at the sight of Raffaele slumped in a graceful sprawl of long limbs in the chair beside the bed. Unshaven with dark stubble framing his strong jaw line and accentuating his mobile mouth, he looked unnervingly familiar and precious to her. 'Why are you still here?' she exclaimed.

'Where else would I be?' he parried levelly. 'I'm part of this too. I couldn't leave you alone.'

'Even though I gave you permission to do exactly that?' Maya glanced away from him again, disturbed by how welcome she found his presence and the sense of security it gave her. The gut reactions Raffaele stirred were misleading and annoying. She always wanted to trust him even when she knew she shouldn't.

'You don't always know what's best for you,' Raffaele fielded.

'And you *do*?' An embarrassed flush lit her heart-shaped face as she heard the edge of scorn lacing her voice.

'I think we both know that if I had ever once considered what was *best* for you, I would never have met you in the first place and offered you the choice that I did,' Raffaele countered drily, sharply disconcerting her.

Maya stared at him in astonishment. Even if he

had chosen not to approach her, her family's debts would still have been called in. Aldo would have seen to that. Her parents would have been made bankrupt and homeless and that was not a development she could have faced any more easily. Raffaele had given her a choice. It might not have been a choice she relished but at the time it *had* seemed the lesser of two evils.

'I suppose you never thought of something like this happening,' she muttered.

'No, I didn't,' he agreed quietly. 'It didn't occur to me that I was taking a gamble on real life and that that is likely to be messier and less predictable than a business transaction.'

'But then you're too accustomed to controlling developments and people and it's made you reckless,' Maya murmured, her heart jumping in her tight chest as he looked up at her through his lashes, his eyes a butterscotch gold that were like a shard of sunlight against his bronzed features.

'When it's a question of how I've treated you, reckless is an acceptable criticism,' Raffaele bit out grudgingly, his lean dark face stormy at having to make that concession. 'I didn't allow for the human factor.'

Involuntarily, Maya smiled. It was only a small smile, just a slight turning-up at the corners of her mouth. 'Who are you and what have you done with Raffaele Manzini?' she quipped.

Raffaele stared steadily back at her, his attention lingering on that unexpected hint of a smile, his golden eyes suddenly ablaze. With disconcerting suddenness, he vaulted upright. 'Would you like something to eat or drink?'

Heat had engulfed Maya, shocking her, her face

burning up as she shook her head and reached for the glass of water beside the bed to raise it to her taut mouth, so unsettled was she by the effect he could have on her at the most inappropriate moments. 'I'm not hungry yet…probably all the medication. You should return to the yacht.'

'I'm booked into a hotel near here,' Raffaele slotted in. 'It's more convenient.'

'Go and get some sleep,' Maya urged.

Raffaele tensed. 'We haven't talked about what happened yet,' he breathed tautly.

Maya paled. 'I really don't want to talk about it. I just want to leave it behind,' she confided.

Raffaele frowned. 'I don't think it's that simple, *bellezza mia*.'

'It can be,' Maya muttered. 'Talking about stuff doesn't always make it better. I'd confide in Izzy but I can't, right now. She's pregnant. If I told her what had happened to me, it would make her sick with worry and it would spoil the pregnancy experience for her. It wouldn't be fair to do that to her.'

'Why do you always put everyone else's needs ahead of your own?' Raffaele demanded in honest bewilderment.

'I don't, not always. I wasn't kind to you last night,' she pointed out guiltily. 'I'm sorry that I lost my head like that.'

'I can take a lot of hard hits without buckling,' he asserted. 'Particularly when I deserve them.'

But Maya was already losing colour, lowering her head back to the pillow with a sinking sensation as she recalled the dark hollow look in his gaze hours earlier when she had accused him of not feeling anything over the loss of their child. That look had stabbed her to the heart. She had hurt him. She *knew* she had hurt him, and her distress was not an excuse. The problem with Raffaele was that he hid everything he felt and she had made assumptions and learnt her mistake the hard way after taking out her grief on him.

Raffaele left the hospital with the sense that once again he was doing the wrong thing because he didn't want to leave Maya alone, even if it was what she seemed to want. He had plans to make though, he reminded himself. Maya needed a distraction and, whether she appreciated it or not, the time and the space to recover from her loss.

Later that day, Maya wakened at lunchtime to a room filled with flowers and magazines and a selection of her own nightwear available. Although she had little appetite, she ate the light meal that arrived for her because she wanted to regain her energy. She went for a shower, dispensed with the hospital gown and doggedly fought the sense of emptiness tugging at her. The loss had happened, and she had to deal with it. Without her agreement, her bright future, shining with the promise of her first child, had reshaped itself. Breathing in deep, she walked back into her room and stiffened when she saw Raffaele poised there, momentarily dazzled by the lustrous energising power of him as he swung round to face her, stunning dark golden eyes gleaming in his lean, beautiful face.

'Did you manage to get much sleep?'

Raffaele shrugged. 'Enough. Sit down. We've got plans to make.'

'The doctor's already been here to see me. We can try again as soon as we like,' Maya declared stiltedly.

'That idea isn't even on the table right now,' Raffaele countered with a level of incredulity he didn't try to conceal.

Maya blinked rapidly, surprise and disappointment flooding her because there was nothing that she wanted more just then than the chance to conceive again. 'What is, then?'

'We're heading back to London so that you can see your family.'

'We can't do that. They don't know about us.'

Raffaele studied her intently. 'They do now. I phoned and *told* them. No, I didn't mention what's just happened because that's private and nobody else needs to know about it. But I did tell your parents that we're married, and they want to meet me.'

So taken aback was Maya that her soft full mouth fell open. 'You told them?' she whispered in astonishment.

'We'll see your family and then we'll go up north to see my father and his,' Raffaele completed with satisfaction.

'You seem to have everything organised,' Maya remarked stiffly.

Raffaele lifted the folder he had set down on the table and tugged some sheets out of it to toss them on the bed. 'And now that I've given instructions for the house on Aoussa to be demolished, I could do with some ideas for the replacement dwelling. The architect wants some ideas from us concerning preferences.'

'*Demolished?* You've started that already?' Maya exclaimed, wide-eyed

'I hate the house. You were right: it has to go.' Raffaele lifted and dropped a shoulder with graceful finality. 'But I could do with some ideas about what to build in its place.'

Maya nodded slowly. She never knew what he was likely to do or say next and it was, she was learning, part of what made him so uniquely fascinating. He didn't think or operate within conventional limits as she did. He made decisions at nuclear speed, followed stray impulses, did what *felt* right to him and stood by it even if, ultimately, it turned out to be a wrong move. She supposed marrying *her*, planning a child with *her*, fell into that latter category and now he was focusing his energies on other things.

But *not* on conceiving another child, she registered in confusion, wondering what that meant and wondering why on earth she should feel weirdly rejected. Was it because she had somehow become attached to him? It wasn't love. It couldn't be love—she wasn't fool enough to fall for a guy in a temporary marriage, particularly one who already had to be thinking of her as flawed and unfit for purpose because she had lost their precious baby within days of conception.

Her brain buzzed with conjecture. What was *his* ultimate plan? What was the bigger picture? To work out Raffaele's goal, she had to start thinking as *he* did. And he was clever and calculating and unscrupulous. All of a sudden he was taking her home for a visit, restoring her to her family. Was it a guilt thing? Was he trying to undo the damage he believed he had caused?

Hadn't he already pretty much admitted that he should never have offered her the chance to marry him in the first place? And never have acted on the plan for them to have a child together? Was it possible that Raffaele was already working towards putting her out of his life again and reclaiming his freedom? And why did that fill her with a sense of panic rather than relief?

CHAPTER EIGHT

THREE LITTLE GIRLS engulfed Raffaele in a wave of giggling, chattering excitement. Andrea was five, Sophie was three and Emily was an adorable toddler with a mop of black curls. And every one of them reminded Maya of their half-brother, Raffaele, and tugged at her heart with a wounding sense of what might have been because, with their dark colouring, they gave her a very good idea of what Raffaele's own children might look like. Clearly, the Manzini genes were strong, for Raffaele bore a striking resemblance to his father, Tommaso.

'The girls are always like a mob of little thugs with Raffaele, all competing for his attention at once,' Claire, a brunette in her early forties, groaned. 'Luckily, they calm down after a while, particularly once the presents are open. I've told him so often not to bring them anything unless it's birthdays or Christmas, but he doesn't listen.'

Tommaso's wife and Raffaele's stepmother, Claire, was a social worker with warm eyes and an even warmer smile. The couple lived in a rambling old farmhouse outside Newcastle and it was very much a family home, from the children's pictures stuck to the fridge door to the clutter that lay around the kitchen. Boots lay in a heap by the back door while piles of kids' toys filled colourful baskets by the wall.

'He does tend to do his own thing,' Maya agreed, accepting the beaker of coffee her hostess passed to her. 'Thanks.'

'He's very generous. He tries to stick to the budget I gave him *most* of the time,' Claire conceded wryly. 'He's fantastic with kids too, much more relaxed with them than he is with adults.'

That was true. Maya had been downright startled watching Raffaele's easy interaction with his little half-sisters. He was very good with them and clearly a man who enjoyed the company of children.

The two women watched the two older girls learn to ride their new scooters in the custom-built playground at the back of the house. After throwing a tantrum because she had not got a scooter as well, Emily had gone down crossly for a nap, still attired in one of her new princess outfits from the wardrobe of dress-up garments she had received.

Raffaele had provided the playground for his half-siblings with all its safety features and the canopied roof that allowed for its use on wet days. Claire had been very frank on the topic of money with Maya, explaining that she and Tommaso only accepted gifts for their children and preferred to maintain their independence, rather than take advantage of Raffaele's wealth and generosity. Across the garden, Raffaele was standing talking to his father, a still-handsome man in his fifties. The two men had the same bone structure but Tommaso was smaller and slighter in build.

'You know, Tommaso was convinced that Raffaele would never marry,' Claire confided quietly.

'My family were equally surprised by our marriage. We were crazily impulsive.' Maya trotted out the same story she had told her own parents and, of course, her mother had thought it was madly romantic because a hasty supposedly love-at-first-sight match mirrored her own courtship history with Maya's father.

'It's amazingly positive to think that Raffaele can do *anything* crazy,' Claire remarked reflectively. 'I used to think that, for his age, he was always a bit too controlled, a bit too sensible and when it comes to women…*well*…' the brunette grimaced '…you're the very first he's brought to meet us and those I've seen him with in the media were pretty…er, trampy, for want of a better word.'

'I knew I should've worn a short skirt and a plunging neckline to fit the mould!' Maya teased with a chuckle, relaxing completely in the other woman's candid company. 'Raffaele likes those sorts of clothes on me, but I *don't*.'

At the sound of her laughter, Raffaele turned his head to look at Maya, noticing with satisfaction the healthy colour blooming in her cheeks and the smile curving her mouth. Maya had been as pale and silent as a wraith after she left the hospital but over the past few weeks she had gradually begun to return to normality. Restored to the company of her family during a lengthy stay in London, she had blossomed, vitality and humour returning to her clear green eyes. Only with him was she still reserved and withdrawn. He thought it was tragic that he had had to resort to using the company of others to draw her out and to make her relax again. But it wasn't surprising, he acknowledged grimly, not after what had happened between them.

For the first time ever, he was doing what he *had* to do even if it wasn't what he wanted to do. He *owed* Maya and he always paid his debts. Maya with her curtain of silky fair hair, long lissom legs and delicate curves, who made no effort whatsoever to be sexy but who could make him rock hard with one playful glance. He shut down hard on that very physical thought, reminding himself that all he could reasonably do was *attempt* to redress the damage he had done before letting her go again. But, regrettably for him, letting go of a woman he still craved didn't come naturally to him. The biter had been bitten, he acknowledged grimly. He was no martyr, no penitent, he wasn't essentially a *good* man, but he would force himself to go through the motions because that was what she deserved from him.

'No, a woman capable of telling Raffaele where to get off is unheard of and exactly what he needs,' Claire opined with a grin. 'From what I've heard, he runs rings round most women. They're too impressed by who he is while you seem to treat him as if he's normal.'

'Which he's not,' Maya conceded.

'And he never will be with that dreadful background of his and all that money,' Claire sighed. 'But he still needs someone to treat him as though he is.'

Only, not necessarily *me*, Maya reflected unhappily, already somewhat stressed by having recently heard her twin's frank opinion of her marriage. Since Maya had told her parents about her marriage, she had spoken to her twin on the phone and given her the same story.

Unhappily, she hadn't felt able to tell Izzy the whole truth either, not about the choice Raffaele had given her, not about their parents' debts being settled with their marriage and certainly not about the baby she had willingly conceived and then lost. Maya refused to burden her pregnant, newly married sister with the disturbing facts of her own situation, deeming it better to let Izzy believe that she had tumbled headlong in love with Raffaele while working for him and had rushed foolishly fast into marrying him.

Ultimately, Izzy had been most shaken by Maya's news only after she had acquainted herself with the online gossip about Raffaele. Izzy had called Maya back purely to raise the topic of Raffaele's raunchy reputation as a womaniser and refer worriedly to the unlikelihood, in *her* apologetic opinion, of such a male choosing to stay faithful on a long-term basis. Her fear that Maya could not possibly hope to find lasting happiness with Raffaele had been unmistakable. Evidently Rafiq, Izzy's new husband and the father of her unborn twins, didn't have that kind of better-left-buried sexual past. Well, bully for him, Maya thought ruefully as she went pink with discomfiture.

Truth to tell, after all, Raffaele's amazing versatility between the sheets was more of a colourful memory for Maya than a current event. Raffaele hadn't shared a bed with Maya, never mind actually touched her in any intimate way, since she had lost their baby, and that distance he had forged between them hurt and made her feel more rejected than ever.

They were based in Raffaele's penthouse apartment in London where they were occupying separate bedrooms. That had been *his* choice. In spite of Maya's clumsy attempts at flirtatious encouragement, Raffaele had made no moves whatsoever. It was as though any sexual attraction she'd had had vanished after her stay in hospital. Evidently he wasn't planning or hoping to get her pregnant again and he wasn't interested enough in her to even approach her for sex. What did that tell her? Well, all it told Maya was that, in Raffaele's eyes, their marriage was already over. He had changed from a guy who couldn't get enough of her into a guy who didn't even seem to appreciate that she was still alive and kicking.

And what about what *she* wanted? Well, that was a ridiculously complicated question, Maya acknowledged ruefully. Every time she looked at Raffaele, she knew she wanted him, and being shot without warning from a passionate relationship into a platonic one was a shattering shock to the system. Naturally, she had told herself that she shouldn't still be attracted to him. Obviously, she had told herself that she should be relieved that he didn't expect to share a bed with her any more. But the logical approach hadn't helped because during the weeks of their marriage, all those sunny lazy days exploring the Mediterranean, she had grown deeply, *illogically* attached to Raffaele.

How had that happened and did it really matter that she didn't know *how*? The reality was that she had fallen in love with Raffaele. His dysfunctional childhood and his experiences since had made him cynical where she was naïve and too trusting; his droll take on his life, born out of those experiences, was nonetheless very entertaining and he often made her laugh. She had also learned that nobody could be kinder or more caring than he. But most of all, on the day he'd told her about his dogs being shot she had caught a glimpse of the broken-hearted, lonely, unloved boy inside him, of the terrible damage done to him and the lingering vulnerability that he worked so hard to hide from the world. And that had been that for Maya: her heart had opened up and taken him in and she knew she would fight like a lioness to protect him from hurt.

Yet *she* had hurt him at the hospital, reminding him of their unlovely beginnings and the child he had persuaded her to conceive to seal a business transaction. And she had seen him acknowledge the wrong that he had done, had witnessed the deeper understanding that he was developing and the care and support he was so determined to give her. She had grasped then that, in many ways, Raffaele had been a case of arrested emotional development ever since his disturbing childhood experiences and now, finally, he was emerging from that shell to change and grow as a man. At the same time, though, she suspected that he was finding the emotions assailing him now almost as confusing and unsettling as she had once found his former emotional detachment.

It was mid-evening when they returned to the London penthouse. They had eaten on the flight back and Raffaele strode off to his room, leaving Maya marooned in the vast reception area with its sumptuous seating and fantastic view of the London skyline as night fell. She had never felt more alone in her life than she did at that moment, wondering why he was avoiding her, barely speaking, wondering why she didn't have the courage to reach out and demand answers from him. Because she was afraid, she accepted numbly, because she was afraid of hearing the truth that their marriage was over. And once Raffaele said those words, he would be free to leave and stay at one of the many, many properties he owned across the world instead. Once he was gone, he would be gone for ever and the very thought of that simply terrified her…and yet, it shouldn't, it *shouldn't*. It would be a return to the life he had taken her from, and she couldn't face the emptiness of that again. She hadn't even known how empty her life was until he'd entered it.

'I'll see you…later,' Raffaele murmured from behind her. 'Probably tomorrow as I won't be back early.'

Maya unfroze with a jerk and glanced across the room at him, shot rudely from her reverie. He had changed into an exquisitely well-tailored suit, a dark claret-shaded shirt with an expensive sheen open at his bronzed throat. 'Where are you going?'

His sculpted mouth compressed. 'Out… I need to go out. I'm feeling…' he shifted a fluid brown hand in almost aggressive emphasis '…cooped up here.'

Already pale, Maya snatched in a deep quivering breath. 'Fancy some company?' she heard herself ask like an over-eager schoolgirl.

Stunning dark golden eyes rich as caramel, Raffaele tensed, his strong jaw clenching. 'Not tonight, I'm afraid,' he told her levelly. 'Tomorrow, we'll talk… OK?'

No, it wasn't OK. Maya didn't want him to go out, didn't trust him to go out in the parlous state of their already broken marriage. She didn't want to be around for the talk he had mentioned either. In fact, she wanted to run and keep on running from that possibility because, unhappy though she was with the current state of affairs, it was infinitely better than being deprived of him entirely. And not only did she not recognise herself in those cowardly reactions, she hated herself for that urge to shrink away and hide from a truth that would hurt.

As Raffaele disappeared into the lift, Maya lifted her phone and stabbed a single button. 'Sal?' she asked as the head of Raffaele's security team answered. 'I need to know where Raffaele is going tonight.'

Troubled silence fell on the line. 'Mrs Manzini...'

'*Please*... I don't want him to do something stupid!' Maya gasped.

And Raffaele was perfectly capable of doing something stupid to break himself out of the marriage he felt trapped in. It wasn't the confinement of the apartment that was making him feel cooped up; no, it was the constraint he had put himself under since she had left the hospital.

'I'll text,' Sal breathed curtly.

'I promise I won't tell him how I found out,' Maya murmured gratefully.

Within minutes the text came, naming a fashionable nightclub that Raffaele owned. And as Maya headed for her room, a voice was screaming in her head that she couldn't do this, couldn't run after him, couldn't force a showdown because that wasn't the dignified way to deal with a husband who didn't want to be a husband any more, who had probably never wanted to be a husband even at the start. But as stubborn, defiant and tough as Raffaele was, he was also still *her* husband.

Maya cursed as she rampaged through her elegant and restrained wardrobe because in the mood she was in, she didn't want elegant and restrained. She dug out the outfit Raffaele had bought for her that first day and wrinkled her nose at the leather and lace corset top and the tight skirt before throwing both items out onto the bed. If that was what he liked, that was what he was getting, she decided, pulling out sky-high heels and hold-up stockings before heading into the bathroom to do her face.

She needed to *do* something, not sit around wringing her hands being passive and letting Raffaele make all the major decisions. She was smart, she was strong and he did do crazy impulsive things, so she had to look out for him even if that meant sticking out a foot and tripping him up hard when he threatened to go in the wrong direction. He also needed to learn that she didn't play games, didn't close her eyes to avoid seeing what she didn't want to see and that she wouldn't dance around the truth when it came to laying down her boundaries.

When Raffaele saw Maya moving towards him in the club, his own security clearing a path through the crush for her benefit, he momentarily thought he was imagining her. How could Maya have found him? Why would she have followed him and why the heck would she be dressed in a way that was decidedly not her style? For some reason she was also sporting enough diamonds to sink a battleship. Maya, who was no fan of conspicuous consumption or showing off his wealth.

The short skirt put her outrageously long legs out on prominent display, legs that were incredibly shapely from slim knee to delicate ankle. Her round small breasts were swelling over the edge of the corset top in a most provocative show and Raffaele hated that he couldn't drag his eyes from her. With her hair draped like a sheet of pale satin down her slender back and framing her beautiful face, her green eyes were glittering as brightly as the diamonds in her ears and at her throat, her sultry peach-tinted lips slightly parted. And he knew right then, if he had ever had any doubt, why not a single woman who had approached him had contrived to awaken his interest. No man went happily from a woman who was a hundred out of ten in the desirability stakes and readily settled for less. In the seconds it took Maya to reach him, Raffaele's slumbering libido raced from zero to sixty, making his heart pound and his trousers tighten.

Rage shot through Maya the instant she saw Raffaele. He wasn't alone in his VIP velvet-upholstered booth, which was cordoned off from the rest of common humanity. Of course, he wasn't by himself, not a lone billionaire on the prowl for company. And when it came to company, Raffaele was surrounded by glamorous options. A half-naked redhead with all the chest development that Maya lacked was lounging up against the side of the booth trying to chat him up while stroking his arm, arching her spine back to ensure that her assets jiggled with her every excited breath. An exotic brunette was coiled sinuously up with a giggling blonde on the seat beside him. Maya wasn't quite sure whether they were with Raffaele or with each other, but it didn't matter, he was still breaking rules.

As far as Maya was concerned, he wasn't allowed within twenty feet of a gaggle of sexy, beautiful women without her around or at the very least her permission. And no way was she giving him permission, not while they were married. The cordon was released to allow her free passage and Maya planted herself directly in front of Raffaele. 'Get rid of your friends,' she instructed quietly. 'Unless you want an audience to what I have to say.'

Spellbound by her belligerent attitude, Raffaele dealt her a slow, assessing smile and dismissed the company he had gathered. '*Madonna mia...* To what do I owe the honour, *bellezza mia*?'

'I wouldn't take that tone unless you want to be drenched by a drink,' Maya bent down to say.

Raffaele snaked out both arms and tumbled her bodily down on his lap. Maya fought that repositioning, which put her in a more submissive position, and wrenched herself over him instead, her tight skirt ripping at the split in the back as she knelt across him, green eyes angry and determined.

'What's the problem?' Raffaele asked, carefully smoothing down the torn skirt as best he could because he didn't want anyone else catching even a glimpse of her panties or her stocking tops.

Maya looked into gleaming golden eyes and spoke from the heart. 'We're married. You're exclusively mine and you're breaking the rules.'

'We don't have any rules now,' Raffaele argued tightly, struggling to suppress the bold arousal her behaviour had induced, wondering if there was a streak of crazy in his bloodline because he was finding her take-no-prisoners public confrontation the sexiest move ever. *You're exclusively mine.* Why did that outrageous statement turn him on even harder and faster? When had he ever wanted to belong to any woman?

'You only get your freedom back if I'm pregnant,' Maya reminded him. 'And I'm *not* pregnant!'

Sheer unvarnished shock reverberated through Raffaele's big powerful frame.

'And you're in default in this marriage contract too,' Maya added informatively. 'You're not even *trying* to get me pregnant.'

'In default? That's an…interesting take on the situation,' Raffaele conceded, seriously stunned by the dialogue. 'I wasn't aware that any further "trying" *could* still be on the agenda. In fact, for the first time ever with a woman, I was attempting to do the decent thing.'

'I don't *want* decent. I don't *want* apologies or pep talks or excuses from you. I want a baby,' Maya interposed bluntly. 'It's very simple.'

'Your grandfather can keep his technology company. I'm walking away from this unholy mess. I started it and I'm finishing it,' Raffaele stressed in a driven undertone.

'No, you're not. You don't get to make this decision for me. I still want a baby…*your* baby. Business doesn't come into this for me,' Maya protested. 'That company has nothing to do with this any more. Try to keep up, Raffaele…you're falling behind. If you try to walk away without fulfilling your obligations to me—'

'Obligations?' Raffaele growled.

Maya laced possessive fingers into his tousled black hair and ground down slowly onto his lap, discovering with secret satisfaction as she met the hard thrust of his arousal why he had been holding her off him. He wanted her, he was just fighting the urge and striving to hide his susceptibility from her.

He had married her, made her fall in love with him and given her a baby she had miscarried. Then in the aftermath, when she was at her most vulnerable, he had suddenly backed off, cruelly cutting the connection he had taught her to crave. Now all her hormones were in uproar and she wanted stuff she shouldn't want but couldn't help wanting. She loved him, she wanted him, oh, dear heaven, did she *want* him, and she also wanted another baby. Not as a replacement, because she would never forget the child she had lost, but she needed a child she could hold in her heart as part of them both after he had ended their marriage.

Big hands framed her hectically flushed face. 'That's *really* what you want most?'

Her eyes stung with tears, but she blinked them back fiercely, a feverish glitter in her green eyes. What she wanted most was his love but that wasn't a very likely development and she was willing to settle for the best she could get. Slowly she nodded in silent serious confirmation.

Raffaele crushed her soft mouth under his and kissed her breathless. And holy hell, he could kiss, she acknowledged.

Her heart was hammering so hard he could feel it against his chest. The hunger flooding him was overwhelming, almost unbearable in its intensity. This wasn't what he had signed up for but giving Maya what she wanted most was what he wanted to do. That felt right, all of a sudden continuing their marriage felt right instead of wrong to him and he consigned every other concern to hell. He had overthought stuff, reached the wrong conclusions, somehow forced her to come to him with a demand. But if it put Maya back in his bed, did she really think he had been likely to argue? And why, underneath the seething hunger he was experiencing, did he feel hollow, even disappointed, when he should be on a high?

CHAPTER NINE

'YOU DON'T NEED to carry me!' Maya scolded as Raffaele scooped her into his arms to carry her out of the limousine into the lift Sal already had waiting for them.

'Your skirt's ripped. I don't want you flashing those beautiful legs for anyone but me,' Raffaele whispered, his mouth close to her ear and lingering to tug at her soft ear lobe and then settle against the quivering pulse point on her neck that sent her temperature rocketing.

Maya had forgotten about that ripping sound she had heard. She was still in shock at the confrontation she had dared to stage and even deeper in shock at its unexpected success. Of course, Raffaele liked bold, he liked honest, he liked straightforward and that was what she had been, telling him what she wanted upfront, leaving no room for misunderstandings, keeping it simple. But there were still some questions to be asked, she reminded herself firmly.

He carried her into the master bedroom where he had left her sleeping alone since their return to London.

'Were you planning to sleep with another woman tonight?' Maya asked bluntly.

'No. I still feel way too married to consider any form of infidelity,' Raffaele admitted with convincing cool. 'I just couldn't face staying in tonight, so close to you and yet not being free to touch you. It plays on my nerves.'

'You're the one who settled himself into a separate bedroom!' Maya reminded him helplessly.

Raffaele settled her down on the bed. 'I thought I was being considerate. I thought the last thing you would want was me anywhere near you!'

'Why? It's not your fault I miscarried,' Maya countered gently. 'It happened and it hit both of us hard but I'm ready to try again…but you're not?'

'Once we were in the separate bedrooms it just seemed to make better sense to continue that way and let it all go,' Raffaele breathed in a raw undertone. 'I made a mistake forcing you into this marriage. I was trying to put it right as much as I could for your benefit.'

'I don't want better sense,' Maya whispered tremulously, welded to the scorching golden turbulence in his eyes and the amount of emotion he was struggling to contain, thinking yet again of how seriously she had underestimated him and his capacity for feeling and of how that could yet prove to be an insuperable barrier between them. Raffaele was feeling stuff again and he didn't like it: his frustration was palpable. There was no guarantee that once he came to terms with what he was feeling he would still even be attracted to her, was there?

'I don't want sense,' she said again. 'I just want you.'

But that definitely wasn't the truth, Raffaele thought grimly, gazing down into her anxious green eyes with a sharp inner pang: she didn't want him for his own sake. She wanted him to get her pregnant and ultimately, hopefully give her another baby. It wasn't that fine a distinction either, he reasoned, considering that any fertile man could have provided the same service. Even so, he would settle for it because he had never wanted any woman the way he wanted Maya and living with her without being intimate with her, he had decided, was an unbearable situation to be in on a daily basis.

And if he had Maya back in his bed again, life would feel *normal* instead of empty and confusing again, wouldn't it? In reality he suspected that it was that sense of normality, occupation and focus that he craved even more than sex. And now he could stop agonising over such intangible responses because they would soon die away again. Sex was simply sex and Maya simply happened to be the sexiest woman alive. Of course, it was only sex with her that he was missing. Why did he persist in seeing complexity where there was none? She wanted a baby and, if he was honest with himself, he did too now. The child they had lost had marked him as well, creating a space where once there hadn't been a space in his world. There was nothing complicated about any of that, was there? *'You're exclusively mine,'* she had said. That was what had stirred up all the weird feelings infiltrating him. He didn't belong to her and she didn't belong to him, regardless of the rings they wore. But if another man so much as looked at Maya, he would kill him. That went without saying. That was normal, sexually possessive behaviour, he told himself calmly.

With a renewed sense of purpose, Raffaele gently turned Maya over and unzipped her skirt. 'I thought you didn't like this outfit.'

'I thought you did.'

'Oh, you put it on for me, did you?' Raffaele laughed softly as he unlaced the back of the leather top. 'Your seduction outfit? I like it even more. But to be brutally frank, anything you wear has the same effect on me. With you, I'm sort of basic in that field, *bellezza mia*.'

Maya tensed as he turned her back round to face him again. She gazed up at him, feeling that wild feverish flutter of excitement burning through her like a brand. 'Basic works for me.'

'It shouldn't. You deserve the flowers and the violins and the smooth stuff,' Raffaele told her earnestly. 'I wouldn't even know where to begin with all that.'

'You're doing just fine,' Maya breathed chokily.

'In the club,' Raffaele muttered raggedly, his nostrils flaring as he shaped his hands to the firm swell of her breasts, catching the straining peaks between his fingers, 'I just wanted to smash you up against the nearest wall and get inside you again. I was so turned on, I felt like an animal. That's what you *do* to me.'

A little quiver snaked through Maya as her nipples tightened and sent a darting arrow of heat down into her pelvis, making her shift, achingly conscious of the damp heat between her thighs. 'That's OK.'

'What would you know about it?' He wrenched off his shirt, angled up his lean hips to unzip his pants, vaulting off the bed to remove them. 'You've only had me…not the best introduction.'

'I like how you make me feel,' she told him confidently, determined not to hide from either him or herself when it came to that reality because he made her feel alive as nobody else ever had. It was as though she had gone through life sleeping until he came along, shattering her expectations but still somehow managing to steal her heart.

Raffaele closed his lips to a pouting pink nipple as he shimmied off her last garment, long fingers tracing the delicate folds between her thighs, and her head fell back and she gasped, hips rising in supplication, her whole body tingling with thrilling arousal. Slender fingers lacing into his black hair, she dragged him up to her and found his mouth again for herself, hungrily, urgently tasting him.

Arranging her beneath him, he drove into her hard and fast, stretching her with his length and girth. A rippling shockwave of delight convulsed her womb. It was electrifying, demanding, everything her desperate body craved. He delivered with every forceful thrust of his lean, powerful body until she was riding wave after wave of sensation. It was no gentle reintroduction to their intimacy; it was wild and elemental and incredibly exciting. He shot her to an explosive climax that sent pulsing paroxysms of pleasure rolling through her and she came back from that slowly with his name still on her parted lips.

Afterwards, Maya gazed up into his lean, breathtaking face, the line of faint colour accentuating his exotic high cheekbones, the stubble outlining his wide masculine mouth, and then she collided with his dark deep-set eyes, a scorching sunset gold with satisfaction and her every thought died away.

'I feel better,' Raffaele confided, smoothing her damp hair back from her brow and then momentarily lifting back from her to gather her tumbled hair off the pillow and push it out of her way so that she could cool down. A wolfish smile slashed his beautiful mouth as he held her possessively close. '*So* much better, *bellezza mia*. Maybe you'll let me take you to visit your sister now.'

Maya tensed with discomfiture because it was far from being the first time that he had mentioned that ambition. 'No, *when* I'm pregnant again, not before. I can't see Izzy and not tell her about the miscarriage, but I can't upset her with that when she's expecting herself. If I'm pregnant again, it'll be OK.'

Raffaele frowned. 'I can't believe you're being so stubborn about this. I know how close you are to your sister and it may take a long time for you to conceive again…we don't know.'

Maya shrugged. 'I know but I didn't think you knew.'

'I've been educating myself,' Raffaele admitted with a hint of amused one-upmanship.

Maya paled. 'Because you're hoping it doesn't take too long? Because you want your freedom back?' she exclaimed.

'No. I want a baby too and, I've got to tell you, I intend to put my *all* into the enterprise,' Raffaele announced, sliding over her, strong and graceful and very sure of himself, shifting against her to acquaint her with his renewed arousal.

Maya laughed in relief, overjoyed that he had warmed to the idea of a child as well, knowing that that would be a powerful link even after they parted.

And if he had been fire and fury the first time round, he was a slow sensual burn the second time, letting the waves of pleasure ebb and then flow and wash over her until she was reaching for the stars again in an exquisite release.

'I've been thinking,' Raffaele mused as she lay in his arms afterwards, scarcely able to credit that they were sharing the same bed. 'We need a house here in the UK.'

'The last thing you need is another house,' Maya told him gently, thinking of the many properties he had inherited from his mother, few of which he used on any regular basis. 'You already have this place—'

'It's not child friendly though. We have to think of that. We'll need outside space for a child to roam. I'll get onto the agents and you can start viewing country properties within easy reach of London,' he completed, his decision evidently made.

'Me?' she exclaimed.

'You don't like it that much here, do you?'

'It's OK.' Maya cringed a little at making that understated description of her palatial opulent surroundings and wondered if just living with Raffaele had already made her insufferably spoiled. 'It's a bit bland but it's central and convenient for you when you have meetings.'

'I'm thinking of you and our child in the future. It makes sense to get the house organised now.'

And the penny of comprehension dropped with Maya then and she felt as winded as if she had been punched. Raffaele was already planning the separation to come, even though it could take months for her to conceive again. What else could he be doing? He saw a future in which they would occupy two separate households, one for him here in the penthouse and one for her and their child safely set at a distance from his. A country house, which naturally he wanted her to choose because he wasn't expecting to be sharing it with her. She breathed in deep and slow to calm herself.

This was what she had signed up for, she reminded herself fiercely as her eyes stung furiously and she blinked rapidly and forced a stiff smile. She had signed up for a marriage, a child and a divorce and, ultimately, Raffaele would stick to the rules. He was comfortable with limits and rules, particularly where relationships were involved. It was typical of Raffaele that he was already working out in advance where to rehome her like a pet he had outgrown. Why on earth had she got the impression that anything between them had essentially changed?

But in the two weeks that followed, it struck her that the ambience between them *had* changed and not for the better. The sex was off-the-charts amazing, but Raffaele was more distant with her out of bed. He was working incredibly long hours and she would see him at breakfast and occasionally for dinner but not much else. He urged her to make a checklist of requirements before she viewed any properties and she spent hours studying houses online to fill her time, discovering that it was anything but easy to find one that ticked every box. And then the inevitable happened: she fell in love with a house.

'I don't understand why you want me to view this place with you,' Raffaele declared with an edge of impatience over breakfast. 'I don't care where I live as long as the usual facilities are available.'

'I would still value your opinion and, as the owners are abroad, you won't even have to make polite conversation with strangers,' Maya pointed out persuasively, wanting him to agree to spending some actual time with her that did not entail sex, wondering if that made her just a little desperate. He was following the rules of their strange marriage and she was trying to break the rules without him noticing.

With a groan, Raffaele agreed while reminding her once again not to organise any viewings for over the weekend.

'I haven't forgotten,' she told him a little tartly. 'You still haven't told me why—'

'It's a surprise. I'll tell you later,' Raffaele parried. 'After you've done a pregnancy test.'

Maya paled at the suggestion. 'It's too soon.'

'No, it's not and you're getting all stressed out over it, which isn't good,' Raffaele countered. 'We could be doing this for months, so let's not make a production out of a simple check. Months… *Madonna mia*…how will I stand all that sex?'

Maya went red as fire. 'Raffaele…'

Raffaele dealt her a wolfish grin. 'I can take everything you can throw at me,' he teased. 'Now give me the brochure for the house.'

Raffaele was picking holes in her choice even before they boarded the chopper that would ferry them to Grey Gables.

'It's at the very limit of a convenient distance from London,' he warned her.

'It's historic,' he pointed out. 'You said you wanted to avoid that because it's a protected building, which makes alterations difficult.

'It's also going to need more bathrooms and you said you didn't want anywhere requiring building work,' he reminded her annoyingly.

'It's got woods, acres and acres of woods,' he commented.

'Didn't you ever want to build a tree house when you were a kid?' she gibed in frustration.

'My play properties were built for me,' Raffaele admitted. 'And I would never have got to run free in the woods because Julieta would have deemed that, like a tree house, too dangerous. She had a whole list of pursuits which I wasn't allowed to follow and places I wasn't allowed to go…her control only loosened after I started boarding school.'

'Yes, but we're not going to be the same with our child,' Maya pointed out brightly, wishing she hadn't mentioned anything to do with his childhood with his troubled mother because that only roused unhappy memories.

Raffaele sent her a sardonic smile and handed the brochure back to her. 'And presumably, you're planning to give me triplets at the very least. Grey Gables has an awful lot of bedrooms.'

'But you'll need those rooms for extra bathrooms,' Maya tossed back, lifting her chin.

A couple of hours later, Raffaele watched as she toured the house while the agent waited outside to give them some privacy. Maya's hair was in a long golden braid, as rigidly contained as she was, slender shapely legs outlined in casual cropped jeans mounting the stairs. She was beautiful, so beautiful, her delicate profile absorbed, her soft mouth still unnaturally taut because he had dared to mention the pregnancy test they had agreed to do every month. Her entire focus was on conception, which was why he was praying that it simply happened, and quickly, to take that complication off the table. Once that was achieved, she would relax, open her eyes, maybe even see what else was on offer…

Raffaele studied the gracious landing, ancient polished boards creaking beneath his feet. Grey Gables was pretty much everything he had avoided throughout his life but that didn't mean that he couldn't see the appeal of the Georgian gem set within its own estate. It was, primarily, a *family* house with a warmth that even he could feel. The owners were downsizing, their children long since grown up, but happy snapshots of the life they had led at Grey Gables, fashionably presented in black and white, abounded. Maya, predictably, paused again and again to study the photos because that was what Maya wanted even if she didn't know it: she wanted a family life, a happy, perfect family life like the one she had grown up with. It galled him to acknowledge that truth but there it was. Maya's debt-ridden parents had still, against all the odds, contrived to raise happy kids.

'So, what's this surprise you won't tell me about?' Maya pressed as she stood at one of the windows in the master bedroom, which looked out across the front lawns.

The main bedroom was a beautiful room in a very elegant house with the delicate ceiling and wall mouldings and gracious marble fireplace still intact. She had already pictured the bedroom with that fire lit on a winter evening and she bit down hard on her lip when she registered that she was imagining Raffaele by her side. By the time winter came, she would very probably be pregnant, and he would be long gone, only reappearing after their child was born. Her heart clenched as if someone had squeezed it and she forced herself to focus on the view instead. Beyond the window, she could see long stretches of well-maintained lawn surrounded by towering graceful lime trees. Their weeping branches of bright green leaves almost touched the ground and beyond the formal gardens stretched a dense belt of natural woodland.

Raffaele strode across the room, opening doors, glancing in at a superb well-appointed bathroom and a pair of formally fitted-out dressing rooms, which she had already inspected. 'At least they didn't stint on the details,' he commented grudgingly.

Maya studied him. Even in faded designer jeans and a shirt, he still contrived to take her breath away at a glance. Nothing he wore said billionaire, aside of the slender gold watch on his wrist and possibly his handstitched shoes. His whole attitude of masculine command and expectation, however, screamed his exclusive status for him. She had seen the female agent's fluttering, hair-tossing instant reaction as Raffaele had vaulted out of the chopper that had brought them to the estate and then paused to lift Maya out with the care he always utilised around her. The agent had had that glazed expression that women often wore in Raffaele's presence.

He was drop-dead gorgeous from his lean, powerfully built, hard body to his chiselled, breathtaking features. All that and money *too*, she had seen the woman thinking as she'd scanned him before staring at Maya as if trying to penetrate the mystery of how Maya had captured such a husband. No mystery, Maya had felt like saying, more of a trap sprung by Aldo, who had made both of them victims.

Raffaele could never just stand still in business. He had a great need to prove himself even if that meant competing against his own best performances year on year, and the prospect of anything new or challenging, like the current underperformance of her grandfather's technology company, had grabbed his interest and held him fast. Maya, in comparison, had become the victim of the belief that she could save her family without harming or changing herself. She thought it was fair to say that neither she nor Raffaele had appreciated quite what they were getting into when they had married. They had thought they could do it without pesky feelings and personalities getting involved and both of them had got it badly wrong.

'The surprise, Raffaele,' Maya prompted a second time, hitching a fair brow in emphasis.

Raffaele lounged back fluidly against the door frame and in that one sleek, graceful movement ensured that her fingers literally tingled with the desire to touch him. She wanted to trail her fingers through that tousled silky black hair, trace the sensual line of that full lower lip, smooth her hand down over his tightly muscled abdomen. 'We have guests coming this weekend.'

Maya struggled to drag her brain back out of the gutter, where his extraordinary physical pulling power had taken her. 'Guests?' she queried in surprise.

'We're holding a big family reunion,' Raffaele extended with a twist of his shapely mouth.

'You don't have family… I mean, apart from Aldo and your father, and London is too far for Aldo to travel,' Maya remarked, her smooth brow furrowing.

'*Your* family,' Raffaele corrected silkily. 'Your Parisi grandparents, your own parents and siblings. All of them are eager to have the chance to get to know each other.'

Maya blinked in bemused disbelief. 'And you just decided to go behind my back and arrange this reunion?' she exclaimed in disbelief. 'Without even discussing the idea with me first?'

'Your grandparents approached me. Someone had to step in and sort things out, although I can't take the kudos in this case. Rafiq, Izzy's husband, contacted me first.'

Maya froze in dismay at that admission. 'Why? Why would Rafiq contact you?'

Raffaele dealt her a pained look. 'Your twin's been worrying about why you haven't visited her or asked her to visit you. You've made a lot of ridiculous excuses and naturally she's worked out that you're avoiding her.'

'I haven't been avoiding her!' Maya raked back at him angrily, outraged that he had got himself involved in something that had nothing to do with him. 'My relationship with my sister is none of your business!'

'I'm not standing by while you endanger a relationship that I know is very important to you, just as Rafiq wasn't prepared to stand by and ignore Izzy worrying that *she's* done something to upset you. I told him about the miscarriage.'

Maya stiffened, all the colour draining from her shocked face. 'You had no blasted right!'

'And he immediately understood why you'd been keeping your distance and why you didn't want to share that experience with Izzy right now. He won't reveal your secret. If it's any consolation, he believes you made the right choice even if I don't. Of course, he's looking at the situation from Izzy's point of view, but I'm looking at it from *yours*.'

'You don't know what you're talking about!' Maya slammed back at him tempestuously.

'I know you're still hurting and that your sister's support might have helped you to adjust. And don't tell me that I don't know what I'm talking about when I do,' Raffaele warned her grimly. 'But don't worry. Izzy hasn't been told and she won't be told unless you choose to tell her. Instead, I've taken the fall to explain your unavailability in recent months.'

'You've taken the fall?' Maya repeated blankly. 'What on earth are you saying?'

'That with Rafiq's agreement, he will inform Izzy that you've been avoiding her because our new marriage has been rocky and you didn't want her to see us together and notice anything wrong and start worrying about you,' he extended curtly. 'It's a good cover story and you can see her tomorrow evening.'

'Tomorrow?' Maya gasped in disbelief. 'Izzy's arriving *tomorrow*?'

Raffaele nodded confirmation. 'In advance of your grandparents. They're arriving the following day. And you can rubbish me in the husband stakes to your heart's content with Izzy. I'm not that sensitive,' he declared curtly.

'I'm not going to be rubbishing anyone!' Maya protested, moving restively off one foot onto another, shaken at the knowledge that she would be with her twin again after months of being deprived of her company. She was torn between joy at the prospect and rage with Raffaele for intruding. 'You shouldn't have interfered.'

'You were making a mistake and you didn't give me a choice.'

'I'm not *still* hurting!' Maya proclaimed hoarsely, her green eyes flashing a defiant challenge.

'Yes, you are, *bellezza mia*, and so am I. That's completely normal,' Raffaele murmured sibilantly, curving an arm to her rigid spine and urging her out of the room.

Her clear eyes prickled. 'You—?'

'*Sì*. I may have got with the programme when it was a little too late but…' Raffaele shrugged a shoulder wordlessly. 'Let's walk through the grounds now.'

Consternation gripped Maya as it occurred to her that her refusal to talk about the miscarriage had also denied Raffaele any way of expressing his feelings, *his* grief. She had hugged her sadness to herself, excluding him, and that knowledge filled her with regret.

'I *can't* tell Izzy,' she whispered apologetically. 'She would be so hurt for me and I'm used to protecting her. I'm used to being the strong one.'

'It's your decision, but she's got Rafiq now and I have the feeling he would stand in the path of a tornado to protect her. You need your family, Maya. You'll need them in the future when we're no longer together,' he bit out in a harsh undertone.

And at those words, Maya broke out in a cold sweat all over her body. She felt sick and dizzy and she pulled away from him to hurry into the cloakroom off the main hall before she disgraced herself. Her head was pounding fiercely, her stomach heaving but, luckily for her, she made it in time and for long moments afterwards, having bathed her clammy face and freshened up as best she could, she rested her brow against the cold tiled wall and breathed in slow and deep in an effort to calm herself down.

When we're no longer together.

He had said it, he had put it into words that could not be unsaid, words that cut through her like slashing knives. He had said out loud what she could not even bear to think about.

How very considerate of Raffaele to ensure that she had her family behind her for support when he walked away! She supposed that set-up would make his life easier, lightening up his conscience, if he would even have an attack of guilt at ditching her. And why would he? Why would he feel guilty when she had *asked* him for another baby? She had made that choice, that plea, that *demand*. Thinking about how she had approached him in the club that night, Maya shuddered with shame and comprehension. She had used sex to hold onto him, hadn't she?

Yes, Raffaele might have stated that he also wanted a child now more than he had at the outset of their marriage, but she had been the one to fling herself brazenly at him in public, spelling out that he could have anything he wanted if he would only stay with her long enough to grant her that one burning wish. The heat in her face climbed even higher as she looked back over the past weeks.

Sex was the lowest common denominator in a relationship, and she had certainly made use of it, she acknowledged in growing mortification. She had spent those weeks engaged in frantically, feverishly swarming over Raffaele every chance she got, like some sort of sex fiend on a roll. And Raffaele had liked that, had revelled in that, of course he had. But at the end of the day, it didn't make her one bit more special than any other casual lover he had taken to his bed. And he would have been downright shocked, she suspected, had he realised that she had *lied* when she'd approached him in that club.

She had said she wanted only a baby, but that was the biggest, most barefaced lie she had ever told. In truth, she wanted him because she loved him, and she wanted him *for ever*. So, she had only herself to blame for the consequences of her behaviour. Raffaele was already envisaging their separation, putting into place the supportive family framework he believed she needed for that future event, not seeming to realise that absolutely nobody in her family was likely to have the power to glue back together the pieces of her broken heart and fix her...

CHAPTER TEN

'CONGRATULATIONS,' THE URBANE private obstetrician told Raffaele and Maya the next morning, when the nurse reappeared with the result and a smile of confirmation.

Maya shivered, suddenly chilled, as Raffaele's hand on her shoulder urged her down into the seat awaiting her. As she had performed a test for herself before leaving the apartment, they had already known that she had conceived again. It had taken all of Raffaele's considerable argumentative skill to persuade her that she also needed to speak to a consultant to deal with the secret fears she had not shared with anyone. Only her fears were apparently not as secret as she had assumed when Raffaele was so readily aware of their existence. It was true, sadly, this time around she was not as innocent, and she couldn't feel joy as yet and couldn't luxuriate in the result as she had before because she was far too afraid that something might go wrong again.

Dr Carruthers spoke at length with ease, determined to allay her very real concerns. A very early miscarriage, such as she had experienced, was extremely common. Indeed, he told her, it often happened before women even realised that they had conceived, so any statistics he quoted her were almost certainly in-accurate. She had no grounds to suspect that there was anything else amiss with her and should approach this new pregnancy without undue concern or stress. At present, he saw no reason for her to take any additional precautions. He was very reassuring and Maya left his smart consulting rooms on Harley Street with a renewed sense of confidence.

'Are you planning to tell your twin?' Raffaele pressed.

'Yes. Not about before but about this, yes.' Maya's glorious smile lit her beautiful face to radiance. 'I can share this.'

Raffaele slotted her back into the limousine and, without even thinking about the intimacy of the gesture, she reached for his hand. 'We're pregnant!' she said foolishly and then flushed with embarrassment.

'Guess that means I'm unlikely to get lucky tonight,' Raffaele teased, dark golden eyes gleaming with amusement.

'Oh, don't you believe that you get off that easily.' Maya laughed. 'My hormones are going crazy right now!'

'I bet you anything that tonight you'll sit up gossiping with Izzy until the early hours of tomorrow morning and forget that I exist. You have so much to catch up on and once your parents and grandparents get together with you tomorrow, you won't have much privacy,' he pointed out.

And that was when she tugged her fingers hurriedly free of his. What on earth was she doing? Clinging to him? Behaving as though they were still a normal couple? Why was she behaving that way when the instant that pregnancy test had shown a positive result their marriage, as such, had become redundant? How had she managed to forget that reality even for a few minutes?

She scanned his teasing, charismatic smile. He was pleased, undeniably he was pleased that she was pregnant again. Naturally, he was because that put his freedom back within view again. Now he was more concerned with getting her settled into a house he had no intention of sharing with her and ensuring that she was once again fully integrated into her family circle. That was to be her solace for his absence, his departure from her life. All of a sudden, Maya felt hollow, the temporary lift of joy in being pregnant again draining away when she was forced to face the prospect of losing the man she loved.

Raffaele was buying Grey Gables for her and he had offered a premium if the owners were willing to vacate the premises quickly. Earlier she had been over the moon that he was as impressed as she was with the property, or, at least, sufficiently impressed to overlook the disadvantages he had outlined. She had nourished foolish dreams about them sharing the house as a new family, dreams utterly removed from reality for that had never been on the cards for them, had it been? And in truth, once Raffaele left the picture, she wasn't so sure that she wanted to move out of London and be at a less convenient distance from her family.

'Where are we going?' Maya asked as she realised the limo had pulled up on a busy street.

'I wanted to mark the occasion. I ordered it weeks ago,' Raffaele admitted confusingly. 'I want you to be wearing it when your sister arrives.'

Her brow furrowed as she glanced up at the logo of the world-famous jeweller's showroom before she was ushered inside, across a quiet shop floor into a private room where she sank down on a chair.

'The occasion,' she prompted, registering that he was giving her another surprise and reflecting on just how much Raffaele enjoyed surprising her, treating her, *spoiling* her with spontaneous unexpected presents. It occurred to her that she would soon be surprising him with the purchase she had already made on his behalf in honour of his twenty-ninth birthday in just over two weeks' time. A little chill tickled at her spine as she recalled the gift that had seemed like such an absolutely brilliant idea at the time she had come up with it, but now she found herself wondering if she had got it right for him or if, in fact, she had actually got it very, *very* wrong. Maybe her gift would be too personal and unwelcome? An unhappy reminder of an experience he preferred to forget? Or a new beginning? Well, there was no point agonising over her decision, she conceded ruefully, because she had already booked and paid for the two puppies, which were being kept until the big day.

The jeweller attending them with the utmost discretion produced an emerald ring for their perusal, waxing with enthusiasm about its perfection, its cut, the simple design of the platinum and diamond setting. It was a magnificent ring. She watched numbly while Raffaele threaded the jewel onto the same finger as her wedding band. 'What do you think?' he asked.

'It's breathtaking…' It was also utterly enormous and she listened intently while Raffaele told her how he had tracked down the stone in a private collection where it had resided for a couple of centuries and how, after persuading the collector to sell it, he had designed the setting. 'It matches your eyes.'

'If I truly had eyes that colour, they'd be in somebody's collection too,' she mumbled in a daze, flexing her finger under that new weight, wondering if she would ever, *ever* understand Raffaele Manzini because he gave her so many mixed messages.

A ring was such a particular gift, literally laden with meaning to most people, and she stared down at the ring, which he had been so careful to place next to her wedding band. 'It…it looks like an engagement ring,' she framed hoarsely when she could finally unglue her tongue from the roof of her mouth.

'It's pretty. It suits you,' Raffaele informed her almost brusquely. 'And since you went with the love-at-first-sight story when you told your sister about our marriage, it will be more normal for you to have a ring.'

'So, this is like a prop to make us look more like a convincing couple?' Maya questioned, her delight in her gorgeous ring ebbing a little.

Raffaele frowned. '*Madonna mia*…of course not. We're way beyond that stage now, aren't we?'

Were they? Here she was waiting to hear when he was planning to leave her now that she was pregnant again and he was busy buying her a truly spectacular ring and putting it on her engagement finger and telling her that it matched her eyes. Raffaele definitely moved to the beat of a different drummer and, while she loved that impulsive, unconventional ability he had to utterly confound and fascinate her, sometimes that exotic individuality was just a little exhausting and unnerving.

'Could we go and…er…look at baby stuff now?'

Maya asked in a discomfited, apologetic undertone only loud enough for him to hear as they returned to the car, her emerald ring glittering on her finger.

'*Baby* stuff?' Raffaele repeated in seeming consternation.

Maya cringed inwardly and outwardly and went pink. 'I just sort of…er…wanted to look—'

'Of course we can go and buy stuff if that's what you want,' Raffaele told her smoothly.

'No…no, we're not going to *buy* anything,' Maya contradicted with an edge of urgency. 'That would be unlucky. No, we're only going to window-shop.'

'I'm not much of a fan and don't have much practice of window-shopping,' Raffaele confided gently.

'Well, then, you can just drop me off to browse. That's all I want to do…it's my treat for me,' she admitted tautly.

'I wouldn't dream of allowing you to treat yourself alone, *bellezza mia*,' Raffaele retorted.

In an opulent department store, Maya almost touched an admiring finger to a tiny pair of cobweb-fine bootees and her eyes stung, excitement flaring through her.

'Come on…let's buy stuff,' Raffaele urged with enthusiasm even while he fully understood her reluctance.

Maya swallowed the thickness in her throat. 'No, not yet…we're just looking,' she repeated, examining a delicate lace shawl with brimming eyes of wonder.

'It's going to be OK this time,' Raffaele told her confidently.

'Why do you think that?' she whispered, closing a hand over his to pull him away from the display.

'Gut instinct and the reality that lightning rarely

strikes twice in the same place,' he murmured bracingly, disturbed by the anxiety she couldn't hide. 'We're going to be parents.'

Ridiculously cheered by that confidence that came so naturally to him, Maya laced her fingers into his and they returned to the penthouse. Maya had a dozen things to do. Raffaele might have organised preparations for her family's arrival behind her back but there were all sorts of little touches she could add to make her relatives feel welcome, like Izzy's favourite magazines in the bedroom, flowers for her grandmother, who adored white roses, and tissues everywhere for her mother because Lucia would probably be crying a lot at being reunited with her parents. Although the two women and her grandfather had been talking on the phone in recent weeks, there had been a certain constraint and nothing could take the place of a face-to-face meeting and a frank conversation.

Raffaele strolled into the bedroom and watched Maya get dressed. She was no longer self-conscious around him, which he enjoyed. The vision of her willowy figure as she donned fine lingerie held him fast. She was still wearing the ring and he supposed that was something to be grateful for. He couldn't concentrate, he acknowledged. He had put everything into place just as they had planned, just as they had agreed, and yet nothing felt right. How could it when he was accustomed to having Maya in his life? Accustomed for the first time ever to sharing everything with another person? That was a huge change in outlook for him. Familiarity did not always breed contempt, as he had once thought it unerringly did with him and women. Disturbingly aware of the teeming turmoil he had been suppressing deep in his mind for weeks, Raffaele turned his brain to a more current topic.

'Has it occurred to you that Izzy's husband could have settled your family's financial problems for you?'

Much struck by the concept, Maya rested wide eyes on him. 'Seriously?'

'Oil-rich, future King of Zenara?' Raffaele prompted gently. 'If you had turned to Izzy for assistance you would never have met me and never have married me.'

'But I didn't know about Rafiq then, who he was, how rich he was or that they were getting married,' Maya pointed out prosaically, but she was involuntarily shocked at the picture he had drawn. 'I had no idea that she might ever be in a position to help. That possibility never even crossed my mind.'

At the same time the very suggestion that she might never have married Raffaele shook her rigid. He had shaken up her and her life, but she couldn't have unwished him, couldn't bear the possibility that she might never have known him. She tugged another pair of cropped jeans from a drawer and teamed them with a casual sleeveless top, sliding her feet into comfortable mules.

Before Izzy arrived, Maya questioned whether she should admit to being pregnant, lest something go wrong again. And then she scolded herself for that pessimistic thought and reminded herself that she could not live her life that way, always expecting the very worst things to happen to her. After all, Raffaele had happened and, while losing him would be bad, she could not regret learning to love him, could not regret anything they had shared and, least of all, the child they had conceived.

Izzy arrived in a welter of buzzing chatter. Maya barely got time to meet her brother-in-law, Rafiq, before Raffaele bore him off into his home office to give Maya and her twin some privacy. Izzy hugged her and bounced around the room, full of energy, the proud curve of her pregnant stomach already obvious.

'Twins,' Maya remarked in awe.

'I know. I still can't believe it!' Izzy exclaimed with a grin. 'Rafiq thinks I'm a living miracle, which is rather nice.'

'I'm pregnant too,' Maya whispered before she could lose her nerve again.

Izzy's eyes rounded in surprise and delight and then she closed her arms around her taller sibling with unashamed affection. 'Wow…that's clever timing. I wasn't expecting *that* news! My goodness, now we'll be able to share stories every step of the way.'

'I'm only just pregnant,' Maya confided.

'Rafiq told me that you and Raffaele had been having problems,' Izzy murmured very quietly, her gaze troubled.

'Oh, that's in the past. Teething troubles,' Maya hastened to assure her twin. 'We probably rushed into getting married too quickly.'

'It was very sudden but, let's face it, when the connection is special, you *know* pretty soon,' Izzy burbled, her obvious anxiety ebbing at Maya's light tone and smile. 'I thought something was wrong and I was losing you.'

'You're never going to lose me,' Maya assured her fondly. 'I was thoughtless, trying to put up a front, that's all.'

And the evening ebbed away, almost without Maya

noticing as she and her sister caught up on all the news. Rafiq and Raffaele joined them for dinner but had to make their own conversation. It was indeed the early hours before Maya finally crept into bed, sliding in beside Raffaele and hooking an arm round him, although there was really no need for her to move that close in the huge bed.

'Feeling happier?' Raffaele asked, startling her because she had assumed he was already asleep and wouldn't have slung that statement possessive arm round him had she known he was still awake.

'Yes,' Maya admitted freely. 'Much happier.'

Her parents arrived early. Her mother, Lucia, was very nervous, and Maya tried to calm the older woman down about her approaching reunion with her once-disapproving parents. Her grandparents arrived an hour later and the surprise they brought with them was her grandfather's niece, Aurora, a stunning blonde model, who had hitched a ride in their private jet because she had an assignment later that day in London.

'I'm so sorry for intruding but I'll only be staying for an hour or so. I did so want to take the opportunity to get to know your side of the family,' Aurora told Maya, easing past her rather as if she weren't there to concentrate her full attention on Raffaele. 'Hi... I'm the marriageable Parisi female possibility whom, sadly, you never even got the chance to meet.'

Stunned to overhear that low-voiced, teasing self-introduction, Maya turned her head to catch Raffaele's flashing smile of amusement. He liked bold, he liked brazen, he liked confident. A shaft of fierce jealousy pierced Maya and it was an effort to concentrate on her grandmother's sobbing reconciliation with her daughter and step in with the occasional soothing sentence and reassuring hugs.

While that was taking place, Raffaele stood across the room chatting to Aurora, a tall, leggy figure clad in a white dress that was the perfect frame for her even more perfect figure.

'She's flirting with him,' Izzy remarked in disbelief. 'What's she even doing here?'

'Apparently she's here to get to know *us*,' Maya said drily, relieved that her sibling hadn't overheard Aurora's opening sally to Raffaele because Izzy would've sought an explanation and the carefully drawn story of Maya's marriage would have fallen apart.

'Not making much effort, then, is she?' Izzy commented. 'Go over there and act like a wife. Warn her off.'

'I trust Raffaele,' Maya fielded stiffly.

But she didn't and the polite lie roused colour in her cheeks. How could she trust a man who wasn't in love with her? How could she trust a man whose right to freedom after she became pregnant had been written into their pre-nup? And there Aurora was, exactly the kind of glossy, self-assured woman whom Raffaele had specialised in before he married Maya. Maya watched Aurora toss her long, unnaturally pale blonde hair while treating Raffaele to flirtatious, covetous looks from her sultry brown eyes and she wanted to slap her and lock Raffaele in a cupboard where no other woman could get near him. Her mood swandived while her temper bubbled.

Maya's parents and grandparents decided to move their reconciliation to the Campbells' house. Lucia and Rory had to be home in time for Matt returning from school and the older couple were eager to meet their youngest grandchild. Izzy and Rafiq accompanied them and then planned to return to the hotel they had organised, Izzy explaining apologetically that she wanted to lie down and nap for a while. After a great deal more hair-tossing and giggling, Aurora departed as well, still as much a stranger to Maya and her immediate family as she had been on her arrival.

'It went well,' Raffaele remarked with satisfaction when their last visitor had departed. 'Fences all mended…and you and Izzy enjoyed yourself.'

'We did.' The silence smouldered. 'Would you have preferred to have married someone like Aurora?' That question just bounced off Maya's tongue before she even knew it was there.

Raffaele dealt her a surprised appraisal and strolled back into the lounge. 'Why are you asking me that?'

Maya compressed her lips and gave a jerky shrug. 'She's definitely more your style than I ever was.'

'Realistically, I don't think it could ever have been a legal option because a niece isn't as close a relative as a granddaughter,' Raffaele fielded. 'When she made that remark, she was only trying to get a rise out of you. I think she's jealous that she missed out on what she would have seen as an opportunity to enrich herself.'

'No, she was jealous because I'm with you.'

'Then, she doesn't know what I put you through,' Raffaele parried. 'Your twin was watching me like a hawk while I was with Aurora. It's pretty obvious that she thinks I'm not to be trusted around other women. I hope that doesn't last.'

'It won't matter if it does, will it?' Maya cut in curtly. 'We'll be separated and you won't be my business any more and I doubt if there'll be any reason for you to meet my sister again.'

Frowning, Raffaele studied her. 'What are you talking about?'

'I get pregnant and then we split up,' Maya reminded him doggedly, choosing to voice her biggest, deepest fear as if throwing it into the open would magically dispel it. She shifted restively as her phone vibrated in her pocket. 'We agreed.'

Raffaele breathed in deep and slow, dark eyes flaring like fireworks. 'I'm not ready to let you go.'

'I thought you played by the rules. That was our business deal.'

'That deal ended in Sicily and we renegotiated,' Raffaele informed her.

'I don't remember renegotiating anything!' Maya slung back at him tartly.

'You came to my club and told me that I was *yours*,' he reminded her.

Maya coloured hotly at having that reminder tossed at her. Her phone vibrated afresh against her hip and with a muttered apology she dug it out and listened to the voicemail, waving her hand at him in a frustrated silencing motion as she tried to listen to the lengthy harassed message left for her. The breeder who had sold her the puppies had been taken into hospital for emergency surgery. The caller was the breeder's daughter and she was ringing to tell Maya that she would be dropping off the pups early because she was unable to look after them while her mother was in hospital. Dismay and disappointment filled Maya and she wondered how much earlier the puppies would arrive because she really had wanted them kept until the day of Raffaele's birthday.

'Why did you tell me that I was yours?' Raffaele asked with icy precision.

'I should think that would be obvious to a man of your intelligence.'

'Oddly enough, it's not,' Raffaele contradicted.

In a storm of turbulent emotions and growing mortification, Maya turned back to him. 'I'm not having this conversation with you right now... I can't think straight!'

As she stalked off towards the bedroom, Raffaele followed her. 'We're having this conversation now.'

'This is not the right moment to be dominant,' Maya told him shakily.

'I need an honest answer.'

'All right, I would have told you *anything* that night to keep you away from other women and get you home,' she admitted between clenched teeth. 'Happy now?'

'You mean...you were *lying* when you said that *all* you wanted from me was another baby?' Raffaele pressed hoarsely.

'Yes, I was lying. I was desperate. I was jealous and scared that you were going to go off and do something really stupid that there would be no coming back from,' she muttered in a bitter surge.

'If the "doing something really stupid" involves me going off with other women, that was never a risk. I don't cheat and I haven't wanted anyone but you since I first laid eyes on you at that hen party and you pretty much told me to go to hell,' Raffaele advanced rawly. 'I'm disappointed that you felt the need to lie to me about anything though. But why were you feeling *desperate* that night?'

The bell buzzed and she heard Sal's voice mingling with their housekeeper's, a strange low whining sound, the noise of something heavy being shifted over the tiled floor and a lot of exclamation from at least two male voices. And then the animal whines penetrated and she realised that the puppies must have been delivered and she shut her eyes tight, wondering what else could possibly go wrong in the space of one short day.

'I was desperate because I love you,' she told Raffaele flatly, assuming that that would end the humiliating dialogue. 'Having another baby was only an excuse to hang onto you. It was the only excuse I could come up with in the time I had. And you *went* for it. You went for the sex, which is OK…you *are* a man and you do like things simple. Excuse me…could you stay in here for a while? I have something to sort out.'

What on earth was she going to do with the puppies? This, the very day their marriage disintegrated, was *not* the moment to gift Raffaele a pair of dogs. But she couldn't ask the breeder's daughter or whoever was delivering them to take them away again because they were now Maya's responsibility.

She loved him.

She had lied to him only because she *loved* him, Raffaele reflected, thunderstruck by that admission. Even after all he had done, she had somehow contrived to fall in love with him? Rafiq had compared the conception of Izzy's twins to the eighth wonder of the world but Maya had pulled off an even bigger wonder in Raffaele's opinion. She loved him. He couldn't be-

lieve it, he just couldn't believe it and, intent on seeking further explanation, he followed her back out of
the bedroom and down the corridor to where Sal and
two of his security team were standing over a giant pet
carrier, Sal's face pale and rigid.

'What's going on?' Raffaele prompted.

The strange woman beside the carrier broke into
a flood of explanation that ranged from her mother's
broken hip to her mother's current incarceration in hospital. 'I couldn't possibly keep them for you the way
my mother promised,' she said apologetically to Maya.
'There's no room in my home for two lively puppies.'

'I understand. It's fine, thank you for bringing
them,' Maya broke in gently.

'I'm afraid I'll have to take the carrier with me but
I've brought a bag of immediate supplies, their vacci-
nation records and current feeding schedule and their
other documentation,' the woman told Maya, indicat-
ing the large sack one of the men carried as she bent
down to release the catch on the carrier. 'Any problems
you have, my phone number is in the bag.'

Maya caught a glimpse of Sal's anxious face as she
bent down and guessed instantly that he knew the same
tragic tale of Raffaele's brief pet ownership as she did
and was concerned about Raffaele's possible reaction
to the animals. A little black nose poked curiously out
of the carrier, swiftly followed by a little squirming
golden puppy body, and then a second explorer appeared.

'They were a gift for your birthday,' Maya whispered weakly to Raffaele as the carrier was withdrawn.
Somehow, she got through the departure of the breed-

er's daughter and said all that was polite before she even dared to glance in Raffaele's direction again.

Raffaele was down on the floor engulfed in puppies. At least he wasn't backing away or fighting them off, she told herself in consolation. He lifted glinting dark golden eyes to hers and smiled. 'Thank you,' he said in a husky undertone.

Maya recognised the tears in his eyes, and she was stunned. Grinning, Sal was already hustling the rest of his team out of the penthouse and their housekeeper was lifting the sack of supplies.

'Puppies,' she said in barely hidden consternation. 'Here.'

'But not for long, Mrs Abram. We're moving out to the country as soon as possible,' Raffaele informed her, a puppy gathered under each arm as he walked back to their bedroom, clumsily hit the button that opened the patio doors onto the balcony and set both little animals down outside. Puddles quickly appeared and he laughed. 'Yes, these two are going to keep us busy.'

'You're not upset?' Maya whispered worriedly. 'It seemed such a great idea but after I thought about what I had done, I started getting second thoughts, but it was too late because I'd already booked and picked and paid for them.'

'It *was* a great idea…and now I believe that you love me,' Raffaele admitted almost buoyantly. 'Because you understand me too. You knew I was afraid to love anything or anyone again.'

'Yes,' she muttered limply. 'You don't mind me loving you?'

'Why would I mind such an honour?' Raffaele demanded. 'If it means you'll consider staying with me for ever? I presume it *does* mean that? I've got you for good?'

Her smooth brow furrowed because she was confused by his attitude. 'For good?'

'We're not a business deal any longer, we're a couple in a normal marriage. That's *all* I want and I can promise you now that I will not do anything to make you regret staying with me,' Raffaele swore feverishly. 'I'll probably annoy you and frustrate you at times, but I will never deliberately hurt you.'

Maya nodded slowly as if she was afraid to break the spell. 'For good,' she agreed. 'But what's changed?'

'I had the stupid idea that all you did want from me was a baby, that you didn't actually want me for me… which was perfectly understandable after the way I'd behaved. But it wasn't something I felt that I could live with long-term,' he explained ruefully. 'You could have had a baby with any man, even had a baby without a man and gone for artificial insemination, so you wanting a baby fathered by me didn't really mean much, just that you knew it was achievable with me because you already knew that I was fertile.'

Maya had paled. 'I never thought of it from that angle.'

'Nobody has ever wanted me for me but you,' Raffaele breathed grimly. 'I've been wanted a hundred times over for my wealth, my looks, my body, for the publicity I attract. I've never been wanted just for me.'

'Oh, I'm sure you have, you probably didn't notice,' Maya opined, dismayed to register once again that she had wounded him by telling him that she only wanted him because he could give her another baby. 'And maybe you haven't always been the most lovable person around other women, but you've been honest and wonderful with me since quite early on, always surprising me with how kind and thoughtful you could be, and tender.'

Raffaele winced. 'I'm really not the tender type.'

She wanted to tell him how amazingly affectionate and demonstrative he could be, but thought that possibly it was wiser for him to slowly recognise that about himself. He needed to accept that his ready affection did not in any way detract from his masculinity, that indeed it only enhanced it.

He had picked her a dream of a wedding gown, had guided her around Egyptian antiquities purely to surprise and please her, had in every way pandered unerringly to her likes and dislikes rather than his own. He had reunited her family, had introduced her to her long-lost grandparents and had searched out and designed a beautiful ring for her pleasure. He had even lied and declared that their marriage was rocky to his brother-in-law to cover up any damage she might have inflicted by avoiding her sister for so long.

And after they had been engulfed by their first crisis when she suffered a miscarriage, he had ignored her attempts to push him away even though that would have offered him an easier path. He had not been detached and even when she had lashed out at him, he had stayed supportive and caring. The more she thought about everything Raffaele had done for her since their first intimidating meeting, the less she marvelled at the love she had for him because he had changed just as much as she had changed and within that change they had grown very close.

'In fact… I may not be tender or sensitive or any of

that stuff that's important to women,' Raffaele admitted gruffly, 'but I do really love you. I couldn't face the idea of life without you. When we viewed Grey Gables, I said, "when we're no longer together" to try and get a reaction out of you...something, *anything* that would give me hope, but instead you succumbed to the pregnancy sickness and afterwards, well, you were a bit quiet but you certainly didn't seem upset to me.'

'You said *that* deliberately?' Maya gasped. 'I was upset and hiding it. Where were your eyes?'

'Well, you're pretty good at hiding being upset. You burbled about the house all the way back here.'

Belatedly she blinked. 'You said that you loved me?'

'You're the only person I've ever loved. I like my father, my little sisters, but I don't think I love them. I don't think I've let myself love them, but I didn't get a choice with you. From the start I was flooded by these feelings about you and I was always burying them and then we lost our baby and...' Raffaele turned in an almost clumsy half-circle. 'Suddenly it was all there in front of me, how much I cared about you, how much it hurt to see you hurting and not be able to fix it for you. I felt helpless. I hated it at first. I was flailing around trying to work out what would be best for you, what would make you happy even if it made me unhappy and that's why I took you to see your family.'

'And that's why you stayed out of bed with me too,' Maya guessed. 'Because you thought letting me go was the kindest thing you could do for me...you idiot!'

'So, you stormed into the club that night and that was so incredibly sexy, such a turn-on.'

'You're easily impressed, Mr Manzini,' Maya teased, looking up at him with her heart in her eyes.

'And such a sweetie behind the nasty front. What did you really think of cousin Aurora?'

'Pushy, fake, not my type but she made you jealous and I liked that, which is why I stayed talking to her. I could see your annoyance,' Raffaele confessed ruefully.

'You can be *so* sneaky sometimes,' Maya sighed, wrapping both arms round him and resting her cheek against his shirtfront, loving the familiar warmth and scent of him.

He tilted back her head and kissed her passionately. 'I want you so much at this moment.'

'You can't have me. We have puppies to take care of,' Maya reminded him ruefully, watching the puppies gambol about the floor.

'All right, we feed them, we play with them, we come up with some names for them and then, we go to bed and they get an early night as well,' Raffaele proposed.

'We'll see. You're happy with them? They weren't a stupid gift?' she checked.

'This is my fresh start in life alongside you. There's nothing stupid about that,' Raffaele assured her fondly, running a fingertip along her cheekbone and leaning down to claim another, longer kiss. 'I love you, I'll love our child and I'll love our dogs.'

It was late when the puppies got fed and several shoes got chewed up in the intervening time, but Raffaele and Maya got to make love and celebrate their newfound happiness and both pets and owners remained delighted with each other.

EPILOGUE

FIVE YEARS LATER, Maya lay back on her sun lounger in the shade with Izzy beside her.

It was gloriously peaceful on the little island of Aoussa. The children and the dogs were down on the beach with their nannies. Izzy was a queen but she didn't act like one in private because Maya was always teasing her about the fact.

Maya had given birth to a little girl called Greta, and she was blonde and dark-eyed and crazy about mechanical things. Maya had had an easy pregnancy and a straightforward delivery but she had been well into the second trimester before she'd stopped fretting about something going wrong again. A year later she had conceived twins and, like her sister, had given birth a few weeks early. She had had two little boys, Pietro and Daniele. Black-haired and green-eyed and identical, they were noisy little boys full of endless energy, she thought with a rueful smile, but wonderfully affectionate and loving. Izzy's family was complete with her two girls, Lucia and Leila, and her son, Nazir, and Maya rather thought her family was complete as well unless Raffaele took another notion and persuaded her otherwise.

Raffaele adored children, his own children in particular. He got out of bed at night when they were babies and got under the feet of their nanny. He changed nappies, built brightly coloured plastic towers of bricks and dressed dolls and combed their hair. He showed their children all the love he himself had lacked but he didn't over-indulge them.

The new house on Aoussa was a rambling ultra-modern property, perfectly suited to family occasions, which was fortunate when pretty much their whole lives revolved around family connections. The sisters got together as often as possible. Maya and Raffaele would fly to Zenara and stay at the palace in the desert with Rafiq and Izzy and their children would race around together kicking up a storm. As couples they got on very well. Maya had long since confided in Izzy about the loss of her very first pregnancy, but she hadn't yet told her twin the truth of why she had married Raffaele. She didn't think that would be fair to him when he had changed so much since then and she didn't want her sister to think less of him. She was as protective of Raffaele as she had ever been.

She saw a great deal of her parents and her grandparents because when she visited Izzy and vice versa, their older relatives were often included in the invitation. Her little brother, Matt, had benefitted hugely from the stem cell treatment and was no longer in a wheelchair but could now get around on crutches. His condition was still improving as he was still undergoing treatment. Raffaele's great-grandfather, Aldo, had died two years earlier and Raffaele regretted never having had the chance to get to know the old man better before his dementia set in. They saw Tommaso, Claire and Raffaele's half-sisters regularly as well.

Raffaele's giant business holdings had begun to take up too much of his time and when Maya complained about the long hours he was working, Raffaele sold off some of his empire, choosing to invest instead. Maya wrote a mathematics textbook, which only sold to very clever people but that didn't bother her. She had Raffaele, her children, the dogs, a large and demanding extended family and entertainment to organise, and in reality she didn't have time for much else.

Now, when she watched Raffaele striding up from the beach, the dogs, Luna and Primo, at his heels, Pietro plodding after his father with his thumb stuck in his mouth, Daniele lazily dribbling a football and Greta dragging her basket of toy cars and diggers behind her, she got to her feet. Behind the group, Rafiq was urging his children towards the house with the nannies in attendance.

There Raffaele was, vital and golden in swim shorts and nothing else, and her heart hammered like crazy inside her chest.

'The nannies are about to feed the tribe and we're... we're taking a nap,' Raffaele announced with a wicked gleam in his dark golden gaze.

Maya turned as red as fire.

'I thought only children need a nap in the middle of the day,' Izzy remarked pointedly.

'The heat drains Maya,' Raffaele countered cheerfully. 'If she doesn't get a nap now, she'll be asleep before we get the BBQ lit.'

Izzy rolled her eyes with amusement and said nothing more.

'Do you have to be so obvious?' Maya hissed as Raffaele urged her upstairs to their secluded bedroom suite, which rejoiced in a spectacular view of the sea and *Manzini One* moored out in the bay.

'You know you wouldn't have me any other way.' Raffaele laughed. 'I don't want to turn into a boring lover who waits for bedtime when you're most tired. No, I'd much rather have you sun-warmed and sexy and sandy, even if you're embarrassed by something as entirely natural as your husband lusting after you.'

'You're never going to be boring in bed or out of it,' she promised him lovingly.

'But that's because I've got you to keep me on my toes and fully diverted.' Raffaele watched her strip off her wrap and bikini and fold sinuously down on the bed, stunning dark golden eyes absorbing her every move. 'You're so beautiful. I don't want to be shallow, but that *is* the very first thing I noticed about you.'

'You're forgiven. It's the very first thing I noticed about you as well,' Maya confided as he sprang up on the bed beside her.

'You blew me off!' Raffaele reminded her accusingly as if that memory still rankled. 'You walked away from me!'

'I don't think you'd have wanted me half as badly if I hadn't done that,' Maya murmured.

Raffaele strung a line of kisses across her collarbone and butterflies danced in her tummy, heat stirring lower down. 'You're probably right, but then I'm convinced that you were made for me, put on this earth just for me to love. Women don't come any more perfect than you.'

'I'm not perfect.'

'You're perfect for me,' he contradicted. 'That's why I love you…we fit.'

Maya trailed her fingers through his tousled wind-blown black hair, her gaze captured by his. 'Yes, we do,' she agreed softly. 'We fit amazingly well, don't we?'

'And I love you more every day, particularly when you agree with me,' Raffaele said with a wolfish grin before he kissed her and then there was no more talking for a long while.

* * * * *

VOWS TO
SAVE HIS CROWN

KATE HEWITT

To Cliff, my partner and my prince!
Love, K.

CHAPTER ONE

'I'M SORRY, MATEO.'

On the computer screen, Mateo Karavitis' mother's elegant face was drawn into weary lines of sadness and resignation—sadness for the position she'd put him in, and resignation that it had come to this. A queen who'd had three healthy, robust sons, an heir and *two* spares, and yet here he was, the unneeded third to the throne, now about to be thrust into the unwanted limelight.

'I know you don't want this,' his mother, Queen Agathe, continued quietly.

Mateo did not reply. He knew who didn't want this: his *mother*. How could she? As the third son, and a late surprise at that, he hadn't been prepared for the throne. He'd never been meant to be King, to rule Kallyria with a gentle manner and an iron fist the way his father had for thirty years, as a revered ruler, kind but strong, beloved by his people, feared by his enemies.

It has been his oldest brother Kosmos who had been taken into training from infancy, told from the cradle who he was and what he would become. Kosmos who had gone to military school, who had met dignitaries and diplomats when he was barely out of nappies, who had been crowned Prince and heir to the throne when he was just fourteen, arrogantly assuming the title that would be his. And it was

Kosmos who had died in a sailing accident ten years ago, when he was only thirty.

His oldest brother's sudden death had shocked his family to the core, and rocked its seemingly stable foundations. His father, King Barak, had diminished visibly in what felt like minutes, his powerful frame suddenly seeming smaller, the thick mane of grey hair turning thin and white. Three months after Kosmos' death, Barak had suffered a mini stroke that had affected his speech and movement but kept him on the throne. Four destabilising years after that, he'd died, aged only sixty-eight, and Mateo's older brother Leo, the true spare, had been crowned King.

How had they got here?

'Have you spoken to Leo?' he asked his mother, his tone brusque. 'Has he given an explanation for his unprecedented actions?'

'He…he just can't do it.' Agathe's voice, normally mellifluous and assured, wavered and broke. 'He's not up to it, Mateo. Not up to anything any more.'

'He is *King*.'

'Not any more,' she reminded him gently. 'Not since he abdicated last night.'

Mateo spun his chair around, hiding his face from his mother, a welter of emotions tangled inside him, too knotted up to discern one from the other. He'd never expected this. Even after Kosmos had died, after his father had died, he'd never expected this. Leo had seemed more than ready to assume their father's mantle. Leo, who had always been in Kosmos' shadow, finally ready to shine. He'd been more than ready for it, eager even. Mateo recalled the gleam in his brother's eye at their father's funeral, and it had sickened him. He'd walked away from Kallyria, intent on pursuing his own life here in England, away from the royal family and all its pressures.

And now he had to come back, because Leo was the

one who was walking away. His brother had been King for more than half a decade, Mateo acknowledged with an iron-edged frustration. How could he just walk away from it all? Where was his sense of duty, of honour?

'I don't understand,' he ground out through gritted teeth. 'This is coming from nowhere.'

'Not nowhere.' Agathe's voice was soft and sad. 'Your brother…he has always struggled to assume his royal duties.'

'Struggled?' His brother hadn't struggled when he'd practically snatched the crown from their father's head. 'He seemed more than ready to become King six years ago.'

Agathe's mouth tightened. 'The reality was far more challenging than the dream.'

'Isn't it always?' If his brother had acted as if being King was a licence to indulge whatever pleasures and whims he had…but Mateo didn't know if he had or not, because he'd chosen to distance himself from Kallyria and all it meant, and that had been fine by everyone, because until now he'd never been needed. 'How has he struggled, exactly?' He turned back to face Agathe, wanting to see the expression on her face.

She shrugged her slim shoulders and spread her manicured hands, her face drawn in lines of weary sorrow. 'You know Leo has always been a bit more highly strung than Kosmos. A bit more sensitive. He feels things deeply. He hides behind his pleasures.' Mateo made a dismissive sound. Leo was thirty-eight years old and had been reigning as King for nearly six. Surely it was more than time to put such boyish indulgences behind him, and act like a man. Like a king. 'With the insurgency in the north of the island,' Agathe continued, 'and the economic talks coming up that are so important…' She sighed sadly. 'He fell apart, Mateo. He simply fell apart. It was a long time coming, but I should have seen this was going to happen. He couldn't handle the pressure.'

Leo was now, according to his mother, in a very private, very expensive clinic in Switzerland, leaving his country rudderless at a critical time. Leaving Mateo as the only one to step up and do his duty. To become King.

But Mateo had never been meant to be King.

Outside, the chapel bells of one of Cambridge's many colleges began to peal, a melodious sound so at odds with the bleak conversation he was having with his mother. His life was here, in the hallowed halls of this university, in the modern laboratories where he conducted important research into chemical processes and their effect on the climate.

He and his colleagues were on the brink of discovering how to neutralise certain chemical emissions and potentially reverse their effect on the climate. How could he leave it all behind, to become King of a country most people hadn't even heard about?

A country that was the linchpin in important economic talks, a country that was, if his mother was to be believed, on the brink of war.

'Mateo,' Agathe said softly, 'I know this is hard. Your life has been in Cambridge. I understand that I am asking so much of you. Your country is.'

'You are not asking any more of me than you asked of my brothers,' Mateo said roughly. Agathe sighed.

'Yes, but they were prepared for it.'

And he wasn't. The implication was glaringly obvious. How could he be a good king, when he'd never been shown or taught? When no one had expected anything of him, except to live his own life as he pleased?

And he had done exactly that—going to Cambridge, becoming a lecturer and researcher, even living under a false name so no one knew he was a prince, eschewing the usual security and privileges to be his own man, free from all the encumbrances of royalty.

But all along he'd belonged to Kallyria.

'Mateo?' Agathe prompted and he gave a terse nod of acceptance.

'I'll fly back to Kallyria tonight.'

Agathe could not hide her relief; it shuddered through her with an audible sound. 'Thank you. Thank you.' Mateo nodded, knowing he was doing no more than his duty, even if it chafed bitterly. Of course he would still do it. There had never been any question of that.

'We must move quickly, to secure your throne,' Agathe continued and Mateo stared at her, his blue-green eyes narrowed to aquamarine slits, his chiselled jaw bunched with tension.

'What do you mean?'

'Leo's abdication was so sudden, so unexpected. It has led to some…instability.'

'You mean from the insurgents?' A tribe of nomadic rabble, as far as he could tell, who hated any innovation or threat of modernity.

Agathe nodded, her forehead creased in worry. 'They are growing in power, Mateo, as well as number. Without any-one visible on the throne, who knows what they may do?'

Mateo's gut clenched at the thought of a war. It was so far from his experience, his *life*, that it was almost laugh-able. Tonight he was meant to be speaking at a fundraising dinner, followed by drinks with some university colleagues. Now those plans seemed ephemeral, ridiculous. He had a country to rule. A war to avoid, and if not, then win.

'I will do my best to put a stop to them,' he said, his tone assured and lethal. He might never have been meant to be King, but heaven knew he would step up to the role now. He would do whatever he had to secure his family, his country, his kingdom.

'I know you will,' Agathe assured him. 'But there is more, Mateo.' His mother looked hesitant, and Mateo frowned. What more could there be than what she had already said—his brother abdicating, his country on the verge of ruin, and the necessity for him to leave his entire life behind? How on earth could there be *more*?

'What do you mean?' he demanded. 'Mitera, what are you talking about?'

'Your rule must be made stable as quickly as possible,' Agathe explained. 'With your father and brothers…so much uncertainty…there must be no doubt, Mateo, that our line will rule. That our house will remain established, through all the foibles and fortunes of war.'

'I am travelling to Kallyria tonight,' Mateo answered, with an edge to his voice that he tried to moderate. His mother looked so worn down, so worried. He didn't want to hurt her or cause her any more concern. 'What else can I do?'

'You must marry,' Agathe told him bluntly. 'As quickly as possible, with an heir as soon as possible after that. I have drawn up a list of suitable brides…'

Mateo jerked upright, his mouth dropping open before he snapped it shut, his teeth grinding together. 'Marry? But Leo never married.' Six years his brother had been King, and he'd never even entertained the thought of a bride, as far as Mateo knew. There had certainly been no whispers of a potential match, never mind an engagement or a wedding. Leo had had numerous affairs with unsuitable women, many of them splashed across the tabloids, none of the fleeting relationships leading anywhere.

'It is different now,' Agathe said with bleak, regal honesty. 'There is no one else left.'

A bride.

He resisted the notion instinctively, with an elemental aversion both to marriage itself, and to marriage to a woman he didn't know or care about, a woman who would no doubt be so very *suitable*.

'And what women are on this list of brides?' he asked, a sardonic note entering his voice. 'As a matter of curiosity.'

'Admittedly, not very many. Your bride will play an important role, Mateo. She must be intelligent, not easily cowed, of the right birth and breeding…'

'So no vacuous socialites need apply?' Thank God. He could not stand the thought of being married to some grasping, faint-hearted miss who only wanted his money or title. Yet what kind of woman would agree to marry a man she'd never met? Not, Mateo suspected, one he wanted to share his life with.

'No, of course not.' Agathe gave him a severe look that reminded him of his childhood, of the days when he'd been unrepentantly unruly, testing all the boundaries to make sure they were there. 'You need a bride to suit your station, Mateo. A woman who will one day become Queen.' As she was. Yet no woman could match his mother for strength, elegance, or grace.

Mateo looked away. He couldn't bear to think about any of it. 'So who is on the list?' he asked after a moment.

'Vanessa de Cruz…a Spanish socialite who has started her own business. Women's wear.'

He made a scoffing sound. 'Why would she want to give all that up and become Queen?'

'You're a catch, Mateo,' Agathe said, a hint of a smile in her voice, despite all her sadness.

'She doesn't even know me,' he dismissed. He did not want to marry a woman who would only marry him for his title, her station in life. 'Who else?'

'A French heiress…a Turkish daughter of a CEO…in today's modern world, you need a woman who is her own person by your side. Not a princess simply waiting for the limelight.' His mother reeled off a few more names Mateo had barely heard of. Strangers, women he had no interest in knowing, much less marrying. He'd never intended to marry at all, and he certainly didn't want to love the woman whom he did, but neither did he want such a soulless arrangement as this.

'Think about it,' Agathe pressed gently. 'We can discuss it more when you arrive tonight.'

Mateo nodded his terse agreement, and a few minutes later he ended the video call. Outside the bells had stopped ringing. Mateo looked around his cluttered study, the research paper he'd been writing discarded on his desk, and accepted that his entire life had changed for ever.

'Something's come up.'

Rachel Lewis looked up from the microscope she'd been bending over to smile a greeting at her closest colleague. Mateo Karras' dazzlingly good looks had stopped stealing her breath years ago, thank goodness, but the academic part of her brain still couldn't help but admire the perfect symmetry of his features every time she saw him—the close-cropped blue-black hair, the aquamarine eyes the exact colour of the Aegean when she'd gone on holiday there a few years ago, the straight nose and square jaw, and of course the lithe and tall powerful figure encased now in battered cords and a creased button-down shirt, his usual work attire.

'Come up?' She wrinkled her nose, noting his rather terse tone, so unlike his usual cheerful briskness as he came into the lab, eager to get started. 'What do you mean?'

'I…' He shook his head, let out a weary breath. 'I'm going to be away for…a while. I'll have to take a leave of absence.'

'A leave of absence?' Rachel stared at him in shock. She and Mateo had been pioneering research on chemical emissions and climate change for the better part of a decade, since they'd both received their PhDs here at Cambridge. They were close, *so* close, to discovering and publishing the crucial evidence that would reduce toxic chemicals' effect on the climate. How could he be walking away from it all? It was too incredible to take in. 'I don't understand.'

'I know. I can't explain it all now. I'm afraid I have a family emergency that has to be dealt with. I… I don't know when I'll be back.'

'But…' Shock was giving way to dismay, and something even deeper that Rachel didn't want to consider too closely. She didn't *feel* anything for Mateo, not like that. It was just that she couldn't imagine working without him. They'd been colleagues and partners in research for so long, they practically knew each other's thoughts without needing to speak. When discussing their research, they'd completed each other's sentences on many occasions, with wry smiles and a rueful laugh.

They had a symmetry, a synchronicity, that had been formed over years of dedicated research, endless hours in the lab, as well as many drinks in pub gardens by the river Cam where they discussed everything from radioactive isotopes to organic compounds, and raced each other as to who could recite the periodic table the fastest. Unfortunately, Mateo always won. He *couldn't* be leaving.

'What's going on, Mateo? What's come up?' After nearly ten years together Rachel thought she surely deserved to know, even as she acknowledged that she and Mateo had shared next to nothing about their personal lives.

She didn't really have one, and Mateo had always been very private about his. She'd seen a few women on his arm over the years, but they hadn't stayed there very long—a date or two, nothing more. He'd never spoken about them, and she'd never dared ask.

She'd also never dared consider herself a candidate for that vaunted position—they were poles apart in terms of their appeal, and she was pragmatic enough to understand that, no matter how well they got along. Mateo would never, ever think of her that way. And, Rachel had reminded herself more than once with only a small pang of loss, it wasn't likely that any man would. She certainly hadn't found one yet, and she'd accepted her single state a long time ago, not that she'd ever admitted as much to Mateo.

Over countless conversations, they'd stuck to chemistry, to research, maybe a bit of university gossip, but nothing more. Nothing personal. Certainly nothing *intimate*. And that had been fine, because their work banter was fun, their research was important, and being with Mateo made her happy.

Yet now Rachel knew she needed to know why he was leaving. Surely he couldn't walk away from it all without giving her a real reason.

'It's difficult to explain,' he said, rubbing a hand wearily over his face. Gone was his easy charm, his wry banter, the glint in his aquamarine eyes that Rachel loved. He looked remote, stony, almost like someone she didn't even know. 'All I can say is, it's a family emergency…'

Rachel realised she didn't know anything about his family. In nearly ten years, he'd never mentioned them once. 'I hope everyone is okay,' she said, feeling as if she were fumbling in the dark. She didn't even know if there was an *everyone*.

'Yes, yes, it will be fine. But…' He paused, and a look of such naked desolation passed over his face that Rachel had the insane urge to go over and give him a hug. Insane, because in nearly ten years she had never touched him, save for a brush of the shoulder as they leaned over a microscope together, or the occasional high five when they had a breakthrough in their research. But they'd never *hugged*. Not even close. It hadn't bothered or even occurred to her, until now.

'Let me know if there's something I can do to help,' she said. 'Anything at all. Are you leaving Cambridge…? Do you need your house looked after?' Although she'd never been to his house, she knew it was a sprawling cottage in the nearby village of Grantchester, a far cry from the terraced garden flat by the railway station that she'd scraped and saved to afford and make a cosy, comfortable home.

'I'm leaving the country.' Mateo spoke flatly. 'And I don't know when I'll be back.'

Rachel gaped at him. 'This sounds really serious, then.'

'It is.'

It also sounded so *final*. 'But you will come back?' Rachel asked. She couldn't imagine him not returning *ever*. 'When it's all sorted?' Whatever it was. 'I can't do this without you, Mateo.' She gestured to the microscope she'd been looking through, encompassing all the research they'd embarked on together, and a look of sadness and regret flashed across Mateo's face like a lightning strike of emotion, before his features ironed out and he offered her a nod.

'I know. I feel the same. I'm sorry.'

'Are you sure there isn't something I can do? Help in some way?' She didn't know what to do, how to help, and she hated that. She wanted to be useful, had spent her entire life trying to be necessary to people, if not actually loved. But Mateo was already shaking his head.

'No, no. You…you've been amazing, Rachel. A great colleague. The best I could ask for.'

She grimaced, struggling to make a joke of it even as horror stole over her at the thought of him leaving in such a final way. 'Don't, you make it sound as if you're dying.'

'It feels a little bit that way.'

'Mateo—'

'No, no, I'm being melodramatic.' He forced a smile to that mobile mouth that had once fascinated Rachel far more than it should have. Thankfully she'd got over that years ago. She'd made herself, because she'd known there was no point. 'Sorry, it's all just been a shock. I'll try to explain when I can. In the meantime…take care of yourself.'

He stepped forward then, and did something Rachel had never, ever expected him to do, although she'd dreamed it more times than she cared to admit. He leant forward and brushed her cheek with his lips. Rachel drew in a shocked breath as the sheer physicality of him assaulted her senses—the clean, citrusy smell of his aftershave, the softness of his lips, the sharp brush of his stubbled cheek against hers. One hand reached out, flailing towards him, looking for purchase, but thankfully her mind hadn't short-circuited quite that much, and she let it fall to her side before she actually touched him.

With a sad, wry smile, Mateo met her gaze and then stepped back. He nodded once more while Rachel stared dumbly, her mind spinning, her cheek buzzing, and then he turned around and left the lab. A second later Rachel heard the door to the block of laboratories close, and she knew he was gone.

CHAPTER TWO

MATEO STARED OUT at the idyllic view of his island home—sparkling sea, pure white beach, and the lovely, landscaped gardens of the royal palace stretching down to the sand, the flowers as bright as jewels amidst all the verdant green. A paradise, which he now knew was rotting at its core.

Everything was worse, far worse, than he'd thought. As soon as he'd arrived in Kallyria, he'd had briefings from all of his cabinet ministers, only to discover that Leo had been running the country—*his* country—into the ground. The economy, the foreign policy, even the domestic affairs that should have ticked over fairly smoothly had suffered under his brother's wildly unstable hand, with decisions being made recklessly, others carelessly reversed, world leaders insulted…the list went on and on, as his brother pursued pleasure and took an interest in affairs only when it suited him.

Mateo didn't know whether to be furious or insulted that no one had informed him what was happening, and had been going on for years. As it was, all he felt was guilt. He should have known. He should have been here.

But then, no one had expected him to be. Certainly no one had ever asked. He turned from the window to glance down at the desk in the palace's study, a room that still reminded him of his father, with its wood-panelled walls and faint, lingering smell of cigar smoke—unless he was imagining that? His father had been gone for six years. Yet the room bore far more of an imprint of him than of Leo, who had, Mateo had discovered, spent more time on his yacht or in Monte Carlo than here, managing the affairs of his country.

Mateo's narrowed gazed scanned the list his mother had written out in her copperplate handwriting—the list of prospective brides. His mouth twisted in distaste at the mercenary nature of the venture; it seemed incredible to him that in this day and age, in a country that professed to be both progressive and enlightened, he was meant to marry a woman he didn't even know.

'Of course, you will get to know her, in time,' Agathe had assured him that morning, a tentative smile curving her mouth, lines of tension bracketing her eyes.

'And then impregnate her as quickly as possible?' Mateo queried sardonically. '*That's* not a recipe for disaster.'

'Arranged marriages can be successful,' his mother stated with quiet dignity. She should know; her own marriage had been arranged, and she'd striven tirelessly to make it work. Mateo knew his father had been a proud and sometimes difficult man; he'd had a great capacity for love and generosity, but also for anger and scorn. Mateo loved his mother; he'd admired his father. But he didn't want to emulate their marriage.

'I know they can, Mitera,' he said with a conciliatory smile, as he raked his hand through his hair. He'd arrived on Kallyria at ten o'clock last night, and only snatched an hour or two of sleep as he'd gone through all the paperwork his brother had left behind, and attended one debriefing meeting after another.

'Is it love you're looking for?' Agathe asked tentatively. 'Because love can grow, Mateo…'

'I don't want *love*.' He spoke the word with a sneer, because he had to. How else was he meant to think of it? 'I've already been in love, and I have no desire to be so again.'

'You mean Cressida.' Mateo didn't bother to reply. Of course he meant Cressida. 'That was a long time ago, Mateo.'

'I know.' He tried not to speak sharply, but he never talked about Cress. Ever. He tried not even to think about her, about the grief and guilt he still felt, like bullets embedded under his skin, a knife sticking out of his back that he couldn't twist around enough to pull out. If he didn't think about it, he didn't feel it, and that was his preferred way of managing the pain.

Agathe was silent for a moment, her hands folded in her lap, her head tilted to one side as she pinned Mateo in place with her perceptive gaze. 'Considering your aversion to that happy state, then, I would think an arranged marriage would suit you.'

Mateo knew she was right, and yet he still resisted the unpalatable notion. 'I want an agreement, not an arrangement,' he said after a moment. 'If I'm going to have my wife rule alongside me, bear and raise my children, be my partner in every way possible... I don't want to trust that role to a stranger who looks good on paper. That seems like the epitome of foolishness.'

'The women on this list have been vetted by several cabinet ministers,' Agathe countered. 'Everything about them is suitable. There is no reason to think they wouldn't be trustworthy, dutiful, admirable in every way.'

'And willing?' Mateo said with a curl of his lip. Agathe shook her head slowly.

'Why is that wrong?'

Mateo didn't answer, because he wasn't sure he could explain it even to himself. All he knew was, after a lifetime of being told he would never be king, he didn't want a woman to marry him only because he finally was. But that felt too complicated and emotional to explain to his mother, and so he straightened his shoulders and reached for the piece of paper with its damned list.

'I'll look it over.'

Several hours later he was no closer to coming to a decision regarding any of the oh-so suitable candidates. He'd searched for information about them online, scanned their social media profiles, and found them all as duly admirable as his mother had insisted. One of his advisors had cautiously told him that initial overtures had been made, and at least four of the women had expressed their interest, despite knowing nothing about him. Having never spoken to him. Knowing only about his wealth and title, his power and prestige. Why did that bother him so much? Why did he *care*?

The whole point was, he didn't want to care. He wouldn't care. Yet he still hated the thought of it all.

His mobile buzzed and Mateo slid it out of his pocket. In the eighteen hours since he'd arrived on Kallyria he hadn't spoken to anyone from his former life, but now he saw with a ripple of undeniable pleasure that the call was from Rachel.

He swiped to take it. 'Yes?'

'Mateo?' She sounded uncertain.

'Yes, it's me.'

'You sounded so different there, for a second,' Rachel told him with an uncertain laugh. 'Like some... I don't know, some really important person.'

Mateo's lips twisted wryly. That was just what he'd become. Of course, he'd been important in his own way before returning to Kallyria; he held a fellow's chair at one of the world's most prestigious universities, and he'd started his own tech company as a side interest, and made millions in the process. Last year he'd been named one of Britain's most eligible bachelors by some ridiculous tabloid. But he hadn't been king.

'How are you?' Rachel asked. 'I've been worried about you.'

'Worried?' Mateo repeated shortly. 'Why?'

'Because you left so suddenly, for a family emergency,' Rachel said, sounding both defensive and a bit exasperated. 'Of course I'd be worried.'

'You needn't be concerned.' Too late Mateo realised how he sounded—brusque to the point of rudeness, and so unlike the usual way he related to his colleague. His *former* colleague. The truth was, he was feeling both raw and uncertain about everything, and he didn't want to admit that to anyone, not even Rachel.

Rachel. She'd been a good friend to him over the years, his closest friend in many ways although she knew little about his life, and he knew less about hers. They'd functioned on an academic plane, both enjoying the thrill of research, of making discoveries, of joking in the lab and discussing theories in the pub. Mateo didn't think he'd ever asked her about her personal life, or she about his. The thought had never occurred to him.

'I'm sorry,' he apologised, for his tone. 'But it's all under control.'

'Is it?' Rachel sounded hopeful. 'So you'll be back in Cambridge soon?'

Realisation thudded through Mateo at the assumption she'd so blithely made. The leave of absence he'd been granted was going to have to become a termination of employment, effective immediately, and yet he resisted the thought. Still, he steeled himself for what he knew had to be both said and done.

'No, I'm afraid I won't. I'm resigning from my position, Rachel.' He heard her soft gasp of surprised distress, and it touched him more than he expected it to. They might have been close colleagues, even friends, but Rachel would be fine without him. She'd find another research partner, maybe even move up in the department. It wasn't as if they'd actually *cared* about each other.

'But why?' she asked softly. 'What's going on, Mateo? Can't you tell me?'

He hesitated, then said, 'I need to take care of the family business. My brother was in charge but he's stepped down rather suddenly.'

'The family business…'

'Yes.' He wasn't ready to tell her the truth, that he was now king of a country. It sounded ridiculous, like something out of some soppy movie, and it made a lie of his life. Besides, she would find out soon enough. It would be in the newspapers, and rumours would ripple through the small, stifling university community. They always did.

'I can't believe it,' Rachel said slowly. 'You're really not coming back at all?'

'No.'

'And there's nothing I can do? No way I can help?'

'No. I'm sorry.' The words sounded so final, and Mateo knew there was no more to say. 'Goodbye, Rachel,' he said, and then he disconnected the call.

Rachel stared at her phone in disbelief. Had Mateo just *hung up* on her? Why was he acting as if he'd *died*?

And yet it felt as if he'd died. In truth, Rachel felt a far greater grief than she'd ever expected to, to have Mateo walk out of her life like that. She knew they hadn't actually been close in the way that most friends were, no matter how much they'd shared together. She suspected they wouldn't keep in touch. Mateo probably wouldn't even think of it. Typical scientist, existing on a mental plane rather than a physical one.

And yet Mateo Karras was a very physical man. Rachel

had noticed it the moment she'd been introduced to him, when they'd both been obtaining their PhDs. Mateo had been in his third year while she'd been in her first, and the rumours had already been swirling around him, with the few female students in the department pretending to swoon whenever his name was mentioned.

Still, Rachel hadn't been prepared for the sheer physical presence of him, the base, animal attraction that had crashed over her, despite the glaring obviousness of their unsuitability. She was plain, nerdy, a little too curvy, with no fashion sense. Mateo might be a brilliant scientist, but he didn't fit the geeky stereotype as so many of his colleagues did.

He was devastatingly attractive, for a start, with close-cropped dark hair and those amazing blue-green eyes, plus a physique that could grace a calendar if he chose. He was also charming and assured, his easy manner and wry jokes disguising the fact that no one actually knew anything about him. Some people wondered at the aloofness under his easy exterior; some had called him a snob. Rachel had felt something else from him. Something like sadness.

In the intervening years, however, she'd disabused herself of that fanciful notion and accepted that Mateo was a man, and a law, unto himself. Charming and urbane, passionate about his work, he didn't need people the way most others did. The way Rachel had, and then learned not to, because it hurt less.

'Rachel? Is that you?' Her mother's wavery voice had Rachel slipping her phone into her pocket and plastering a smile on her face. The last thing she wanted to do was worry her mother about anything, not that she would even be worried. Or notice.

Carol Lewis had been diagnosed with Alzheimer's two years ago, and since then her decline had been dispiritingly steady. She'd moved into the second bedroom of Rachel's flat eighteen months ago. After living on her own since she was eighteen, Rachel had struggled to get used to her mother's company, as well as her many needs…and the fact that her mother had never actually seemed to *like* her very much. Neither of her parents had, and that had been something Rachel had made peace with, or thought she had. Having her mother here tended to be an unwelcome reminder of the lack in their relationship.

'Hey, Mum.' Rachel smiled as her mother shuffled into the room, squinting at her suspiciously.

'Why were you making so much noise?'

She'd been talking quietly, but never mind. 'Sorry, I was on the phone.'

'Was it your father? Is he going to be late again?'

Her father had been dead for eight years. 'No, Mum, it was just a friend.' Although perhaps she couldn't call Mateo that any more. Perhaps she never could have called him that. 'Do you want to watch one of your shows, Mum?' Gently Rachel took her mother's arm and propelled her back to the bedroom, which had been kitted out with an adjustable bed and a large-screen TV. 'I think that bargain-hunter one might be on.' Since being diagnosed, her mother had developed an affinity for trashy TV, something that made Rachel both smile and feel sad. Before the disease, her mother had only watched documentaries, the obscurer and more intellectual the better. Now she gorged herself on talk shows and reality TV.

Carol let herself be settled back into her bed, still seeming grumpy as Rachel folded the blanket over her knees and turned on the TV. 'I could make you a toastie,' she suggested. 'Cheese and Marmite?'

Another aspect of the disease—her mother ate the same thing over and over again, for breakfast, lunch, and dinner. Rachel had gone through more jars of Marmite than she'd ever thought possible, especially considering that she didn't even like the stuff.

'All right,' Carol said, as if she were granting Rachel a favour. 'Fine.'

Alone in the kitchen, Rachel set to buttering bread and slicing cheese, Mateo's strangely brusque call weighing on her heavily. She was going to miss him. Maybe she shouldn't, but she knew she was. She already did.

Looking around the small kitchen—the tinny sound of the TV in the background, the uninspiring view of a tiny courtyard from her window—Rachel was struck with how *little* her life was.

She didn't go out. Her few friends in the department were married with children, existing in a separate, busy universe from her. Occasionally they invited her to what Rachel thought of as pity dinners, where they paraded their children in front of her and asked sympathetically if she wanted to be set up. Rachel could endure one of those about every six months, but she always left them with a huge sigh of relief.

The truth was, she hadn't felt the need or desire to go out, to have a social life, when she'd been working with Mateo for eight hours every day. Their banter, their companionable silence, their occasional debates over drinks... all of it had been enough for her. More than enough, since she'd dealt with the stupid crush she'd had on him ages ago, like lancing a wound. Painful but necessary. Thank goodness she'd made herself get over that, otherwise she'd be in real trouble now.

'Rachel? Is my sandwich ready?'

With a sigh Rachel turned on the grill.

Three days later it was bucketing down rain as Rachel sprinted down the street towards her flat. She was utterly soaked, and even more dispirited by Mateo's disappearance from her life. She'd tried to be cheerful about gaining a new research partner, but the person put forward by the new chair was a smarmy colleague who liked to make disparaging comments about women and then hold his hands up, eyebrows raised, as he told her not to be so sensitive. Work had gone from being a joy to a disaster, and, considering the state of the rest of her life, that was a blow indeed.

She fumbled with the key to her flat, grateful that she'd have half an hour or so of peace and quiet before her mother came home. Carol spent her weekdays at a centre for the memory impaired, and was brought home by a kindly bus service run by the centre, which made Rachel's life a lot easier.

She was just pushing the door open when someone stepped out of the alleyway that led around to the back courtyard and the bins. Rachel let out a little scream at the sight of the figure looming out of the gloom and rain, yanking her key out of the door, ready to use it as an admittedly feeble weapon.

'Rachel, it's me.' The low thrum of his voice, with the faintest hint of an accent, had Rachel dropping her keys onto the concrete with a clatter.

'Mateo...?'

'Yes.' He took another step towards her and smiled. Rachel stared at him in wonder and disbelief.

'What are you doing here?'

'I wanted to see you.'

Rachel shook her head, sending raindrops splattering, too shocked even to think something coherent, much less say it. She realised just how glad she was to see him.

'May I come in? We're both getting soaked.'

'Yes, of course.' She scooped her keys up from the floor and pushed open the door. Mateo followed her into the flat, and as Rachel switched on the light she realised how small her flat probably seemed to him, and also that she

had three ratty-looking bras drying over the radiator, and
the remains of her jam-smeared toast on the coffee table,
next to a romance novel with a cringingly lurid cover. Welcome to her life.

She turned to face Mateo, her eyes widening at the sight
of him. He looked completely different, dressed in an ex-
pertly cut three-piece suit of dark grey, his jaw closely
shaven, everything about him sleek and sophisticated and
rich. He'd always emanated a certain assured confidence,
but he was on another level entirely now. The disparity of
their appearances—her hair was in rat's tails and she was
wearing a baggy trouser suit with a mayonnaise stain on
the lapel—made her cringe.

She shook her head slowly, still amazed he was in her
flat. *Why?*

'Mateo,' she said questioningly, as if he might suddenly
admit it wasn't really him. 'What are you doing here?'

CHAPTER THREE

THAT, MATEO REFLECTED, was a very good question. When the idea had come to him twenty-four hours ago, after his initial disastrous meeting with Vanessa de Cruz, it had seemed wonderfully obvious. Blindingly simple. Now he wasn't so sure.

'I wanted to see you,' he said, because that much was true.

'You did?' Rachel pushed her wet hair out of her eyes and gave him an incredulous look. 'Why?'

Another good question. In his mind's eye Mateo pictured Vanessa's narrowed gaze of avaricious speculation, the pouty pursing of her lips that he'd instinctively disliked. She'd been sleek and beautiful and so very cold.

'Of course we'll have a prenup,' she'd said.

He'd stiffened at that, even though he'd supposed it made sense.

'I believe marriage is for life.'

'Oh, no—you're not old-fashioned, are you?'

Mateo had never considered himself so before. In fact, he had always thought of himself as progressive, enlightened, at least by most standards. But when it came to marriage? To vows made between a man and a woman? Then, yes, apparently he was old-fashioned.

'Hold on,' Rachel said. 'I'm soaking wet and I think we could both use a cup of tea.' She shrugged off her sopping jacket, revealing a crumpled white blouse underneath that was becoming see-through from the damp, making Mateo uncomfortably aware of how generously endowed his former colleague was. He looked away, only to have his gaze fasten on some rather greying bras draped over the radiator.

Rachel tracked his gaze and then quickly swept them from the radiator, bundling them into a ball as she hurried into the kitchen. A few seconds later Mateo heard the distinctive clink of the kettle being filled and then switched on.

He shrugged off his cashmere overcoat and draped it over a chair at the small table taking up half of the cosy sitting room. The other half was taken up with a sofa covered in a colourful throw. He glanced around the flat, noting that, despite its smallness, it was a warm and welcoming place, with botanical prints on the walls and a tangle of house plants on the wide windowsill.

He scanned the titles in the bookcase, and then the pile of post on a marble-topped table by the front door. These little hints into Rachel's life, a life lived away from the chemistry lab, made him realise afresh that he didn't know anything about his former research partner.

Yes, you do. She worked hard and well for ten years. She can take a joke, but she knows what to take seriously. You've had fun with her, and, more importantly, you trust her.

Yes, he decided as he lowered himself onto the sofa, he knew enough.

The kettle switched off and a few minutes later Rachel came back into the sitting room with two cups of tea. She'd taken the opportunity to tidy herself up, putting her damp hair back in a ponytail, although curly tendrils had escaped to frame her face. She'd also changed her wet trouser suit for a heather-grey jumper that clung to her generous curves, and a pair of skinny jeans that showcased her just as curvy legs.

Mateo had never once looked at Rachel Lewis with anything remotely resembling sexual interest, yet now he supposed he ought to. At least, he ought to decide if he could.

'Here you are.' She handed him a cup of tea, black as he preferred, and then took her own, milky and sweet, and went to perch on the edge of an armchair that had a tottering pile of folded washing on it. 'Sorry for the mess,' she said with a wry grimace. 'If I'd known you were coming, I certainly wouldn't have left my bras out.'

'Or this?' He picked up the romance novel splayed out on the table, his lips quirking at the sight of the heaving bosom on the cover. '"Lady Arabella Fordham-Smythe is fascinated by the dark stranger who comes to her father's castle late one night…"'

'A girl's got to dream.' Humour glinted in her eyes again, reminding Mateo of how much fun she could be, although her cheeks had reddened a little in embarrassment. 'So why are you here, Mateo? Not that I'm not delighted to see you, of course.' Another rueful grimace, the glint in her eyes turning into a positive sparkle. 'Despite the lack of warning.'

'And the underwear.' *Why* were they talking about her underwear? Why was he imagining, not the worn-out bras she'd bundled away, but a slip in taupe silk, edged with ivory lace, one strap sliding from her shoulder…

The image jolted Mateo to the core, forcing him to straighten where he sat, and meet Rachel's laughing gaze once more.

Her eyes were quite lovely, he acknowledged. A deep, soft chocolate brown, with thick lashes fringing them, making her look like a gentle doe. A doe with a good sense of humour and a terrific work ethic.

'Have you heard who has taken over as chair?' she asked, her grimace without any humour this time, and Mateo frowned.

'No. Who?'

'Supercilious Simon.' She made a face. 'I know I shouldn't call him that, but he is *so* irritating.'

Mateo's lip curled. 'That was the best they could do?' He was insulted that Simon Thayer, a mediocre researcher at best and a pompous ass to boot, had been selected to take his place.

'I know, I know.' Rachel shook her head as she blew on her tea. 'But he's always played the game. Cosied up to anyone important.' The sparkle in her eye had dimmed, and Mateo didn't like it. 'Working with him is going to be hell, frankly. I've even thought about going somewhere else, not that I could.' For a second she looked so desolate Mateo had a bizarre and discomfiting urge to comfort her. *How?* 'Anyway, never mind about that.' She shook her head, cheer resolutely restored. 'How are you? How is the family emergency?'

'Still in a state of emergency, but a bit better, I suppose.'

'Really?' Her eyes softened, if that were possible. Could eyes soften? Mateo felt uncomfortable just thinking about it. It was not the way he normally thought about eyes, or anyone. 'So why are you here, Mateo? Because you haven't actually said yet.'

'I know.' He took a sip of tea, mainly to stall for time, something he wasn't used to doing. When it came to chemistry, he was decisive. He knew what to do, no matter what the scientific conundrum. He saw a problem and he broke down the solution into steps, taking them one at a time, each one making sense.

So that was what he would have to do here. Take her through his reasoning, step by careful, analytical step. Rachel raised her eyebrows, a little smile playing about her generous mouth. Her lips, Mateo noticed irrelevantly, were rosy and lush.

And instead of starting at the beginning, and explaining it

all coherently, he found himself doing the exact opposite—blurting out the end point, with no lead-up or context.

'I want you to marry me,' he said.

Rachel was sure she'd misheard. It had almost sounded as if Mateo had just asked her to marry him. In fact, that was *exactly* what it had sounded like, which couldn't be right. Obviously.

Unless he'd been joking…?

She gave him a quizzical little smile, as if she was unfazed, perhaps a bit nonplussed, rather than completely spinning inside and, worse, suddenly deathly afraid that he *was* joking. That it was so obviously a joke…as it had been once before. She'd been able to take it from Josh all those years ago, but she didn't think she could take it from Mateo, someone she both liked and trusted. *Please, please don't make me the butt of your joke.* 'Sorry,' she said lightly. 'Come again?'

'I didn't phrase that properly.'

Was there another way to phrase it? Rachel took a sip of her tea, mostly to hide her expression, which she feared was looking horribly hopeful. This was starting to feel like something out of the novel on the coffee table, and she knew, she *knew* real life wasn't like that. Mateo Karras did not want to marry her. No way. No how. It was impossible. Obviously.

'I want you to marry me,' he said again. 'But let me explain.'

'O…kay.'

'I'm not who you think I am.'

Now this was really beginning to seem melodramatic. Rachel had a sudden urge to laugh. 'Okay,' she said. 'Who are you?'

Mateo grimaced and put down his cup of tea. 'My full

name and title? Prince Mateo Aegeus Karavitis, heir to the
throne of the island kingdom of Kallyria.'

Rachel stared at him dumbly. He *had* to be joking. Mateo
had liked to play a practical joke or two, back in the lab.
Nothing serious or dangerous, but sometimes he'd rela-
bel a test tube with some funny little slogan, and they had
an ongoing contest of who could come up with the worst
chemistry joke.

*If H2O is the formula for water, what is the formula for
ice? H2O cubed.*

Was that what he was doing here? Was he making fun of
her? Her cheeks stung with mortification at the thought, and
her heart felt as if it were shrivelling inside her. Please, no…

'I'm sorry,' she said stiffly. 'I don't get it.'

Mateo frowned, the dark slashes of his brows drawing together. Why did he have to be so handsome? Rachel
wondered irritably. It didn't make this any easier, or less
painful. 'Get it?'

'The punchline,' she said flatly.

'There's no punchline, Rachel. I mean it. I accept this
comes as a surprise, and it's not the most romantic proposal
of marriage, but please let me explain.'

'Fine.' She put down her tea and folded her arms, feeling angry all of a sudden. If this was some long, drawn-
out practical joke, it was in decided poor taste. 'Explain.'

Mateo looked a little startled by her hard tone, but he
continued, 'Five days ago my brother Leo abdicated his
throne.'

'Abdicated? He was King of this Kall—?'

'Kallyria, yes. He's been king for six years, since my
father died.'

He spoke matter-of-factly and Rachel goggled at him.
Was he actually serious? 'Mateo, why did you never say
anything about this before? You're a *prince*—'

'I didn't say anything because I didn't want anyone to

know. I wanted to succeed on my terms, as my own man. And that's exactly what I did. I used a different name, forewent any security protocols, and established myself on my own credentials.' His voice blazed with passion and purpose. 'No one at Cambridge knows who I truly am.'

'No one?'

'No one.'

For a terrible second Rachel wondered if Mateo was deluded somehow. It had happened before to scientists who spent too much time in the lab. They cracked. And the way he'd left so suddenly, this family emergency…what if it was all some weird delusion?

Her face crumpled in compassionate horror at the thought, and Mateo let out an exasperated breath. 'You don't believe me, do you?'

'It's not that…'

Mateo said something in Greek, most likely a swear word. 'You think I'm actually making it up!'

'Not making it up,' Rachel soothed. 'I think you *believe* you're a prince…'

Mateo swore again, this time in English. He rose from her battered sofa in one fluid movement of lethal grace. 'Do I look or act like someone who is insane?' he demanded, and Rachel cringed a little.

No, he most definitely did not. In fact, with his eyes blazing blue-green fire, in a suit that looked as if it cost more than she made in a month, he *did* look like a prince. She sagged against the back of her chair, causing the pile of laundry to fall in a heap to the floor, as the realisation thudded through her.

'You really are a prince.'

'Of course I am. And in a week's time I am to be crowned king.'

He sounded so assured, so arrogant, that Rachel wondered how she could have doubted him for a minute. A second. And as for being deluded…of course he wasn't. She'd never seen a more sane, focused, determined individual in her life.

'But what does this have to do with me?' she asked shakily, as she remembered what he'd said. He wanted to *marry* her…

Surely not. *Surely not.*

'As King of Kallyria, I'll need a bride,' Mateo resumed his explanation as he paced the small confines of her sitting room. 'A queen by my side.'

Rachel shook her head slowly. She could not reconcile that statement with him wanting to marry her. Not in any way or form. 'Maybe I'm thick, Mateo, but I still don't understand.'

'You are not thick, Rachel.' He turned to face her. 'You are the smartest woman I know. A brilliant scientist, an incredibly hard worker, and a good friend.'

Her cheeks warmed and her eyes stung. He was speaking in a flat, matter-of-fact tone, but his words warmed her heart and touched her soul. She couldn't remember the last time she'd been given so much sincere praise.

'Thank you,' she whispered.

'I must marry immediately, to help stabilise my country. And produce an heir.'

Wait, what? Rachel stared at him blankly, still unable to take it in. She must be thick, no matter what Mateo had just said. 'And…and you want to marry *me*?' she asked in a disbelieving whisper. Even now she expected him to suddenly smile, laugh, and say of *course* it was a joke, and could she help him him to think of anyone suitable?

Yet she knew, just looking at him, that it wasn't. He'd come back to Cambridge; he'd come to her flat to find her. He looked deadly serious, incredibly intent.

Mateo Karras—no, Karavitis—Prince—no, *King* of a country—wanted to marry her. *Her.* When no man had ever truly wanted her before. Still, she felt uncertain. Doubtful. Josh's words, spoken over a decade before, still seared her brain and, worse, her heart.

How could any man want you?

'Why?' Rachel whispered. Mateo didn't pretend to misunderstand.

'Because I know you. I trust you. I *like* you. And we work well together.'

'In a chemistry lab—'

'Why not in a kingdom?' He shrugged. 'Why should it be any different?'

'But…' Rachel shook her head slowly '…you're not offering me the vice-presidency, Mateo. You're asking me to be your *wife*. There's a huge difference.'

'Not that much.' Mateo spread his hands. 'We'd be a partnership, a team. I'd need you by my side, supporting me, supporting my country. We'd be working together.'

'We'd be *married*.' An image slammed through her head, one she had no business thinking of. A wedding night, candles all around, the slide of burnished skin on skin…

Like something out of the book on the table. *No.* That wasn't real. That wasn't her. And Mateo certainly didn't mean that kind of marriage.

Except he'd mentioned needing an heir. As soon as possible.

'Yes,' Mateo agreed evenly. 'We'd be married.'

Rachel stared at him helplessly. 'Mateo, this is crazy.'

'I know it's unexpected—'

'I have a *job*,' she emphasised, belatedly remembering the life she'd built for herself, just as Mateo had, on her own terms. She'd won her place first at Oxford and then Cambridge, and finally her research fellowship, all on her own merit, not as the daughter of esteemed physicist, William Lewis, with his society wife Carol. She'd made no mention of her parents in any of her applications, had made sure nobody knew. She'd wanted to prove herself, and she *had*.

And Mateo was now thinking she might leave it all behind, everything she'd worked so hard for, simply to be his trophy wife, a mannequin on his arm? She started to shake her head, but Mateo forestalled her, his voice calm and incisive.

'I realise I am asking you to sacrifice much. But you would have limitless opportunity as Queen of Kallyria—to promote girls' involvement in STEM subjects; to fund research and support charities and causes that align with your interests; to travel the world in the name of science.'

'Science? Or politics?' she asked, her voice shaking with the enormity of it all. She couldn't grasp what he was asking her on so many incredible levels.

'Both,' Mateo replied, unfazed. 'Naturally. As king, one of my priorities will be scientific research. Kallyria has a university in its capital city of Constanza. Admittedly, it is not on the same level as Cambridge or Oxford, but it is esteemed among Mediterranean countries.'

'I don't even know where Kallyria is,' Rachel admitted. 'I'm not sure I've ever heard of it before.'

'It is a small island country in the eastern Mediterranean Sea. It was settled by Greek and Turkish traders, over two thousand years ago. It has never been conquered.'

And he was asking her to be its *Queen*. Rachel felt as if her head were going to explode.

'I don't…' she began, not even sure what she was going to say. And then the front doorknob rattled, and her mother shuffled into the house, looking between her and Mateo with hostile suspicion.

'Rachel,' she demanded, her voice rising querulously. 'Who is this?'

CHAPTER FOUR

MATEO STARED DISPASSIONATELY at the old woman who was glaring back at him.

'Mum,' Rachel said faintly. 'This is…' She glanced uncertainly at Mateo, clearly not sure how to introduce him.

'My name is Mateo Karavitis,' Mateo intercepted smoothly as he stepped forward and offered his hand. 'A former colleague of your daughter's.'

Rachel's mother looked him up and down, seeming unimpressed. 'Why are you visiting here?' She turned back to Rachel. 'I'm hungry.'

'I'll make you a toastie,' Rachel said soothingly.

She threw Mateo a look that was half apology, half exasperation. He gave her an assured, blandly unfazed smile in return.

So Rachel had a mother who was clearly dependent on her care. It was a surprise, but it did not deter him. If anything, it offered her an added incentive to agree to his proposal, since he would be able to offer her mother top-of-the-line care, either here in England or back in Kallyria.

Not, Mateo reflected as Rachel hurried to the kitchen and her mother harrumphed her way to her bedroom, that she needed much incentive. Judging from everything he'd seen so far of her life outside work, there was nothing much compelling her to stay.

He fully anticipated, after Rachel had got over the sheer

shock of it, that she'd agree to his proposal. How could she not?

He came over to stand in the doorway of the kitchen. Rachel was looking harassed, slicing cheese as fast as she could.

'How long has your mother been living with you?' he asked.

'About eighteen months.' She reached for a jar of Marmite and Mateo stepped forward.

'May I help?'

'What?' Rachel looked both frazzled and bewildered, her hair falling into her eyes. 'No—'

Deftly he unscrewed the jar of Marmite she seemed to have forgotten she was holding. Plucking the knife from her other hand, he began to spread the Marmite across the bread. 'Cheese and Marmite toastie, yes?'

'What?' She stared at him blankly, then down to the bread he was preparing. 'Oh. Er… Yes.'

Mateo finished making the sandwich and placed it on the hot grill. 'Shouldn't be a moment.'

'I don't understand,' Rachel said helplessly. Mateo arched an eyebrow.

'How to make a toastie? You did seem to be having trouble mastering the basics, but I was happy to step in.'

A smile twitched her lips, and Mateo realised how much he'd missed their banter. 'Thank goodness for capable males,' she quipped. 'What on earth would I have done if you hadn't been here?'

His lips quirked back a response. 'Heaven only knows.'

'I shudder to think. Careful it doesn't burn.' She nodded to the grill. 'I'll make my mother a cup of tea—do you want another one?'

'Not unless it has a generous splash of whisky in it.'

'Sorry, I'm afraid that's not possible. Not unless you want to nip out to the off-licence on the corner.'

He stepped closer to her. 'What I really want is to take you to dinner to discuss my proposal properly.'

A look of fear flashed across Rachel's face, surprising him. He didn't think he'd ever seen her actually look afraid before. 'Mateo, I don't think there's any point—'

'I think there is, and, considering how long we have known each other, I also think it's fair to ask for an evening of your time. Assuming your mother can be left for a few hours?'

'As long as she's eaten and the TV's on,' Rachel answered with clear reluctance. 'I suppose.'

'Good. Then I will make arrangements.' He slid his phone out of his pocket and quickly thumbed a text to the security guard he had waiting outside in a hired sedan.

Smoke began to pour out of the oven. 'I think you've burned my mother's toastie,' Rachel said tartly, and with a wry grimace Mateo hurried to rescue the sandwich from the grill.

Half an hour later, Carol Lewis was settled in front of a lurid-looking programme, a toastie and cup of tea on her lap tray.

'I'll be back in about an hour, Mum,' Rachel said, sounding anxious. 'If you need anything, you can always knock on Jim's door.'

'Jim?' Carol demanded. 'Who's Jim?'

'Mr Fairley,' Rachel reminded her patiently. 'He lives in the flat upstairs, number two?' Her mother harrumphed and Rachel gave Mateo an apologetic look as she closed her bedroom door. 'Do I need to change?'

Mateo swept his glance over her figure, noting the way the soft grey cashmere clung to her breasts. 'You look fine.'

Her lips twisted at that, although Mateo wasn't sure why, and she nodded. 'Fine. Let's get this over with.'

Not a promising start, but Mateo was more than hopeful. The more he saw of Rachel's life, the more he was sure she would agree...eventually.

Outside the drenching downpour had tapered off to a misty drizzle, and an autumnal breeze chilled the air. Rachel had shrugged on a navy duffel coat and a rainbow-colored scarf, and Mateo took her elbow as he led her to the waiting car.

'We're not walking?'

'I made a reservation at Cotto.'

'That posh place in the Gonville Hotel?' She pulled her arm away from him, appalled. 'It's so expensive. And I'm not dressed appropriately—'

'You'll be fine. And we're in a private room, anyway.'

She shook her head slowly, not looking impressed so much as uncertain. 'Who *are* you?'

'You know who I am.'

'You never did this before. Private rooms, hired cars—'

'I need to take necessary precautions for my privacy and security, as well as yours. Once it becomes known that I am the King of Kallyria—'

'I can't help but think you're deluded when you say that,' Rachel murmured.

Mateo allowed himself a small smile. 'I assure you, I am not.'

'I know, I really do believe you. I just...don't believe this situation.'

The driver hopped out to open the passenger door of the luxury sedan. Mateo gestured for Rachel to get in first, and she slid inside, running one hand over the sumptuous leather seats.

'Wow,' she murmured, and then turned to face the window.

Mateo slid in beside her, his thigh brushing hers. She moved away. He thought about pressing closer, just to see, but decided now was not the time. The physical side of their potential arrangement was something that would have to be negotiated carefully, and there were certainly other considerations to deal with first.

They didn't speak as the driver navigated Cambridge's traffic through the dark and rain, and finally pulled up in front of the elegant Georgian façade of the Gonville Hotel. A single snap of his fingers at the concierge had the man running towards him, and practically tripping over himself to accommodate such an illustrious personage as the Crown Prince, soon to be King.

Rachel stayed silent as they were ushered into a sumptuous private room, with wood-panelled walls and a mahogany table laid for two with the finest porcelain and silver.

'I've never seen you like this before,' she said once the concierge had closed the door behind them, after Mateo had dismissed him, not wanting to endure his fawning attentions any longer. She shrugged off her coat and slowly unwound her scarf.

'Seen me like what?' Mateo pulled out her chair and she sat down with murmured thanks.

'Acting like…like a king, I suppose. Like you own the place. I mean, you were always a little *arrogant*,' she conceded as she rested her chin in her hand, 'but I thought it was just about your brain.'

Mateo huffed a laugh. 'I'm wondering if I should be offended by that.'

'No, you shouldn't be. I'm basically telling you you're smart.'

'Well, then.'

'Except,' Rachel continued, 'I don't think you're making a very smart decision here.'

Mateo's gaze narrowed as he flicked an uninterested glance at the menu. 'Oh?'

'No, I don't. Really, Mateo, I'd make a terrible queen.'

* * *

Rachel eyed him mischievously, her chin still in her hand. It was actually a bit amusing, to see this self-assured man, who was kind of scaring her in his fancy suit, look so discomfited. It helped her take her mind off the fact that he'd asked her to marry him, and she still had absolutely no idea how to feel about that. Flattered? Furious? Afraid? Appalled? All four, and more.

'I disagree with that assessment,' Mateo said calmly.

'I can't imagine why.'

He frowned, and even when he was looking so ferocious, Rachel couldn't help but acknowledge how devastatingly handsome he was. The crisp white shirt and cobalt-blue tie were the perfect foil for his olive skin and bright blue-green eyes. He'd looked amazing in rumpled shirts and old cords; he looked unbelievably, mouth-dryingly gorgeous now. And it was yet another reminder that they couldn't possibly marry each other.

'I don't understand why you are putting yourself down,' he said, and Rachel squirmed a bit at that. It made her feel pathetic, and she wasn't. A long time ago she'd accepted who she was…and who she wasn't. And she'd been okay with that. She'd made herself be okay, despite the hurt, the lack of self-confidence, the deliberate decision to take potential romance out of the equation of her life.

On the plus side, she had a good brain, a job she loved— or at least she'd *had*—and she had a few good friends, who admittedly had moved on in life in a way she hadn't, but *still*. She'd taken stock of herself and her life and had decided it was all good.

'I'm not putting myself down. I'm just being realistic.'

'Realistic?' Mateo's dark eyebrows rose, his eyes narrowed in aquamarine assessment. 'About not being a good queen? How would you even know?'

'I'm terrible at public speaking.' It was the first thing

she could think of, even though it had so little to do with her argument it was laughable.

Mateo's eyebrows rose further. 'You are not. I have heard you deliver research papers to a full auditorium on many occasions.'

'Yes, but that was research. Chemistry.'

'So?'

She sighed, wondering why she was continuing this ridiculous line of discussion, even as she recognised it was safer than many others. 'I can talk about chemistry. But other things...'

'Because you are passionate about it,' Mateo agreed with a swift nod. Rachel felt her face go pink at the word passionate, which was embarrassing. He wasn't talking about passion in *that* way, and in any case she couldn't think about that aspect of a marriage between them without feeling as if she might scream—or self-combust. 'So you will have to find other things you are passionate about,' he continued calmly. 'I am sure there are many.'

Now her face was fiery, which was ridiculous. Rachel snatched up her menu. 'Why don't we order?'

'I have already ordered. The menu is simply so you can see their offerings.'

'You ordered for me?' Her feminist principles prickled instinctively.

Mateo gave a small smile. 'Only to save on time, since I know you are concerned about your mother, and also because I know what you like.'

'I've never even been to the restaurant.' Now she was a bit insulted, which was easier than feeling all the other emotions jostling for space in her head and heart.

'All right.' Mateo leaned back in his chair, his arms folded, a cat-like smile curling his mobile mouth. A mouth she seemed to have trouble looking away from. 'Look at the menu and tell me what you would order.'

'Why? It's too late—'

'Humour me. And be honest, because if you order the black truffle and parmesan soufflé, I'll know you're lying. You hate truffles.'

How did he know that?

One of their seemingly innocuous conversations in the lab or the pub, Rachel supposed. They might not have shared the intimate details of their personal lives, but food likes and dislikes had always been a safe subject for discussion.

She glanced down at the menu, feeling self-conscious and weirdly exposed, even though they were just talking about choices at a restaurant. Across the table Mateo lounged back in his chair, that small smile playing about his lips, looking supremely confident. He was so sure he knew what she was going to order.

Rachel continued to peruse the offerings, tempted to pick something unlikely, yet knowing Mateo would see through such a silly ploy.

'Fine.' She put the menu down and gave him a knowing look. 'The beetroot and goat cheese salad to start, and the asparagus risotto for my main.'

His smile widened slightly as his gaze fastened on hers, making little lightning bolts run up and down her arms. Now, *that* was alarming. She'd inoculated herself against Mateo's obvious attraction years ago. She'd had to.

You couldn't work with someone day in and day out, heads bent close together, and feel sparkly inside while the person next to you so obviously felt nothing. It was positively soul-deadening, not to mention ego-destroying, and Rachel had had enough of both of those. And so she'd made herself not respond to him, not even *think* about responding to him.

Yet now she was.

'So is that what you ordered for me?' she asked, a little bolshily, to hide her discomfort and awareness.

'Let's find out, shall we?' As if on cue, a waiter came quietly into the private room, two silver-domed dishes in his hands. He set them at their places, and then lifted the lids with a flourish. Rachel stared down at her beetroot and goat cheese salad and felt ridiculously annoyed.

'You just like winning,' she told him as she took her fork. The salad did look delicious. 'I mean, how many hours did you practise reciting the periodic table just to beat me?'

'Practise,' Mateo scoffed. 'As if.'

She shook her head slowly as she toyed with a curly piece of radicchio. 'You might know what I like to eat, but that's all.'

'All?'

'That is not a challenge. I just mean…we don't actually know each other, Mateo.' She swallowed, uncomfortably aware of the throb of feeling in her voice. 'I know we've worked together for ten years, and we could call each other friends, but… I didn't even know you were a prince.'

'No one knew I was a prince.'

'And you don't know anything about me. We've never really talked about our personal lives.'

She felt a ripple of frustration from Mateo, like a wavelength in the air. He shrugged as he stabbed a delicate slice of carpaccio on his plate. 'So talk. Tell me whatever it is you wish me to know.'

'What an inviting prospect. Why don't I just give you my CV?'

'I've seen your CV, but do feel free.'

Rachel shook her head. 'It's not just a matter of processing some information, Mateo. It's *why* we don't know anything about each other. Ten years working together, and you don't even know…' she cast about for a salient fact '…my middle name.'

'Anne,' Mateo answered immediately. And at her blank look, 'It's on your CV.'

Rachel rolled her eyes. 'Fine, something else, then. Something that's not on my CV.'

Mateo cocked his head, his gaze sweeping slowly over her, warming everywhere it touched, as if she were bathed in sunlight. 'I'm not going to know something you haven't told me,' he said after a moment. 'So it's pointless to play a guessing game. But I know more about you than perhaps you realise.'

Which was a very uncomfortable thought. Rachel squirmed in her seat at the thought of how much Mateo could divine from having worked so closely with her for ten years. All her quirks, idiosyncrasies, annoyances… She really did not want to have the excoriating experience of having him list everything he'd noticed over the past decade.

He was a scientist, trained in matters of observation. He would have noticed *a lot*, and she should have noticed the same amount about him, but the trouble was she'd been exerting so much energy trying *not* to notice him that she wasn't sure she had.

Which put him at a distinct and disturbing advantage.

'Look, that isn't really the point,' she said quickly. 'This is not even about you knowing or not knowing me.'

'Is it not? Then what is it about?'

Rachel stared at him helplessly. She wasn't going to say it. She wasn't going to humiliate herself by pointing out the glaringly obvious discrepancies in their stations in life, in their *looks*. She didn't want to enumerate in how many ways she was not his equal, how absurd the idea of a marriage between them would seem, because she'd been in this position before and it had been the worst experience of her life.

'It's about the fact that I don't want to marry you,' she said in as flat and final a tone as she could. 'And I certainly don't want to be queen of a country.'

Something flickered across Mateo's beautiful face and then was gone. His gaze remained steady on hers as he answered. 'While I will naturally accept your decision if that is truly how you feel, I do not believe you have given it proper consideration.'

'That's because it is so outrageous—'

He leaned forward, eyes glinting, mouth curved, everything in him alert and aware and somehow predatory. Rachel tried not to shrink back in her seat. She'd never seen Mateo look so intent.

'I think,' he said, 'it is my turn to give my arguments.'

CHAPTER FIVE

RACHEL'S EYES WIDENED at his pronouncement, lush lashes framing their dark softness in a way that made Mateo want to reach across the table and touch her. Cup her cheek and see if her skin was as soft as it looked. He realised he hadn't actually *touched* his former colleague very much over the last ten years. Brushed shoulders, perhaps, but not much more. But that was something to explore later.

Right now she needed convincing, and he was more than ready to begin. He'd patiently listened to her paltry arguments, sensing that she wasn't saying what she really felt. What she really feared. And he'd get to that in time, but now it was his turn to explain why this was such a very good idea.

Because, after an evening in her presence, Mateo was more convinced than ever that it was. Rachel was smart and focused and, more importantly, he *liked* her. And best of all, he *only* liked her. While he sensed a spark of attraction for her that could surely be fanned into an acceptable flame, he knew he didn't feel anything more than that.

No overwhelming emotion, no flood of longing, desire, or something deeper. And if he didn't feel that after ten years basically by her side, he would never feel it.

Which was a very good thing.

'All right,' Rachel said, her voice wavering slightly although her gaze was sharp and focused, her arms folded. 'I'm waiting for these brilliant arguments.'

'I didn't say they were brilliant,' Mateo replied with a small smile. 'But of course they are.'

Rachel rolled her eyes. 'Of course.'

Mateo paused, enjoying their back and forth as he considered how best to approach the subject. 'The real question, I suppose,' he said slowly, 'is why *wouldn't* we get married?' He let that notion hover in the air between them, before it landed with a thud.

'Why wouldn't we?' Rachel repeated disbelievingly. 'Please, Mateo. You're a *scientist*. Don't give me an argument from fallacy. Neither of us is married. Therefore we should marry. That is *not* how it works.'

'That is not how science works,' Mateo agreed, hiding his smile at her response. She was so fiery. He'd never enjoyed it quite so much before. 'But this isn't science.'

'Isn't it?' she challenged, a gleam in her eye that looked a little too much like vulnerability. 'Because I'm not sure what else it could be.'

She had him on the back foot, and he didn't enjoy the sensation. Mateo took a sip of the wine the waiter had brought—a Rioja because he knew Rachel liked fruity reds—to stall for time. 'Elucidate, please.'

'Fine, I'll *elucidate*.' She lifted her chin slightly, her eyes still gleaming, making Mateo feel even more uncomfortable. Something more was going on here than what was apparent, and it made him a little nervous. 'You came back to Cambridge to convince me to marry you. Considering we've never dated or even thought about dating for an entire decade, it's hardly love or physical attraction that brought you to my doorstep.' She spoke matter-of-factly, which was a relief. He must have been imagining that unnerving note of vulnerability in her voice, of something close to hurt. Yes, he had to have been.

'True,' Mateo was willing to concede with a brief nod.

'So the reasons for wanting me to marry you are scientific, or at least expedient, ones. Let me guess.' She paused, and Mateo almost interrupted her. He wasn't sure he wanted his arguments framed in her perspective.

'All right,' he said after a moment, leaning back in his chair to make it seem as if he were more relaxed than he was. 'Guess.'

Rachel pursed her lips, her gaze becoming distant as she considered. Mateo waited, feeling tense, expectant, almost eager now to hear what she thought.

'We get along,' she said at last. 'We have a fairly good rapport, which I imagine would be important if we were working together to rule a country.' She shook her head, smiling ruefully. 'I can't believe I'm even *saying* that.'

'I take exception to *fairly*,' Mateo interjected with a small smile, willing her to smile back. She did, tightly.

'Fine. We get along well. Very well, even.'

He inclined his head. 'Thank you.'

Rachel let out a breath. 'And we know each other, on a basic level.'

'More than a basic—'

'You said you trust me,' she cut across him.

'I do.' His heartfelt words seemed to reverberate between them, and Mateo watched with interest as her cheeks went pink.

'Still,' Rachel pressed. 'None of that is reason to get married.'

Mateo arched an eyebrow. 'Is it not?'

'If it was, you should have asked Leonore Worth to marry you,' she flung at him a bit tartly.

'Leonore?' She was a lecturer in biology at the university, a pointy woman with a nasal laugh whom he'd escorted to a department function once. He hadn't made that mistake again. But why was Rachel mentioning *her*? 'Why would I do that?' he asked.

'Because she's...' Rachel paused, drawing a hitched breath. Her cheeks were turning red. 'More suited to the role than I am,' she finished.

Mateo stared at her, mystified. 'I am wondering, from a purely scientific view, of course, how you arrived at that conclusion.'

She shook her head, looking tired, even angry. 'Come on, Mateo,' she said in a low voice. 'Stop it.'

'Stop what?'

'Pretending you don't know what I'm talking about.'

'I don't.' Of that he was sure. They were skirting around something big and dark but damned if he knew what it was.

Rachel flung her arms out, nearly knocking her plate of almost untouched salad to the floor. 'I am not queen material.'

'Define your terms, please,' Mateo said. Perhaps it would be easier if they did make this as scientific as possible: What is queen material?

'Oh, this is pointless,' she cried. 'I'm not going to marry you. I'm not going to leave my job—'

'Toadying up to smarmy Simon?' he interjected. 'You've already said you're considering looking elsewhere.'

'I didn't really mean that.'

'Your job has changed, Rachel, and not for the better. I'm offering you a greater opportunity.'

'To hang on your arm?' Her sneer was insulting.

'Of course not. If I wanted a mere trophy wife, I would have picked one of the eminently suitable candidates on the list my mother drew up.'

Rachel nearly choked at that, her soft brown eyes going shocked and wide. 'There's a list?'

'Yes, more's the pity. I don't want a trophy wife, one who ticks all the boxes. I want someone I can trust. Someone who makes me laugh. Someone who, dare I sound so sentimental, *gets* me.'

Tears filled her eyes, appalling him. He'd been trying for humour, but he feared he'd only sounded twee. 'Rachel…'

'Why are you making this so hard?' she whispered, blinking back tears. Her teeth sank into her lower lip, creating two rosy indents he had the urge to soothe away— with his tongue. Mateo forced the unwanted and unhelpful image back.

'I'm making it hard because I want you to agree.'

'And if I did?'

The thrill of victory raced through his veins, roared in his ears. Never mind that she sounded a bit sad, a touch defeated. *She was actually considering it.*

'Then I'd arrange for you to travel back to Kallyria with me as soon as possible. We'd be married as soon as possible after that, in the Cathedral of Saint Theodora. Everyone in the royal family has been married in the Greek Orthodox church. I hope that is acceptable to you.'

'Mateo, I was speaking hypothetically.'

He shrugged, refusing to be deterred. 'So was I.'

'But after the ceremony? What then?'

'Then we live together as man and wife. You accompany me to state functions, on royal tours. You decide on which charitable institutions you wish to pioneer or support.'

'And I give you an heir?' She met his gaze even though her cheeks were fiery now. 'That's a part of this marriage deal you haven't actually mentioned yet.'

'No, I haven't,' Mateo agreed after a moment. He wished he knew why she was blushing—was it just because they were talking about sex? Or was it something else, something more? 'It seemed fairly obvious.'

'That this would be a marriage in…in every sense of the word?'

'If, by that phrase, you mean we'd consummate it, then

yes.' He held her gaze evenly despite the images dancing through his mind. Images he'd never, ever indulged in before, of Rachel in slips of silk and lace, smiling up at him from a canopied bed in the royal palace, her thick, wavy hair spread across the pillow in a chocolate river...

'Don't you think that's kind of a big thing to discuss?' Rachel asked, her voice sounding a little strangled. 'Obvious as it may seem?'

'Fine.' Mateo spread his hands as a waiter came in to quickly and quietly clear their dishes. 'Then let's discuss it.'

What had she got herself into? Rachel sat in silent mortification, willing her blush to recede, as the waiter cleared their plates and Mateo waited, completely unfazed by the turn in the conversation, just as he'd been unfazed by everything that had already been said.

He was like a bulldozer, flattening her every objection, making his proposal seem obvious, as if she should have been expecting it. And meanwhile Rachel felt as if she kept stumbling down rabbit holes and across minefields, dodging all the dangers and pitfalls, as she was accosted by yet another reason why a marriage between them would never work.

'You're not attracted to me,' she stated baldly. It hurt to say it; it humiliated her beyond all measure, in fact, and brought up too many bad memories or, really, just one in particular, but Rachel had long ago realised that confronting the elephant in the room, naming and shaming it, was the only way forward for her dignity. She'd done it before and she'd do it again, and she'd come out stronger for it. That much had been her promise to herself, made when she was a shy and naïve twenty and still holding true today, twelve years later.

She held his gaze and watched his lips purse as an expression flickered across his face that she would have given her eye teeth to identify, but could not.

'Sexual attraction is not a strong foundation for a marriage,' he said at last, and Rachel swallowed, trying not to let the sting of those words penetrate too deeply.

'It's not the most important part, perhaps,' she allowed. 'But it matters.'

Another lengthy silence, which told her just how unattracted to her he had to be. Rachel took a sip of wine, her gaze lowered, as she did her best to keep Mateo from knowing how much he was hurting her.

'I don't believe it will be an obstacle to our state of matrimony,' he said at last. 'Unless you have an intense aversion to me?' He said this with such smiling, smug self-assurance that Rachel had the sudden urge to throw her wine in his face. Oh, no, of *course* it couldn't be the case that she found him undesirable. Of course *that* was a joke.

'It might surprise you,' she said with a decided edge to her voice, 'but I want more from a potential marriage than the idea that my attractiveness, or lack of it, won't be an *obstacle.*'

Mateo's eyes widened as he acknowledged her tone, the rise and fall of her chest. She saw his lips compress and his pupils flare and knew he didn't like her sudden display of emotion. Well, she didn't like it, either.

She was far too agitated for either of their own good, and their reasonable, scientific discussion had morphed into something emotional and, well, *awful*. Because she really didn't want any more explanations about how he was willing to sacrifice sexual attraction on the altar of— what? His duty? Their compatibility? Logic? Whatever it was, Rachel didn't want to know. She'd had enough of being patronised. Enough of being felt as if she'd just about do. She'd had enough of that before this absurd conversation had even begun.

'Please.' She raised one hand to forestall any explanations he might have felt compelled to give, throwing her napkin onto the table with the other. 'Please don't say anything more, because I really don't want to hear it. Any of it. I am not going to marry you, Mateo, end of. Thanks anyway.'

She rose from the table on unsteady legs, her chest still heaving. She had to get out of here before she did something truly terrible, like start to cry.

But before she could even grab her coat, Mateo had risen from his own seat and crossed the small table to take her by the arms, his grip firm and sure.

'If you will not believe my words,' he said in a voice bordering a growl, 'then perhaps you will believe my actions.'

And then he kissed her.

It had been a long time since Rachel had been kissed. So long, in fact, that she'd sort of forgotten she had lips. Lips that could be touched and explored and licked. Lips that Mateo was moving over with his own, his tongue tracing the seam of her mouth before delving inward, making her knees weaken. She'd never known knees to actually do that before. She'd considered it a metaphor rather than scientific fact.

His lips felt both hard and soft, warm and cool. A thousand sensations exploded inside her as she parted her own lips, inviting him in. He reached up and cupped her cheek with his big, warm hand, his thumb stroking her skin, making her both shiver and shudder. Everything felt as if it were on fire.

The kiss went on and on, deeper and deeper, fireworks exploding all over her body. She'd never been kissed like this. She'd never *felt* like this.

Her hands came up of their own accord to clutch at his hard shoulders, fingers clawing at him, begging him for more.

And he gave it, one knee sliding between her own willing legs, the length of his hard, taut body pressed against hers for one glorious second before he stepped away, looking as composed to Rachel's dazed gaze as if they'd just shaken hands.

While she…she was in pieces. *Pieces*, scattered on the floor, with her mind spinning too much to even start to pick them up.

'I think that proves,' Mateo said in a clipped voice as he straightened his suit jacket, 'that attraction is not an issue.'

He stood there, a faint smile curling his mouth, his eyes gleaming with unmistakable triumph, while Rachel was still gasping and reeling from what had obviously been an unremarkable kiss to him. Meanwhile it had rocked her world right off its axis. Heaven only knew if she'd be able to straighten it again.

Standing in front of her, his arms folded, his eyebrows raised, he looked so confident, so utterly assured of his undeniable masculine appeal, that Rachel wanted to scream. Claw the face she'd just kissed. Had he really felt it necessary to prove how in thrall to him she could be?

While he seemed almost at pains to show how utterly unaffected he was—his expression composed, his breathing even, his manner bland.

Damn him.

'If you thought that was meant to win me over, you were wrong,' Rachel choked out, unable to hide the tears of mortification that had sprung to her eyes. She couldn't stand another minute of this utter humiliation. When she'd felt it once before, she'd vowed never to expose herself to it again, and so she wouldn't. This meeting was over.

While Mateo looked on, seeming distinctly nonplussed, she grabbed her coat and yanked it on, winding the scarf tightly around her neck, needing as many barriers between him and her as she could get.

'Rachel…' He stretched out one hand, his brows knitted together. He didn't understand. He thought she should be grateful for his attention, for the fact that he could kiss like a cross between Prince Charming and Casanova. And that made Rachel even more furious, so her voice shook as she spoke her next words.

'You might think you're God's greatest gift to women, Mateo Karr—whatever, but that doesn't mean I'm about to fall into your lap like a plum ripe for the picking. As much as you so obviously thought I would.' She jabbed a finger into his powerful pecs for good measure, making his eyes widen.

'So you're handsome. So you're a good kisser. So you're an out-and-out prince. I don't care! I don't care a—a *fig* about any of it. I am *not* marrying you.' And with that final battle cry, the tears she'd tried to keep back spilling from her eyes, Rachel stalked out of the room.

CHAPTER SIX

WELL. THAT HADN'T gone exactly as he'd expected. In fact, it hadn't gone the way he'd expected at *all*—a failed experiment, if there ever was one.

Because if he'd truly been conducting an experiment, Mateo acknowledged with a grimace, he would have first made his aim.

To convince Rachel Lewis to marry him, and that physical compatibility would not be an issue for them.

And his prediction? That she would agree, and it wouldn't. And the variables? Well, how attracted they both would be, he supposed. And those had been *variable* indeed.

In fact, he didn't really like to think how variable their attraction had been. He'd been acting on instinct at first, sensing that Rachel needed proof that physicality between them would not be a problem. And from the moment his lips had brushed hers—no, from the moment he'd put his hands on her arms, felt her warm softness, and drawn her to him—he'd known there was no problem at all.

In fact, the *lack* of problem suggested a problem. Because Mateo hadn't expected that variable, hadn't expected to want more and more from the woman who had become so pliant in his arms.

Well, he told himself now, there had been another variable—the fact that he hadn't had sex in a very long time, and so his response had to have been predicated on that. Explainable. Simple. It didn't *mean* anything. It certainly didn't mean he had some sort of ridiculously overwhelming attraction to Rachel Lewis, when he hadn't looked at her that way even once in ten years.

Which right now felt like a comfort. He could be attracted to her, but it wasn't a force in his life. It wasn't something he would have to keep under control.

Not that it mattered anyway, because she'd stormed out of here as if she never intended seeing him again.

So what should his next step be? Why had she been so offended by his kiss? He'd felt her response, so he knew it wasn't some sort of maidenly revulsion. He thought of her words—*'You might think you're God's greatest gift to women...'*

He hardly thought that, of course. Admittedly, he'd never had trouble finding sexual partners, not that he'd had all that many. He was too focused on his work and too discerning in his companions to sleep around, but it certainly wasn't for lack of interest on women's—*many* women's— part. But Mateo didn't think he was arrogant about it, and he hadn't been proving to Rachel how attractive she found him, but rather how good they could be together.

And the answer was they could be quite surprisingly good indeed.

So why had she been annoyed? Why had she seemed, rather alarmingly, *hurt*?

Mateo was still musing on this when there was a tap on the door. Expecting the waiter back, to deliver the main course they now wouldn't be eating, he barked a command to enter.

The door creaked open slowly and Rachel appeared. Her hair was in damp tendrils around her face, and the shoulders of her coat were wet. The look she gave him was one of abashed humour.

'I think I may have been a little bit of a drama queen there,' she said, and Mateo nearly laughed with the relief of having her back, smiling at him.

'At least you were a queen,' he returned with a small smile. 'I knew you had it in you.'

She laughed ruefully and shook her head. 'This is all so crazy, Mateo.'

'I agree that it seems crazy, but how many experiments have we conducted over the years that others said were crazy? Or pointless? Or just wouldn't work?'

She bit her lip, white teeth sinking into pink lushness, making Mateo remember exactly how those lips had felt. Tasted. 'Quite a few.'

'And this is just another experiment. The ultimate experiment.' It sounded so clever and neat, but a shadow had entered Rachel's eyes.

'And what happens when the experiment fails?'

'It won't.' He answered swiftly, too swiftly. She wasn't convinced.

'We write up the lab results? Draw some conclusions? *Marriages between princes and commoners are not a good idea.*'

'I admit, the experiment analogy only goes so far. And you only have to look at this country's royal family to know that a marriage between a prince and a commoner has an excellent chance of success.'

'Or not.'

'The point is, our marriage can be successful. There's absolutely no reason for it not to be.'

'Isn't there?' There was a note of sorrowful vulnerability in her voice that made Mateo tense. And this had all been starting to look so promising.

'Are you referring to something specific?' he asked in as reasonable a tone as he could manage.

She sighed, shrugging off her wet coat as she sat back

down at the table. It seemed they would be eating their main course, after all. 'Yes and no, I suppose.'

Mateo took his own seat. 'As you know, there are no yes-and-no situations in science.'

'This isn't science. But it may be chemistry.' She met his gaze evenly, her expression determined.

'Physical chemistry,' Mateo stated, because it was obvious. 'You think we don't have it? I thought I proved—'

'You proved you were a good kisser,' Rachel cut across him. 'And that you can…make me respond to you.'

He frowned, wishing he could figure out what was bothering her, and why it was so much. 'And that is a problem?'

'It's not a problem. It's just…an inequality.' She looked away, blinking rapidly, and Mateo realised that no matter her seemingly calm and practical exterior, something about their kiss had affected her deeply, and not on a physical level.

'Why were you a drama queen, Rachel?' he asked slowly, feeling his way through the words. 'What made you respond so…emotionally?'

She was silent, her expression distant as she looked away from him, and Mateo decided not to press.

'When are our main courses coming?' she finally asked. 'I stormed out of here without eating my salad, and I'm starving.'

'So why did you storm out of here, exactly?' Mateo asked, taking the obvious opening. Rachel paused, her once determined gaze sliding away from his. Whatever it was, she clearly didn't want to tell him. 'Rachel,' he said gently, 'if we're going to be married, I need to know.'

She swung back towards him, her face drawn in lines of laughing disbelief. '"If we're going to be married"? A little cocksure, aren't you, Mateo?'

'I meant hypothetically,' he returned smoothly. 'If it's

something you're thinking about even remotely…and you must be, because you came back here.'

'Maybe I came back here because I value your friendship.'

'That too.'

'And I didn't want to look like a prima donna.'

'Three reasons, then.'

She laughed and shook her head. 'Oh, Mateo. If we don't get married, I will miss you.'

Something leapt inside him and he leaned forward. 'Then marry me, Rachel.' His voice throbbed with more intent than he wanted to reveal. More desire.

Her eyes widened as her gaze moved over his face, as if she were trying to plumb the depths of him, and Mateo didn't want that. He held her gaze but he schooled his expression into something calm and determined. How he really felt.

'The reason I might have overreacted,' she said slowly, her gaze still on his face, 'is because I've… I've been burned before. By an arrogant man who thought I'd be grateful for his attentions, and then made a joke of them afterwards.'

Mateo didn't like the sound of that at *all*. Everything in him tightened as he answered levelly, 'Tell me more.'

She shrugged, spreading her hands. 'Sadly there's not much more to tell. He was a doctoral student when I was in my second year at Oxford—he paid me special attention, I thought he cared. He didn't, and he let people know it.' Her lips tightened as she looked away.

What was that supposed to mean? 'He hurt you?' Mateo asked, amazed at how much he disliked the thought. Not just disliked, but *detested*, with a deep, gut-churning emotion he didn't expect or want to feel.

'Emotionally, yes, he did. But I got over it.' Rachel lifted her chin, a gesture born of bravery. 'I didn't love him, not like that. But my ego was bruised, and I felt humiliated and hurt, and I decided for myself that I was never going to let another man treat me that way ever again, and so far I haven't.'

Realisation trickled icily through him and he jerked back a little. 'And you think I did? Was?'

'It felt like that at the time, but, I admit, I probably over-reacted, due to my past experience.' She shrugged again. 'So now you know.'

Yet he didn't know, not really. He didn't know what this vile man had done, or how exactly he'd humiliated Rachel. He didn't know how she'd responded, or how long it had taken her to recover and heal. But Mateo was reluctant to ask any more, to know any more. It was her private pain, and she'd tell him if she wanted to. Besides, information was responsibility, and he had enough of that to be going on with.

'I'm sorry,' he said. 'For what happened. And how I made you feel.'

'You didn't mean to. At least I don't think you did. Which is why I'm still here.' She gave him one of her old grins. 'That, and the risotto that had better be here soon.'

'I assure you, it is.' Mateo reached for his phone and texted the maître d' of the restaurant, whom he'd contacted earlier to make the reservation. Within seconds the waiter was back, with two more silver-domed dishes.

'So if you really are a prince,' Rachel asked after he'd whisked the lids off and left, 'where's your security detail? Why isn't there a guy in a dark suit with a walkie-talkie in the corner of the room?'

'That would be a rather unpleasant breach of privacy,' Mateo returned. 'He's outside in the hall.'

Rachel nearly dropped her fork. '*Is* he?'

'Of course.'

She shook her head slowly. 'Did you have security all the time in Cambridge? Was I just completely blind?'

'No, I didn't. I chose not to. As the third in line to the throne, I had that freedom.'

'But you don't any more.'

His lips and gut both tightened. 'No.'

Rachel watched Mateo's expression shutter with a flicker of curiosity, and a deeper ripple of compassion. 'Do you want to be king?' she asked and he stiffened, the shutter coming down even more.

'It's not a question of want. It's my duty.'

'You didn't actually answer me.'

His mouth thinned as he inclined his head. 'Very well. I want to do my duty.'

Which sounded rather grim. Rachel took a forkful of risotto and chewed slowly. It was delicious, rich and creamy, but she barely registered the flavour as her mind whirled. Was she really thinking seriously about saying yes to Mateo's shocking proposal?

It had struck her, as she'd stormed away from the restaurant and got soaked in the process, that she was a little too outraged. It was easier to feel outraged, to wrap herself in it like a cloak of armour, than to think seriously about what Mateo was suggesting.

And yet the farther she'd walked, the more she'd realised she had to be sensible about this. She had to be the scientist she'd always been. She couldn't sail on the high tide of emotion, not for long. It simply wasn't in her nature.

And so she'd gone back, and now she was here, thinking seriously about saying yes.

'So what would a marriage between us look like?' she asked. 'On a day-to-day basis?'

'We'd live in the royal palace in Constanza,' Mateo answered with calm swiftness. 'It is a beautiful place, built five hundred years ago, right on the sea.'

'Okay…'

'As I said before, you could choose your involvement in various charities and initiatives. Admittedly, there would be a fair amount of ribbon cutting and clapping, that sort of thing. It's unavoidable, I'm afraid.'

'I don't mind that. But I don't exactly look the part, do I?' She had to say it.

Mateo looked distinctly nonplussed. 'So you've intimated before. If you mean clothes, I assure you, you will be provided with a complete wardrobe of your choice, along with personal stylists and hairdressers as you wish.'

'So like Cinderella.' She didn't know how she felt about that. A little excited? A little insulted? A little afraid? All three, and more than a little.

Mateo shrugged. 'Like any royal princess—or queen.'

'And what about children?' Rachel asked. Her stomach quivered at the thought. 'You mentioned needing an heir as soon as possible.'

'Yes.'

'That's kind of a big thing, Mateo.'

'I agree.'

'You don't even know if I want children.'

'I assume we would not be having this discussion if you were completely averse to the idea.'

Rachel sighed and laid down her fork. Her stomach was churning too much to eat. 'I don't even know,' she admitted. 'I haven't let myself think about it.'

Mateo frowned, his gaze searching her face. 'Let yourself?'

'I'm thirty-two, and I haven't had a serious relationship since university. I assumed it wasn't likely to happen.'

'Well, now you can assume differently.'

'Assuming I can get pregnant in the first place.'

He shrugged. 'Is there any reason you believe you cannot?'

'No.' She couldn't believe they were talking about having a baby together so clinically, and yet somehow it didn't surprise her at all. Mateo was approaching the whole matter of their marriage in as scientific a way as possible, which she didn't mind, not exactly.

'What about love?' she asked baldly. 'I know you didn't approach me because of love, but is it something that could happen in time? Something you'd hope for?' A long silence ensued, which told her everything.

'Is that something you would wish?' Mateo asked finally. 'Something you would hope for?'

Which sounded pathetic, and was the exact reason why she'd thought this whole idea was ridiculous in the first place. Well, that and a lot of other reasons, too.

And yet...was it? Did she want the fairy-tale romance, to fall head over heels in love with someone? With *Mateo*? Falling head over heels sounded painful. And from her limited experience with Josh, it had been. Did she really want that again, just because everyone around her—on TV, in books—seemed to assume it was?

When she and Mateo had first started working together, she'd had a bit of a crush on him and she'd worked to get over it. And she *had*. Did she really want to feel that soul-pinching, gut-churning sensation of liking someone more than he liked you, and in this case to a much more serious degree? Wouldn't it be easier if they just both agreed to keep that off the table for ever?

'Honestly, I don't know,' she said slowly. 'It's what everyone assumes you should want.'

'Maybe between the pages of a book like the one on your coffee table, but not in real life. Feelings like that fade, Rachel. What we have—what we could have—would be real.'

'You don't need to sound quite so dismissive about the whole idea,' Rachel returned.

'Not dismissive,' Mateo countered. 'Sensible. And I think you're sensible, as well.' He held her gaze, his aquamarine eyes like lasers. Not for the first time, Rachel wondered why he had to be so beautiful. It would be so much easier if he was more normal looking. Average.

'So you're not interested in falling in love?' she asked, unsure if her tone was pathetic or joking or somewhere in between. 'I just want to make sure.'

Mateo was silent for a long, painful moment. 'No,' he said finally. 'I am not.'

She nodded, absorbing that, recognising that at least then the whole issue would be off the table. Not something to be discussed or hoped for, ever. Could she live with that? Was she *sensible* enough? 'I have my mother to consider,' she said at last, hardly able to believe they were now talking about real practicalities. 'She has Alzheimer's. She needs my care.'

'That is not a problem. She can accompany us to Kallyria, where she will receive top medical care, her own suite of rooms, and a full-time nurse.'

'I don't know if she could cope with that much change. She struggled to move here from Sussex.'

'If it is preferable, she could stay in Cambridge. I can arrange her care at the best residential facility in the area immediately.'

Rachel sighed. Thinking of her mother made her feel anxious—and guilty. Because the thought of escaping the mundanity of her life with her mother, the constant complaining and criticism that she'd faced her whole life and that had become only worse with her mother's disease, was wonderfully liberating.

'I don't know,' she said at last. 'I suppose I could discuss it with her.' A prospect that made her stomach cramp.

'If it helps, I could do that with you,' Mateo said, and for a second Rachel felt as if she'd put on a pair of 3D glasses. She could see the whole world in an entirely different dimension.

If she married Mateo, she wouldn't have to do everything alone. She'd have someone advocating for her, supporting her, and backing her up. Someone to laugh with, to share life with, to discuss ideas and sleep next to. What did love have on any of that? Suddenly, blindingly, it was obvious. Wonderfully obvious.

'Thank you,' she said after a moment, her voice shaky, her mind still spinning.

'It's not a problem at all.' Mateo paused, his hands flat on the table as he gave her a direct look. 'While I recognise the seriousness of your decision, and the understandable need for time to consider, I am afraid matters are quite pressing. The situation in my country is urgent.'

'Urgent?'

'The instability of rule has led to a rise in insurgency. Nothing that cannot be dealt with, but it means I need to be back in Kallyria, firmly on my throne, my wife at my side, as soon as possible.'

'How soon as possible do you mean?' Rachel asked as she grappled with the whole idea of insurgency and Mateo needing to deal with it.

'Tomorrow would be best.'

'*Tomorrow...?*' She gaped at him. 'Mateo, I'd have to give at least a term's notice—'

'That can be dealt with.'

'My mother—'

'Again, it can be dealt with.'

'My flat...'

'I can arrange for it to be sold or kept, as you wish.'

She'd worked hard to save for that flat. Prices in Cambridge had skyrocketed over the last decade and, even on a researcher's salary, buying the flat had been a stretch. Rachel took a quick, steadying breath. 'I don't know. This is a lot quicker than I expected.'

'I understand.' Yet his tone was implacable. He understood, but he would not change the terms. And that, Rachel realised, was an attitude she would encounter and have to accept again and again if she said yes.

'I don't know,' she said at last. 'Can I think about it for a little while, at least? A night, and I'll tell you first thing in the morning?'

Mateo hesitated, and Rachel knew even that felt like too long to him. Then he gave a brief nod. 'Very well. But if you do say yes, Rachel, I will have to put things in motion very quickly.'

'I understand.'

He hesitated, then reached over and covered her hand with his own, his palm warm and large and comforting on hers. 'I know this all seems quite overwhelming. There are so many different things to consider. But I do believe, Rachel, I believe completely, that we could have a very successful and happy marriage. I wouldn't be here if I didn't believe that absolutely.'

She nodded, pressing her lips together to keep them from trembling. Already she knew what her answer would be.

CHAPTER SEVEN

RACHEL PEERED OUT of the window as the misty grey fog of an English autumn grew smaller below and the plane lifted into a bright azure sky. It was the day after Mateo's proposal, and they were on the royal Kallyrian jet, for an overnight flight to Constanza.

Rachel's head was still spinning from how quickly everything had happened. Mateo had escorted her home, kissed her cheek, and told her he would ring her at seven in the morning for her answer.

Back in her flat, with her mother parked in front of a television on highest volume and the burnt smell of her toastie still hanging in the air, Rachel had felt the smallness of her existence descend on her like a thick fog. When she'd opened a patronising email from Supercilious Simon, it had been the push she hadn't even needed.

She was going to say yes. As crazy as it seemed, as risky as it might be, she believed in her heart that life was meant for living, not just existing, and without Mateo in it that was what hers had become. A matter of survival.

She spent a sleepless night trying to imagine her future and unable to come up with anything more than hazy, vague scenes out of a Grace Kelly film, or maybe *The Princess Diaries*. When her mobile buzzed next to her bed at seven o'clock precisely, her stomach whirled with nerves—but also excitement.

'Mateo?'

'Have you decided?'

She took a breath, let it fill her lungs. She felt as if she were leaping and twirling into outer space. 'Yes,' she said softly. 'I say yes.'

Mateo had sprung instantly into action. He'd disconnected the call almost immediately, saying he would come over within the next half-hour to begin arrangements.

'My mother…' Rachel had begun, starting to panic. 'She doesn't do well with change…'

'We will make her transition as smooth as possible,' Mateo promised her, and it had been. He'd left her mother speechless and simpering under the full wattage of his charm, and that very afternoon the three of them had toured the high-end nursing home on the outskirts of Cambridge that had a private facility for memory-impaired residents.

Carol had seemed remarkably pleased with it all—the private room was far larger and more luxurious than the one she currently had, and the nursing home had a full schedule of activities. And when Rachel had explained she would be moving away, her mother hadn't been bothered in the least. Not, Rachel acknowledged with a sigh, that that had been much of a surprise.

Still, it all seemed so incredibly, head-spinningly fast. Her mother was already settled in the nursing home; Rachel and Mateo had moved her over that very evening. A lump had formed in Rachel's throat as she'd hugged her mother goodbye. Who knew when or if she'd see her again? Yet her mother had barely seemed aware of her departure; she'd turned away quickly, intent on investigating the lounge area with its large flat-screen TV. As she'd watched her mother shuffle away, it had seemed hard to believe that she'd once been the sophisticated and erudite wife of a prominent academic.

'Bye, Mum,' she'd whispered, and then she'd walked away without looking back.

Back at her flat, Rachel had packed her things up in a single suitcase, since Mateo had assured her she would not need anything once she was in Kallyria; all would be provided. He advised only to take keepsakes and mementoes, of which she had very few.

It felt a little sad, a bit pathetic, to leave an entire life behind so easily. She'd email her friends once she reached Kallyria, and Mateo had promised her that he would pay for anyone she wished to attend the wedding to be flown over. He'd dealt with her job situation, and she'd felt a flicker of sorrow that, after ten years, she could both walk away and be let go so easily. But Cambridge was a transient place; people moved in and out all the time. Even after ten years, she was just one more.

Still, Rachel told herself as the royal jet levelled out, there was no point in being melancholy. She was about to embark on the adventure of a lifetime, and she wanted to enjoy it.

She glanced at Matteo, who was sitting across from her in a sumptuous seat of white leather, frowning down at his laptop. Since securing her hand in marriage, he had paid very little attention to her, but Rachel hadn't minded. He had much to attend to, a country to rule and, besides, she wasn't one to want to be fussed over.

Still, she wouldn't have minded a bit of conversation now.

'I feel like we should have champagne,' she said a bit playfully, and Mateo looked up from his screen with a frown.

'Champagne? Of course.' He snapped his fingers and a steward materialised silently, as if plucked from the air.

'Yes, Your Highness?'

That was something that was going to take a lot of getting used to. Despite Mateo's obvious and understated displays of both wealth and power, she realised she hadn't fully believed in the whole king thing until she'd stepped on the royal jet, and everyone had started bowing and curtseying and 'Your Highnessing' him. It had been weird.

The steward produced a bottle of bubbly with the kind of label Rachel could only dream of, popped the cork and poured two crystalline flutes full.

'Cheers,' Rachel said a bit tartly. During this whole elegant procedure, Mateo hadn't so much as looked up from his screen.

She took a large sip of the champagne, which was crisp and delicious on her tongue. Another sip, and finally Mateo looked up.

He took in the open bottle chilling in a silver bucket, his untouched flute, and Rachel's expression with a small, rueful smile.

'I apologise.' He reached for his glass and touched it to hers, his gaze warm and intent. 'As we say in Kallyria, *yamas*.'

'I don't even know what language that is,' Rachel confessed, wrinkling her nose. 'Or what language you speak in Kallyria.'

'It is Greek, and it means health or, more prosaically, cheers.'

'Do you speak Greek?'

'Yes, and Turkish.'

'Wow.' She realised how little she knew about, well, *anything*. 'I should have done an Internet search on you last night.'

He arched an eyebrow. 'You didn't?'

'I was too busy thinking about whether or not I was going to marry you.' Although really she'd already decided. She'd spent most of the evening walking around in a daze, doing nothing productive.

'You can ask me what you like. There will be a lot to learn.'

'Yes.' Rachel could see that already. 'What's going to happen when we land?'

'I've had our arrival at Constanza embargoed—'

'What does that mean?'

'I am not alerting the media and no press will be allowed.'

'Okay.' She tried to process that for a moment, and failed. 'Why?'

'Because I want to control all the information,' Mateo answered swiftly. 'When we arrive at the royal palace, I will take you to meet my mother.'

Rachel swallowed. 'Have you told her about me?'

'Yes, she is greatly looking forward to making your acquaintance.'

'That's nice,' Rachel said faintly. She didn't know why she was starting to feel so alarmed; she'd known this was the kind of thing she was signing up for. And yet now it was starting to feel so very *real*. 'And then what?'

'Then you will meet with your stylist and hairdresser,' Mateo answered. 'They are temporary only, as I am sure you will like to select your own staff when the times comes.'

'I've never had staff before,' Rachel said with a nervous laugh. She took a gulp of champagne to steady her nerves.

'You do now.' Mateo nodded towards the stewards in the front cabin of the aircraft. 'Everyone who works for me works for you.'

'Right.' Something else she could not get her head around.

'When you have finished with the stylists, you will be introduced to Kallyria.'

'Introduced to a country? How is that meant to happen?' Already her mouth was drying, her heart beginning to hammer at the thought.

'There is a balcony from where royalty has traditionally made all such announcements. I shall introduce you, we will wave, and then retire into the palace. Some time in the next week we will hold an engagement ball where you will meet all the dignitaries and statesmen you need to, and then we will marry next Saturday.'

'Wait, what? That's only a week from now.'

Mateo's brows snapped together as he regarded her evenly, his flute of champagne held between two long, lean fingers. 'Is that a problem? You are aware of the urgency of the situation.'

Rachel swallowed dryly. 'It's not a problem. Just…give me a moment to get my head around it.'

'Very well.' Mateo turned back to his laptop, and Rachel sipped the last of her champagne, her mind feeling like so much buzzing noise. After a few moments she excused herself with a murmur and went to the back of the plane, where there was a sumptuous bedroom with a king-sized bed and an en suite bathroom all in marble.

Rachel sank onto the bed and looked around her in as much of a daze as ever, if not more. What was she doing here, really?

Mateo straightened the cuffs of his suit as he waited for Rachel to emerge from the bedroom where she was changing into a fresh outfit to exit the plane.

He'd spent the majority of the flight working, grabbing an hour of sleep in his seat while Rachel had retired to the bedroom as soon as she'd drunk her champagne, and she hadn't come out again until an hour before landing.

Mateo had checked in on her halfway through the flight, and seen her still in her clothes, curled up on top of the covers, fast asleep. Her hair was spread across the pillow just as he'd once imagined, and as he gazed at her he realised he'd never seen her sleep before, and yet from now on he would many times over.

The thought had brought a shaft of—something—to him. Something he wasn't sure he wanted to name, because he couldn't discern how it made him feel.

He'd rushed into marriage because he'd had to, and he'd done it with Rachel because at least he knew and trusted her. But watching her sleep, he was accosted by the realisation of how intimate their lives together would have to be, no matter how much he kept a certain part of himself closed off, a part that he hadn't accessed in fifteen years, since Cressida.

No matter how physically intimate they might be, no matter how close they might become, Mateo knew there was only so much he could ever offer Rachel. Only so much he knew how to give, and he had to trust that it would be enough. It certainly would be for him, and it had better be for her, because he didn't have anything else.

Straightening his tie, he gave his reflection one last glance before he went to knock on the bedroom door.

'We're landing in twenty minutes, Rachel. We need to take our seats.'

'All right.' She opened the door, throwing her shoulders back as she gave him a smile that bordered on terrified. 'Do I look all right?'

'You look fine,' Mateo assured her, because the media wouldn't be there and so it didn't matter. In truth he acknowledged that she would benefit from the help of a stylist. The shapeless trouser suit and plain ponytail that had served her so well for over ten years in academia were not exactly the right look for a queen, something he suspected Rachel was completely aware of. She certainly seemed aware of any potential deficiencies in her persona, and Mateo was determined to assuage her concerns.

'Did you sleep well?' he asked as he took her elbow

and escorted her to the front of the plane. She gave him a strange look, and he realised it wasn't something he would have normally done...*touch* her. Yet he acknowledged he needed to start acting like a husband, not a colleague, and in any case he found he wanted to do it, his fingers light on her elbow, her breast brushing his arm as they walked. Was she aware of it? She didn't seem to be, but he most certainly was.

'Better than I expected,' Rachel answered with a little laugh. 'I think I was so exhausted because I didn't sleep a wink the night before!'

'Didn't you?'

She gave him a wry, laughing look. 'No, I most certainly did not. I stayed up the entire night wondering if I was going to marry you, and trying to imagine what that would look like, because frankly I still find it impossible.'

'Yet very soon you will find out.'

'I know.' She fiddled with the seat buckle, her gaze lowered so her ponytail fell forward onto her shoulder, like a curling ribbon of chocolate-brown silk. For some reason he couldn't quite understand, Mateo reached forward and flicked it back. Rachel glanced at him, startled. He smiled blandly.

'Tell me about your mother,' she blurted.

'My mother? Her name is Agathe and she is a very strong and gracious woman. I admire her very much.'

'She sounds completely intimidating.'

Mateo frowned. 'She isn't.'

'I don't believe you. You're intimidating.' Rachel gave him a teasing smile, but Mateo knew she was serious—and scared. He could see it in her eyes, in the way she blinked rapidly, her lush lashes fanning downwards again and again as she moistened her lips with the tip of a delectably pink tongue.

'You've known me for ten years, Rachel,' he pointed out reasonably. 'How can I be intimidating?'

'You're different now,' she answered with a shrug. 'Until yesterday, I never saw you snap your fingers at someone before.'

Mateo acknowledged the point with a rueful nod. 'I don't think I had, at least not while at Cambridge.'

'You seem so used to all this luxury and wealth. I mean, I suppose you grew up with it, and I knew you had a fancy house in Cambridge because of some investments or something…'

He raised his eyebrows. 'Is that courtesy of the university gossips?'

Rachel smiled, unabashed. 'Yes.'

'Well, it wasn't investments. It was a company I founded. Lyric Tech.'

'What, you just *founded* a company in your spare time?'

He shrugged. 'I had an idea for a music app and it went from there.'

'As it does.' Rachel pursed her lips, looking troubled. 'See, when you say stuff like that, I feel as if I really don't know you at all.'

'You know me, Rachel.' He hadn't meant his voice to sound so low and meaningful, or to caress the syllables of her name quite so much, but they did. Her eyes widened and a faint blush touched her cheeks as she stared at him for a second before looking away.

'Maybe we should talk about molecular electrocatalysis or something?' she suggested shakily. 'Just to feel like our old selves again.'

'If you like.' Mateo relaxed back into his seat. He was always happy to talk shop. 'What are your thoughts on the metal-to-metal hydrogen atom transfer?'

Rachel looked surprised that he was playing along, but then a little smile curved her mouth and she considered the question properly. 'I suppose you're talking about iron and chromium?'

'Indeed.'

'There are some limitations, of course.' They spent the next fifteen minutes discussing the potential benefits of the new research on various forms of renewable energy, and she became so engrossed in the discussion that Rachel didn't even notice the plane landing, or taxiing along the private airstrip. It was only when she glanced out of the window and saw several blacked-out sedans with a small army of people in front of them that her face paled and she gulped audibly.

'Mateo, I don't know if I can do this.'

'Of course you can,' he answered calmly. He meant it; he'd seen her handle a dozen more demanding situations back at Cambridge. All she had to do now was walk out of the plane and into a waiting car. 'You are going to be my queen, Rachel. The only one who doubts whether you are up for the role is you.'

She gave him a wry look. 'Are you sure about that?'

'Positive.' If anyone else doubted it, he would make sure they stopped immediately. He would not allow for anyone to doubt or deride his chosen queen.

Rachel glanced back out at the sedans, and the flank of waiting security, all looking suitably blank-faced, and Mateo watched with pride as the iron entered her soul. She nodded slowly as she straightened her shoulders, her chin tilting upward as her eyes blazed briefly with gold.

'All right,' she said. 'Let's do this.'

Moments later the security team were opening the door to the plane, and Mateo reached for Rachel's hand. Hers was icy-cold and he twined his fingers through hers and gently drew her closer to his side. Her smile trembled on her lips as she shot him a questioning look. This closeness was new to both of them, but Mateo didn't mind it.

'Ready?' he asked softly, and, setting her jaw, she nodded.

Then together they stepped out of the plane, onto the stairs. They walked side by side down the rather rickety stairs to the waiting car, and Mateo nodded at the security team, who all bowed in response, their faces remaining impressively impassive. Mateo did not explain who Rachel was; they would find out soon enough. They could almost certainly guess.

Pride blossomed in his soul as she kept her chin tilted and her back ramrod straight as she walked from the bottom of the stairs to the waiting car. She was, Mateo acknowledged with a deep tremor of satisfaction, fit to be his queen.

CHAPTER EIGHT

THE WORLD BLURRED by as Rachel sat in the sedan and it sped along wide boulevards, the sea glittering blue on the other side of the road, palm trees proudly pointing to an azure sky.

Since exiting the plane, Rachel had felt as if she were disembodied, watching everything unfold as if from far above. She couldn't possibly be sitting in a luxury sedan with blacked-out windows, an armed guard travelling before and behind and a man set to be king brooding next to her, on her way to an actual palace?

It had been utterly surreal to walk down those steps and see the guards bowing to Mateo—and her. She'd seen their impassive faces and recognised the look of people well trained to keep their expressions to themselves. Had they guessed she was Mateo's bride, their next queen? Or did they assume she was some dowdy secretary brought along to take dictation? That was what she would have assumed, if she'd been in their place.

As much as she was trying to keep from getting down on herself, Rachel had to acknowledge the struggle was real. Her trouser suit was five years old and bought on the bargain rack, because she'd never cared about clothes. She had no make-up on because when she tried to use it, she looked like a clown. Her hair hadn't been cut in six months at least. Yes, she was definitely feeling like the dowdy secretary rather than the defiant queen.

'If I'd known I was going to become a queen this week,' she quipped to Mateo, 'I would have had my hair cut and lost a stone.'

He turned to her, his expression strangely fierce, his face drawn into stark lines of determination. 'Neither is necessary, I assure you.'

She eyed him sceptically. 'Didn't you mention a team of stylists and beauticians waiting at the palace to turn me into some kind of post-godmother Cinderella?'

'It doesn't mean you need to change.'

Rachel glanced down at her trouser suit. 'I think I might,' she said. 'At least this outfit.' She didn't want to dwell on all the other ways she might need to change, and so she chose to change the subject. 'So what is the royal palace like? Besides being palatial, naturally.'

A small smile twitched the corner of Mateo's mouth. 'And royal.'

'Obvs.'

'It's five hundred years old, built on the sea, looking east. It has magnificent gardens leading down to the beach, and many beautiful terraces and balconies. You will occupy the Queen's suite of rooms after our marriage.'

'You need to stop saying stuff like that, because I feel like I'm living in a fairy tale.'

His smile deepened as he glanced down at her, aquamarine eyes sparkling. 'But it's true.'

'And where will I be before our marriage?' Which was now in six *days*, something she couldn't let herself think about without panicking.

'A guest suite. But first, remember, my mother wishes to meet you.'

'Right away?' Rachel swallowed hard. 'Before anything else?'

'It is important.'

And terrifying. Rachel tried to moderate her breathing as the car sped on, past whitewashed buildings with terracotta roofs, flowers blooming everywhere, spilling out of pots and window boxes. She gazed at a woman with a basket of oranges on her head, and a man with a white turban riding a rusty bicycle. Kallyria was a place where the east and west met, full of history and colour and life. And it was now her home.

The reality of it all, the enormity of the choice she had made, slammed into her again and again, leaving her breathless.

After about ten minutes, the motorcade drove through high, ornate gates of wrought iron, and then down a sweeping drive, a palace of sparkling white stone visible in the distance. It was a combination of fairy-tale castle and luxury Greek villa—complete with terraces and turrets, latticed shutters and trailing bougainvillea at every window, and Rachel thought there had to be at least a hundred.

'Welcome home,' Mateo said with a smile, and she nearly choked. She felt as if she were caught up in a riptide of officialdom as she was ushered out of the car and into the soaring marble foyer of the palace, a twisting, double staircase leading to a balcony above, and then onwards. A cupola high above them let in dazzling sunlight, and at least a dozen staff, the royal insignia on their uniform, were lined up waiting to bow or curtsey to Mateo.

'My mother is waiting upstairs, in her private parlour,' Mateo murmured, and, taking her by the elbow, he led her upstairs.

'Mitera?' he called, knocking on the wood-panelled door once, and when a mellifluous voice bid them to enter, he did.

Rachel followed, her knees practically knocking together. What if Mateo's mother didn't like her? What if she looked at her and wondered why on earth he'd chosen her as his bride? His queen?

The woman rising from a loveseat at one end of the elegant and spacious room was exactly what Rachel had expected, even though she had never seen a photograph of Agathe Karavitis.

She was tall and elegant, her dark blonde hair barely streaked with silver drawn back in a loose chignon. She wore a chic silk blouse tucked into wide-leg trousers and as she came forward, a welcoming smile on her face, her arms outstretched, she moved with an unconscious grace. Rachel felt like the dowdiest of dowds in comparison, and she tried not to let it show in her face as Agathe kissed both her cheeks and pressed her hands between her own.

'Rachel. I am so very delighted to make your acquaintance.'

'As I am yours,' Rachel managed to stammer. She felt woefully and wholly inadequate.

'I must check on a few things before we appear publicly,' Mateo informed her. Rachel tried not to gape at him in panic. He was leaving?

'She is in safe hands, I assure you,' Agathe said.

'We will appear on the balcony at two…' Mateo gave his mother a significant look.

'She will be ready.' She waved at him with an elegant hand. 'Go.'

Mateo gave Rachel a quick smile that did not reassure her at all and then strode out of the room.

'I have called for tea,' Agathe said once he had left, the door clicking firmly shut behind him. 'You must be exhausted.'

'I'm a bit tired, yes,' Rachel said carefully. She realised she had no idea how to handle this meeting. Despite Agathe's air of gracious friendliness, she had no idea how the woman really thought of her. According to Mateo, Agathe had drawn up a list of suitable brides, and Rachel had most certainly not been on it.

'Come sit down,' Agathe invited, patting the seat next to her. 'We have little time today to get to know one another, but tomorrow I have arranged for us to have breakfast together.'

'That's very kind.' Rachel perched on the edge of the loveseat while Agathe eyed her far too appraisingly. Rachel knew how she looked—how limp her ponytail, how creased her suit, how pasty her skin. She tried to smile.

'I suppose you are surprised,' she said finally, because as always she preferred confronting the truth rather than hiding from it. 'I am not the expected choice for your son's bride.'

'You are not,' Agathe agreed with a nod. 'And yet I think you might be exactly right.'

That surprised Rachel, and for the first time in what felt like for ever she actually started to relax. 'You do?'

'Don't sound so surprised,' Agathe returned with a tinkling laugh. 'Did you think I would not approve?'

'I wondered.'

'More than anything, I wish my son to be happy,' Agathe said quietly. 'And the fact that he chose you, that he knows you and calls you his friend…that is important. Far more important than having the right pedigree or something similar.' She shrugged slim shoulders. 'It is a modern world. We are no longer in the days of princes and kings needing to marry young women of suitable social standing, thank goodness.'

Rachel wasn't sure how to reply. Her father had been a well-regarded academic, if a commoner, but she doubted that held much water in the world of royalty. 'Thank you for your understanding,' she said at last.

An attendant came in with a tea tray, and Agathe served, her movements as elegant as ever. 'I am afraid we have only a few moments, if we wish you to be ready for the announcement.'

Rachel's stomach cramped as she took a soothing sip of the tea. Swallowing, she said, 'I don't think I'll ever be ready.'

'Nonsense,' Agathe said briskly. 'You just need the right tools.'

Mateo felt the weight of responsibility drop heavily onto his shoulders as he took a seat at his father's desk. His desk now. How long would it take him to think of it like that? To think of himself as King?

Two days away had taken their toll, and now his narrowed gaze scanned the various reports that had come in during his absence. Increased unrest in the north of the country; the important economic talks on a knife edge; domestic policy careening towards a crisis. An emergency on every front, and in just three hours he and Rachel would step in front of the waiting crowds and he would announce his choice of bride.

At least he did not regret taking that decision. Although she clearly had doubts about her suitability, Mateo did not. His only concern was making sure their relationship did not veer into the overly emotional or intimate. As long as they stayed friends, they would be fine. He would make sure of it.

Mateo spent an hour going over reports before he decided to check on Rachel's progress with the stylists he'd engaged. After a member of staff informed him of their whereabouts, he strode towards the east wing of the palace, where the guest suites were housed. From behind the first door on the corridor he heard the accented trill of the woman who dressed his mother.

'Of course we will have to do something about those eyebrows...' Mateo stopped outside the door, frowning.

'And that *chin*...' The despair, bordering on disgust, in the woman's voice tightened his gut. 'Fortunately some—how do they say in the English?—contouring will help. As for the clothes...something flowing, to hide the worst.'

The worst?

Furious now, as well as incredulous, Mateo flung open the door. Four women, matchstick-thin and officious, buzzed around Rachel, who sat in a chair in front of a mirror, looking horribly resigned. At his entrance the women turned to him, wide-eyed, mouths open.

'What is going on here?' Mateo demanded, his voice a low growl of barely suppressed outrage.

The women all swept panicked curtsies that Mateo ignored.

'Your Highness...'

'What is going on?'

'We were just attending to Kyria Lewis...'

'In a manner I find most displeasing. You are all dismissed at once.' A shocked intake of breath was the only response he got, followed by a frozen silence.

'Mateo,' Rachel said softly. He turned his gaze to her, saw her giving him one of her wonderfully wry smiles. 'Remember when I was being a drama queen? Don't be a drama king. They're just doing their job.'

'They insulted you,' he objected, his voice pulsating with fury. 'I will not have it.'

'They were just being pragmatic, and in any case they weren't saying anything I haven't said myself a thousand times before. I really don't like my chin.'

'Your chin is fine.'

Rachel's mouth quirked. 'Shall we argue about it?'

'Their comments and attitude are *not* acceptable.' He would not back down, no matter what damage mitigation Rachel felt she needed to do.

'Your Highness,' Francesca, the main stylist, said in a

hesitant voice. 'Please accept my deepest apologies for my remarks. I was thinking out loud…but you are right, it was unacceptable.' She bowed her head. 'If you will give me this opportunity to style Kyria Lewis, I will do my utmost to help her succeed.'

'She will succeed with or without you,' Mateo snapped. 'You are not here to make her succeed, but simply to provide her with the right clothes and make-up.'

Francesca's head dipped lower. 'As you say,' she murmured.

'Mateo.' Rachel's voice was gentle. 'Honestly, it's okay.'

But it wasn't. He saw so clearly how she accepted being belittled, how she thought because she was curvy and dressed in shapeless clothes she wasn't worth the same as a woman with a wasp-like waist and a similar attitude. Mateo hated it.

'You will dress and style Kyria Lewis,' he instructed the women, his eyes like lasers on the penitent Francesca. 'I will review the terms of your contract with the palace myself before the day is out.'

The women murmured their thanks and he strode out of the room, still battling an inexplicable fury. Why did he care so much? Rachel didn't. Why couldn't he just let it go? Yet he found he couldn't.

He'd never considered Rachel's feelings in such a specific way before he'd decided to marry her. He'd never considered *anyone's* feelings, he acknowledged with wry grimness, not really.

Not since Cressida, whose feelings he had considered both far too much and not nearly enough. The paradox of his relationship with her, the manic highs and terrible lows, was something he knew he wasn't strong enough to experience again. And even though Rachel was entirely different, he feared the root cause of those emotions was the same. *Love.* Best to avoid.

And yet now, despite his determination to keep a certain aloofness, and for reasons he did not wish to probe too deeply, he felt as if he was changing. Now he cared—admittedly about something relatively small, but still. It mattered. It mattered to him.

Wanting to leave such disturbing thoughts behind, Mateo went to meet with the palace press officer and arrange the last details of their appearance on the main balcony. All the country's press would be assembled in the courtyard below, along with most of Europe's and some of Asia's.

Kallyria was a small country, but since the discovery of oil beneath its lands, it had become a major player on the world stage. The whole world would be waiting for and watching this announcement. Mateo wanted to make sure everything was ready—and perfect.

At quarter to two, the door to the reception room whose French windows opened onto the main balcony opened, and Francesca ushered Rachel in, beaming with pride.

Mateo gave her a level look, still unimpressed by her behaviour, before turning his attention to his soon-to-be wife…and then trying not to let his jaw drop.

Rachel looked…like Rachel, yet more. Her hair had been trimmed and was styled in loose waves about her face, soft and glossy. She wore minimal make-up, but it highlighted everything Mateo liked about her—her lush and rosy lips, her dark eyes with their luxuriant lashes, and cheekbones that he hadn't actually noticed before but now couldn't tear his gaze away from.

She wore a simple wrap dress in forest-green silk—a dress that clung without being too revealing and made the most of the generous curves Mateo longed to touch and explore. Her shapely calves were encased in sheer tights, and accentuated by a pair of elegant black heels.

'Well?' Her voice held a questioning lilt that bordered on uncertainty. 'Will I pass?'

'You will more than pass.' Mateo gave Francesca a grudging nod. 'I meant what I said earlier, but I will admit you have done well.'

'Thank you, Your Highness.' She bobbed a curtsey and then was gone. Rachel walked slowly towards him, grimacing a little.

'I'm tottering. I know it. I'm not used to heels.'

'All you'll have to do is step through those doors and stand still.'

She shot a worried look towards the gauze-covered windows. 'How many people are out there?'

Mateo knew there was no point in dissembling. 'Quite a few.'

Rachel nodded and ran her hands down the sides of her dress. 'Okay.' She threw back her shoulders and lifted her chin, as she'd done before when she was gathering her courage. He loved to see it.

'I don't look ridiculous, do I?' she asked in a low voice. 'You know, silk purse, sow's ear…'

'*Rachel.*' Mateo stared at her incredulously. 'You look amazing. Gorgeous, vibrant, full of life, *sexy.*' The words spilled from him with conviction; they *had* to be said.

She stared at him for a moment, her lips parting, her eyes widening. Belatedly Mateo realised how intent he'd sounded, how involved. He cleared his throat, but before he could say anything more the press officer stepped forward.

'If we could go over the schedule, Your Highness?'

'Yes, in a moment.' He waved the man aside before drawing the small black velvet box out of his jacket pocket. 'You need one more thing to complete your outfit.' Her eyes had widened at the sight of the box, and she didn't speak. Mateo opened it to reveal a blue diamond encircled with smaller white diamonds, set on a ring of white gold. 'This

is the Kallyrian Blue. It has been in the royal family for
six hundred years.'

'Oh, my goodness…' She looked up at him with genuine
panic. 'Can I please wear a fake? I cannot be responsible
for a jewel that size.'

'It is heavily insured, don't worry. And it belongs to
you now. It has always been the Queen's engagement ring.'

'Your mother…'

'Was more than happy to pass it on.'

Rachel let out a shaky breath. 'Whoo, boy.' She held
out her hand, and Mateo slipped the ring onto her finger.

'There. Perfect.'

'It's so heavy.' She let out a breathy, incredulous laugh.
'I feel like I'm doing finger weights, or something.'

'You'll get used to it.' Mateo gestured to the press officer, and he stepped forward. 'Now, the schedule?'

The next ten minutes passed quickly as they rehearsed
their brief performance—step out on the balcony, smile
and wave, and then Mateo would introduce Rachel as his
queen, with their wedding and joint coronation on Saturday to be celebrated as a national holiday.

'That's *insane*,' Rachel murmured, and the press officer
gave her an odd look.

'It's quite normal for royal weddings,' Mateo remarked
calmly.

'Your Highness, it's time!'

Mateo glanced at Rachel, who had suddenly morphed
into the proverbial deer snared by headlights. She threw
him a panicked look.

'I can't…'

'You can.' His voice was low and sure as he reached for
her hand. 'All you have to do is take a single step, smile
and wave.'

She nodded rather frantically. 'Smile and wave. Smile
and wave.'

'That's it.'

Two attendants threw open the French windows that led out to the balcony, the massed crowd visible below in a colourful blur.

'Oh, my heavens,' Rachel whispered. 'There are thousands of people down there.'

And even more watching the live video stream, but Mateo chose not to enlighten her.

'Let's do this,' he said, echoing her words from before. She gave him a small smile of recognition, and then he drew her out onto the balcony, the applause crashing over them in a deafening wave as they appeared. He turned to Rachel, his mouth curving in pleasure and pride as she offered the crowds below a radiant smile and a decidedly royal wave.

After a few moments of cheering and clapping, Mateo made his announcement, which was met with even more applause and excited calls. Then a cry rose up: *'Fili! Fili!'*

Rachel's forehead wrinkled slightly as she gave him a questioning look. She didn't know what they were calling for, but Mateo did.

Kiss.

And it seemed like the most natural thing to do, to take her in his arms, her curves fitting snugly against him, and kiss her on the lips.

CHAPTER NINE

RACHEL GAZED DOWN at the list of potential charities to support and marvelled for about the hundredth time that this was now her life.

The last three days had felt like a dream. She had, quite deliberately, chosen to enjoy all the good and ignore the worrisome or flat-out terrifying. And there was a lot of good—not least the people who surrounded her, who were determined to help her to succeed.

The day after her arrival and the announcement on the balcony, Agathe had invited Rachel to her private rooms for breakfast. Eighteen hours later, Rachel's lips had been practically still buzzing from the quick yet thorough kiss Mateo had given her, to the uproarious approval of the crowds below. He'd given her a fleeting, self-satisfied smile afterwards, his eyes glinting with both knowledge and possession, while Rachel had tottered back into the palace on unsteady legs that had had nothing to do with her heels.

She and Agathe had chatted easily over croissants and Greek yogurt withsweet golden honey and slices of succulent melon.

'I can see now more than ever that my son has made a good choice,' Agathe said with a little smile and Rachel blushed as she recalled that kiss yet again.

'It's not like that,' she felt compelled to protest. 'We're only friends. What I mean is, that's all we've been.'

'And it is a good, strong foundation for a marriage. Much better than—' She stopped abruptly, making Rachel frown in confusion.

'Much better than what?' she prompted.

'Oh, you know.' Agathe laughed lightly as she poured them both more of the strong Greek coffee. 'The usual fleeting attraction or empty charm.'

Yet as Agathe dazzled her with a determinedly bright smile, Rachel couldn't shake the feeling that she'd been about to say something else, something she'd decided not to.

Despite that brief moment of awkwardness, the rest of the conversation was easy and comfortable, and Rachel's initial concerns about being intimidated by Mateo's elegant mother proved to be as ill-founded as she might have hoped.

After breakfast, the over-the-top unreality of her situation continued as her personal assistant Monica—a neatly efficient woman in her late twenties—introduced herself and put herself entirely at Rachel's disposal.

Then came another session with Francesca, who was becoming a firm friend. Rachel knew, despite Mateo's outrage, that the stylist had been merely pragmatic in her assessment of Rachel's looks, although she apologised yet again when they met to discuss her wardrobe, and in particular her evening gown for the ball in a few days' time, and also for her wedding in less than a week.

Rachel's head continued to spin as she was outfitted beyond her wildest imaginings—yet with an eye to what she liked and felt comfortable in. Instead of shapeless trouser suits, she had chic separates in jewel-toned colours that Francesca assured her highlighted her 'flawless skin' and 'gorgeous eyes and hair'. Rachel had never heard herself described in such glowing terms, and some battered part of her that she hadn't let herself acknowledge began to heal…just as it had when Mateo told her she was gorgeous and sexy.

But surely he couldn't have meant that…?

Whether he did or not was not something Rachel let herself dwell on for too long, because either way they were getting married. She'd already told herself she could manage without love, and that included desire, too. At least the kind of head-over-heels, can't-live-without-you desire she knew Mateo didn't feel for her, no matter what he had said.

The trouble was, she felt a little of it for him. Looking at him was starting to send shivery sparks racing along her nerve-endings, and sometimes when she was watching him she had an almost irresistible urge to touch him. Run her hand along the smooth-shaven sleekness of his jaw, or trail her fingertips along the defined pecs she saw beneath the crisp cotton of his shirt.

She didn't, of course, not that she had any opportunity. In the three days since she'd arrived on Kallyria, she'd barely seen Mateo at all. Which was fine, she reminded herself more than once, because he had a country to run and she had a wedding—a whole life—to prepare for.

Rachel made a few ticks next to charities she was interested in supporting before laying the paper aside. She was in her private study, on the ground floor of the palace, a spacious and elegant room with long, sashed windows open to the fragrant gardens outside. Even though it was autumn, the air was still warm, far balmier than the best British summer.

Despite all the beauty and opulence surrounding her, Rachel felt a little flicker of homesickness that she did her best to banish. As wonderful as all this was, as kind as people were, it was still all incredibly unfamiliar. She kept feeling as if she were living someone else's life, and as small as her own had been, at least it had been hers.

At least she'd been able to email her friends and have regular updates about her mother. Her friends had been amazed and thrilled by her change in circumstances; apparently her and Mateo's kiss had been on the cover of several British tabloids. Rachel hadn't felt brave enough to look at any of it online. The thought of seeing herself splashed on the covers of national magazines was both too surreal and scary even to contemplate, much less actually inspect.

Several of her friends and former colleagues from Cambridge were coming to the wedding, all at Mateo's expense, a prospect that lifted her spirits a bit. She wasn't completely cut off from her old life, even if sometimes she felt as if she were.

Rachel rested her chin on her hand as she gazed outside. A bright tropical butterfly landed on a crimson hibiscus blossom, the sight as incredible as anything she might find in the pages of a nature magazine, and yet commonplace in this new world of hers.

She supposed she was bound to feel a bit uncertain and out of sorts, at least at the start. Everything had happened so fast, and the change had been so enormous. She wished she'd seen more of Mateo, because she recognised that he grounded her, and his reassurance would go a long way. But when she'd asked that morning, one of the palace staff had informed her he'd left for the north of the country last night, and wouldn't be back until this evening. He hadn't even told her he was leaving. And she kept telling herself not to mind.

But that didn't mean she had to sit and do nothing about it.

Rachel was busy for the rest of the afternoon, between fittings for her evening gown and wedding dress, and lessons on comportment that Agathe had gently advised her to attend. Rachel hadn't even known what those were until she'd shown up for her first one, and Agathe had begun to explain how to both sit and stand in public; how to make small talk with strangers; how to navigate a table setting with six separate forks, knives, and spoons.

At first Rachel had bristled slightly at the instruction; she wasn't a complete yokel, after all. She knew how to behave in public, surely, and she'd made small talk with plenty of people over her years in academia. Still, it hadn't taken her long to realise, when it came to royalty, she was out of her element, and Agathe was here to help her. She had only a week to become royalty-ready, and she—and Agathe—were determined to make the most of every moment.

As evening fell, the sky scattered with stars, Rachel heard the sound she hadn't even realised she'd been waiting for—the loud, persistent whirr of a helicopter. From the window of her bedroom she watched the royal helicopter touch down on the palace's helipad.

Mateo was back…and she was going to find him.

Mateo scrubbed his gritty eyes as he tried to refocus on the report he was reading. He'd barely slept last night, having spent the last forty-eight hours on the move in the north, trying to arrange a meeting with the leader of the insurgents gathering there.

Despite the unrest, the realisation of his marriage and ascension to the throne had made them more willing to consider a compromise, thank heaven. His marriage to Rachel was already paying dividends.

Rachel. He hadn't seen her in several days, and barely before that. Barely since the kiss on the balcony, when they'd as good as sealed the deal. He wondered how she was now, if she was coping with all the change and busyness. He told himself she was too sensible to have cold feet, but he wished he could see her. He'd make time tomorrow, he promised himself. At least, he'd try to.

A soft footfall outside had him tensing. The palace was nearly impregnable and teeming with security. He wasn't nervous, not exactly…just conscious that he'd spent the last few days negotiating with desperate men who were little more than terrorists, and if they wanted to put an end to him, before his wedding would be the time to do it.

'Mateo…?' The voice was soft, low, and wonderfully familiar.

'In here.'

The door creaked open and Rachel peeked her head in, smiling with relief when she saw him. 'I've been wandering around in my nightgown, which I realised is probably not the best idea. Certainly not queenly behaviour.'

'Well, you're not a queen yet.' Mateo smiled, pleasure at seeing her like honey in his veins. She was wearing an ivory dressing gown that was all silk and lace and hugged her sweet curves lovingly.

She caught him looking at her and, grimacing, spread her arms wide. 'Isn't this the most ridiculous thing ever? Francesca insists it's perfectly appropriate night-time attire for a queen, but I feel a bit like—I don't know—Lady Godiva.'

'As I recall, Lady Godiva was meant to be naked, as well as on a horse.'

'Right.' Rachel laughed huskily. 'Well, you know what I mean.'

Yes, he did. Just as he knew that with the lamplight behind her and her arms spread, Rachel might as well be naked. Out of decency he knew he should inform her of the fact, but he didn't want to embarrass her—and he was enjoying the view.

'Anyway.' She dropped her arms and moved towards him, so the robe became seemly again, more was the pity. 'Where have you been? How *are* you? I haven't seen you since—well, since the balcony.'

She blushed at that, which Mateo liked. He might have been trying to keep Rachel at arm's length, but the memory of that kiss was scorched onto his brain. And after several days of having her much farther away than his arm, he was enjoying her company far too much to put up the usual barriers.

'I know, I'm sorry. I'm afraid I have had much to command my attention.'

'You don't have to apologise.' She perched on the edge of his desk, giving him a small smile. 'You were up north?'

'Trying to set up some peace talks, yes.'

'And were you successful?'

'I believe so.'

'And now?' She nodded towards the stack of files on his desk. 'What are you working on now?'

He paused, because he had already developed the instinct to keep his royal work private, and yet this was the woman he'd hashed out every potential problem with for a decade. They'd wrangled and wrestled with countless theorems and difficulties, had debated the best way forward on countless experiments, had worked side by side most days. He'd wanted to marry her for just those reasons, and yet sharing this work did not come naturally to him.

'Mateo?'

'I'm trying to decide who to place in my cabinet of ministers,' he said at last. 'When a new king ascends to the throne, it is his privilege and right to choose his own cabinet.'

'Is it? That's a lot of power to hand to one person.'

'Indeed, but his choices must be ratified by sixty per cent of parliament, which helps to keep things balanced.'

'So what's the problem?'

Mateo gestured to the stack of files, each one containing information on potential ministers. 'I don't actually know any of these people. I've been away from Kallyria for too long.' He could not keep the recrimination from his voice. This was his fault.

'Then you can get to know them, surely.' Rachel edged closer, so her hip was brushing Mateo's hand. She leaned over so she could glance at the files, and gave him a delightful view down the front of her dressing gown.

'I can, but it's a matter of time. I need things settled and stabilised as quickly as possible.' With what was surely a herculean effort, he dragged his gaze away from Rachel's front.

'You must have some top contenders.' She reached for the first file, her narrowed gaze scanning it quickly. Mateo leaned back and watched her work, enjoying the sight—her hair spilling over her shoulders, her breasts nearly spilling out of her nightgown. He could practically hear her brain ticking over. Smart *and* sexy.

'You're looking at one of them.'

'Mm.' She continued to read the file before tossing it aside. 'No.'

'No?' Mateo repeated in surprise. 'Why not?'

'Look at his voting pattern.' She gestured to the third sheet of the file. 'Entirely inconsistent. He can't be trusted.'

Mateo leaned forward to glance at the relevant part of the document. 'I wouldn't say it's entirely inconsistent. I think it was more of knowing which way the wind was blowing.'

'You want people with principles. Otherwise they will be swayed—sometimes by you, and sometimes not.'

'True,' Mateo acknowledged. He realised how much he appreciated her input, and how much he was enjoying the sight of her. 'What about the next one?'

Over the next few hours, they went through every single file, creating piles of yes, maybe, and definitely not. Mateo was grateful for Rachel's input, and as they discussed the different candidates they fell into a familiar pattern of bouncing ideas off one another, along with the banter between them that he'd always enjoyed.

'You just like him because he went to Cambridge,' Rachel scoffed. 'You are so biased.'

'And you're not?'

'Of course not.' She smiled at him, chocolate eyes glinting, and quite suddenly as well as quite absolutely, Mateo found he had to kiss her.

'Come here,' he said softly, and Rachel's eyes widened as he reached for the sash of her robe and tugged on it.

'I'm afraid that's not going to do it,' she said with a husky laugh. 'Silk isn't strong enough.'

'But I am.' He anchored his hands on her hips as he pulled her towards him—and she came, a little breathlessly, a little nervously, but she came.

Mateo settled her on his lap, enjoying the soft, silky armful of her. Her hair brushed his jaw as she placed her hands tentatively on his shoulders.

'This feels a bit weird,' she whispered.

He chuckled. 'Good weird or bad weird?'

'Oh, definitely good.' Her anxious gaze scanned his face. 'Don't you think?'

'I definitely think,' Mateo murmured, 'that we should stop talking.'

Rachel's mouth snapped shut and Mateo angled his head so his lips were a breath away from hers. He could feel her tremble. 'Don't you think?' he whispered.

'Oh, um, yes.'

That was all he needed to settle his mouth on hers, her lips parting softly as a sigh of pleasure escaped her. Her hands clenched on his shoulders and he drew her closer so he could feel the delicious press of her breasts against his chest.

He deepened the kiss, sweeping his tongue inside the velvet softness of her mouth. She let out a little mewl, which enflamed his senses all the more. The need to kiss her became the need to possess her, with an urgency that raced through his veins and turned his insides to fire.

He slid his hand along the silky length of her thigh, spreading her legs so she was straddling him, the softest part of her pressed hard against his arousal. He flexed his hips instinctively, and she moaned against his mouth and pressed back.

He was going to explode. Literally. Figuratively. In every way possible. Mateo pressed against her once more as his brain blurred. Her hands were like claws on his shoulders, her breasts flattened against his chest. He slid his hands under her robe to fill them with those generous curves, everything in him short-circuiting.

If he didn't stop this now, he was going to humiliate himself—and her. They couldn't have their wedding night in a *chair*.

Gasping, he tore his mouth away from hers and with shaky hands set her back on the desk. Her lips were swollen from his kisses, her hair in a dark tangle about her flushed face, her nightgown in delicious disarray. Mateo dragged his hands through his hair as he sought to calm his breathing.

'We need to stop.'

'Do we?' Rachel asked shakily. She pulled her robe closed, her fingers trembling.

'Yes. This isn't…' He shook his head, appalled at how affected he was. The blood was still roaring through his veins, and he most definitely needed an ice-cold shower. He couldn't remember the last time he'd felt this way about a woman.

Yes, you can.

Abruptly he rose from the chair and stalked to the window, his back to Rachel. 'I'm sorry,' he managed to choke out. 'I shouldn't have taken such advantage.'

'Was that what you were doing?' Rachel asked with a husky yet uncertain laugh.

'We're not married yet,' Mateo stated flatly.

'I'm a grown-up, Mateo, and we're getting married in

three days. I think it was allowed.' She sounded wry, but also confused. He still couldn't look at her.

Their relationship wasn't supposed to be like this. Yes, he enjoyed their camaraderie, and the physical attraction was an added bonus he hadn't expected. But the way his need for her had consumed him? The way it had obliterated all rational thought?

No, that wasn't something he was willing to feel. He could not sacrifice his self-control to his marriage.

'You should go to bed,' he said, his voice brusque, and a long silence ensued. He waited, not willing to turn, and then finally he heard the swish of silk as she slid off the table.

'Goodnight, Mateo,' she said softly, and then he heard the click of the door closing as she left the room.

CHAPTER TEN

RACHEL GAZED AT her reflection anxiously as the flurry of nerves in her stomach threatened to make their way up her throat. In just fifteen minutes she was going to enter the palace ballroom on Mateo's arm, and be presented to all Kallyrian society as his bride-to-be.

Their wedding was in less than forty-eight hours, a fact that kept bouncing off Rachel's brain, refusing to penetrate. In forty-eight hours they would be *married*, and then crowned King and Queen in a joint ceremony.

A fact which would have filled her with excitement last night, when she and Mateo had worked together on the list of potential cabinet ministers, and then he'd kissed her.

Oh, how he'd kissed her. Rachel had never been kissed like that in her life, and she'd been in a ferment of desire since, longing to be kissed again—and more. So much more. To feel his hands on her, his mouth possessing her, his gloriously hard body beneath her…

But since he'd rather unceremoniously pushed her off his lap, Mateo had avoided her like the proverbial plague. At least, it felt that way. Rachel told herself he had to be busy, but she knew it was more than that, after the way he'd ended their kiss and turned his back, quite literally, to her.

She had no idea what had made him back off so abruptly, but the fact that he had filled her with both disappointment and fear. Was she a clumsy kisser? Heaven knew, it was perfectly possible. It wasn't as if she'd had loads of experience. Or maybe he'd gone off her for some reason—when he'd touched her? She knew she was a little overweight. Maybe Mateo now knew it too.

The thought made her stomach clench as she frowned at her reflection, all her old insecurities, the ones she'd fought so hard to master, rising up in her again. Whatever it was, he'd ended the kiss and then avoided her ever since, so she hadn't seen him from that moment to this. At least, she hoped she'd see him in this moment—they were meant to enter the ball together, after all, in just a few minutes.

Taking a deep breath, Rachel ran her hands down the sides of her gown, a fairy-tale dress if there ever was one. Made of bronze silk, it was strapless with a nipped-in waist and a delightfully full skirt that shimmered every time she moved. The dress was complemented with a parure from the Kallyrian crown jewels—a tiara made of topaz and diamonds, with a matching necklace, bracelet, and teardrop diamond earrings. She truly was Cinderella; the only question was when and if midnight would strike.

A knock sounded on the door of her bedroom, and, with her heart fluttering along with her nerves, Rachel croaked, 'Come in.'

The door opened and Mateo stood there, looking devastatingly handsome in white tie and tails. They were the perfect foil for his olive skin and black hair, his eyes an impossibly bright blue-green in his tanned face.

'Well?' Rachel asked shakily as she straightened her shoulders. 'Will I do?'

'You look stunning.' The compliment, delivered with such quiet sincerity, made a lump form in her throat.

Why did you push me away? She longed to ask, but didn't dare. She wasn't brave or strong enough to hear the answer.

'These jewels are stunning,' she said, nervously touching one of her earrings. 'When Francesca showed them to me, I couldn't believe I was meant to wear them.'

'Who else should wear them?' Mateo countered. 'You are Queen.'

'Technically, I'm not. Not for another forty-eight hours.'

'It is as good as done. Tonight, in the eyes of the world, you are my Queen.'

Rachel shook her head slowly. 'I feel like I'm living in a dream.'

'Is that a bad thing?' Mateo asked, his gaze fastened on hers.

'No, but the thing with dreams is…you have to wake up.'

'Maybe with this one you don't. Maybe it will go on for ever.'

She laughed uncertainly. 'No dream lasts for ever, Mateo.'

He acknowledged her point with a nod. 'True.'

What, Rachel wondered, were they really talking about? She felt an undercurrent to their conversation, to the tension tautening the air between them. He extended his hand, and she took it, the feel of his warm, dry palm under hers sending little shocks along her arm. She would never stop responding to him, and yet it seemed he could turn his physical response to her off like a tap.

She pushed the thought away. She had enough insecurity to deal with already, appearing in public, knowing there would be whispers and rumours, criticisms as well as compliments. It was the nature of being a public figure, which, amazingly, she had now become.

'Ready?' Mateo asked softly, and she nodded.

They walked in silence from her bedroom in the palace's east wing, along the plushly carpeted corridor to the double staircase that led down to the palace's main entrance hall. The hall had been cleared for their entrance, save for a few security men flanking the doors to the ballroom, where a thousand guests were waiting.

Dizziness assailed Rachel and she nearly stumbled in the heels she still wasn't used to wearing.

'Breathe,' Mateo murmured, his hand steady on her elbow.

'You try breathing when you're wearing knickers that are nearly cutting you in half,' Rachel returned tartly, and was gratified to see his mouth quirk in a smile. No matter how Mateo did or did not feel about her physically, Rachel didn't want to lose his friendship. As he'd said before, it was a good foundation for a marriage. She needed to remember that. She needed to remind herself of how important it was.

'Here we go,' Mateo said, and two white-gloved footmen opened the double doors to the ballroom. Taking a deep breath, Rachel held her head high as she sailed into the room on Mateo's arm.

The crowd in the ballroom parted like the Red Sea as they entered under the glittering lights of a dozen chandeliers. The guests naturally formed an aisle that Mateo and Rachel walked down, hands linked and held aloft.

'We'll have to dance,' Mateo murmured. 'The first waltz. It is expected.'

'*Dance?*' Rachel whispered back as she nearly tripped on the trailing hem of her gown. 'No one told me that! I don't dance.'

'It's a simple box step. Follow my lead and you'll be fine.' They were almost at the end of the aisle, and panic was icing Rachel's insides.

'No, really,' she said out of the side of her mouth, her gaze still straight ahead. She felt like a bad ventriloquist. 'I. Don't. Dance. At *all*. Two left feet would be a kind way of putting it.'

Why hadn't Agathe covered this in her comportment lessons? Or had she just assumed that Rachel could dance?

She risked a glance at Mateo's face; he wore the faint smile he'd had on since they'd entered the ballroom. He was so handsome it hurt. And she was about to humiliate herself publicly in front of a thousand people, and, really, the whole world. She was wearing a dress worthy of Beauty in *Beauty and the Beast*, but in this case she felt like the beast.

'Mateo—'

'Just follow my lead.'

'I *can't*—'

'Trust me.' The two words, simply spoken and heartfelt, were enough to allay her fears, or almost. Whatever he had planned, she knew she would follow along.

The crowds parted to reveal an empty expanse of gleaming parquet, a string orchestra poised at the other end. As Mateo escorted her to the centre of the floor, they struck up a familiar waltz tune: 'Gold and Silver'.

Rachel stared at him in blind panic.

'Put your feet on top of mine,' Mateo murmured, so low she almost didn't hear the words.

'On top? I'll kill your feet—'

'Do it.'

She did, and Mateo didn't even wince as she practically crushed his toes.

'Hold on,' he said, slipping one hand around her waist, and the next thing Rachel knew she was flying around the dance floor, her skirt swinging out in an elegant bell as Mateo moved them both around in a perfectly elegant waltz.

'Are you in agony?' she whispered as he arced around, carrying her easily without even seeming to do it.

'Smile.'

She did. Two more minutes of soaring music and graceful moves when she felt as if she were flying, and then finally, thankfully, the waltz was over. The crowd erupted into applause and Mateo looked at Rachel and winked.

* * *

His feet were killing him, it was true, but the sight of Rachel looking at him in wonder and admiration and maybe even something more made it worth it. More than worth it. The look she gave him could have powered a city. Or perhaps the feeling inside him could have.

Whatever it was, Mateo felt like a king—of the whole world.

'Your Highness.' A local dignitary, someone whose name Mateo had forgotten, approached him with a bow. 'That was exceptional. Please let me introduce you to my wife…'

The next hour passed in a blur of introductions and small talk. Just as he'd known she would, Rachel shone. She wasn't one to give tinkling laughs or arch looks; she was far too genuine for that. But she talked to everyone as if she wanted to, and she listened as if she was really interested in what they had to say. Mateo was proud to have her on his arm and, more importantly, she seemed happy to be there. The evening, he knew, would be deemed a great success.

He didn't think anything of it when Rachel was escorted into dinner by Lukas Diakis, a senior minister from his father's cabinet. Nor when she listened politely to his Aunt Karolina, her gaze darting occasionally to him. He smiled back every time, but her own smiles became smaller and smaller until they were barely a stretching of his lips, and then they weren't there at all, because she'd stopped looking at him.

Mateo told himself not to be concerned. What on earth could a doddering retired minister or an elderly spinster aunt possibly say to Rachel to make her seem so thoughtful and pale?

Still Mateo couldn't shake his unease through the six-course meal. Even though they were at opposite ends of the table, he felt her disquiet. Or was he just being fanciful? It wasn't as if they had some sort of mental or, heaven forbid, emotional connection. He didn't even want that.

At the end of the meal Rachel left first, arm in arm with Diakis. Mateo watched them go, but by the time he'd made it back to the ballroom she was lost in the crowd and annoyance bit at him. She was his wife. He'd already told her they would spend much of the evening apart, mingling and chatting, but now he wanted her by his side.

He needed her there, which would have alarmed him except right now he didn't care. He just wanted to find her.

Another hour of mingling passed, endless and interminable. Occasionally Mateo glimpsed Rachel across the room, but it would have been impolite, if not downright impossible, to storm through the crowds and approach her. Besides, as the minutes ran into hours, Mateo managed to convince himself that nothing was amiss…and he certainly didn't *need* anything or anyone. He breathed a sigh of relief at the thought.

Finally the evening came to an end. It was two in the morning, the sky full of stars, as the guests departed in a laughing stream, while Mateo, Rachel, and his mother all stood by the door, saying their official farewells. Rachel looked ready to wilt.

'Such a success!' Agathe kissed Rachel on both cheeks. 'You were marvellous, my dear. Absolutely marvellous.' She turned to Mateo. 'Wasn't it a success, Mateo? An absolute triumph!'

'It was.' He glanced searchingly at Rachel, but her gaze flitted away. What was going on?

'I must say goodnight,' Agathe said on a sigh. 'I am absolutely exhausted, as you both must be.' She kissed Mateo's cheek. 'You've done so well.'

'Thank you, Mitera.'

His mother headed upstairs, and the staff melted away

to clean up after the ball. They were alone in the great entrance hall, the space stretching into shadows under the dimmed lights of the chandelier high above. From outside someone laughed, and a car door slammed before an engine purred away.

'You really were wonderful,' Mateo told her.

'Your feet must be killing you.' Rachel reached up and took out the teardrop earrings. 'These are lovely, but they're agony to wear. I haven't worn earrings since my uni days.'

'You look amazing.'

'Thank you.' She still wasn't looking at him, and Mateo bit back his annoyance. What game was she playing?

'I think I'll go to bed.' Rachel let out a little laugh that sounded brittle as she started towards the staircase. 'I think I could fall asleep right here.'

'It's been a long evening.'

'Yes.' She glanced back at him, like a beautiful flame in her bronze gown with the topazes and diamonds glinting in her hair and at her throat and wrists. 'Goodnight, Mateo.' She almost sounded sad, and that irritated him further.

They'd had a brilliant evening, they were getting married the day after tomorrow, and she was playing some passive-aggressive game of showing him she was sad without actually saying it.

'Why don't you just tell me what's going on, Rachel?' His voice came out hard, harder than he'd meant it to, but he'd never liked these games. Not with Cressida, when he'd so often had to guess the reason for her pique, and not with Rachel. Not with anyone.

Her eyes widened as she stilled, one hand on the banister. 'What…what do you mean?'

'You know what I mean.'

She stiffened, her eyes flashing with affront at his tone. 'I really don't.'

'Are you sure about that?' Mateo knew he was handling this all wrong, but hours of wondering and worrying that something was amiss had strung him tighter than he'd realised. He was ready to snap now, and it was hard to pull back.

'Yes, I'm quite sure. I'm tired, Mateo, and I want to go to bed.'

So he should let her go. He knew that, and yet somehow he couldn't. 'Why did you keep giving me looks all evening?'

'Looks?'

'During dinner. As if...' He struggled to put a name to the expression in her eyes. 'As if you were disappointed in me.' The realisation that that was indeed what her look had been was a heaviness in his gut.

Recognition flashed in Rachel's eyes, and Mateo knew he was right. Something was wrong...and she didn't want to tell him what it was. She wanted him to guess, and beg, and plead. He'd been here before, and he hated it. He wouldn't play that game.

'You know what? Never mind.' He shook his head, the movement abrupt, dismissive. 'I don't care what it is. If you can't be bothered to tell me, I can't be bothered to find out.'

'Why are you so angry?' She sounded bewildered, and rightly so. He was overreacting, he knew it, and yet he still couldn't keep himself from it. Because this was bringing back too many old, painful memories, memories he'd suppressed for fifteen years. He really didn't want them rising up now.

'I'm not angry.' His tone made his words a lie.

She gave a little shrug, as if the point wasn't worth arguing, which it probably wasn't. His hands balled into fists at his sides.

'Rachel...'

'Fine, Mateo, if you want to do this now.' She let out a weary sigh that shuddered through her whole body before she gave him a look that was both direct and sorrowful. 'Who is Cressida?'

CHAPTER ELEVEN

SHE HADN'T WANTED to confront him. She'd told herself there was no point. And yet Mateo had forced an argument, much to her own shock, because he'd never acted in such an emotional and unreasonable way before. And now they were here, and she'd asked the question that had been burning on her tongue since Karolina had patted her hand at dinner and said in a dreamy way, *'You're so much better for him than Cressida, my dear.'*

When Rachel had smiled politely in return, the conversation had moved on, but then the man who had escorted her from the table had said something similar.

'Thank God he didn't marry Cressida.'

And Rachel had started to feel…unmoored. She couldn't have explained it better than that, that the sudden emergence of this unknown woman that Mateo must have considered marrying had left her feeling entirely and unsettlingly adrift. And so she'd asked, and now she wasn't sure she wanted to know the answer.

Who is Cressida?

Mateo stared at her unsmilingly, his hands still in fists by his sides. 'Where did you hear that name?' he asked tonelessly, but with a seething undercurrent of anger that Rachel sensed all the way from the stairs.

'Does it matter?'

'Where?'

She stiffened at his tone. She'd never seen Mateo like this, and it frightened her. It made her wonder if she knew him at all.

Who *was* Cressida?

Did she really want to know?

'Karolina told me,' she said. 'And then Lukas Diakis, the minister.'

'What did they say?'

She stared at him, willing the fierce mask to crack. Why was he looking so terribly ferocious? She shrugged, deciding to play it straight, as she played everything. She was never one for machinations, manipulations, a sly tone, a leading question, no matter what Mateo had just accused her of.

'Karolina said she thought I was better for you than Cressida, and Lukas said he was glad you didn't marry her.' Mateo's face darkened, his brows drawing together in a black slash. Rachel took a step backwards on the stairs and nearly stumbled on her gown.

'They should not have spoken of her.'

His icy tone should have kept her from saying anything, but Rachel sensed that if they didn't talk about Cressida now, they never would.

'Who is she, Mateo? Why have you never mentioned her before?'

'Why should I have?'

'She's obviously someone important to you.' Rachel struggled to keep her tone reasonable even though she had an almost uncontrollable urge to burst into tears.

It was past two in the morning, she'd had the longest and most stressful night of her life, wonderful as it had been, and she knew she was feeling far too fragile to handle a big discussion right now...just as she knew they needed to have it. 'You dated her,' she said, making it not quite a question.

'Yes.' Mateo's mouth thinned to a hard, unforgiving line. 'It was a long time ago. It's not important.'

Not important? Was he serious?

'She seemed like someone important to you, judging from your reaction now.'

'My reaction,' Mateo informed her in as chilly a tone as she'd ever heard from him, 'was because my relatives and civil servants were gossiping about me like a bunch of fishwives.'

'It wasn't like that—'

'It was exactly like that.' Mateo strode past her, up the stairs. Rachel watched him go with a sense of incredulity. This was so unlike Mateo, it was almost funny. He wasn't this cold, autocratic, ridiculous dictator of a man. He just *wasn't*.

And yet right now he was.

'Why won't you tell me about her, Mateo?' she called up the stairs. 'We're about to be *married*—'

He did not break his stride as he answered. 'It is not to be discussed.'

Rachel watched him disappear up the stairs, dazed by how quickly things had spiralled out of control. Alone in the soaring entrance hall, she strained her ears to hear the distant sound of Mateo's bedroom door closing.

She glanced around the empty hall and swallowed hard. She felt numb inside, too numb to cry. Had they just had their first argument?

Or their last?

Slowly she walked up the stairs. She was still in her gown and jewels, but the clock had definitely struck midnight. The party was over.

Francesca was waiting for her in her bedroom, eager to hear about the party as she helped her undress.

'You wowed them all, I am sure,' she exclaimed. 'So beautiful…'

Rachel forced a smile as she bent her head and allowed Francesca to undo the clasp of her necklace. She remained quiet as she took off the rest of her jewels, and the stylist put them away in a black velvet case that would be returned directly to the vault where all the crown jewels were kept.

Then Francesca undid the zip of her gown, and Rachel carefully stepped out of it, and into the waiting robe.

'I drew you a bath,' Francesca said as she swathed the dress in a protective bag. 'I know it's late, but I thought you might want to relax.'

'Thank you, Francesca, you're a saint.' Since their first meeting, when Mateo had glowered at and almost fired her, Francesca had proved to be a stalwart stylist and a good friend. Rachel was grateful for the other woman's support.

With the dress draped over one arm, Francesca frowned at her. 'Is everything all right?'

Rachel managed another wan smile. 'Just tired. Exhausted, really.' She considered asking Francesca if she knew who Cressida was, but she could imagine Mateo's reaction if he discovered she was asking around. Clearly, for him, the woman was off-limits to everyone, even Rachel. Especially Rachel.

'Have a bath and get some sleep,' Francesca advised. 'It's a big day tomorrow.'

'Another one?' Every day had been a big day.

'We have the final fitting for your dress, a rehearsal for the ceremony, and a dinner in the evening with about thirty guests.'

Rachel's head drooped at the thought of it. 'Right. Okay.'

'You're sure everything is all right?' Francesca looked at her, worry clouding her eyes.

For a second Rachel wanted to confide in the other woman. She wanted to confess to all the doubts that were now crowding her heart and mind.

I don't know if I can cope with this. I'm not sure I'm queen material after all. I'm afraid the man I'm about to marry is still in love with another woman.

'I'm fine,' Rachel said as firmly as she could. 'Thank you.'

Francesca patted her on the shoulder and left the room, and Rachel sagged visibly once the woman had gone, unable to put up a front any longer.

She nearly fell asleep in the bath, the hot water doing its best to loosen the knots tightening her shoulder blades. When she finally got out of the bathroom, dripping wet and aching with both tiredness and sorrow, she fell across the bed, pulling the duvet across her, her hair still in a wet tangle, and didn't stir until bright autumn sunshine was pouring through the windows whose shutters she'd forgotten to close.

In the morning light, everything seemed a little better. At least, Rachel felt more resolved. Last night she'd been blindsided by Mateo's sudden change in attitude, the way he'd morphed from the charming, easy-going man she'd known into some parody of a cold, frosty stranger. She knew the pressures of his kingship weighed on him heavily, but he'd never taken that tone with her before, and Rachel had no intention of setting some sort of awful precedent now.

She showered and dressed, blow-dried her hair into artful waves and chose one of her new outfits to boost her confidence—a pair of wide-leg trousers and a cowl-necked topped in soft maroon jersey. Her engagement ring glinted as she moved, reminding her of the promises they'd already made to each other. They'd get through this. They were getting married tomorrow, after all.

Finding Mateo, however, was not as easy as Rachel hoped. After a buffet breakfast in the palace dining room by herself, she was whisked away by Monica, her personal assistant, to the final fitting of her wedding gown.

Rachel loved the pure simplicity of the white silk gown, with its edging of antique lace on the sleeves and hem, and the long veil of matching lace. When she wore it, she truly felt like a princess. A queen.

After the fitting, Monica met with her in the study Rachel was to call her own, going over the schedule of events on tomorrow's big day. Rachel scanned down the list— wedding ceremony and coronation in the cathedral across the square, and then a walkabout through the plaza to greet well-wishers before returning to the palace for a wedding breakfast. Then a turn around the city in a horse and carriage before returning to the palace for a ball, and finally spending their wedding night there in a private suite. Considering Mateo's responsibilities, there would be no honeymoon.

'That looks like a very full day,' Rachel said with a smile, trying to ignore the butterflies swarming in her middle. Even though she was getting a little bit used to being in the public eye, the thought of all those events made her feel dizzy with anxiety. What if she tripped and fell flat on her face? What if she was sick? Considering how nervous she was, she knew it was perfectly possible. She could utterly humiliate herself in front of thousands of people, not to mention those watching from their homes, since everything was to be broadcast live.

Don't think about it, she instructed herself. *When the times comes, you'll just do it. You'll have to.*

She turned to Monica with as bright a smile as she could manage. 'Do you know where the king is?'

The wind streamed by him, making his eyes water, as Mateo bent low over the horse and gave it its head. The world was a blur of sea, sand, and sky as the stallion raced over the dunes.

When he'd woken up that morning after a few hours of restless sleep, he'd known he needed to get out of the palace. Out of his own head. And riding one of the many horses in the royal stables was the perfect way to do it.

Mateo hadn't been on a horse in years, but as soon as he'd settled himself atop Mesonyktio, the Greek word for midnight, he'd felt as if he were coming home. And feeling the world fall away, even if just for a few minutes, was a blessed and much-needed relief.

He was still angry with himself for the way he'd handled the altercation with Rachel. He was also angry with his meddling relatives and colleagues for mentioning Cressida; he'd only brought her to Kallyria once, fifteen years ago, but they remembered.

He remembered. He'd been so besotted. So sure that she was the only, the ultimate, woman for him.

Of course she hadn't been. His gut tightened and he leaned farther over Mesonyktio's head, letting the wind and speed chase away the last of his tumultuous thoughts.

By the time he arrived back at the stables, he was tired enough not to have to think too much about last night, or how he regretted the way he'd handled that tense and unexpected situation with Rachel.

He slid off Mesonyktio's back and led him by the reins into the dim coolness of the palace stables, only to stiffen when he heard a familiar voice say quietly, 'Mateo.'

He blinked in the gloom, breathing in the smell of horse and hay, and then focused his gaze on Rachel, standing in front of him, chin tilted, eyes direct.

'What are you doing here?'

'I wanted to talk to you.'

He drew a deep breath, forcing himself to relax. 'All right. Let me see to the horse first.'

She nodded and stepped out of the way as he brought Mesonyktio to his stall and began to unfasten his saddle.

'I didn't even know you rode.'

'Not much time or space for it, back in Cambridge.'

'No, I suppose not.'

She remained quiet as he rubbed the horse down, taking his time to delay the moment when he'd have to face her. He should apologise. He knew that. Yet somehow the words wouldn't come.

Finally there was nothing more to do with Mesonyktio, and Mateo knew he could not delay the inevitable. He turned around and faced his bride-to-be. She looked lovely in a pair of tailored trousers and a soft top in burgundy that made the most of her curves. Her hair was loose about her shoulders, her eyes wide and dark and fastened on him.

'I want to talk about last night,' she said without preamble. Rachel was no shrinking violet, never had been. She had always been willing to be confrontational at work, politely so, but still. Mateo should have known she wouldn't let last night go, no matter how foreboding he might have seemed.

'I'm sorry if I seemed a bit abrupt,' he said. 'It's a sensitive subject.'

Her eyebrows rose. 'You seemed a bit abrupt? Nice try, Mateo, but I'm not having that.'

Despite the tension coiling inside him, he almost smiled. 'You're not?'

'No. We're about to be married.' She glanced at her watch, an elegant strip of diamond-encrusted gold that was part of her trousseau. 'In less than twenty-four hours. I'm not having you go all glowery on me and refuse to discuss something that is clearly important. The whole point of marrying me, or so you said, was because we were friends, and we liked and trusted one another. So don't pull the Scary King act on me, okay?'

'I don't think "glowery" is actually a word.'

'Well, it should be. And if it was in the dictionary, you'd be next to the definition.' She blew out a breath. 'So, look. Just tell me what the deal with Cressida is.'

Even now, when she'd played her hand straight, the way she always did, he was reluctant to reveal the truth, and what details he gave her he would do so sparingly.

'I told you all you need to know, Rachel. I dated her back in university. We were both young. The relationship ended.'

'There must be more to it than that.'

'I don't ask you about your relationship with that man who broke your heart,' he retorted, and she flinched.

'He didn't break my heart. I told you that. I said I was never in love with him.' She paused, seeming to weigh whether she wanted to ask the question he already knew was coming. 'Were you in love with her? Cressida?'

Mateo stood still, doing his best to keep his face bland, his body relaxed. It took effort. 'I suppose I was. Yes.'

She nodded slowly, as if absorbing a blow. 'I wish you had told me before.'

'Before? When, exactly?'

'When you asked me to marry you.' A crumpled note of hurt entered her voice, and she took a breath, clearly striving to hold onto her composure.

'Would it have made a difference?'

'I don't know, but you know as well as I do, Mateo, that when a scientist does not have all the relevant information regarding an experiment, they cannot draw an accurate conclusion.'

Mateo folded his arms and attempted to stare her down. He should have known he wouldn't succeed. Rachel had never been one to be cowed. 'What happened before has no relevance on the present or the future, Rachel. Our future. It was a long time ago. Fifteen years.'

'Yet you can't say her name,' she said softly. 'You haven't said it once since we've started talking about her.'

Everything in him tightened. 'I admit, it was a painful time. I do not wish to revisit it.'

'So fifteen years on, you still have trouble speaking about it? About her?' She shook her head sorrowfully. 'That does make a difference, Mateo.'

'Why?' he demanded. 'It ended a long time ago, Rachel. It doesn't matter any more.'

'Is she the reason you want a loveless marriage?' Rachel asked stonily.

'I didn't say that—'

'You as good as did. One based on friendship and trust, rather than love. That's been clear all along, Mateo. You told me you weren't interested in falling in love. I just... I didn't realise it was because you'd been in love before.'

He flinched at that, but did not deny it.

'So.' Rachel nodded slowly. 'That's how it is.'

'This really doesn't need to change things, Rachel. Like I said, it was a long time ago.'

'What happened?' Rachel asked. 'I deserve to know that much. How did it end? Did she leave you?'

Mateo struggled to keep his expression even, his voice neutral. 'She died.'

'Oh.' The sound that escaped her was soft and sad. 'I'm so sorry.' He nodded jerkily, not willing to say more. To reveal more. 'So if she hadn't died...' Rachel said quietly, almost to herself, and Mateo did not finish that thought. She nodded again, then looked up at him. 'You should have told me,' she stated quietly. 'No matter how long ago it happened. I should have known.'

'I didn't realise it mattered.'

'Then you are not nearly as emotionally astute as I thought you were,' she retorted with dignity. 'You talked about how you trusted me, Mateo, but what about whether I can trust you?'

'This is not about trust—'

'Isn't it?' The two words were quiet and sad, and she didn't wait for his answer as she walked out of the stables.

CHAPTER TWELVE

TODAY WAS HER wedding day. Rachel gazed into the mirror at her princess-like reflection and tried to banish the foreboding that fell over her like a dark cloud.

Ever since her confrontation with Mateo in the stables yesterday, she'd felt as if she were walking under it, blundering forward in a storm of uncertainty, trying to make peace with this new knowledge of her husband-to-be, and what it might mean for their marriage.

So he'd had his heart broken. He'd been deeply in love with a woman, and she'd died. It wasn't a deal-breaker, surely, but Rachel would have appreciated knowing and adjusting to the fact before she was about to walk down the aisle.

No matter what Mateo might insist, it made a difference knowing he'd loved and lost rather than believing he'd never been interested in loving at all.

All through yesterday, as she'd gone through the motions of their wedding rehearsal, and chatted over dinner with dignitaries whose names she couldn't remember, a battle had been raging in her head.

Should I? Shouldn't I?

But at the end of the day, when she'd gone up to her suite of rooms and seen her wedding gown swathed in plastic and ready for her to wear in the morning, she'd known there wasn't a battle at all.

Her wedding was the next day. Her marriage was already set in motion. She had a *coin* with her name minted on it, as Mateo had informed her that evening. She couldn't walk away from this, just because the situation was a little bit messier than she'd anticipated. There was far, far more riding on this marriage than her own happiness.

And yet…it caused a pain like grief deep inside her to know that Mateo had loved another woman, loved her enough to not want to love someone else ever again. It was, she told herself, a grief she could get used to, and would ultimately have to live with, but a grief, nonetheless.

Since their confrontation in the stables, Rachel had felt a coolness between her and Mateo that definitely hadn't been there before, and it saddened her. It was no way to start a marriage, to say vows, with this tension between them.

And yet that was how it seemed it was going to be.

She'd woken that morning to bright sunshine and pealing bells—apparently they would ring all morning, until the wedding. Rachel tried to tune them out as Francesca helped her dress, giving her understated make-up and sweeping her hair into an elegant up-do.

'This feels crazy,' Rachel murmured numbly as she stood in front of the mirror and gazed at the vision she beheld. 'That can't be me.'

'It is,' Francesca said with a wide smile. 'You look utterly fabulous.'

'All thanks to you.'

'Not all,' the stylist answered with a wink. 'But I'll take a *tiny* bit of credit.'

Rachel moved to the window that overlooked the front of the palace and the large square that stretched to the cathedral on the other side, already crowded with spectators even though it was still several hours until the ceremony.

Many looked as if they had set up early, with camping

chairs and flasks of coffee, and others were waving flags or banners. All for her…her and Mateo.

Since coming to Kallyria, Rachel had been too busy and overwhelmed to look online and find out what the media was saying about her and Mateo, and in truth she wasn't sure she wanted to know. Now, however, as she eyed a banner that said simply *True Love*, she wondered.

'Francesca,' she asked slowly. 'What are they saying about Mateo and me?'

The stylist, who was tidying away the many cosmetics she'd used to create Rachel's natural look, glanced up with an arched eyebrow. 'Hmm?'

'What are they saying about us? Are they asking why we're marrying?' Rachel caught sight of a sign that read *A Real-life Fairy Tale*!

'Well…' Francesca paused as she mentally reviewed all she'd heard and read. 'Nothing bad, if you're worried about that. Everyone thinks it's incredibly romantic that you've worked together for so long and that now he's king Mateo wants you by his side. I mean, it *is* romantic, right?'

Rachel forced her lips upwards in what she suspected was a parody of a smile. 'Right.'

'I mean, Mateo could have chosen anyone…but he wanted you. People are saying you're the luckiest woman in the world.'

'Right,' Rachel said again. She turned back to the window, not wanting Francesca to see the expression on her face.

The luckiest woman in the world.

Why did she not feel that way right now? Why did she feel as if she were living a lie?

A short while later, it was time to go. Francesca arranged her veil to spread out behind her as Rachel headed down the staircase to the palace's entrance hall, for a round of official photographs.

Her cheeks ached from smiling, and the heavy satin of the dress felt as if it was weighing her down, as Rachel posed for photograph after photograph. This was what she'd agreed to, she reminded herself. She was lucky, even if she was filled with doubts right now. Mateo was a good man, a man she liked and trusted, even if love was never going to come into their particular equation. She had more, so much more, than most women of the world. She certainly wasn't going to complain.

But her heart felt as heavy as her dress as she prepared to make her official exit from the palace, and walk alone across the crowd-packed square to the cathedral where her groom—and a thousand guests—awaited.

As the doors were flung open, the bright sunlight streamed in, making Rachel squint. Francesca's hand was at her back, her voice a murmur in her ear.

'Chin up, eyes straight ahead. Nod, don't wave, in case you drop your bouquet.'

Rachel glanced down at the magnificent selection of white roses and lilies she'd been given for the photos. She gulped. 'Okay.'

'Walk slowly—right foot forward, feet together, and so on. It will feel a lot slower than you're used to. Count it in your head.'

'Okay,' Rachel said again. She wished they'd rehearsed this part, and not just what happened in the church, but it had sounded simple when the square was empty. All she had to do was walk across it.

'Go,' Francesca urged, and gave her a little push. Rachel stepped through the palace doors. The noise greeted her first, like a towering wave crashing over her. They were cheering. She, the nobody who had been overlooked by everyone for most of her life, even by her parents, now had what felt like the entire world screaming their approval. It was daunting, terrifying even, but also, surprisingly and amazingly, wonderful.

'Go,' Francesca whispered, and Rachel started down the shallow steps towards the square, her gown fanning behind her in an elegant arc of lace-edged satin. She knew she was meant to keep her gaze straight ahead, on the path that had been cleared through the crowd, with crowd barriers keeping everyone at bay, but she couldn't help but meet the gazes of some of the people who had queued for hours simply to be here, to see her.

'Queen Rachel!' someone called, and she nearly jerked in surprise. Queen Rachel. If that didn't sound crazily weird…

'You're so beautiful!' someone else shouted, and she let her gaze move amidst the crowd, settling on as many faces as she could and offering them her smile. Her bouquet was too heavy for her to free one hand to wave, and she hoped her smile was enough.

'Thank you,' she heard herself saying. And then, *'Efharisto. Efharisto!'*

The cheers continued all the way across the square, which felt like a hundred miles instead of the equivalent in metres. On impulse, at the doors to the cathedral, she handed her bouquet to a waiting attendant and lifted her hand in a wave that sent the crowd cheering even more wildly. Then she reached for her bouquet and headed into the cool, hushed interior of the cathedral.

She blinked in the candle-flickering gloom, the brightly painted icons of saints visible high in the shadows of the huge cathedral. She took in the pews and pews filled with guests in their wedding finery, and there, at the start of a very long aisle, Mateo, standing by himself, looking devastating in a white tie and tails, bright red and blue royal regalia pinned to his chest. A king. *Her* king. Waiting to escort her down the aisle and to the ceremony.

For a second, poised on the threshold of her entire life, Rachel hesitated as a thousand thoughts tilted and slid through her mind. Her hands tightened on the bouquet as organ music crashed and swelled.

This was happening. She was doing this. *They* were doing this. And she hoped and prayed that somehow it would be the right thing for them both.

Mateo's gaze was fixed on his bride as she turned to face him. Her veil flowed over her shoulders in a lace river, her dress belling out behind in her in a floaty arc of satin. He reached out a hand and, with her gaze fixed on him, she took it. Her fingers slid across his and then tightened. The moment felt suspended, stretching on in significance, before Mateo turned and together they began to walk down the aisle.

He glanced at her as they walked—her chin tilted proudly, her shoulders back, her gaze straight ahead. She was elegant. Regal. Magnificent. Mateo's heart swelled with pride and something else, something dangerously deeper, as they walked towards the altar. All the unspoken tension and coolness that had existed between them for the last two days fell away in that moment. They were walking towards their future together, and she would soon be his.

The ceremony passed in a dazed blur. As was tradition, every vow was repeated three times, and wedding crowns of laurel placed on their heads, rings slipped onto their right hands, the hand of blessing. The music swelled and Mateo lifted her veil. She smiled at him tremulously, everything she felt and more in her eyes. He kissed her, barely a brush of her lips, but it felt like fireworks exploding in his head.

How was he going to stand this? How was he going to maintain that necessary distance for his own safety, as well as hers?

The questions fell into the tumult of his mind and were

lost as the ceremony continued, into their coronation. Now husband and wife, they ascended the steps of the cathedral and knelt, hand in hand, before the two thrones there.

The bishop placed the historic crowns on their heads; the weight was surprising, and Mateo glanced at Rachel, a tremor rippling through him at the beautiful sight of her—wearing both a crown and a wedding dress. His bride. His Queen.

Then the ceremony was over, the crowns removed, and the music started again. After helping her to rise, Mateo escorted her back down the aisle. They were married. Husband and wife, for ever.

'Did that actually happen?' Rachel asked shakily as they stood on the steps of the cathedral, blinking in the bright sunlight.

'It most certainly did.' Mateo glanced down at the ring sparkling on his hand. He felt changed in a way he hadn't expected, on a molecular level. His whole *being* was changed, as if he'd undergone a chemical reaction without realising. He could never go back, and neither could Rachel.

'What do we do now?' Rachel asked. 'I know I've been told, but everything feels different now.'

'It does, doesn't it?' He felt a rush of gratitude and even joy that she felt the same as he did. They were *changed*.

'I mean, there's people, for one.' She gestured to the crowds who had been waiting for them to emerge. 'It's completely different, to walk across that square when it's filled with people.'

'Of course.' Mateo looked away, annoyed with himself for rushing to such a stupid, sentimental conclusion. They were changed. Right.

'So should we go? Or do we wait?'

'We can go.' His jaw tightened as he reached for her hand. 'Might as well get this over with.'

Hurt flashed in her eyes as she looked at him. 'Is that really how you see it, Mateo?' she asked quietly.

'I didn't mean anything by it,' he said a bit shortly, even though he had. He'd been reminding himself as well as her of what their marriage was really based on, and it wasn't some stupid rush of emotion.

'This is our wedding day,' Rachel stated with quiet dignity. 'The only one we'll ever have, God willing. Can't we enjoy it?'

He felt like a cad then, a real joy-stealing jerk. 'I'm sorry,' he said. 'Of course we can. Why don't we give them a kiss?'

'Wait—what?'

'A kiss,' he said more firmly, and took her into his arms. She came willingly, and as he settled his mouth on hers he felt a deep sense of satisfaction as well as a rush of desire. This part of their marriage, at least, didn't have to be so complicated.

Rachel's mouth opened like a flower under his and she reached up to cup his cheek with one hand, in an unsettlingly tender gesture. The crowd roared and stamped and whistled their approval. Reluctantly Mateo broke the kiss. His breathing was ragged and so was Rachel's.

'That's a deposit towards later,' he said, and she let out a little breathless laugh.

'Good to know.'

They started the traditional wedding walk across the square to the palace, where they would have a formal wedding breakfast, followed by the carriage ride and then later by a ball. People continued to cheer, reaching their hands across the barriers. It was usual royal protocol to ignore such gestures, but Rachel broke ranks and starting shaking people's hands, and Mateo started to restrain her before he saw how people were responding to her—with both devotion and joy.

Mateo had always intended to model his kingship on his father's, to be dignified, a bit austere and remote, but also sincere and hardworking. His father would never have shaken a commoner's hand, never mind posing for a selfie as Rachel was now doing. And yet when Mateo saw the reaction of his people, their unfettered delight, he realised that this might be what was needed.

His father had kept the public at a distance, thinking he was above them, and Leo had ignored them in pursuit of his own private pleasure. Maybe it was time for Mateo to be different. For the King and Queen to engage with their people, to love them as their own.

The thought was novel, a bit alarming, and yet also strangely exciting.

'They love you,' Mateo murmured as they finally cleared the crowds and entered the palace. 'They really love you.'

'It's so strange,' she murmured, shaking her head, looking dazed. 'I've never…' She stopped, but something in her tone made Mateo turn to her.

'You never what?'

She paused, biting her lip as she gazed at him uncertainly. 'I've never been loved before,' she confessed with a shaky laugh. 'By anyone. But I think I could get used to it.'

It was such a dramatic statement that Mateo shook his head instinctively. 'Of course you've been loved.'

'No, not really.'

'Your mother. Your parents—'

'No. Not like that, anyway.'

He frowned, searching her face, looking for self-pity but finding only her usual good-humoured pragmatism. 'What are you talking about, Rachel?'

'My parents didn't love me,' she said simply. 'Or at least, they didn't like me. Which is worse, do you think?' She posed it like an academic question.

'Of course your parents loved you.' Even though he'd

rebelled as a youth, even though he'd resented being seen as unnecessary in the line to the throne, and walked away from everything as a result, he'd never doubted his parents' love. *Never.* Yet Rachel spoke about her loveless parents as if she was simply stating facts.

'I suppose they loved me after a fashion,' she said after a moment. 'I mean, they provided for me, certainly. But they didn't act as if they loved me, or wanted me in their lives, so I didn't feel loved.' She shrugged. 'But why on earth are we talking about this now? We need to go into the wedding breakfast.'

'They must have loved you.' Mateo didn't know why he was labouring the point, only that he really hated the idea that Rachel had grown up unloved. Disliked, even. *Rachel.* 'Maybe they were just reticent...'

She rolled her eyes. 'Okay. Sure. That's what they were. Can we go now?'

It was obvious she wanted to drop it, and now was hardly the time or place for some sort of emotional discussion—the kind of discussion he'd never really wanted to have—and yet Mateo was realising what a fool he'd been, to think he could separate parts of his life—his heart—like oil and water, never mixing. Marriage wasn't like that. It was a chemical reaction, just as he'd felt in himself; two separate entities combining and becoming something new. Hydrogen and oxygen turning into life-giving water. Or perhaps caesium and water, causing a life-threatening explosion. *Which was it?*

Only time would tell. And whichever it was, Mateo knew he couldn't take the affection and the trust and the physical desire and compartmentalise them all, neatly labelled, put away in a drawer and never causing him any bother. As much as he wanted to, needed to, he couldn't.

And that was when Mateo knew he was in big trouble.

CHAPTER THIRTEEN

RACHEL'S HEART FLUTTERED like a wild thing in her chest as Mateo closed the door of the bedroom. They were in the honeymoon suite, tucked away in a tower in a far wing of the palace, with a view of the sea shimmering under the moonlight from its high windows.

The circular room was something out of another fairy tale—*Rapunzel*, perhaps—with a twisting staircase that led up to this lovely room, a cosy fire crackling in the grate, and a canopied king-sized bed draped in silks and satins of various shades of ivory and taupe taking pride of place.

Rachel released a shuddery breath she hadn't even realised she'd been holding. It had been a long day, an endless day, from the ceremony and coronation this morning to the formal wedding breakfast with speeches and toasts, posing for photo after photo, and then the carriage ride around the old city, and finally a ball to finish. She'd changed into another gown, the one she wore now, a strapless ball gown in taupe satin and a diamanté-encrusted band around her waist.

At least she and Mateo hadn't had to dance in front of everyone, although after three glasses of champagne she'd managed a simple swaying with him to a modern pop song. Mateo had smiled down at her as they had danced, but she hadn't been able to gauge his mood, just as she hadn't been able to all day. Just as she couldn't now.

He turned from the door, his expression inscrutable as he loosened his white tie. Rachel watched him, feeling like a mouse being observed by a hawk, although there was nothing particularly predatory about his cool blue-green gaze. She was just feeling uncertain and vulnerable now that they'd finally reached this moment, the moment when they were alone together. When they would truly become husband and wife.

'It's very late,' Mateo remarked. 'We don't have to do anything tonight.'

Rachel couldn't keep disappointment from swooping inside her. Clearly he wasn't in any rush.

'We might as well get it over with,' she tossed back at him, echoing his words from this morning that had hurt her more than they should have.

'Is that how you view it?' His lips twisted and he tossed his tie aside.

'It's not how I want to view it,' she returned. The last thing she wanted to do was argue *now*. 'I'm not trying to sound snippy, but I have no idea how you feel about this, Mateo.'

'This?'

'Us.' She gestured to the bed. 'You *know*.'

'Sex?' he stated baldly, and for some reason she flinched. He made it sound like some sort of physical procedure they had to perform, rather than the joyful consummation of their marriage.

'Yes,' she muttered, and suddenly found herself fighting tears. She turned away from him, not wanting him to see, but he caught her arm.

'Rachel.'

'What…?' she managed thickly, blinking as fast as she could to keep the tears back. A few fell anyway.

'I'm sorry. I think I'm being an ass.'

'You think?'

'All right. I am. I'm sorry. I don't…' He blew out a breath. 'This is strange for me too.'

'Not as strange as it is for me,' she returned tartly, and he frowned at her.

'What do you mean?'

'I have a feeling that my experience is significantly more limited than yours,' she informed him, knowing it needed to be said even as she wished that it didn't.

'Oh?' Mateo gazed at her appraisingly. 'You might be wrong.'

She almost laughed at that. 'I don't think so.'

'I'm not some Lothario, Rachel. Work has been my mistress more than any woman.' His mouth curved in a crooked smile. 'I've spent far more time with you than anyone else, you know.'

'As gratified as I am to hear that, I still stand by my statement.' She felt her cheeks heat as she confessed, 'I have *very* little experience, Mateo.'

His narrowed gaze scanned her face. 'You're…you're not a virgin,' he stated, not quite making it a question.

'No…but almost.'

'How can you be almost?'

She pressed her hands to her cheeks, willing her blush to fade. 'This is seriously embarrassing, you know?'

'You don't have to be embarrassed with me.' He made it sound so obvious, but it wasn't.

'I do, especially when you turn all brooding and remote on me, and make me feel as if I don't know you at all.'

'Brooding and remote?' The corner of his mouth lifted in a smile. 'Just slap me when I do that.'

'I might.'

'Seriously, Rachel.' He took a step towards her, his shirt open at the throat, his gaze a bit hooded, his eyes so bright and his hair so dark and his jaw so hard… He was just too beautiful. It should have been a crime. It certainly wasn't fair. 'Tell me.'

'Tell you what? How little experience I have when it comes to this?' She gestured to the bed.

'Only if it would make you feel better, to have me know.'

'One time, okay?' The words rang out and she closed her eyes in mortification. 'I've done it one time, and, trust me, it was completely forgettable.' There. It was out. Thirty-two years old and she'd had sex *once*, with a guy who had turned out to be a complete cad. But she didn't want to go into those humiliating details now.

'Okay,' Mateo said after a moment.

'Okay?' Rachel stared at him uncertainly.

'Now I know.' Mateo shrugged. 'It doesn't make any difference to me. I'm not put off, if that's what you're afraid of.'

'Not *yet*.'

'Not ever. A lack of experience isn't a turn-off, Rachel, trust me.'

'That's assuming you're turned *on* in the first place,' she muttered. She felt tears again, and tried to hide it. This was all getting a bit too much.

'Why would you think I wouldn't be?'

'Why would I think you would?' she challenged. 'We've known each other for ten years, Mateo, and you haven't felt anything like that for me in all that time.'

'And nor have you for me,' Mateo countered. Rachel decided to remain silent on that point. There was only so much honesty she could take. 'It's changed now. We're looking at each other differently now.'

'You haven't exactly had trouble keeping your hands off me,' she felt compelled to point out. 'Quite the opposite. We've kissed exactly three times since we've been engaged.'

Mateo's lids lowered as he looked at her meaningfully. 'We've done more than kiss.'

'Barely. And even then you were pretty quick to haul me off your lap.' The humiliation of that moment stung all over again, and a tear fell. She dashed it away hurriedly and Mateo swore under his breath.

'Rachel, I had no idea you felt this way.' He looked flummoxed; the colour leached from his face as he shook his head slowly.

'I'm not expecting you to fall in love with me,' she managed stiltedly. 'Or even be wild with passion for me. I know I'm not exactly—'

'*Don't* say it.' Mateo sounded fierce. 'Don't run yourself down, Rachel. You're amazing. You're beautiful. You're my *wife*.'

'Then show me,' she whispered brokenly. '*Show me.*'

Mateo held her gaze for one blazing second and then he swiftly crossed the room and, cupping her face in his hands, kissed her deeply.

He'd kissed her before, and it had always made her senses spin. Now was no different, as his mouth slanted and then settled over hers and his tongue swept the softness inside, making her body sag and her knees weaken. He kissed her as if he *knew* her. And that made all the difference.

Rachel wrapped her arms around his hard body and he pressed closer, one knee sliding between the billowing folds of her gown as his kiss took possession of her, and her spinning senses started to drown. She was overwhelmed. Overloaded. Undone. And all by one kiss.

When he finally lifted his head to give her a questioning, demanding look, she managed the weakest smile she'd ever given.

'That's a start.'

'A *start*?' he growled, and he kissed her again. Deeper this time, until she was truly and utterly lost, and yet at the same time found. She'd never been kissed like this before. She'd never felt like this before. And she wanted more.

Mateo broke the kiss to give her another one of his burning looks. Then he began to unbutton his shirt. Rachel swallowed hard.

'I've never seen you without your shirt on before,' she remarked conversationally, except her voice came out in a croak.

'You're going to see me with a whole lot less on than that.'

Rachel gulped—and then thought of her wobbly bits that she wasn't sure she wanted Mateo seeing. 'Maybe we should move to the bed,' she suggested. 'Get under the covers.'

Mateo arched an eyebrow. 'Are you trying to hide from me?'

'A little,' she confessed. 'Let's face it, Mateo, when it comes to basic good looks—'

He laid a finger against her lips. 'I don't want to hear it. Not one more disparaging word. This is our wedding night, Rachel, and you are a beautiful, gorgeous, sexy *queen*. Don't ever forget it.'

His finger was still against her lips as she regarded him with wide eyes. 'I won't,' she whispered, and then Mateo lifted his finger from her lips and finished unbuttoning his shirt, shrugging it off his broad shoulders in one sinuous movement.

He was breathtakingly beautiful, all hard, sculpted muscles, pecs and abs burnished and defined, making Rachel long to touch him, but she felt too timid.

Mateo met her shyly questioning gaze. 'Touch me,' he commanded, and so she did.

The trail of Rachel's fingertips along his abdomen had Mateo's muscles flexing involuntarily. Her hesitant caress was positively enflaming, with an intensity he hadn't expected. He *responded* to this woman, and it wasn't just merely physical. Her artless confession, her shy looks, that small smile, *everything*…

It humbled him, that Rachel was so honest. She'd experienced so little in life—so little love, so little desire—and yet she'd still held onto her pragmatic attitude, her good humour. And even though the intensity of his own feeling, as well as the intimacy of Rachel's confession, had Mateo instinctively wanting to throw up all the old barricades, he didn't.

Because this wasn't about him, or at least not just him. It was about Rachel, and showing her how beautiful and desirable she was. It was about making her feel cherished and wanted, because right now Mateo realised he wanted that for her more than anything. More than his instinct for self-protection. He could give her this. He *needed* to give her this.

Her fingers skimmed up his chest and she looked at him with a question in her eyes. 'You can touch me a lot more than that,' he told her. 'But first we need to get some clothes off.'

Her eyes widened and she bit her lip. She was nervous about being naked in front of him. Mateo knew that, and it felt like a gift. He would cherish it. Cherish her.

'Turn around,' he said softly, and slowly she did.

Her ball gown had about a thousand tiny buttons from the middle of her back right down to the base. Mateo began undoing them one by one as Rachel sucked in a hard breath.

'I think there's a lovely nightgown around here somewhere,' she said shakily. 'Francesca picked it out…'

'We'll save it for later.' His fingers skimmed her skin as he slid each button from its hole, revealing the smooth, silky expanse of her back. He spread his hands, enjoying the whisper-soft feel of her skin against his palms. With the last button undone, the dress fell about her waist. The gown had had a built-in bra, and so there was nothing on her top half and Mateo liked it that way.

He reached around and filled his hands with the warm softness of her breasts, and she let out a shocked gasp at his touch. After a second she leaned back against him and he brushed his thumbs across her nipples, making them both shudder. Her gown slithered lower on her hips, and it only took one swift tug to have it falling in a crumpled heap around her calves.

Taking a deep breath, Rachel stepped out of it, and then turned to face him, her heart—and all her fear—in her eyes. She wore nothing but a lacy slip of underwear, and a pair of stockings with lace garters. Her hair had half fallen out of the elegant up-do, and lay in tumbled, chestnut waves over her shoulders. Her cheeks were flushed, her lips bee-stung, her eyes like stars. And her *body*…all the blood rushed from his head as Mateo gazed upon her.

'Rachel,' he said in a voice that throbbed both with sincerity and desire. 'You are truly beautiful.'

'I feel beautiful,' she whispered, sounding amazed, and Mateo reached for her. The press of her breasts against his bare chest was exquisite, but he wanted more. He let her go to briefly shrug out of his clothes, muttering with impatience as he fumbled with his waistcoat, the faff of his trouser buttons. Finally he was free, as nearly naked as she was, and he drew her to the bed.

They fell upon it in a tangle of covers and limbs, and Mateo ran one hand from her ankle to her hip, revelling in the silken sweetness of her skin.

'Touch me, too,' he whispered and she pressed her palm flat against his chest, before an impish smile came over her face and she trailed her hand down and down, wrapping her fingers around the throbbing heat of him.

'I've never done this before,' she whispered as her fingers explored and stroked. 'Am I doing it right?'

Mateo could not keep from groaning aloud. 'Yes,' he told her as she continued her artless, and very effective, caresses. *'Yes.'*

She continued to stroke and explore, her caresses becoming less and less hesitant, making his blood heat and his mind blur. He was going to lose his self-control very, very soon.

'This might surprise you,' he managed as he gently but firmly removed her hand, 'but I am not nearly as experienced as you seem to think I am, and it has been rather a long time since I have been in this type of situation.'

Her eyes widened as she looked at him. 'Really?'

'Really. And if you keep doing what you're doing, our wedding night will be rather short and, I fear, even more disappointing. So let me touch you now.'

A small smile curved her mouth as he gently pushed her onto her back. 'All right.'

Mateo kissed her on her mouth, savouring the sweetness of her lips, before he moved lower, kissing his way from her jaw to her throat, and then taking his time to lavish each of her lovely breasts with his full attention. The mewling sounds she made enflamed him further, and he moved lower, his tongue skimming the gently rounded beauty of her belly to settle happily between her thighs.

'Mateo...' Her fingers threaded through his hair as her hips lifted instinctively and Mateo tasted his fill.

Rachel's cry shattered the air as her body shuddered with her first climax. Mateo intended there to be several.

'Oh, my goodness...' she managed faintly, and Mateo smiled against her skin. 'I've never...'

'Now you have.'

She laughed at that and he rolled on top of her, bracing himself on his forearms, as he looked down at her, flushed and sated, yet clearly ready for more. 'Oh...' she breathed as he nudged at her entrance. She wriggled underneath him, a look of concentration on her face as she angled herself upwards, ever the scientist looking for the perfect conditions for an experiment.

And the conditions were perfect, Mateo acknowledged as he slid slowly, inch by exquisite inch, inside her. Rachel's eyes widened and her lips parted and she hooked one leg around his waist to draw him even deeper, so their bodies felt totally enmeshed, utterly entwined. *As one.*

Here was the ultimate chemical reaction, where something new was created from two separate substances, and could never, ever be torn apart.

Mateo began to move, and Rachel moved with him, hesitant at first but then with sinuous certainty, and they found their rhythm together as easily as if they'd always known it, minds and bodies and hearts all melded.

It was wonderfully strange and yet as natural as breathing, as they climbed higher and higher towards the pleasure that was promised both of them, just out of reach until it burst upon them like a dazzling firework, and then, with a gasp and a cry, they fell apart, reassembling themselves together, as one, their bodies still entwined, their arms around each other as their releases shuddered through them.

Mateo rolled onto his back, taking Rachel with him, their hearts thudding against one another with frantic beats.

He'd meant to offer this—himself—as a gift to her, but it wasn't, he realised now, that simple an exchange. He couldn't give without receiving. He couldn't offer himself and at the same time keep himself separate.

If he'd thought he was in trouble this morning, after the ceremony, he knew he was utterly lost now. Lost—and yet found. And the thought terrified him, not for his own safety or self-protection, but for Rachel's.

He could not hold her heart in his hands. He could not bear to, for he would surely, surely shatter it.

CHAPTER FOURTEEN

'THANK YOU SO much for your contribution, Your Highness.'

Rachel smiled and nodded graciously at the head teacher of the girls' high school in Constanza, where she'd been part of a round-table discussion on encouraging female pupils to study STEM subjects. The conversation had been wide-ranging and invigorating, and she'd enjoyed every minute of it.

'Thank you for inviting me,' she said as she took her leave, pausing for a photo op before shaking hands with everyone at the table. A few minutes later she was in the back of a black SUV, speeding back towards the palace.

It had been a month since her wedding, and Rachel had done her best to fully involve herself as Queen. She'd selected several charities to support, and said yes to almost every engagement at which she'd been asked to appear. Maybe if she kept herself busy enough, she wouldn't notice the empty space in her heart.

She had nothing to complain about, Rachel reminded herself severely. It was a talking-to she had to give herself almost every day. Absolutely nothing to complain about, because she'd agreed to this; she'd known what she was getting into; she'd accepted the deal with full understanding of what it had meant.

She just hadn't realised how it would *feel*.

Since their wonderful and frankly earth-shattering wed-

ding night, Rachel had had hopes that something more—
something a lot like love—would blossom between them,
in time. When Mateo had held her to him, moved inside
her, buried his face in her hair…

She'd been so sure. Everything had felt possible.

But in the month since that night, that incandescent sense
of possibility had begun to fade, day by day and night by
night. Mateo wasn't cruel, or cold, or even cool. He was
exactly what he'd said he'd be—a trusted friend, an affectionate partner. But he didn't love her, Rachel knew that
full well, and while she'd agreed in theory to a marriage
based on friendship rather than love, she'd assumed it would
mean that neither of them loved the other.

Not, Rachel acknowledged hollowly as she watched the
streets of Constanza slide by, that she would fall in love
with a man who was determined not to love her. Who kept
part of his heart clearly roped off, who had a shadow in his
eyes and a certain distance in his demeanour that even a
passionate night of lovemaking—not that she could even
call it lovemaking—could banish.

And meanwhile she felt herself tumbling headlong into
something she was afraid was love. The kind of soul-deep,
long-abiding love she had never expected to feel for anyone. But Mateo had been so kind…had made her feel so
valued…had held her like a treasure and laughed with her
and given her joy. Of course she'd fallen in love with him.

It was just he hadn't fallen in love with her, and had no
intention of ever doing so, as far as Rachel could see.

The SUV drove through the palace gates and then up
to the front doors. A footman hurried out to open Rachel's
door, bowing as she stepped out. Four weeks of this kind
of treatment and it still felt surreal. Rachel thanked him
and then walked into the palace, heading for her private
suite of rooms. It still felt strange, to live in a palace rather
than her own home.

Although Mateo had assured her she could redecorate her suite as she liked, Rachel hadn't dared touch any of the antiques or oil paintings, the silk hangings and fine furnishings. As a result she felt as if she lived in a five-star hotel rather than a home, which was sometimes nice and sometimes a bit disconcerting.

'Your Highness, you're back.'

Rachel turned to give her personal assistant a smile. 'Yes, I am.'

'The discussion was productive?'

'Very much so, I believe. Do I have anything scheduled for the rest of the day, Monica?'

'I don't believe there is anything on your schedule until a dinner tomorrow night.'

'Right.' Rachel paused as she took off the heels she still hadn't got used to wearing. 'And do you happen to know where the King is?' she asked casually.

Monica's face was carefully blank. 'I believe he is out.'

'Thank you.' She dismissed her assistant with a smile and a small wave.

Alone in her suite Rachel drifted around, grateful for an unscheduled afternoon and yet still feeling a bit lost. She'd seen very little of Mateo in the last month, besides formal events and nights—nights which were seared on her mind and made her body tingle. Still, she missed spending time with him, missed the easy friendship they'd once had, when it hadn't been complicated by the demands of royalty—and marriage. Even if he would never love her, she wished he'd spend time with her.

She had just changed into comfortable clothes and settled on a sofa by the window with her laptop, hoping to catch up on some emails to friends, when a light knock sounded on her door.

'Yes?'

'Hello.' Mateo popped his head around the door, giving her a wry smile. 'Are you busy?'

'Busy? No.' Rachel closed her laptop, trying to temper the feeling of delight that was spreading through her like warm, golden honey. Perhaps he just had a quick question to ask, and then he'd be on his way…

'I thought we could spend the afternoon together,' Mateo said, an unusual note of hesitation in his voice. 'If you wanted to.'

If? The smile that bloomed across Rachel's face was impossible to suppress, not that she even wanted to. 'I'd love that.'

'Good.'

'What did you have in mind?'

'I thought we could go sailing, just the two of us.'

'On our own?' After being shadowed by security and staff for the last month, the prospect was wonderfully liberating.

'We'll leave the security on the shore. They can't live in my pocket all the time.'

Rachel frowned. 'Are you sure it will be safe?'

'No one's knows where we're going.' Mateo shrugged. 'It would be good to get away.'

Yes, it would. And the fact that Mateo wanted to spend time alone with her was intoxicating. 'All right,' Rachel said. 'When do you want to go?'

'How long until you're ready?'

She laughed. 'Five minutes.'

And it was only five minutes later that they were driving in a dark green convertible, a palace car Rachel hadn't seen before, but much preferred to the heavy SUVS with their blacked-out windows.

With the sky bright blue above them and the sea sparkling below, the day felt full of promise.

'Where are we going, exactly?' Rachel asked.

'A private marina where there's a sailboat.'

'I didn't even know you could sail,' she said with a laugh. Mateo threw her a glinting smile.

'There's a lot of things you don't know about me.'

Today, with the sun shining and the sky so blue, that felt like a promise rather than a warning. Rachel smiled back.

Half an hour later they were on a small sailing raft heading out into the shimmering blue-green waters of the Mediterranean Sea, with not a security officer or staff member in sight.

'Where are we going now?' Rachel asked as she tilted her face to the sun. 'Do you have a destination?'

'As a matter of fact, I do. There is a small island out here—not much more than a speck of land, but it has a nice beach. I used to go here when I was younger.'

'To get away from it all?' Rachel teased, and Mateo gave a grimacing nod.

'Actually, yes. When I was out here, I could forget I was a prince.'

'Was that something you wanted to forget?' Rachel asked softly. She was aware, not for the first time, of all she didn't know. She didn't know about Mateo's family, really, only that he was the youngest of three brothers. One had died, and one had walked away. Both, she realised now, must have left scars.

'Sometimes it was,' Mateo answered after a moment, his narrowed gaze on the glinting sea. 'I'd always get punished for trying to escape. Sent to my room with no dinner. I suppose I deserved it.'

'Your parents must have been worried about you.'

'I suppose.'

'You don't sound convinced.'

He shrugged. 'As the third son, and a later surprise at that, I was a bit of an afterthought.'

Rachel frowned. 'Were you neglected?'

'No, not at all. In some ways, it was a blessing—I had so much more freedom than either Kosmos or Leo.'

'Tell me about your brothers,' she said. 'I've never heard you speak of them before.'

'I suppose I haven't had much to say.' He nodded towards the sea ahead of them, and the shape of an island now visible. 'Let me get us to the shore.'

They spent the next few moments navigating the waters, and then mooring the boat in an inlet of a postage-stamp-sized island, no more than a strip of beach and a bit of scrub. With the sea stretching in every direction, Rachel couldn't imagine a lonelier or lovelier spot.

'I brought a picnic,' Mateo told her as he reached for a wicker basket. 'Or rather, I had the kitchen make one for me.'

'Isn't that how kings always do things?' Rachel teased as she took his hand and he helped her out of the boat. She couldn't remember when they'd last talked so much, or when she'd felt so happy. This was what she'd imagined, what she'd longed for—their friendship back, but something more as well.

They strolled hand in hand onto the beach, and Mateo spread out a blanket before opening the picnic basket and setting out a variety of tempting goodies—strawberries, smoked salmon, crusty bread, a ripe cheese, and, of course, champagne.

It was perfect, Rachel thought as he popped the cork on the bottle and poured them both glasses.

Everything was perfect.

Mateo hadn't planned any of this. It was strange, but his own actions were taking him by surprise. It felt as if one moment he'd been sitting in his study, staring out at the blue sky, and the next he'd jumped into a boat and sailed for the blue yonder.

Not that he regretted what he'd done. In fact, he couldn't remember the last time he'd felt so relaxed, so free. He took a sip of champagne and closed his eyes, enjoying the sunlight on his face.

He realised he didn't even mind talking to Rachel about things he tried never to think about, never mind discuss—his family, his brothers, the deep-seated desire he'd had not to be a prince—or even a king. Yet somehow it felt different out here, sipping champagne on the sand, the barriers gone or at least a little lowered, the whole world wide open.

'When did your older brother die?' Rachel asked quietly, her generous mouth curved downwards, her eyes as soft as a bed of pansies.

'Ten years ago. A sailing accident.'

'Sailing…' Those soft eyes widened and she glanced instinctively at the little boat bobbing gently on the waves.

'Kosmos was a risk-taker. He loved living dangerously. He took a boat out during dangerous conditions, and sailed through a storm.' Mateo remembered the shock of hearing the news, the sudden fury that his older brother, more of a distant, admired figure than someone he'd felt truly close to, could be so careless.

'That was right when we started working together.' Rachel frowned. 'You never told me.'

'We barely knew each other then.'

'It's more than that, Mateo.' She paused, seeming to weigh her words. 'Why did you never confide in me? I don't mean about the royalty thing, which I actually do understand keeping to yourself. But other things. Your brother's death. Your father's death.'

Mateo considered the question for a moment, rather than dismiss it out of hand, as he normally would have, saying, *I never talk about myself.* Or, *There was never a good time.*

'I don't know,' he said at last. 'I suppose because, in doing so, I would have revealed something about myself.'

As soon as he said the words, he felt weirdly vulnerable, and yet also relieved.

Rachel kept her soft gaze steady on him. 'Something you didn't want others to see?'

He shrugged. 'I was never that close to Kosmos or Leo. I looked up to them, but they were both older than me and they were very close themselves. They had a similar set of experiences—the heir and spare preparing for a life in the royal spotlight, while I was left to do more or less as I pleased.'

'That sounds lonely.'

'Like I said before, it had its benefits.'

'Even so.' Her quietly compassionate tone was nearly the undoing of him. Emotions he hadn't even realised he'd been holding onto, buried deep, started to bubble up. Mateo took a sip of champagne in an effort to keep it all at bay. 'It must have been a shock, when you were told you had to be King.'

'It was,' he agreed. He thought his voice was neutral but something must have given him away because Rachel leaned forward and laid her hand over his.

'You're doing an amazing job, Mateo. *You're* amazing. I know I don't even know a tenth of what you do, and with the talk of insurgency and this economic thing...' She laughed softly. 'I don't know much about it, but I know you are doing the best job you can, giving two hundred per cent all the time.'

'As a scientist, you should know better than to use the erroneous phrase two hundred per cent,' he quipped, because to take her seriously would be to very nearly weep.

'I'm a scientist, not a mathematician,' she retorted with a smile. 'And I'm not taking back any of it.'

He shook his head, smiling to cover how much her words meant, how thankful he was for her. He wanted to tell her as much, but he couldn't manage it because he felt too much and he wasn't used to it.

For fifteen years he'd kept himself from deep relationships, from love, because he was afraid of being hurt the way he'd been before, but more importantly, more deeply, because he was afraid of hurting another person. He couldn't live with that kind of guilt and grief again, and yet here he was, treading on the thinnest of ice, in telling Rachel these things. In starting to care, and letting her care about him.

He should stop it right now, but the truth was he didn't want to. It felt too much, but part of that was good. It was wonderful.

'I know you don't want to hear anything soppy,' she continued with an uncertain smile, 'but I'm going to tell you anyway.'

'I consider myself warned,' he said lightly, although his heart gave an unpleasant little lurch. Was she going to tell him she loved him? He would not know how to handle that.

'You've given me such confidence, Mateo,' Rachel said quietly. 'I haven't told you much about Josh except that he didn't break my heart. And he really didn't. But he broke my confidence—not that I had that much to begin with.'

'How…?' Mateo asked, although from what Rachel had already told him, he thought he could guess. She sighed.

'He was older than me, worldly and sophisticated. I had a crush on him. I suppose it was obvious.'

'So what happened, exactly?' Mateo asked, although judging by Rachel's tone, the look of resignation and remembrance in her eyes, he wasn't sure he wanted to know.

'I suppose if it had been a romance novel, I would have said he seduced me. But if it was a romance, he wasn't the hero.'

'The one time?' Mateo surmised.

She nodded. 'And the worst part was, afterwards he acted as if he didn't know me. I bounced into class the next day, full of hope, of certainty. I thought we were a couple.

He acted as if he couldn't remember my name. Literally.' She tried to laugh but didn't quite manage it. 'And then I overheard him joking to his friends, about how it would have to be a really desperate guy who was willing to…you know…with me.'

'Oh, Rachel.' Mateo couldn't get any other words out. He hated the bastard Josh for what he'd done—the careless, callous disregard he'd shown for someone as lovely and genuine and pure as Rachel.

'Anyway, I was telling you all this not to throw myself a pity party, but because you've changed that, Mateo. You've changed *me*. I used to always feel about myself—my body, my looks—the way he did. As if I was beneath notice. Easily forgettable. But when you look at me…' Her voice trailed off and blush pinked her cheeks as she tremulously met his gaze. 'I feel different. I feel…desirable. For the first time in my life. And that's been wonderful.' She gave an uncertain little laugh and Mateo did the only thing he could do, the only thing he wanted to do. He leaned forward and kissed her.

Her lips were soft and tasted of champagne and she let out a breathy sigh as he deepened the kiss. She grabbed his shoulder to steady herself but even so they ended up sprawled on the sand, the kiss going on and on and on.

He slipped his hand under her T-shirt and revelled in the warm softness of her body. As he tugged on her capri bottoms she let out a little laugh.

'Here…?'

'Why not? It's not as if anyone can see.' He smiled down at her and she blinked up at him, a look of wonder in her eyes. She cupped his face with her hands and for a second Mateo's heart felt like a cracked vessel that had been filled to the brim—overflowing and leaking, going everywhere. She'd done this to him. She'd awakened the heart he'd thought had been frozen for ever behind a paralysing wall of grief and fear. Love was too dangerous to consider, and yet here he was. Here *they* were.

'Rachel…' He couldn't bring himself to say the words, but he *felt* them, and he thought she saw it in his eyes as she brought his face down to hers and kissed him with both sweet innocence and passionate fervour. With everything she had. And Mateo responded in kind, moulding his body to hers, wanting only to keep this moment between them for ever.

CHAPTER FIFTEEN

RACHEL WAS HAPPY. It was a frail, fragile thing, like gossamer thread or a rose just about to bloom—all it would take was a gentle breeze to blow it all away. But, still, she was happy.

Since their afternoon on the island, Rachel had sensed a shift in Mateo, a softening. He'd willingly talked about his family, his emotions—things that Rachel had sensed had been off-limits before. The aloofness she'd felt from him since their marriage—the shadow lurking in his eyes, the slight repressiveness of his tone—had gone. Mostly.

Mateo, Rachel suspected, was a man at war with himself. He was starting to fall in love with her—if only she really could believe that!—but he didn't want to. At least, that was her take on the matter, and Agathe surprised her by agreeing.

They'd been having lunch in one of the palace's many salons when Agathe had said quite out of the blue, 'You must be patient with him, my dear.'

Rachel had nearly choked on a scallop. 'Pardon?'

'Mateo. I know he can be…difficult. Remote. It's his way of coping.'

Rachel absorbed that remark, tried not to let it hurt. 'What is he coping with?' she asked even as she thought, *Me?* Was his marriage something her husband had to *cope* with?

'Everything,' Agathe answered with a sad little sigh. 'The pressures of the kingship, certainly. His father was the same.'

'Was he?' Once again Rachel realised how little she knew about the Karavitis family.

'My husband believed he needed to keep a certain distance between him and his people. It was a matter of respect and authority. I don't know if he was right or not, but Mateo feels the responsibility, especially when he was never meant to have any royal role at all. I am afraid we did not prepare him as we should have.'

'Yet he is rising to the challenge,' Rachel returned, a fierce note of pride in her voice.

'Indeed he is, but at what cost?' Agathe smiled sadly. 'But it is more than that. Mateo has lost so many people… if he closes himself off, it's because he doesn't want to risk losing anyone else. Losing you. But it doesn't mean he doesn't love you.'

'You don't know that,' Rachel said after a moment. She paused, deliberating whether she should mention the person who was still utterly off-limits. 'Sometimes I wonder if he has any more room to love, after…' she took a quick breath '…after Cressida.'

Agathe's face softened into sympathetic lines. 'Of course he does. His relationship to Cressida…that was no more than schoolboy infatuation.'

'He doesn't talk about it like that,' Rachel said, even though she desperately wanted to believe it. 'He won't talk about it at all.' Agathe nodded slowly, and Rachel looked down at her plate. 'I shouldn't be talking to you about this. I know Mateo wouldn't like it.' He'd feel as if she'd betrayed him, and she couldn't stand that thought.

'Give him time,' Agathe said by way of answer. 'Be patient…and believe.'

Rachel was still holding onto those words, praying they

were a promise, when she got ready for an engagement in Constanza one foggy afternoon in November. She and Mateo had been married for six weeks, and winter had finally hit the island country, with thick, rolling fog and damp, freezing temperatures.

Mateo remained as busy as ever, but not as aloof, and Rachel continued to feel she had reason to hope. To believe. And, she reminded herself, she was happy.

A knock on her bedroom door had her turning, expecting Monica to tell her the car was ready to take her into the city. To her surprise, Mateo stood there, stealing her breath as he always did, wearing a navy-blue suit with a dark green tie that brought out the brightness of his eyes.

'You have an engagement?' he asked and she nodded as she fastened the second of her pearl earrings. 'Yes, at the bazaar in the city. Supporting women stallholders.'

'In the bazaar?' Mateo frowned. 'That's not the safest place.'

'I'll have my usual security.' Rachel glanced at him in concern. 'Has something happened? Are you worried?'

'No, I just don't like you being in such an exposed, rough place.'

'It's a market, not a Mafia den,' Rachel told him with a little laugh. 'I'm sure I'll be fine.'

Mateo nodded slowly, still looking less than pleased. 'I suppose so.'

He didn't sound convinced and Rachel laid a hand on his arm. 'Is there something you're not telling me, Mateo?'

He hesitated, his lowered gaze on her hand still resting on his arm. 'The insurgents are still active,' he admitted after a moment.

'But in the north…'

'Yes, but it isn't that far away.'

Nerves fluttered in Rachel's stomach at his grim tone.

'Surely they're not in the bazaar?' she asked, trying for a light tone and almost managing it.

Mateo was silent for a long moment, his gaze still lowered. 'No,' he said at last. 'Of course not.'

'Then I'll be fine.' She looked at him directly, willing him to meet her gaze. When he did, the look on his face—a mixture of resolution and despair—made her want to put her arms around him. Tell him she wouldn't go.

But then his lips curved in a quick smile and he nodded. 'It will be fine, I'm sure. I'll see you later today, for dinner.'

'All right.' He gave her a quick kiss on the cheek and as Rachel watched him walk away she had a strange, tumbling sensation that she forced herself to banish. Mateo's worries were just that—worries. Worries of a king who cared too much, who had lost people before. She was just going to the city's bazaar; she'd be surrounded by security. And really, she should be pleased that Mateo cared so much. Another sign, she wondered, that he was coming to love her? Or just wishful thinking?

An hour later Rachel had banished all her concerns as well as Mateo's as she entered the colourful bazaar with its rickety stalls and colourful banners. She spent an enjoyable hour meeting with the female stallholders and chatting about the goods they sold—handmade batik cloth; small honey cakes dotted with sesame seeds; hand-tooled leather wallets and purses.

She was impressed by their ingenuity and determination, and charmed by their ready smiles and cheerful demeanour. They faced far more challenges than she ever had, and yet they'd kept their heads as well as their smiles.

She was just saying goodbye when she felt the heavy hand of one of her security guards, Matthias, on her shoulder.

'Your Royal Highness, we need to go.'

'We're not in a rush—' Rachel began, only to have Matthias grip her elbow firmly and start to hustle her through the crowds and alleyways of the bazaar.

'There is a disturbance.'

'A disturbance—?' Rachel began, craning her neck to see what he meant.

In her six weeks as a royal, she'd become used to being guarded, even as she'd believed it to be unnecessary. There had never been any 'disturbances', and the unrest Mateo spoke of in the north was nothing more than a vague idea.

Now, as she saw Matthias with one hand on her elbow, one hand on the pistol at his hip, she felt a flicker of the kind of fear she'd never experienced before.

This couldn't be happening. This couldn't be *real*. It felt as impossible as Mateo's proposal, as her arrival in Kallyria, as her over-the-top wedding. Just another moment that she couldn't compute in this crazy life of hers.

'Get her in the car,' Matthias growled into his mouthpiece, and Rachel saw another guard emerge from behind an SUV with blacked-out windows, and Matthias started to hand her off.

Then she heard a sizzle and a crack and the next thing she knew the world had exploded.

Mateo could not ignore the tension banding his temples and tightening his gut as he tried to focus on the briefing one of his cabinet ministers was giving.

There was no reason to feel particularly anxious about Rachel's visit to the bazaar, but he did. Maybe it was a sixth sense. Maybe it was just paranoia. Or maybe it was the fact that he was finally acknowledging to himself that he cared about Rachel. Hell, he might even love her, and this was the result. This gut-twisting fear. This sense that he could never relax, never rest, never even breathe.

Love was fear. Love was failure. Love was dealing with both for ever, and it was why, after his experience with Cressida, he'd chosen never to pursue that dangerous, deadly emotion again. Yet like the worst of enemies, it had come for him anyway.

'Your Highness…'

Mateo blinked the minister back into focus, realising he'd stopped speaking some moments ago, and everyone was waiting for him to respond.

'Thank you,' he said gruffly, shuffling some papers in front of him, hating how distracted he was. How he couldn't stop thinking of Rachel, for good or ill, for better or worse. Just like the marriage vows he'd made.

But it wasn't supposed to be this way.

He'd been so sure, when he'd first come up with his great plan, that with Rachel he'd be immune. He'd had ten years of inoculation, after all. How could he possibly fall in love with her after all that time together? How could he barely keep his hands off her, when for an entire decade he hadn't even considered touching her?

How had everything changed since their vows had been spoken, most of all himself? Because loving Rachel felt both as natural as breathing, as terrifying as deliberately stepping off a cliff.

He was already in free fall, because he knew it was too late. He already loved her. He'd been fighting it for weeks now, fighting it and revelling in it at the same time, to his own confusion and despair.

He knew Rachel saw the struggle in him, just as he knew she was patiently waiting for him to resolve it. He saw the hope in her eyes when she looked at him, and that made everything worse, because he knew he was going to disappoint her, no matter what.

'Your Highness.'

He'd stopped listening to the conversation again. Irritated with himself beyond all measure, Mateo made himself focus on the minister again, only to realise he wasn't the one speaking.

A guard who had entered the stateroom was, and Mateo suddenly felt as if he'd been plunged underwater, as if everything were at a distance and he could only hear every third word. *Bazaar...bomb...wounded.*

He lurched up from the table, panic icing his insides, making it hard to breathe. Impossible to think. Rachel was in danger...and it was his fault. He'd been here before. He knew *exactly* how this felt.

'Is she alive?' he rasped.

'She's being taken to the hospital—'

'Get me there,' Mateo commanded, and he strode out of the room.

Half an hour later he was at the Royal Hospital on the outskirts of the city, the wintry fog obscuring the view of the terracotta roofs and onion domes of his city, his kingdom, so all was grey.

On the way there Rachel's security team had briefed him on what had happened—a clumsy, homemade bomb thrown into the bazaar; the explosion had hurled Rachel in the air and she'd hit her head on a concrete kerb. Two other people had received non-life-threatening injuries, including her personal bodyguard, Matthias; they were both being treated.

'And the Queen?' Mateo demanded. 'How is she?'

'She sustained an injury to the head,' the doctor, an olive-skinned man with kind eyes, was telling him, although Mateo found it hard to listen to a word he said. His mind kept skittering back to other doctors, other sterile rooms, the awful surreal sensation of hearing what had happened and knowing he was to blame. Just him.

There was nothing we could do...so sorry...by the time she made it to the hospital, it was too late.

'Is she in a coma?' Mateo asked brusquely. 'Is there… brain damage?'

The doctor looked at him strangely and Mateo gritted his teeth. He couldn't bear not knowing. He couldn't bear being in the same place, knowing the life of the woman he loved was hanging in the balance, and it was all because of him. 'Well?' he demanded in a throaty rasp.

'She is conscious, Your Highness,' the doctor said, looking unnerved by his sovereign's unprecedented display of emotion. 'She regained consciousness almost immediately.' Mateo stared at him, not comprehending. Not possibly being able to understand what this meant. 'She needed to have six stitches to a cut on her forehead,' the doctor continued, 'but other than that she is fine.'

'Stitches?' Mateo repeated dumbly.

'She might have a small scar by her left eyebrow,' the doctor said in an apologetic tone, and Mateo just stared.

Stitches? Her *eyebrow*?

'She's…?' He found he could barely speak. 'She's not…?'

The doctor smiled then, seeming to understand the nature of Mateo's fear. 'She's fine. I will take you to her, if you like.'

Mateo found he could only nod.

A few minutes later he walked into a private room where Rachel was sitting up in bed, looking tired and a bit exasperated.

'I'm quite sure I don't need to stay overnight,' she was telling one of the nurses who fussed around her. '*Den… Chei… Efharisto…*'

He almost smiled at her halting attempts at Greek, which the nurses resolutely ignored with cheerful smiles, but he felt too emotional to manage it. He stood in the doorway and simply drank her in, his heart beating hard from the adrenalin rush of believing, of being so *certain*, she was in danger. Of thinking he was to blame.

Rachel turned and caught sight of him, smiling wryly. 'No one seems to be listening to me,' she said with a little shrug of her shoulders. Her gaze clouded as she caught the look on his face, although Mateo didn't even know what it was. 'Mateo...'

He didn't answer. He simply walked over to her and kissed her hard on the mouth. The nurses scattered like a flock of sparrows.

Mateo eased back and studied the six neat stitches by her eyebrow.

She was all right.

'I'll have quite a cool scar,' Rachel joked uncertainly, looking at him with worry in her eyes.

'I thought you were dead.'

Her lovely, lush mouth turned downward as she realised what he'd gone through, although of course she didn't realise at all. 'Oh, Mateo...'

He shook his head, the remembered emotion, the absolute terror of it, closing his throat. 'Dead,' he forced out, 'or in a coma. A traumatic brain injury...'

'Barely more than a graze.' Her fingers fluttered on his wrist. 'I'm okay, Mateo.'

Now that he knew she was all right, he couldn't escape the awful knowledge that this could have been so much worse...just as it could have been avoided. 'I knew it was dangerous.'

She shook her head. 'It wasn't the rebels. Just some poor deranged man acting on his own. No one could have predicted—'

'This time.'

'Mateo—'

'You should never have gone to the bazaar. I shouldn't

have let you.' The words came out savagely, a rod for his own back.

'You can't keep me in a cage, you know.' Rachel's voice was deliberately light as her concerned gaze scanned his face. Mateo had no idea what she saw there. He felt as if he were a jumble of disparate parts; he'd been so terrified, and then so relieved, and now, inexplicably, he felt possessed by a fearsome, towering rage. He wanted to shout at the doctors. He wanted to tear apart the lone assailant with his bare hands. He wanted to hold Rachel and never let her go.

As the feelings coursed through him, each one more powerful and frightening than the last, he knew he couldn't handle this tempestuous seesaw of emotions any more. He couldn't live with the endless cycle of fear, relief, hope and guilt that had been his two years with Cressida. It had left him a husk of a man fifteen years ago, and he couldn't bear to have it happen again. He couldn't bear for Rachel to see it…or worse, far worse, for her not to see it, because one time it *wouldn't* be six stitches above her eyebrow.

This was what love wrought—grief and guilt, fear and failure. And he didn't want any part of it. He couldn't.

Rachel pressed her hand against Mateo's cheek and he closed his eyes. 'It's okay, Mateo.'

'It isn't.' He opened his eyes and stared at her, imprinting her on his brain, his heart. 'I can't do this,' he said, and he walked out of the room.

CHAPTER SIXTEEN

IT HAD BEEN raining for over a week. It was late November, and Kallyria was in the grip of the worst weather the island had seen in a century, or so her staff had told Rachel.

She liked the rain; it fitted her mood. It reminded her of England, and of everything she'd left behind. And while she couldn't bring herself to regret the choice she'd made, she still felt sad about it.

Ever since the day in the bazaar, Mateo had changed. When he'd walked out of her hospital proclaiming he couldn't do this—and Rachel was frankly terrified to ask him what 'this' meant—he'd kept his distance. The fledgling feeling that she'd been hoping had been growing between them seemed to have withered at the root, before it had had a chance to blossom.

And yet it had blossomed for her; she was in love with him, had been slowly and surely falling in love with him since their wedding, or, really, before then. Really, Rachel acknowledged to herself, she'd been falling in love with him since she'd first met him, when he'd introduced himself as her research partner and her breath had caught in her chest.

For ten years she'd kept herself from falling, because she knew, of *course* she knew, how impossible a relationship between them could be. Yet he'd asked her to marry him, and made her feel beautiful, and even though the kind of relationship she really wanted still felt impossible, she knew the truth.

She loved him. And he didn't love her back. Worse than that, far worse, was that he was choosing not to love her. Actively. Intentionally. And it was that knowledge, rather than him not loving her at all, that was bringing her closer to true despair than she'd ever felt before.

'So we have a round-table discussion today,' Francesca said, bustling into Rachel's bedroom with a briskly officious air and a quick smile. 'And a private engagement with the head of a girls' school tomorrow…'

'Right.' Rachel managed a tired smile. At least, she hoped she did. She hadn't slept well last night, with Mateo lying so silent and stony behind her, and she wondered if she ever would again. *I can't do this,'* he'd said two weeks ago. Well, neither could she.

Francesca looked at her closely. 'Is everything all right? You're looking a bit peaky.'

Rachel just shrugged. As close a confidante as her stylist had become, she wasn't willing to share this particular heartache.

'Is it PMT?' Francesca asked sympathetically. 'I think it's that time of the month, isn't it?' Rachel stared at her blankly and she gave her an impish little smile. 'One of the things it helps to keep track of, when considering your wardrobe choices.'

Rachel's mind ticked over and she shook her head. 'I don't have PMT.'

'No?' Francesca was already in the enormous walk-in wardrobe that was now filled with clothes for a queen.

'I'm late,' Rachel said quietly. And she was never late. Of course, it shouldn't surprise her. She and Mateo had not been using any birth control, since he'd been upfront for his need for an heir as soon as possible. And yet somehow, in the midst of all the busyness of being, Rachel had forgotten she could fall pregnant. Mateo seemed to have forgotten it as well, for he'd certainly never mentioned it.

And yet here she was, just two months into her marriage, and her period six days late. She shouldn't be shocked, and yet she was.

'I was thinking something bright today,' Francesca said. 'To make you stand out in this endless rain...' She brandished a canary-yellow coat dress Rachel had never worn before. 'What do you think?'

Could she really be pregnant? And how would she find out? Rachel's mind raced. She couldn't exactly pop out to the nearest chemist's, at least not without a security detail and half the palace staff knowing what she was up to.

She glanced at Francesca. 'Francesca, can you be discreet?'

Her stylist didn't miss a beat as she answered, 'My middle name.'

'Could you go to the chemist for me?'

'The chemist?' Francesca's eyes narrowed. 'What for?'

Rachel swallowed dryly. 'A pregnancy test.'

Francesca, to her credit, merely gave a swift nod. 'Of course.'

Just twenty minutes later, Rachel knew. It felt strangely surreal to perch on the edge of the sunken marble tub in the adjoining bathroom and wait the requisite three minutes to read the test. She'd never taken one before, and she'd spent ten minutes studying the instructions before she'd done what she'd needed to do.

And now she had turned over the little stick, seen the two blazing pink lines, and knew. She was pregnant.

'This is good news, yes?' Francesca asked cautiously as Rachel came out of the bathroom. She knew the expression on her face wasn't one of undiluted joy. 'The King needs an heir...'

'Yes, it's good news.' Her voice sounded a bit wooden.

'You want to be a mother?' the stylist pressed.

'Yes.' Rachel was sure of that. She might have given up on the hope of motherhood years ago, when her romantic possibilities had been nil, but one of the reasons she'd said yes to Mateo's unconventional proposal had been for the possibility of children.

'So…' Francesca waited for Rachel to fill in the blanks, but she couldn't. She didn't want to talk of something so private and sacred to anyone—but Mateo. And she didn't know what she was going to say to him.

She spent all afternoon in a daze, going through the motions of her meetings, her mind elsewhere. Mateo was engaged on other business until the evening, so it wasn't until dinner that she had the chance to talk to him, and by that time she was resolved.

Agathe was otherwise engaged, which meant it was just her and Mateo in one of the palace's smaller dining rooms, the curtains drawn against the night and the rain, candles flickering on the table between them.

A member of staff served them the first course and withdrew. They were seated at opposite ends of the table that seated twelve, a dozen silver dishes between them along with all that hadn't been said.

Rachel gazed at her husband's face and felt an ache of longing for how she'd hoped for things to be. Oh, how she'd hoped. And yet one glance at Mateo's set jaw forced her to acknowledge that those were all they'd ever be. Hopes. Disappointed hopes.

They ate the first course in silence, as had become their habit in recent weeks, and Rachel tried to work up the courage to say what was on her mind—and heart.

Finally, when their main course had been delivered, she forced herself to speak.

'Mateo, I need to talk to you.'

He looked up, his expression already guarded. 'Yes?'

'Two weeks ago you left my room at the hospital, saying, "I can't do this."' She paused, waiting for him to respond, or say anything, but he simply remained silent, his jaw tense, his eyes narrowed. 'What was it you couldn't do, Mateo?'

'Why are you asking?'

'Don't I have a right to know?'

He sighed, the sound impatient. 'Rachel…'

'You've been shutting me out ever since then,' Rachel stated with quiet, trembling dignity. 'Did you expect me not to notice? Not to *care*?' Her voice caught on a wavering note and she sucked in a quick breath, determined to stay composed.

Mateo laid his hands flat on the table. 'No, of course not. I'm sorry. I know… I know I'm not being fair to you.'

'But you'll do it anyway?'

'The truth is, I don't know how to be.' The look of naked vulnerability on his face seared her heart. 'I don't… I don't know how to love someone. And if that's what you want…'

'Don't know? Or don't want to?'

He hesitated, a familiar, obdurate cast on his features. 'Both, I suppose.'

'Why?'

'I don't want to hurt you—'

'You already have,' Rachel cut across him, trying to sound matter-of-fact and not bitter. 'So if that's your only reason…'

'Why can't we be happy the way we were?' Mateo said. 'As friends.'

'Because you're not acting like my friend, Mateo. You're acting cold and stony and basically a big, fat jerk.' He let out a huff of surprised laughter and Rachel squared her shoulders, knowing what more she needed to say, even if saying it would break her heart clean in half.

'I've been thinking about this quite a lot lately,' she said quietly. 'About you and me, and whether I'd be happy to live without love.'

'I do care for you—'

'But the thing is,' Rachel interjected sadly, 'you don't want to. You're fighting it. Fighting me. Maybe it's because you loved someone before and it hurt. I understand that, Mateo. You've lost a lot of people in your life. Your father, your brother.' She paused. 'Cressida.' Mateo did not reply, but his eyes flashed and his jaw tightened. Even now he couldn't bear to have her name mentioned, and that felt like the saddest thing of all.

'What I'm saying is, I'm not going to fight you back. Part of me wants to, a large part. To fight for you, for *us*. But the funny thing is…' her voice wavered and almost caught on a sob that she managed to hold back '… I'm not going to, because you made me feel I was worth more than that. All my life I've tried to make myself useful or needed, because I'd convinced myself that was almost as good as being loved. I told you my parents didn't love me, and I made myself not mind, because it was easier that way. They weren't bad people, really. They loved their jobs and their social life and they didn't really want an awkward, nerdy girl messing it all up.'

Mateo opened his mouth and Rachel held up a hand to keep him from interrupting. 'I'm not saying this to gain your pity. I really don't want that. I'm just trying to explain. Between them and the whole thing with Josh…well, you were the first person in my life who made me feel I was worth loving.'

'Rachel…'

'You made me feel beautiful and lovely and lovable. And you woke me up to the reality that I shouldn't have to settle for anything less.'

Mateo's eyes widened as he stared at her. 'What are you saying?'

'Don't worry,' she said calmly. She felt empty inside, now that it was all being said. 'I'm not going to leave you. I made vows, and I know my duty. I will stay by your side, as your Queen.' Another breath, to buoy her. This felt like the hardest part. 'But I'm not going to try any longer, Mateo. I'm not going to try to make you love me, and I'm going to do my best not to love you back. It's too hard to handle the ups and downs—the days when you decide to relax enough to let me in, and then the days when you don't.'

'I don't…' Mateo began helplessly, shaking his head. He looked shell-shocked.

'It's not fair on me,' Rachel stated, 'and it wouldn't be fair on our child. Because that is something else I've realised. I don't want a child of mine growing up thinking one of their parents doesn't love them.'

'I would love my child,' Mateo declared in a near growl.

'Would you? How can I possibly believe or trust that?'

'Because—'

'You don't have a great track record,' Rachel cut across him. 'But I accept that you will be involved in our child's life.'

'Of *course* I will—'

'But as for us, I want us to live separately. I'll still live in the palace, but in a separate wing. I'll continue with my own interests and charitable causes, and I'll appear with you in public, but privately we won't spend time together or have a relationship.'

'What…?' Mateo's mouth gaped open as he stared at her. 'But…'

'I think you'll find this works best for both of us,' Rachel said firmly, even though she felt as if her heart were being torn into little pieces and then stamped on. How could this be better? And yet how could she survive otherwise?

'We're married, Rachel—'

'A marriage of convenience only.'

'I still need an heir—'

'That's no longer an issue,' Rachel told him woodenly. 'Because I'm pregnant.'

Mateo stared at Rachel, his mind spinning uselessly, as she told him she was expecting his child and then rose from the table and walked out of the dining room with stiff, wounded dignity.

He slumped back in his chair, hardly able to take it all in. Rachel living separately from him. Trying not to love him. *Pregnant with his child...*

A sound close to a moan escaped him as he raked his hands through his hair. How had this happened? And why did he not feel relieved—that Rachel was suggesting exactly the sort of arrangement that should suit him? No complications. No messy emotions. No danger, no risk, no guilt or grief.

This should be exactly what he wanted, but in that moment Mateo knew it wasn't. It wasn't what he wanted at *all*. Instead of feeling relieved, he was gutted. Eviscerated, as if the heart of him had been drawn right out, replaced by an empty shell, the wind whistling through him.

He didn't know how long he sat there, his mind and heart both empty, but eventually a member of staff came to clear the plates, and Mateo stumbled out of the room.

He must have fallen asleep at some point in the night, although time seemed to have lost all meaning. He spent most of those endless hours simply staring into space, his mind empty of coherent thought and yet full of memories.

Memories of Rachel...ones he hadn't even realised he'd had, and yet now held so dear. The way she'd stick a pencil in her messy bun as she was working, and then forget she had it there and search for one uselessly around her until Mateo drew the stub out of her hair and handed it to her with a laugh.

Evenings at their local pub, him with a pint and her with a shandy—such a funny, old-fashioned drink—testing each other on the periodic table. She'd come up with the game first, insisting she could name all the elements faster than he could. Even though he'd won that first time, they'd continued to play the game, finding it funnier with each playing.

And then later, far sweeter memories—Rachel in her wedding gown, her heart in her eyes, and then Rachel with nothing on at all, her hair spread out in a dark wave against the pillow as she looked up at him with so much trust and desire and love.

Yes, love. She loved him. He knew that; he felt it, just as he felt his own love for her, like a river or a force field, something that couldn't be controlled. Why didn't he just stop fighting it?

'Mateo.' His mother's gentle voice broke into his thoughts, and Mateo looked up, surprised to see his mother in the doorway of his study. Had he gone to bed? He couldn't even remember, but sunlight was now streaming through the windows, the fog finally breaking apart.

'What time is it?' he asked as he scrubbed his eyes and tried to clear the cobwebs from his mind.

'Seven in the morning. Have you slept at all?'

'I don't know.'

Agathe came into the room, her smile sorrowful and sympathetic as her gaze swept over her son. 'Is it Rachel?' she asked quietly.

'How did you know?'

'I have been watching you both all this time, and seeing how you love one another. Knowing you would fight it.'

'I made such a mess of my last relationship,' Mateo said in a low voice. 'My love was toxic.' He choked the words, barely able to get them out.

'Mateo, that wasn't your fault.'

'Wasn't it?' He stared at her hopelessly. '*She* said it was.'

'Cressida was a fragile, damaged individual,' Agathe said gently. 'Her death was not your fault. And,' she continued firmly, 'Rachel is not Cressida. She's strong, and she knows her own mind.'

'She's leaving me.'

'What…?'

'Not properly,' he amended as he scrubbed his eyes. 'We'll remain married. But she wants us to live separate lives.'

'Ah.' Agathe nodded slowly. 'I was afraid of something like this.'

'Were you?' Mateo dropped his fists from his eyes to look at his mother, the weariness and memory etched into every line of her face.

'It's not easy to love someone who doesn't love you back quite as much, or even at all.'

It took Mateo a moment to make sense of his mother's meaning. 'Do you mean Father…?'

'The Karavitis men are strong and stubborn. They don't want to need anybody.'

'But you had such a successful marriage.'

'There are different definitions of success. I choose to believe in one that is about love and happiness, as well as duty and service.'

'I'm sorry,' Mateo said after a moment. 'I never knew.'

'We were happy, in our way,' Agathe said. 'I learned to be happy. But I want more for you…and for Rachel.'

'So do I,' Mateo said, his voice throbbing with the strength of his feeling. 'That's why…'

'Oh, Mateo. Do you honestly think she'd be happy without you?'

'She doesn't know—'

'Then tell her,' Agathe urged, her voice full of sorrow and love. 'For heaven's sake, tell her.'

* * *

He found her in the gardens. The fog had finally lifted, and the day was crisp and clear, the sun surprisingly warm as it shone down on the rain-washed gardens.

Mateo had gone to her suite of rooms first, and everything in him had lurched at the sight of several blank-faced members of staff moving her things out.

'Where are you putting those?' he'd demanded hoarsely, and someone had told him Queen Rachel was intending to reside in the south wing, about as far from him as possible. He felt both angry and lost, and yet he couldn't blame her.

So he'd left her rooms and gone to the south wing, but she wasn't there either, and when Francesca had told him, a look of naked pity on her face, that Rachel had wanted some fresh air, he'd come out here, and now he'd found her, in a small octagonal-shaped rose garden, the branches now pruned back and bare.

'Rachel.' His voice sounded hoarse and he cleared his throat. 'Rachel,' he said again, and she looked up.

'Mateo.'

'You're having your things moved.' It wasn't what he wanted to say, but he couldn't manage anything else right then.

'I told you I would.'

'I know.' He took a step towards her. She was sitting on a stone bench by a fountain that had filled with autumn leaves. Her hair was back in a plait and she was wearing a forest-green turtleneck in soft, snug cashmere and a grey skirt. She looked every inch the Queen, every bit his wife, and so wonderfully beautiful. *His.* She had to be his.

'I don't want you to,' he said and she started to shake her head. 'Please. Hear me out. I heard everything you said last night, and I've been thinking about nothing else since. But now…now I want a turn to tell you about what I've been thinking.'

A guarded expression came over her face, and she nodded. 'All right.'

Mateo moved to sit down next to her on the bench. 'You told me how your parents shaped how you felt about yourself. Well, in a fashion, mine did as well. I knew I was loved—I never doubted that. But I didn't feel important.'

'Because you weren't the heir?'

'My parents thought they were doing me a kindness, and I suppose in a way they were. They shielded me from all the intensity and pressure of the royal life. They gave me the freedom to pursue my own dreams—which led me to chemistry, and Cambridge, and you.' He swallowed hard. 'But I suppose I struggled with feeling a bit less than. I rebelled as a child, and then I turned away from all things royal. And then I met Cressida.'

Rachel's eyes widened as she gazed at him. 'You're going to tell me about her?'

'Yes, I'm going to tell you about her.' He took a deep breath, willing himself to begin, to open the old wounds and let them bleed out. 'Cressida was…fragile. She'd had a difficult if privileged upbringing and she liked—she needed—people to take care of her. I liked that at first. When I was with her, I felt important. I was eighteen, young and foolish, and Cressida made me feel like I was essential to her well-being. I craved that feeling of someone needing me absolutely. It stroked my ego, I'm ashamed to say.'

'That's understandable,' Rachel murmured. Her gaze was still guarded.

'But then she became unstable.' He shook his head, impatient with himself. 'Or, more to the point, I realised she was unstable. I should have seen it earlier. The warning signs were all there, but I thought that was just Cressida. How she was.'

'What happened?' Rachel asked softly.

'Her moods swung wildly. Something I said, something

seemingly insignificant, could send her into a depression for days. She wouldn't even tell me what it was—I had to guess, and I usually got it wrong.' He paused, the memories of so desperately trying to make Cressida feel better, and never being able to, reverberating through him. 'I tried so hard, but it was never enough. She spiralled into severe depression on several occasions. I'll spare you some of the more harrowing details, but she started hurting herself, or going days without speaking or even getting up from bed. Her grades started to suffer—she was studying English— and she was close to being sent down from university.'

'That sounds so difficult,' Rachel murmured. Mateo couldn't tell from her tone whether she truly empathised with him or not. She looked cautious, as if she didn't know what was coming.

'It was incredibly complicated. I wanted to break up with her, but I was afraid to—both for her sake and mine. We'd become so caught up in one another, so dependent. It wasn't healthy, and it didn't make either of us happy, and I don't think it was really love at all.' Even though it had felt like it at the time, and made him never want to experience it again. 'But it consumed us, in its way, and then…' A pause while he gathered his courage. 'In our third year, Cressida killed herself.'

Rachel let out a soft gasp. 'Oh, Mateo…'

'She left a note,' he continued in a hard voice he didn't recognise as his own. Hard and bleak. 'I found it. I found *her*. She'd overdosed on antidepressants and alcohol—I rushed her to the hospital, but it was too late. That's why, I think, I acted so crazily when you were at the hospital. I was right back there, fearing Cressida was dead, and then knowing she was.'

'I'm so sorry…'

'But you know what the note said? It said she was killing herself because of me. Because I made her so unhappy.' His throat had thickened but he forced himself to go on. 'And you know what? She was right. I did make her unhappy. I must have done, because when she was gone, for a second I felt relieved.' His voice choked as he gasped out the words, 'How could I have felt that? What kind of man feels that?' He'd never told anyone that before. Never dared to reveal the shameful secret at the very heart of himself, but Rachel didn't recoil or even blink.

'Oh, Mateo.' Her face softened in sympathy as her arms came around him and he rested his face against her shoulder, the hot press of tears against his lids.

'I'm so sorry,' she whispered, one hand resting on his hair. 'So, so sorry.'

'I'm the one who's sorry,' Mateo said raggedly, swallowing down the threat of tears. He eased back, determined to look at her as he said these words. 'You're right, Rachel, I have been fighting you. I'm scared to love you, scared *for* you. I don't want to make you unhappy, and I don't want to feel the guilt and grief of knowing that I did.'

'Love is a two-way street, Mateo,' Rachel said gently. 'You don't bear the sole responsibility for my happiness. What you had with Cressida…'

'I know it wasn't really love. It was toxic and childish and incredibly dysfunctional. I know that. I've known that for a long time. But you can know one thing and feel something else entirely.'

'Yes,' Rachel agreed quietly. 'You can.'

'But when you left me last night—left me emotionally if not physically—I felt as if you'd died. I felt even more bereft than when I lost Cressida, and without that treacherous little flicker of relief. I was just…grief-stricken.'

Rachel stared at him, searching his face. 'What…what are you saying?' she finally asked.

'That I love you. That I've been falling in love with you for ten years without realising it, and then fighting it for the last few weeks when I started to understand how hard I'd fallen. But I don't want to fight any more. I know I'll get things wrong, and I'm terrified of hurting you, but I want to love you, Rachel. I want to live a life of loving you. If… if…you do love me.'

Rachel let out a sound, half laugh, half sob. 'Of course I love you. I think I fell in love with you a long time ago, but I tried to stop myself. Maybe we're not so different in that respect.' She gave a trembling laugh as she wiped the tears from her eyes.

'Maybe we're not.' Mateo took her hands in his. 'Can you forgive me, Rachel? For fighting you for so long, and hurting you in the process? I was trying not to hurt you, but I knew I was. I'm a fool.'

'As long as you're a love-struck fool, I don't mind,' she promised him as she squeezed his hands.

'I am,' Mateo assured her solemnly. 'Utterly and over-whelmingly in love with you. Now and for always. I know it doesn't mean everything will be perfect, or that we'll never hurt each other, but I really do love you.'

'And I love you,' Rachel told him. 'More than I ever thought possible. Getting to know you these last weeks… it's made me realise how much I love you. And if you love me back…'

'I do.'

'Then that's all that matters. That's what will get us through the ups and downs. That's what will last.'

'Yes, it will,' Mateo agreed, and then leaned forward to kiss her. He settled his mouth softly on hers, and it felt as if he was finally coming home, the two of them together, now and for ever.

EPILOGUE

Three years later

'Mama, Mama, look at me!'

Rachel laughed and clapped her hands as her daughter, Daphne, ran towards her, her dark hair tumbling over her shoulders, her blue-green eyes alight with happiness and mischief.

It was a bright, sunny day, the sky picture-postcard-blue, the white sand of Kallyria's famous beaches stretching out before them. They were holidaying at the royal summer palace on the western coast of Kallyria. In the three years since Mateo had taken the crown, he'd dealt with the insurgents, stabilised the country's economy, and been a leader in bringing Kallyria into a modern and progressive world. It hadn't always been easy, but Rachel had been with him every step of the way.

She'd expanded into the role of Queen with energy and grace, not in small part down to Mateo's unwavering support and love. She'd also taken a six-week research position at the university in Athens last year, which he'd wholeheartedly supported.

But her heart was in Kallyria with her King and her family, and she knew there was nowhere else she'd rather be.

A year ago her mother had died, and Rachel had had the privilege of being with her at the end. To her surprise, although her mother hadn't remembered who she was in months, she'd turned to her suddenly, grasping her hand with surprising vigour, and said, 'I'm sorry. Do you know that, Rachel? That I'm sorry?'

And Rachel, with tears in her eyes, had said she had.

Now she scooped up her daughter and pressed her lips to her sun-warmed cheek, revelling in the simple joy of the moment. From behind her she heard Mateo coming through the French windows of the palace that led directly onto the beach.

'This one's up and ready for his mama.'

With a smile Rachel exchanged armfuls with her husband—he took Daphne and she took her three-month-old son, Kosmos, who nuzzled into her neck.

'Come on, *moraki mou*,' he said cheerfully as he tossed Daphne over his shoulder and tickled her tummy. 'Time for lunch.'

'And this one is ready for lunch too,' Rachel said as she followed him inside.

Sunlight streamed across the floor and Mateo caught her eye as he settled Daphne at the table, and Rachel curled up on the sofa to feed Kosmos.

The look he gave her was lingering, full of love as well as promise. Was it possible to be this happy? This thankful? This amazed?

Meeting her husband's loving gaze, feeling the warmth of it right down to her toes, Rachel knew it was, and with her heart full to bursting she smiled back.

* * * * *

MILLS & BOON

Coming next month

ITALY'S MOST SCANDALOUS VIRGIN
Carol Marinelli

Dante's want for her was perpetual, a lit fuse he was constantly stamping out, but it was getting harder and harder to keep it up. His breathing was ragged; there was a shift in the air and he desperately fought to throw petrol on the row, for his resistance was fast fading. 'What did you think, Mia, that we were going to walk into the church together? A family united? Don't make me laugh…'

No one was laughing.

'Take your tea and go to bed.' Dante dismissed her with an angry wave of his hand, but even as he did so he halted, for it was not his place to send her to bed. 'I didn't mean that. Do what you will. I will leave.'

'It's fine. I'm going up.' She retrieved the tray.

'We leave tomorrow at eleven,' he said again as they headed through to the entrance.

'Yes.'

She turned then and gave him a tight smile, and saw his black eyes meet hers, and there was that look again between them, the one they had shared at the dining table. It was a look that she dared not decipher.

His lips, which were usually plump and red, the only splash of colour in his black and white features, were for once pale. There was a muscle leaping in his cheek, and she was almost sure it was pure contempt, except her body was misreading it as something else.

She had always been aware of his potent sexuality, but now Mia was suddenly aware of her own.

Conscious that she was naked beneath the gown, her breasts felt full and heavy, aware of the lust that danced inappropriately in the air between them. The prison gates were parting further and she was terrified to step out. 'Goodnight,' she croaked, and climbed the stairs, almost tipping the tray and only able to breathe when she heard the door slam.

Tea forgotten, she lay on the bed, frantic and unsettled. So much for the Ice Queen! She was burning for him in a way she had never known until she'd met Dante.

Mia had thought for a long time that there was something wrong with her, something missing in her make-up, for she'd had little to no interest in sex. Even back at school she would listen in on her peers, quietly bemused by their obsessive talking about boys and the things they did that to Mia sounded filthy. Her mother's awkward talk about the facts of life had left Mia revolted. The *fact of Mia's life*: it was something she didn't want! There was no reason she could find. There had been no trauma, nothing she could pin it to. Just for her, those feelings simply did not exist. Mia had tried to ignite the absent fire and had been on a couple of dates, but had found she couldn't even tolerate kisses, and tongues positively revolted her. She couldn't bear to consider anything else.

And while this marriage had given her a unique chance to heal from the appalling disaster that had befallen her family, the deeper truth was that it had given her a chance to hide from something she perhaps ought to address.

A no-sex marriage had felt like a blessing when she and Rafael had agreed to it.

Yet the ink had barely dried on the contract when she had found out that though those feelings might be buried deep, they were there after all.

Mia had been just a few days into the pretend position of Rafael's PA, and the carefully engineered rumours had just started to fly, when Dante Romano had walked in. A mere moment with him had helped her understand all she had been missing, for with just a look she found herself reacting in a way she never had before.

His dark eyes had transfixed her, the deep growl of his voice had elicited a shiver low in her stomach, and even his scent, as it reached her, went straight to form a perfect memory. When Dante had asked who she was, his voice and his presence had alerted, startled and awoken her. So much so that she had half expected him to snap his fingers like a genie right before her scalding face.

Three wishes?

You.

You.

You.

Continue reading
ITALY'S MOST SCANDALOUS VIRGIN
Carol Marinelli

Available next month
www.millsandboon.co.uk